The Achilles Legend

Andrew Clawson

This book is a work of fiction. The characters, incidents, and dialogue are drawn from the author's imagination and are not to be construed as real. Any resemblance to actual events or persons, living or dead, is entirely coincidental.

Get Your FREE Copy of the Harry Fox story *THE NAPOLEON CIPHER*.

Sign up for my VIP reader mailing list, and I'll send you the novel for free.

Details can be found at the end of this book.

Chapter 1

Windsor, England

The flying spears nearly got him.

Harry Fox stood rigid as a statue. One of his feet hovered millimeters above the ancient stone floor. He'd foolishly looked everywhere but down as he entered the hallway. The intricate carvings covering the walls had entranced him, ancient stone deities standing vigilant against those who dared trespass. Harry was definitely a trespasser, one who'd nearly gotten himself killed just now because he wasn't paying attention. He'd missed the tiny lines underfoot, grooves in the floor that told him the floor wasn't solid. No, it was one big, lethal trap.

Harry carefully pulled his foot back. A warm breeze drifted down the gloomy passageway. He knelt, then lay flat on the floor. From this close he could see a line of pressure traps stretching the length of the passage, all the way to where it twisted at a ninety-degree angle ahead. Harry looked to either side where holes had been carved into the stone walls, holes that he suspected sent spears hurtling out toward anyone who stepped on the wrong part of the floor.

Harry stood and wiped his brow. He pulled out the handwritten journal containing every bit of information he had about this hidden temple. The only notebook like it in the world. His research had indicated the passageway was booby-trapped, but he didn't have all the details. He needed to think like the person who'd built it. A person whose goal was to make sure no one but them made it through the

1

gauntlet alive.

Too bad for them Harry Fox was here. He'd done his homework and knew where many of the traps waited, which parts of the floor to avoid and what steps would lead to his doom. He frowned. Nothing he'd read mentioned these floor traps.

He hadn't come all this way to stop now. Harry touched the amulet under his shirt. The answers his father sought might be just ahead. Answers his father had never found.

White light fell through openings in the stone roof overhead, just enough for him to see in the gloomy passageway. Moving softly, he skirted the pressure traps on the floor, hopping between them until he was halfway down the passage. Another thirty feet and he was in the clear. Eyes down, he readied himself to move when he noticed the walls had changed. Harry looked up. There were no holes in them now.

Why did the holes stop halfway down the passageway? There must be a reason, but darned if he knew what it was. He'd skirted the faulty steps coming in—big, wide steps that might hold you, or they might collapse and dump you into a spike-lined pit. But now he was in this booby-trapped passageway, which seemed to give up partway through. Harry squinted at the wall. *No, not there.* He looked up. *Uh-oh.*

Archways ran the length of the ceiling, curved stone supports that until now had been undecorated stone. From this point on, the arches were intricately carved, with decorative holes punched through each of them. The carvings were placed all along the bottoms of the support arches, each one cut so it looked almost like a handle. And they were closer together. Much closer.

He knelt again to study the floor. The same pressure traps ran the length of the floor ahead, only now they were so close together you couldn't possibly walk between them. More holes were along the bottoms of the walls, the same size as before but now running at ground level like some kind of deadly baseboard decorations. He closed his eyes, visualizing the journal contents he'd procured, the information offering clues on how to survive this gauntlet. He recalled the crude diagrams, some direct, others seemingly random. He'd committed it all to memory. One image jumped out. A diagram of a man swinging through the air as though he were on a giant set of monkey bars.

These arches weren't decorative. They were his way ahead. He skirted the floor until one carving was directly above him, reached up and grabbed it like a handhold. Harry eyed the next arch. It would be a stretch, but he could make it. Probably. Harry took a step back, his arm stretched to its limit, then launched himself toward the next arch.

He got it. Latched on, he swung back and forth, building momentum until he could let go of the first arch and use the second one to swing himself forward. After a half-dozen swings he reached the last one and flung himself ahead to where the passageway ended. He landed softly and held his breath. No spears flew from the walls, no blades sliced him open. A look behind him showed his heel had cleared the last pressure trap by about six inches.

That was close. He couldn't help but grin.

Checking the floor for traps ahead and finding none, he crept forward to where the passageway turned. Reddish light flickered across the stone floor. Harry peered around the corner to find lit torches lining both sides of the passage. The row of flames pushed away the darkness and led to the reason he'd risked his life to come here. But Harry didn't have eyes for what lay ahead yet. The torches had him spooked.

"Why are they all lit?" In his years hunting artifacts, their original owners had usually been long dead. They didn't keep the lights on. This was odd, but then again, nothing about this was normal. Harry Fox may have been avoiding lethal devices meant to protect a priceless relic in a place that looked thousands of years old, but it was all a mirage.

The stone passageway was within the English town of Windsor, home of Windsor Castle, the Queen's main residence. The traps along this ancient-looking hallway worked because they were not ancient. An eccentric Russian oligarch had installed them to protect his world-class collection of antiquities, acquired mostly on the black market. Evgeny

Smolov had made a fortune in his homeland after the Soviet Union collapsed, then ran afoul of the tyrant who now ruled in Russia. Forced to flee, he'd built this massive home in Windsor and designed a unique security system, one inspired by every deadly temple trap known to man.

Evgeny had designed his personal museum to resemble an ancient temple. Or at least what he imagined one to be. The building was modern on the outside, but once you entered, it was as though a portal opened and transported you to another world, one in a forgotten land where a lost civilization had crafted a deadly temple to protect their treasures. A temple you could enter, but never leave.

Yet Evgeny's system was not foolproof. Harry had managed to sneak into the facility without the posted guards spotting him, and there were no cameras installed in the booby-trapped passageways. Evgeny could disable all the traps by pressing a button, and his assumption that no one would be skilled enough to sneak in and live to test the traps would be his downfall. Harry Fox had the guts to do it. All for a prize that was Harry's destiny.

Harry peered through the passageway's gloom as dim light danced across the walls. An object came into view, resting on a circular stone platform. A golden crown that had once belonged to Mark Antony. The Civic Crown.

Its gold gleamed with a familiar sharpness, though it was the precious stones dotting each of the woven oak leaves that shone the brightest. The Civic Crown was most often associated with Julius Caesar, partner of Cleopatra before Mark Antony. Harry paused to appreciate the brilliant red, green and blue light reflected over the stone walls of the chamber. The crown was exactly as he'd seen it in a mural preserved in the ruins of Pompeii. A mural that had served as a marker on the mysterious path Harry now followed. A path laid out by Antony and Cleopatra.

The torchlight revealed a smooth floor devoid of visible traps.

Harry rubbed his chin. It couldn't be this easy. No obvious barrier stood in his way, which was why only a fool would stride up to the platform and touch the crown. Harry took a single step forward, then another. His foot edged ahead until the first flickers of torchlight reflected dully on his boot. Harry stopped when a sound caught his ear.

He jumped back as a torrent of flame spewed down from the torch to engulf the spot where he'd been standing an instant earlier. The incredible heat seared his face. He tumbled to the ground, twisting to look at the torch. No, not at the torch. Behind it. He squinted. *There*. A nozzle protruded from the wall. When it sprayed liquid, the torch flames created a flamethrower. Harry shivered, then looked more closely: Latin letters had been inscribed on the wall under each torch. The language of Mark Antony and Cleopatra. And one Harry could read. He turned to his left and translated the message.

Follow the true gods to Antony's crown. The false path leads to where Orcus dwells.

Orcus. The Roman god of the underworld, punisher of those who broke oaths and one who lived in dark places surrounded by fire.

An image of Orcus had been carved beneath the written warning. A monstrous creation, with large eyes and a gaping mouth, the stuff of nightmares. The same warning was written on the opposite side of the hall underneath that torch, with a different figure carved beneath it. Harry tilted his head. Same words, different deity. A bearded man this time. The dog carved beside its master gave it away. Only Hades had a three-headed dog as a pet. Cerberus, his faithful companion and guardian of the underworld.

A Roman god on the left and his Greek counterpart on the right. Intentional, like everything Evgeny had done. Evgeny was adept at using either a hammer or a scalpel to guard his treasure. This time he had chosen the latter.

More images had been carved under the next set of torches as well. They were hard to make out in the shifting light, but they appeared to be helmeted men carrying weaponry. Mars and Ares, the Roman and Greek gods of war. Mars was on the same side as Hades, Ares down the wall from Orcus. The sides had switched. Why?

Harry frowned. His research didn't give an answer. The information in his notebook mainly came from an engineer who helped build Evgeny's temple. No one man had worked on the entire project, for security reasons, but this engineer had been so intrigued by the unusual work that he had jotted down what he saw, bits and pieces that didn't reveal the entire picture. But he must not have worked on this part of the temple.

Yet Evgeny himself had left clues. The writings and pictures. Clues, as though he wanted to give intruders a fair shot. Or fair warning.

Harry snapped his fingers. *That's it.* The alternating deities didn't make sense until you stepped back and looked at the trap as a whole. The answer to surviving was right in front of him.

Follow the true gods. Two sets of gods adorned the walls. Which was true? These gods were protecting Mark Antony's crown. Antony was a Roman. To him, Orcus was true. Hades, a mere shadow.

Cool air snuck up Harry's shirt. The nozzles hadn't spewed gas until his foot edged into the light cast by the torch. There must be sensors that were tripped when anything blocked the light. He checked again. There were nozzles running down the hallway, one behind each torch. He edged a toe toward the light coming from above Orcus. The flames jumped, shadows going in and out until suddenly the wind blew them so the light cast by the torch covered his entire boot.

No flames spewed forth. Harry took a long step and stood squarely in front of Orcus. Now the torchlight covered him entirely. He turned and looked across the hall. The light from Hades' torch didn't quite reach the middle of the floor, and neither did the light from the others, leaving a dark strip running down the center of the entire hall. Not so wide you could walk down it, but it seemed almost as though the torches had been arranged to create that thin, dark strip.

Nothing moved ahead of him. He looked over his shoulder.

Nothing behind him. He'd avoided the human guards by approaching the property on foot, following hedgerows through the early moonlight until he reached the rear of the building, then shimmying up a drainpipe to the roof, where he'd found an unlocked window he could open and slide through by dangling from the gutter. That window had been slightly ajar each time he'd surveilled the property the past two days. For the moment, nobody knew he was here. As long as he didn't trigger a trap and get himself killed, no one would know he'd been here until morning, when some poor sod found the empty stone platform. Harry didn't envy them.

Harry didn't give himself more time to think before he stepped diagonally across the floor. The next set of opposing deities was indeed the war gods Mars and Ares. Whereas Orcus had adorned the left wall, this time the Roman god Mars was on the right. He stayed closer to Mars. No flames. Two choices down, two left. Harry looked at the next set of deities and found two men who looked exactly alike. From the eagles on their shoulders to the lightning bolts in their hands, the carvings were identical. Zeus and Jupiter, Greek and Roman gods of the sky and all it contained.

Both used eagles to retrieve their lightning bolts. Both were massive and bearded, clad in robes. Both wore crowns to symbolize their rule over all other gods and humans. It all made sense according to myth and legend. Yet it offered no clear choice for Harry, no path forward. He couldn't just flip a coin.

He stood motionless, thinking. Evgeny wouldn't do this. It didn't fit. There had to be some way to tell them apart. Perhaps there was and it was escaping him at the moment. He couldn't use his cell phone for fear of revealing himself, so no Google searches to help. Clearly this temple wasn't constructed solely to kill you. It gave you a chance—a fighting chance.

Think, Harry. You've been in places like this before. He looked to one side, then the other. Both images appeared to be identical. He didn't dare step closer to inspect either one in more detail. He pulled a flashlight out of his pocket and aimed it at the image on his left, chasing away the darkness under the flaming torch. An eagle sitting on the shoulder. Lightning bolt in hand. Robes slung over one shoulder. Harry turned to the one on his right and repeated the search. Check, check, check. All the same, from the sandals on his feet to the crown atop his head. Harry flicked his light back to the left.

A quick flash of brightness sparked as his light moved off the image on the right. He moved his light to and fro. There it was again. A small flash of red at the top of the crown. Zeus or Jupiter? It didn't matter. Until it did. This one on the right had a ruby-red dot atop his crown. The one on the left didn't. He double-checked to be certain. These images were different in the smallest detail.

Harry grinned. He looked ahead to the object on the circular platform and found what he sought: a red ruby in Antony's crown, right at the top. Zeus didn't have a ruby on his. Jupiter did.

Harry stepped ahead, staying to the right side of the hall. No flames roasted him. He paused, took a breath, then aimed his light at the final images at the end of the tunnel. A female figure had been carved into the wall on each side. Both had short hair. An owl pictured flying beside each one gave the identities away.

One was Athena, the Greek goddess of wisdom and warfare; the other was Minerva, Roman goddess of the same. Both were commonly pictured with an owl, the symbol of knowledge; both women wore helmets to indicate their ties to war. But neither of these helmets had a unique jewel or anything else to give Harry a clue as to who was who.

Harry had to make a choice. He was now far enough along to see that the area beyond Antony's crown was under active construction. It looked to be the beginnings of another exhibit, and it was very possible Evgeny had workers or guards on site at all hours.

Harry's light played over each image. What was that? Hidden in the folds of the goddess's robe to his right was a necklace, tucked away so that he'd nearly missed it. A circular pendant dangled from the chain. He leaned closer. The pendant contained a face. A hideous face with curled hair and bulging eyes above a protruding tongue. Horrible to look at, it was the prettiest thing Harry had seen all night. It was a Gorgon, a deity even older than the ones carved on these walls. This was a protective amulet worn by two deities, Athena and Zeus, royalty in the pantheon of Greek gods.

The female goddess to Harry's left also had a necklace in the folds of her robe, but there was no such face on her pendant. This goddess was the Roman Minerva.

Left it was. Harry hopped diagonally across, then stepped out of the tunnel to stand directly in front of the stone platform. Antony's crown was his. No obvious traps here, so he stretched an arm out toward it. Harry glanced across the platform to where construction materials sat piled along the hallway. He'd slip down there, see what Evgeny was building next, then get out. Maybe there was another artifact to sell on the open market. Harry's finger brushed Antony's crown.

A uniformed guard rounded the corner down the hallway. Harry dropped out of sight. He tensed, ready to grab the crown and run if the man shouted. He held his breath and cocked an ear. Nothing but silence, then the soft footsteps of a man in no hurry to get anywhere.

Harry crouched and pressed his back to the circular platform. It was wide enough to hide his entire body. If the guard did a circle, Harry could stay ahead of him, sliding around the platform to keep out of sight. Two things stuck in Harry's mind. The first was that this guard hadn't been looking up as he rounded the corner, so he likely had no idea Harry was there. The second was the gun holstered at the man's side. A big gun.

The sound of footsteps got closer. Harry got on the balls of his feet, crouched against the stone and ready to slide around in either direction to stay out of sight if the guard poked his head around. The *click* of the guard's shoes on marble came from the other side of the platform. Then they stopped.

Harry counted to ten. Nothing. Then the guard belched.

The guard was facing the other way from the sound of it, looking back down the hall he'd come from. He was standing too close to the crown for Harry to reach up for it. The tiniest scrape of metal on stone would alert the guard, and the crown must be heavy. Harry's luck had held so far, but now he was pressing it. He'd parked his electric motorcycle far enough away that no one should find it. The entire place would go on high alert if anyone did. There was also the chance that someone could lock the window, his only escape route. Or perhaps another guard would call this one, tell him to check out the hallway of flames because one of them had ignited. So many things could go wrong. The longer Harry stayed, the worse his chances became.

He chose another option: take the fight to them. One unsuspecting guard should be no problem. Harry reached soundlessly into his pocket and felt the cool comfort of his ceramic knuckledusters as he slipped them over his fingers. His secret weapon in tough times. He wasn't a big man, and he'd learned to fight on the streets of Brooklyn. They didn't give silver medals where he came from.

Harry rose until he could just see above the platform. The guard stood mere feet away, arms crossed in front of him, his back to Harry. The guy started to whistle tunelessly. He was big.

Harry flexed his fingers. He slid around the platform until he was behind the guard, then reached up and tapped the guy once on the shoulder. The man started, turning to look behind him. His chin made it around at the same time Harry's fist connected with it. A direct hit. The guard dropped like a stone. Harry darted over and checked the man's breathing. No blood, and it didn't look like the jaw was broken. The guard would have a headache for sure, but he'd be all right.

Harry wasn't waiting around for anyone else to show up. He grabbed the crown, turned around and headed back toward freedom. He made it one step and stopped.

What exhibit was under construction? Evgeny Smolov was worth north of eleven billion dollars. If Evgeny was building another display, the artifact had to be good. He should take a quick look. Just one.

He turned and moved beyond the pedestal, crown in hand as he walked quickly down the hall. The guard hadn't taken any precautions on his rounds; that told Harry that this hallway clearly wasn't yet staged with deadly traps. Harry stepped over a pile of building materials and followed the hallway to the left, nearly running headlong into a half-finished display case.

Ten feet tall and half again as wide, the case was all glass and white marble. Dark spotlights were on the ceiling, with all the light coming from a wide window framing the moon. A rectangular stone with writing engraved on it was mounted in front of the half-finished case. Whatever was to be stored here hadn't arrived. Across the room a wooden box taller than him stood against the wall. Writing he couldn't decipher ran across the surface. Harry tilted his head. *Is that Turkish?*

He headed to the stone and found writing in two languages. One was Cyrillic, of which Harry could read only bits and pieces. The other was Greek, a language he could more fully decipher. He frowned as he read the first line of text.

What stands before you gave birth to the modern world. What did that mean?

A man's voice broke the still air. "Hey! Who are you?"

Harry whirled around. A second guard was looking at him from down the hall.

"Identify yourself," the guard shouted in heavily accented English. Definitely Russian. He started running toward Harry, one hand on the gun holstered at his side. "Do not move."

Harry turned and ran back toward the tunnel. The guard shouted again, though Harry didn't catch it as he ran the safe path in reverse. Stay to the left. No, the right. Remember, it's backwards. He slowed, wasting precious seconds as he thought it through. Yes, to the left.

"He has the crown." A new voice. The guard Harry had clocked was awake. Harry looked back to see him getting groggily to his feet as the second guard ran past. "Take him out," the fallen man shouted.

The second guard already had his pistol out. He took aim. Harry turned, leaping diagonally across the floor as a gunshot boomed. Supersonic metal pinged off the stone with a flash as Harry jumped ahead. Left side again, then hop to the right. No more torches after that. He completed the route and raced to where the passageway turned.

The fallen guard shouted again as another gunshot rang out. "Wait!"

His friend didn't listen. A third shot buzzed Harry's head. Screams followed. Not Harry's, but the quick shriek of a guard engulfed in flames. Harry didn't look back as he rounded the final corner, jammed the crown in his waistband and took a running leap at the closest arch. His grip was true. Flying with the momentum you only got as bullets chased you, he swung down the hallway, his feet never coming close to the floor. He threw himself off the last arch and landed to the side of the pressure traps. One long leap took him clear of the traps underfoot, then he stopped. That remaining guard was wary. His buddy had just been fricasseed. Maybe the guard needed one more thing to worry about.

Harry turned back to the closest pressure trap. He lay down flat on his belly as the sounds of a big man not used to acrobatics hesitantly jumped across the floor, cursing in Russian all the while. Harry reached out and touched the closest pressure plate, pulling his hand back in a flash.

A spear as long as his arm ejected from the wall and banged off the far side with a clang. It bounced toward Harry, who scooped it up. He crouched against the wall and cocked his arm. The ongoing Russian swearing told him the guard was getting close. An armed guard, so this throw had better count. Harry waited until it sounded like the man was rounding the corner before he took aim, waited a beat, and fired his spear at the first glimpse of movement.

The guard caught sight of the spear hurtling at his chest and jumped back awkwardly, his feet going out from under him. Metal clanged as his pistol clattered off the floor. Harry was halfway down the main hallway by then, headed for the window he'd left cracked open and a drainpipe to freedom.

A bullet shattered the stone wall inches from Harry's head. He kept running, flinging himself around a corner and up a flight of modern stairs. The temple structure started after a sparkling entranceway, all glass and steel. Visitors entered what appeared to be a modern building only to soon discover Evgeny had built a secret museum. A museum with the power to kill any uninvited guests.

The window ahead was still open. An alarm sounded as Harry leapt at the wall and kicked himself up, using a trick his buddy had shown him, a parkour move used to climb walls without a rope. He caught the lip beneath the window and clambered onto the sill. Slipping through onto the roof, he ran through the bright moonlight to the roof's edge. The rope he'd left hidden in a drainpipe was still there. Without it, he was trapped. Nobody could jump thirty feet to the ground and not break something.

The grounds of Evgeny's estate were coming alive now. A siren blared, shouts rang out, and guards ran out of the building, their flashlights waving everywhere in a frantic search. Nobody looked up, not yet.

Harry grinned and touched the amulet around his neck. *Send me some luck, Dad.* He secured the rope around an exhaust pipe, tugged on it to be sure it was tight, then twisted it around his body in a rappelling technique meant for emergencies. He'd never done this with armed men on his tail, and the one thing he knew was this would hurt. Under his legs, around his waist, over the shoulder. Harry threw the rest of the rope over then leapt into the void below.

The wall rushed up to meet his feet. Kicking and sliding, he descended as fast as he dared; his hands started to burn from the friction of letting the rope out. One guard aimed his light toward Harry. He cinched tight, holding himself in place, biting his tongue as the raw skin on his hands screamed. The light passed beneath him and Harry kept going until, out of nowhere, the hard ground appeared and he smashed to earth in a heap.

The crown. It was still in his waistband, sharp as a knife. He pulled it free, wiggled his toes and found them in working order, then stood up.

He immediately dropped down again as another light flashed his way. The shouting was close now, too close, men yelling at each other in Russian. What they were saying he had no idea, but it wasn't good.

The manicured lawn stretched interminably in front of him until it reached a tall hedgerow. On the other side of the thick brush was his electric motorcycle and the road that would take him to Windsor. Beyond that waited a plane, headed home. Cool grass brushed his chin as he crawled over the lawn while the guards shouted at each other and searched for him. Thank goodness Evgeny wasn't in residence at the moment, or there would be three times as many guards. Evgeny Smolov had made an enemy of the current Russian president, a man known to poison or abduct his enemies, or simply make them disappear. Hence, Evgeny had put a substantial portion of those billions of dollars of his toward an elite security team that traveled everywhere with him.

Harry crawled on. The hedges were fifty feet away now, close enough he considered making a break for it before a guard's light bounced on the foliage. Harry hugged the darkness as a guard passed within mere yards of him on his way to the property line. This guard was running right for the spot where Harry's motorcycle was hidden. Harry had dropped it out of sight, but if the guard found it, so much for getting out of here.

The guard stopped at the hedges and turned, looking back toward the facility. He was standing no more than five feet from the concealed bike. Harry stayed low. *Get out of there. Nothing to see.*

The guard started walking again—on a direct line toward Harry, headed back to the building. Harry shoved his face deeper into the dirt and didn't breathe. The guard's footsteps sounded in the crisp grass, coming so close the ground vibrated beneath Harry's fingertips. The footsteps passed. Harry counted to ten before twisting his head around. The guy was still walking away.

Enough of this. Scrambling across the lawn faster than he should, Harry made it to the hedges, bursting underneath them and promptly smacking his face on a handlebar. At least the bike was still here. It was the work of a moment to drag it from under cover and pull the machine upright. He pushed the bike along as fast as he could go, the hairs on his neck standing up as he waited for a car to come around from the main entrance or a guard to poke his head between the hedges. The moon hung full overhead as he ran along the open road with the bike, fully exposed with nowhere to hide. Several hundred yards on and he'd had enough.

The motorcycle's storage compartment popped open when he touched it. Out came a pair of night-vision goggles, in went the crown. Hopping astride the bike, Harry fired the electric motor and hit the throttle. The soft whine was nearly inaudible this far from Evgeny's museum, a low shrill that whipped Harry into the dark night. He rode with no lights as the world turned into a blur of green-tinted open road. A road headed straight back to Brooklyn.

Chapter 2

Brooklyn, New York

"How much did you pay for it?"

Sara Hamed and Harry Fox were sitting at the table in his apartment. She turned the crown over in her hands as she asked, watching Harry all the while. "It's worth a fortune."

He pretended to think. "Not what you think," he finally said. "But it was worth every penny."

She aimed a finger between his eyes. "Don't lie to me. I thought we were past that."

They were, and he was. *Damn.* Harry sighed. "Hear me out."

Sara set the crown down. She pulled a lock of auburn hair off her forehead and crossed her arms. "The truth. All of it."

Forty-eight hours ago he'd been racing away from Evgeny Smolov's museum with the crown. Now he faced a new trial, just as precarious. Harry reached for his half-empty glass of beer to buy time. The glass was nearly empty when he set it back down. "I tried to purchase it," he said. "The owner wasn't selling."

A look crossed her face that pained him more than anything she could shout. "You lied to me."

"I want to protect you," he said. "That's the truth. You don't know who we're dealing with."

"I know you work for a mobster," Sara said. "And you also work undercover for the Manhattan district attorney's office recovering trafficked antiquities." The finger again, this time jabbing his chest. "That means you work with lots of bad people. I met some of them. Now tell me what happened." Her face softened. "I know you live and work in a gray area, Harry." Her lips turned up in a half-smile. "It can be exciting."

Funny how working with the D.A.'s office had changed her tune on that. "Fine. Here's the whole story. Don't tell anyone, because they wouldn't believe you."

Harry laid it all out. Yes, he'd told Sara he knew who had Antony's crown, and that he was trying to purchase it. He had tried, until he discovered Evgeny Smolov owned it.

"I asked a few questions," Harry said. "Quietly. It turns out Evgeny Smolov built a private museum in Windsor."

Sara started. "One moment." She touched the crown. "Evgeny Smolov owned this. The Russian oligarch."

Harry nodded. "Offering him money is pointless. He would never sell it."

"How do you know?"

"All the people I spoke with made it clear Evgeny treasures this crown."

"Hence building a private museum," Sara said. She lifted an eyebrow. "Did you go there?" Harry confirmed that he had. "You stole it, didn't you?"

"I did."

Silence filled the air. Sara watched him as she took a drink of wine. She looked at the crown, then reached out to touch it again. "It was the only way you could get it," she said. "To continue following the path." She leaned over and reached for the amulet hidden under his shirt. He flinched back, stopped himself, then pulled it out. "The path your father left for you," she said.

Sara Hamed was the only person who'd ever touched his father's amulet since it became Harry's. "Yes," Harry said. "It was the only way."

They'd met little more than a year earlier. Sara Hamed was a professor of Egyptology at Trier University in Germany. Harry Fox hunted relics and artifacts for the mob. A more unlikely match was difficult to imagine.

"This crown is a remarkable piece of history," she said. "It shouldn't be locked away for one man's pleasure. I'm certain it will find a better home after we finish." The look on her face made it clear disagreement wasn't an option.

A wise man picks his battles. "It will," he said. "When we're done."

Sara touched a particularly fine ruby on the crown. "What else was in this private museum?" She didn't look at him as she spoke.

"I only saw one other exhibit. It wasn't finished." He described the half-done showcase with Greek and Cyrillic writing on it. "The tablet said 'What stands before you gave birth to the modern world.'"

"You didn't see anything else inside?"

"I was on a tight schedule."

Six months ago Sara wouldn't have dropped it. Now she did. "I see," she said, though her expression said the opposite. "I'm grateful you're safe and that you found the crown. It's the next step on the trail Antony and Cleopatra left behind."

It had all started with Harry's amulet. A gift bequeathed by his father far too soon. The mysterious amulet had led them to an ancient scarab medallion commemorating Antony and Cleopatra's last great military victory, which then pointed Harry and Sara to a necklace worn by Cleopatra, one that Harry had recovered. The necklace indicated that a mural preserved in the ruins of Pompeii held the next clue, which was a hidden message leading to Antony's crown—the one in front of him now. Harry had no idea what came next, or more importantly, what the trail ultimately led to.

"Cleopatra was wearing the necklace in the Pompeii mural," Harry said. "And *VERITAS* was written above Antony's crown."

"Truth," Sara said.

"She was telling us the *truth* could be found in Antony's crown. A crown often displayed publicly."

"But the crown was accessible only to certain people. Which makes me suspect there is a person who they intended to follow this path."

Harry grinned. "You don't think Antony and Cleopatra left this for us?"

"If they did, you were a terrible choice." She laughed as she rubbed his forearm. "Whoever was truly meant to find it never did. Now it's our turn."

Sara angled the crown so light caught the inside. A phrase had been engraved on the gold. "This Latin engraving is where we start."

She opened a notebook and wrote the phrase in it. *CSILAH.*

"You think it's Latin because that was the language of Rome in their time," Harry said. "But this isn't a Latin word. It's not a word in any language." He'd scoured every conceivable language for a possible match and come up empty. Sara wasn't happy with him jumping ahead like that. For an academic like her, a methodical search was as important as the artifact.

"It's still the most logical conclusion," Sara said. "Cleopatra spoke many languages. Antony spoke Latin and Greek. They likely communicated in their common language of Greek, which suggests this writing is Greek. However, I've read thousands of documents from their time. These letters are clearly written as part of a Latin phrase."

"Then why can't we understand it?"

She glared at him. "That's what we figure out."

Harry took the crown from her. "If Antony and Cleopatra intended for someone specific to find their messages, we can assume they likely knew this person well."

"That doesn't narrow it down very much."

"I'm not trying to narrow the list down," Harry said. "What I'm saying is perhaps these letters, whether Latin or Greek, aren't the message."

"Then why inscribe them?"

"No idea. Any number of people in their time could possibly have deciphered a written message like this. It's likely this is a code or a message that should only make sense to the person they chose."

"A code, or perhaps part of a cultural or local reference."

"Exactly. One we can't easily understand two thousand years later. If I'm correct, a straightforward written message isn't secure. They'd need something else, a different way to communicate to one specific person."

"In a way others wouldn't recognize." Sara tapped the crown. "How?"

"That's what I'm working on." He lifted the crown, holding it up to look at the underside. "The mural scene had several paintings detailed in it. They all related to Greek gods, which isn't surprising given Cleopatra would have been intimately familiar with those myths."

He paused. "Did you know Hades never lived on Mount Olympus even though he was Zeus's brother? I didn't. He's not considered an Olympian."

"I did," Sara said. "Does that mean anything for our search?"

"Other than I was surprised to find out it has nothing to do with the Olympic games? No." Harry shrugged. "I looked at the possibility of a local or cultural reference, but that seems too obvious. My gut says there's something more."

Sara had uncovered relics with him in Iran and England. She knew by now Harry's instincts should be heeded. Unless they shouldn't. "I'm listening. How else could the crown be a message?"

Harry frowned and glared at the crown. He didn't answer.

"This is a textbook example of the Civic Crown," Sara said. "It's actually a military decoration, but Emperor Augustus wore it as emperor." She pointed to the gold oak leaves woven in a circular shape. "The gemstones on each oak leaf are an interesting touch. Other than that, it's quite typical."

Harry pointed to the rear leaf. "This is the only amethyst. It's purple, the same color as the cloaks worn by emperors. Every other stone is on here twice. Two diamonds, sapphires, emeralds, and of course rubies."

"Red was the color of war in Rome."

"Why put the amethyst at the rear?" Harry asked. "It represents royalty. Why make it so hard to see?"

"It's a magnificent stone," Sara said. "The biggest one."

He'd noticed. An incredible amethyst that dazzled when the light hit it, the sort of stone a Roman potentate would show off, not hide. It made no sense for Mark Antony to tuck this gem back in the shadows. Or, to be more accurate, it made no sense for Cleopatra to do it, for she had certainly played a role in creating the crown. A woman who had risen to such power knew the value of displaying it.

"They did this on purpose," Harry said softly. "It's in the back for a reason."

But darned if he knew what it was. The crown was likely twenty-two-carat gold. It was heavy enough for him to tell it wasn't hollow. He spun it around. A diamond on the front leaf, then a ruby, an emerald and a sapphire. The order repeated itself around the entire crown, except for the amethyst. Was it a code?

"How do you say these gemstones in Latin?" Harry asked. "Diamond, ruby, emerald, sapphire."

"*Adamantem, rubeus, smaragdus, sapphirus.* Amethyst is *amethystus.*"

He put the first letters in a row. He chuckled. "Does *arssa* mean anything to you?"

Sara thought for a moment. "No."

"Could it be an anagram?" He rearranged the letters in his head. "I can't think of anything that makes sense in Latin or Greek."

"Neither can I."

Harry was studying the front leaf when Sara reached across the table and lifted the back side, where the amethyst had been placed. "Angle this up to the light," she said.

He did. "Do you see something?"

"No." His face fell. "That's what's wrong," she continued. "I don't see the amethyst dispersing light as it should. There's not enough 'fire' in it."

Harry tried to flip the crown around, but she held it in place. "A stone of this quality should come alive at the right angle."

"It doesn't?" he asked.

"Nothing really happens when you tilt it toward the light. Look." Sara took the crown from him and spun it around. "It shines, yes, but not like it should."

She was right. The purple gem was the size of his knuckle, yet it didn't do much of anything even in direct light. The other stones exploded with color. The amethyst did not.

"The crown is made of gold," Harry said. "If anything, the metal backing should make it more impressive." He drained the last of his beer. "Hold the crown steady," he said. "Point the amethyst at me."

Sara angled it toward his face. He lifted his empty glass and held it right above the purple stone. This close, the bottom of the glass served as a magnifying glass, bringing the stone into clear focus. Harry blinked. The breath caught in his throat. "There's something wrong with the stone."

She pulled the crown away. "What do you mean?"

"Use this glass." Harry gave her the empty glass and took the crown. Sara held his glass over the stone just as he had. "See anything?" he asked.

She twisted the glass back and forth. A second later she visibly started. "There's a crevice running through the stone. Along the rear of it. No, crevice isn't the right word."

"A dark streak," Harry said. "Ever seen anything like that in a gem?" Sara said she hadn't. "I didn't think so, because I don't think it's part of the stone."

"It could be an imperfection in the metal," Sara said. "Though I doubt it. The rest of the crown is perfect. The craftsmanship is exceptional."

She didn't see it. Perhaps Sara wasn't devious enough. If she actually followed through on her thoughts about taking a semester off and spending it with Harry, maybe he could change that. "Nothing's wrong with the crown," Harry said. "It's intentional. There's something *behind* the stone."

Everything made sense once you had it. Sara got it an instant later. "Oh my." She leaned closer to the stone, looking through his beer glass. "There *is* something behind the stone."

"There's an opening carved behind the amethyst," Harry said. "That's what we see in the back. You hardly notice the imperfection, even in the light. At the back it's practically invisible. I suspect that's also why these letters are carved on the rear side." Harry tapped the mysterious engraving. "They're directly below the hollow spot."

"A way to mark it," Sara said. She jumped from her chair and circled the table to wrap her arms around him. "Nice work."

He inhaled the scent of lavender in her hair. "Thanks."

Sara let go just as quickly as she'd grabbed him. "You realize this artifact is priceless."

"I'm not going to destroy it," Harry said. "Only pop one gem out. Whoever put it there wanted the stone to come out eventually."

"Who will repair it? We can't just walk into a local jeweler and ask him to fix it."

Harry winked. "Don't worry. I know a guy who can keep a secret."

Sara shook her head, but there was a smile on her lips. "Don't you always."

"Let me grab my toolbox." Harry jumped up and darted into his basement, where he grabbed an oversized toolbox and a pair of headlamps. "Here," he said when he got back to the table. "Put this on."

The headlamps went on both their foreheads and illuminated the crown as well as any spotlight. Sara stayed his hand as Harry reached for the toolbox. "Gold is soft," she said. "You can easily damage it."

"I'm a bit of a craftsman myself."

"Of destruction, perhaps. I've seen your handiwork."

He grumbled, mainly because it was true. "I'll be careful." Still, he selected a smaller screwdriver than was necessary. "I only want to pop the stone out." He touched the screwdriver to the crown, then stopped. "What do you think is behind it?"

"I have no idea, but it must be thin." Sara drummed her fingers against the table. "A message from Mark Antony and Cleopatra?"

"If it is, there aren't many of those around."

"We'd be obligated to share it with the world," Sara said. "Its historical value cannot be overstated."

"We will," Harry said. "After we unravel its meaning."

"Along with any steps that come next?"

"That's my thought."

"Fine."

Harry paused. A year ago, Sara had thought him merely an interesting man who was always caught up in a deadly, often illegal race to locate artifacts. Now he liaised with the authorities to help preserve cultural relics for everyone. Mostly. To her, it made all the difference in the world.

"Keep your eyes open," he said. "I don't want to dig this stone out of the air duct."

Harry leaned over the crown. Sara stood at his shoulder, the light from their headlamps bringing the stones to life as he touched the narrow screwdriver to where the purple stone lay snug against the crown. It didn't budge. He bit his tongue and pushed harder. "Hold the crown steady," he said.

"Wait." Sara ran to the kitchen and grabbed a dish towel, which she placed under the crown. "Don't want it to scratch your table," she said. "I've got it now."

The towel actually made it easier, giving him purchase to push on the crown while he worked. He wiggled the screwdriver back and forth until it nudged between stone and crown. The tool left a tiny groove in the metal.

"Be careful," Sara said. "You're damaging it."

"Gold is soft. I'm about to do worse." The screwdriver slid in further until it stuck. Harry bit his lip, leaned on the tool, and the stone came loose as though shot out of a cannon. "Watch out."

The screwdriver clattered down as he grabbed for the stone, missed it, then managed to hit it with his other hand to send the purple rock flying across the room. His chair toppled as Harry jumped up and gave chase. Once, twice, he clipped it before finally diving on top of the amethyst.

"Got it," he called over a shoulder. Sara didn't respond. He was flat on the floor as he checked whether the stone was trapped beneath him. It was. "It's right here." He lifted his closed fist. Still nothing from Sara.

"Are you okay?" he asked as he stood and turned. "I said I got it."

"Come look at this."

She was hunched over at the table. Harry got to his feet, moved carefully back to the table and found her leaning over a piece of dark fabric. "What is that?" he asked.

"It was behind the stone. This is the imperfection we spotted." He reached for it. She slapped his hand away. "Are you crazy? Don't touch it. This material could disintegrate."

She pushed him into the chair beside her. "It's rolled. Get me some tweezers and a safety pin."

Harry set the amethyst in a bowl before retrieving the items. Sara took them. "We should be in a laboratory."

"Don't even think about it," Harry said. "You're as qualified as anyone to do it. And if you say you don't want to open it now, I won't believe you."

She hesitated. "I won't say it." She poked and prodded the rolled material with her tweezers. "It's sturdier than I thought. Thicker, too. There could be something inside of it."

"*On* it, more likely." Harry had seen this sort of thing before. "It looks like a scroll."

She grabbed his shoulder and made him lean forward. "Keep your head steady. I need more light."

Sara bent over the rolled fabric. The dark material resembled vellum, though it appeared to have been stretched and scraped, the process making it much thinner and offering the added benefit of making the surface area larger. More surface area meant more room to write—if Harry's idea was correct. The unrolled scroll was every bit of two inches tall.

"What can you see?" he asked.

"Nothing with you moving around like that."

He kept still as Sara cautiously unrolled the scrap of fabric to reveal dark ink. She stopped and looked up. "You were correct. Nicely done."

He didn't try to keep the grin off his face. A minute of delicate work later and the little scroll turned out to not be so little. It was twice as long as it was high; lettering covered the translucent vellum document. Greek letters.

"Greek was Cleopatra's native language." Sara's voice barely reached his ears. "These may be her words."

"The only other person who could have written it is Antony."

"I understand part of it." Sara copied the text down onto her notepad, her lips moving silently as she wrote. "But not all of it. This is Koine Greek."

Harry's Greek was borderline non-existent. Not that he could read the tiny, cramped script with Sara hovering over it. "Do people still speak it?"

"The Greek Orthodox church does, so yes. Now let me concentrate."

By concentrate she meant copy the rest of the text and then grab her phone. Harry absently reached out to touch the crown at the same time as a car engine roared outside his window and tires screamed on asphalt. He started, knocked the crown over, and cursed his nerves. "My fault."

"I would be jumpy too if someone had tried to kill me in my own apartment." She looked up. "You never did fix those bullet holes outside."

"They give the place character." He didn't remind her that that had been over a year ago. He'd survived.

The crown had been upended. He picked it up, twisted the leafy headpiece around, and his chest went cold. "Sara."

"I'm busy," she said.

"Look at this."

Hidden in the depths where the impressive amethyst had been were letters, etched into the gold where the hidden missive had been stored. "Latin," Harry said. "*In posterum.*"

"The future," Sara translated.

"What future?" Harry tilted the crown to get a better look. "There's nothing else."

"Put that mystery on the back burner," Sara said. "We have one we can unravel right here."

The small scroll was now completely open. "These are directions," she said. "To somewhere in Egypt."

Harry leaned over her shoulder. "Do you recognize it? This piece is two thousand years old."

Sara didn't answer, but began reading.

Seek the southern sanctuary where the pharaohs are born. Summit Ramses II. Look to the obelisk nearest Helios for your destiny. You are the future.

"There's that part about the future again," Harry said. "What does it mean?"

Sara didn't respond. Her lips were moving as she read the passage again. Harry kept quiet until she was ready to speak. "If we're correct that this message was meant for someone specific, then we have a problem."

"Too many people to choose from."

"Yes. Family members, advisors, plus any number of hangers-on. And there could be other people we would never suspect."

"We can start to narrow it down," Harry said. "The person they have in mind would be educated."

Sara got a look in her eye. The one he imagined she had when quizzing an overly confident student. "Why?"

"The intended person must be literate."

"No more than five percent of ancient Egyptians were literate," Sara said. "Go on."

"The messages are in two languages, so we have someone who's multilingual. Beyond language skills, this person would also need a working knowledge of religion and geography."

"Why do you say that?"

Harry winked. "I won't steal your thunder."

She frowned as though confused. "What?"

Harry hurried on with his analysis. "Finally, this person needed the resources to follow this path wherever it led. A path that includes having access to Antony's crown. Even if it was on display, not just anyone could walk up and touch it."

"Or rip an amethyst out," Sara said. "I agree with everything."

Harry sat back, more than a little pleased with himself. Half a lifetime of doing this had taught him a few things, yet Sara was often head and shoulders above him in decoding the past.

"And I appreciate you not—how did you say it?" Sara asked.

"Stealing your thunder."

Sara shook her head and chuckled. "You Americans and your sayings." Sara turned to the exposed scroll. "These are directions. *Southern sanctuary.* Does that mean anything to you?"

Harry puzzled it over. "No."

"This refers to the Luxor Temple. Which still stands in Egypt, on the banks of the Nile in the city of Luxor. Antony and Cleopatra knew it as Thebes. Numerous pharaohs were crowned there."

"Where their reign was *born*," Harry said. "What about *Ramses II*?"

She frowned. "Let's skip that for now."

Odd, but if she said so. "Are there any *obelisks* in Luxor?"

"Not as many now as then. Two great obelisks used to stand on either side of the entrance, one larger than the other. This message directs us to the taller one. It is closer to *Helios*, the sun god."

"Hold on. You said there used to be two obelisks. How many are there now?"

"One. The other is in Paris. An Egyptian ruler gave it to the French as a gift two hundred years ago. Lucky for us he gave them the shorter one."

Harry smacked the table. "We're still in business."

"Perhaps. I know where this message points us, and the obelisk referenced is still there. However, I'm uncertain about the reference to Ramses II."

"Remind me who he was again?"

"The third pharaoh of the nineteenth dynasty." Sara fired it off without blinking. "Ramses was dead for over a thousand years before Antony or Cleopatra came along. That's why there is a statue of him at the entrance to Luxor. The statue is nearly forty feet tall, and until a few years ago, was in pieces on the ground. It shattered during a long-ago earthquake and was only discovered in the fifties."

"Can you see the obelisk from on top of it?"

"You've had more than a few crazy ideas since I met you. That may be the worst."

He turned his palms to the ceiling. "Why? That's what the message says to do."

"That's what you *think* it says. Forget for a moment that anyone caught climbing the statue in Cleopatra's time would have been executed. It's tall enough that you could die if you fell."

Her lack of faith was not his concern. "How far is it from the statue to the obelisk?"

"Not far," she admitted.

"Then what if we're supposed to do what the directions say? Climb the statue, look at the obelisk, and see what's written there. I'll bet there are hieroglyphs all over the obelisk." Her silence confirmed it. "Thought so. This solves two problems. First, it tells us what we're supposed to do next. Second, it further narrows down who this path was meant for. Someone who had the status to climb Ramses and not be killed for it."

He could tell she was fighting the idea, not only because it made too much sense, but because she loved it. Sara Hamed was a respected Egyptologist. A year ago, she would have dismissed such a wild notion as heresy. After twelve months of knowing Harry Fox and chasing relics at his side, she was changed. Now, she found the idea worth considering.

"It's possible. But not only for the reasons you think," she said quickly. "There's no telling what line of text you would see standing atop Ramses."

"Or what else might be apparent."

"There could be an image or drawing on top of the statue that helps you understand what to focus on," Sara said. "Or on the temple itself."

She was warming to it. "Then what are we waiting for?" Harry asked. "We need to get to Luxor."

Sara laughed. "You have clearly never been there. Luxor Temple is the city's main tourist attraction. It's a sprawling complex connected to the Karnak Temple by a nine-thousand-foot-long Avenue of Sphinxes."

"What's that?"

"Exactly what it sounds like. A road guarded by sphinx statues, itself also a tourist attraction. The area is patrolled by armed guards at all hours."

"Does it close at night?"

"The entire—what? Of course it closes at night."

"Then there won't be nearly as many guards around after the sun sets."

Sara shook her head. "No way. As I was saying, this entire idea is crazy. What we should do is use my connections in Egypt. I know faculty members at Luxor University. I can apply for a research permit so we can do this without fear of injury or incarceration."

She had to be joking. "The second you tell anyone about this, the word will spread and half of Luxor will join our search." She didn't argue. "No," Harry continued. "My idea isn't the safest, but it's our only option if we want to find out what this"—here he touched his amulet—"is hiding. That's what I want." He paused. "Don't you?"

"It's still a terrible idea." She twirled a strand of hair around her finger. "Despite your being correct." Sara tapped a finger on the tabletop as though it had offended her. "Let's talk through the challenges. The statue of Ramses you propose to climb is nearly forty feet tall. There are no steps, no guiderails. How would you climb it?"

"I've climbed a number of vertical faces outside the city for exercise. Getting up a forty-foot statue won't be a problem. In fact, I guarantee you could do it if I showed you how to use the climbing gear."

The glare she offered struck fear in his heart. "Thank you for explaining how climbing is done. In Germany we call it mountaineering, and it is quite popular. I don't need you to show me how climbing gear works. I've used it in the Bavarian Alps."

The woman never stopped surprising him. "I'm sorry."

She frowned at him for a long moment. "Apology accepted. A word of advice. The next time you have the urge to explain anything to a woman, myself included, don't."

"Fair enough."

"I hate to say this, but I agree. We should go to Luxor. Reconnoiter the area, see what we can find without clambering atop a statue. We may be able to identify what this scroll is pointing us to without climbing."

"And if not, we do it my way."

"In that case, we regroup."

Harry flashed a grin. "I'll take that as a maybe." He pointed to the crown. "Which still doesn't answer what *the future* means."

Sara frowned. She pulled at a strand of hair. Harry kept quiet. "Perhaps it will become clear later," she finally said.

"Fair enough." Harry's father, Fred Fox, had had more than his fair share of sayings. One jumped to mind. "Focus on the big picture."

"Yes," Sara said. "We know where to go. If that message plays a role, it's likely we'll realize it when we need it." She opened her laptop. "I'll book two tickets to Luxor." Keys clicked. "After I buy a top-shelf pair of binoculars. Climbing the Ramses statue is a foolhardy errand. Binoculars may save me from your incredibly thick skull."

Sara had already pulled up an outfitter's website when Harry's doorbell rang. They both went still. A moment later knocking sounded, the sort that said whoever was outside had no plans to go away. Harry knew only one person with so little patience for waiting. "I think I know who it is."

Lines had creased Sara's forehead. "Should you answer it?" Evidently she was still worried about gunmen in the area.

"Watch this," Harry said. He grabbed his phone and dialed a number he hadn't expected to call so soon. A moment later the knocking stopped. Harry hung up and went to the door. "She's the only person I know who tries to beat down every door," he called to Sara over his shoulder.

He pulled the door open to reveal Nora Doyle standing outside, a phone pressed to her ear.

"Good evening," Harry said.

A streetlight flickered behind her. "I have a problem," Nora said. "You're going to help me with it."

Chapter 3

Windsor

A circular saw whined as sawdust filled the air. Hammers banged like gunshots while a man wielded an acetylene torch nearby, sparks bouncing off his helmet as he sliced through metal tubing. The noise of the controlled chaos rang off the stone walls and floor of the newly constructed building, the dust contained by long plastic sheets draped from the ceiling and walls. Two men wielded laser measuring tools as they inspected different areas under construction, one taking notes on a pad. A wooden box taller than a man stood to one side. Turkish writing ran across the surface.

Across the room, one of the plastic sheets moved aside to reveal a squat man. A hand far too large for his short body replaced the sheet again as he walked in. The cacophonous production ceased moments later. All the contractors watched as the man made his way to the center of the hallway. He paused in front of the welder, hands behind his back as he surveyed the scene. He seemed to notice a speck of dust on his hand-made suit. A silk handkerchief came out of the man's jacket pocket, which he used to wipe the dust away. Everybody watched until the handkerchief disappeared again. No one made a sound.

"*Skol'ko yeshche?*"

The suited man directed his question to the foreman, one of the men taking measurements. The foreman considered the question. For too long, it seemed. The man repeated his question, the hard consonants of his native tongue like rocks cracking together. "*Skol'ko yeshche?"* How much longer?

"One week," the foreman replied in Russian. "Two at most."

The suited man reached up and clapped one of his massive hands on the foreman's shoulder. The foreman stood a foot taller. Even so, he flinched.

"One, and no more."

The foreman agreed. "Yes, Mr. Smolov. One week."

Mr. Smolov flashed his teeth. "Yes." He eyed the wooden box with Turkish writing on it. He nodded before turning around.

Silence hung for several beats as he retreated before the foreman shouted, "*Vernut'sya k rabote!* Back to work!"

The plastic sheeting opened, Mr. Smolov walked through, and the tension in the air vanished. Not that Mr. Smolov noticed as he stepped into a golf cart. It was a long walk to the portion of the estate he used as his private residence. He was aware of the impact he had on others, though he rarely worried about other people unless they could do something for him. There were only a few people in the world who could.

Financial publications reported that Evgeny Smolov was worth somewhere in the neighborhood of eleven billion dollars. He knew it was actually a bit less than that, but why correct them? In truth, he was impressed the journalists had gotten so close to the real figure. Sifting through the murky finances of an oligarch was difficult. Even more so when such detective work came with the unspoken but clear threat of physical harm for any journalist foolish enough to anger the man.

Evgeny had worked hard to cultivate his image. Fortunately, he no longer had much need to dirty his hands. That's what his employees were for.

His office door opened to reveal a room large enough to comfortably hold two hundred people. Evgeny knew because he had once hosted a party of that size in here, a birthday gathering for one of the few men from the old country who still darkened his door. Evgeny stopped on the threshold. That had been a night to remember, and one that had cost him a few million. He didn't have many friends, not any more. Most of them were now in shallow, unmarked graves somewhere in his former homeland. A homeland controlled with an iron fist by the new tsar.

Evgeny realized he was grinding his teeth. Take a breath, Evgeny. You beat him. Now you are untouchable.

The same line he repeated to himself every time those memories surfaced. He'd beaten the soulless tyrant at his own game. Now Evgeny was rich beyond imagination. All it had cost him was everything.

A restrained knocking sounded on the door. "Mr. Smolov."

Evgeny turned to find his butler at the door with one white-gloved hand upraised. "Come in, Poole."

The Englishman walked as though skating on invisible wheels. His legs hardly seemed to move. Evgeny loved that. "Your appointment is here, sir."

"Send him in."

Evgeny leaned against one of the overstuffed chairs arranged around a coffee table in the corner. He crossed his arms on his chest, and he waited.

Poole reappeared and ushered a man into Evgeny's office. The new man's eyes were drawn to the towering windows behind Evgeny's desk across the room. A manicured lawn stretched into the distance, dotted with horses feeding in oversized plots, all of it meant to impress. The man took in the view for a fraction of a second before his eyes fell to Evgeny.

Evgeny showed the man all his expensive teeth. "Oleg, come in."

Oleg found the carpet quite interesting as he walked. He stopped well back from Evgeny as Poole closed the door without a sound.

"Over here." Evgeny smacked the chair he was leaning on. "Have a seat."

Oleg sat, while Evgeny remained standing behind him. He could see Oleg's shoulders shaking. "Would you like something to drink?" Evgeny asked. He touched Oleg and the man jumped. "It will help."

Evgeny walked to the drinks cart and poured two glasses of champagne. Evgeny already knew Oleg was more of a vodka man. A pity. Most vodka was garbage, and even the quality ones ruined your senses.

"*Dlya vashevo zdorov'ya.*" Evgeny tapped Oleg's glass with his own, spilling several drops of very expensive liquid on the seated man. "To your health, Oleg."

Evgeny drained his glass, then waited for Oleg to do the same. The man hesitated. "You think it is poisoned?" Evgeny laughed. Oleg didn't answer. He didn't have to. "Give it to me," Evgeny said in Russian. He grabbed the glass, drained it in one go, then refilled them both. "Now, drink."

Only after Oleg had tasted the champagne did Evgeny sit down. His chair was adjacent to Oleg's, with a table between them. Evgeny dropped the overpriced bottle of champagne onto it. "Relax, Oleg. If I wanted to kill you, I wouldn't do it here." He pointed to the floor. "Blood is difficult to get out of this rug."

Oleg burrowed into his chair as Evgeny erupted, smacking his leg and laughing like no one was listening.

"A joke! I am joking."

Eventually Oleg smiled, looking like a man who would give anything to be out of the room.

"Relax," Evgeny told him. "I am not upset about the crown."

Oleg was a battle-hardened Russian soldier. He was also scared to death of Evgeny Smolov, who had rescued Oleg and his family from the bland, oppressive existence of their native land. Evgeny had been Oleg's ticket to a better life, and for that he demanded complete loyalty. The same story could be repeated dozens of times, one for each of the men Evgeny paid exorbitantly to protect him and his properties.

Evgeny paid well, and he also did nothing to dissuade his loyal guards of the notion he would kill anyone who crossed him. He didn't because it was, to a degree, completely true. Failure he could accept. Betrayal he could not.

"I am deeply sorry, Mr. Smolov." Oleg licked his lips as he spoke in their native tongue, eyeing the champagne. "I will do whatever is required to retrieve it."

"Have more champagne." Evgeny refilled their glasses. "What I require is an explanation. Tell me what happened."

Evgeny had been out of the country when an intruder broke into his private museum and stole the crown belonging to Mark Antony. One of his guards had died during the ensuing chase. The man's stupidity had killed him.

"I was walking my round," Oleg said. "I stopped in front of the crown display."

Evgeny leaned forward. "Do you always do this?"

Oleg flinched, then sat straight. "Not in the same place. I change my routine. My patrol must be unpredictable."

"Yes, it must. What happened next?"

"A hand tapped my shoulder."

"Which one?"

Oleg paused. "This one." He touched his left shoulder. "It startled me."

"You never saw the man who touched you?"

"Not until the end," Oleg said. "When Alexei ran after him."

"Yes, Alexei." Evgeny opened a drawer in the small table and removed a remote control. He aimed it at the massive fireplace not far from them, pushed a button, and a fire burst to life. "He made a grave mistake."

Oleg couldn't take his eyes off the fire. "Yes. A tragedy."

"What happened after the intruder touched you?"

"He punched me as I turned."

"It must have been a hard punch," Evgeny said. "One hit knocked you down."

Oleg's eyes darkened, the first sign of life from the big man. "It was not. The intruder wore knuckledusters. You can see the marks." Oleg tapped the row of dark indents along his jawline.

"It was the only way he could take you out," Evgeny assured him. "What then?"

Oleg sat noticeably straighter now. "I lost my senses for a moment. I got up as Alexei ran past. He was chasing the intruder."

"And he forgot about the traps."

"Yes." Oleg studied his hands for a moment. "He will be missed."

"He will. I hope you do not ever make the same mistake."

"I would never, sir."

Now to the part Evgeny truly cared about. "How did the intruder escape? I designed the traps myself. No one outside of your team knows how they work. Not even the men who installed them."

Oleg's eyes widened. "I swear I did not reveal the secret."

"I am not saying you did." Though he had been, sort of. He needed to see Oleg's reaction. "I trust you completely. You would know if I did not."

Oleg clearly wasn't sure how to respond to that. He played it safe. "Yes, sir."

"The escape?"

"The intruder knew to use alternate squares," Oleg said quickly. "He jumped from one side to the other."

"It is possible he deciphered the clues," Evgeny said to himself.

"What, sir?"

Evgeny waved a hand. "Nothing." He hadn't told his men what the message referencing the *true gods* meant, and they knew to avoid the hallway with the pressure traps unless they deactivated the security system first. Even then, none of them entered it other than to clean. They were too afraid. "Perhaps this man was meant to survive my security traps," Evgeny said. His face hardened. "That is why you are there. To stop anyone who survives."

Oleg said nothing. Evgeny let him stew a moment longer. "However, no one is perfect. I forgive you, Oleg." He reached out. Oleg accepted the crushing handshake. "Do not let it happen again."

"I swear on my life, Mr. Smolov. I will not let you down."

"Go watch the men unloading my newest piece," Evgeny said. "Be sure they do not damage it."

Evgeny sent Oleg on his way. On the whole, it had gone well. He'd confirmed his suspicion that Oleg wasn't involved, and more importantly, reinforced that Oleg was his man for life. You could buy other crowns, but unwavering loyalty had to be earned. Equally important was the question of who had the gall to sneak into his private museum, the intellect to avoid his traps, and the skills to escape. To have one quality was not uncommon. Two, less so. But all three? That was a man Evgeny needed to know about, in large part because such a man could trouble him in the future.

Evgeny already had several of his top men working on identifying the intruder. They had little to go on. A short man, possibly Italian. Or perhaps from South America, though what country it was hard to say. No usable fingerprints had been found, and the facial images Evgeny sent to one of his friends with access to Interpol records came up empty. Same with the search for an escape vehicle. The man had hopped on a motorcycle and disappeared.

In short, he had nothing. Evgeny poured more champagne and moved to look out the towering windows. Clouds covered the sky in a typical English embrace. Evgeny might get his crown back, or he might not. Either way, his collecting continued. A new exhibit space down the hall from where he displayed the crown would hold his finest acquisition yet, a piece tied to the other new artifact about to be put on display. A recently acquired statue, yet it was merely a prelude to what he now sought. A relic that had only been whispered about for centuries, an artifact kept alive in stories passed down through generations, though no one truly believed it could exist.

Except Evgeny. Bubbly liquid tickled his throat as he drank. He believed. He had chased down the legend, and now he was closer than anyone to uncovering the truth. So close he was already building the exhibit. However, one thing stood in his way. Evgeny was a collector, not an archaeologist. He'd built his fortune handling money. First for oligarchs in Russia, old and new, now for anyone around the globe who required financial services. Freedom fighters, terrorists, despots or gangsters. It didn't matter. If they had cash, Evgeny managed it for them. He made it grow, without fail. For a fee, of course.

He left finding the actual artifacts to experts. And it was amazing who wanted to find an artifact for you when you offered a five-million-dollar finder's fee. Evgeny wouldn't work with just anyone. You had to be someone he could trust. Who did he trust? Mostly no one, though if the person had done business with Evgeny before, he might. Right now he was sorting through several offers. Whoever he selected would receive a message Evgeny had uncovered. A message, lost to time, that led to the ancient artifact that would be the centerpiece of his museum.

He drained the glass. A single framed photograph looked back at him from atop his desk. Faded and worn, it was the only image he had left of her. Over thirty years she had been gone, yet he thought of her every day. She was why he had come so far in life. If his sister hadn't died after the Soviet Union collapsed, Evgeny would never have understood how much dangerous work it took to become the man he was today. The world took from you. It never gave. The only way a man got what he wanted was by taking it. As many had said before, power is never given. It is always taken.

His sister was taken from him by men who meant to take what their family had. Her death allowed Evgeny to realize he must take what he deserved in the world from that day on. It didn't matter who he worked with. All that mattered was power. And Evgeny knew the golden rule. The one with the gold makes the rules.

He shook his head. Enough of that. He lifted a file from his desk and opened it. A photo lay inside, taken the day his newest piece had been acquired, a day not long ago in Turkey. The piece being put on display now. This piece had the message Evgeny had been seeking for so long. A message telling him how to find the greatest relic of all.

Chapter 4

Brooklyn

"Give me a second."

Harry closed the door in Nora's face and darted back to where Sara waited. "Put my amulet research away," he said. "We have company."

Sara jumped from her chair. "Who?"

"An old friend. It's safe. But do me a favor and don't mention anything about this." He touched the amulet hidden under his shirt. "It's personal."

"I won't," Sara said.

Harry walked back over and opened his front door. Nora stood backlit by the streetlight, arms crossed on her chest, chin jutting out. A leather bag hung from one shoulder. "Finished hiding everything?" Nora asked.

"Only the stuff you can't know about," Harry said as he opened the door and stood back. "Come in. There's someone here you'd like to see."

"I know she came back." Nora brushed past him. "I can't imagine why."

"How do you know? I never told you."

"You didn't have to. It was written all over her face the last time I saw her."

Which had been a month ago. Nora had given Harry a lifeline, a chance to go semi-straight. Her offer of employment had convinced Sara that the man she had grown close to through deadly adventures in

Iran and Britain was worth pursuing despite the fact that Harry was employed by a man who many called a gangster—because he was. Nora didn't have to help him, but she did, and Harry would not forget it.

"What's that mean?"

"Why do you think she's hanging around here?" Nora waved a hand to encompass Harry's apartment. "It's not for the food."

Harry turned on the charm. "Told you she was smart."

Nora was not impressed. "Which is why I'm so confused about what she sees in you. Where is she?"

Nora didn't wait for Harry to lead on, walking deeper into the apartment until she spotted her friend. "I hope I'm not intruding," Nora said.

Sara put a hand on her chest. "Nora. I'm so glad it's you. Strangers coming to Harry's door make me nervous."

"It's always good to be on your toes." Nora gave Sara a genuine smile as she stuck out her hand. "It's good to see you again."

Sara went straight in for the hug. "You too."

The table they stood around was mercifully empty. Harry saw no evidence of the amulet research. "Have a seat," Harry said. He indicated the bag she carried. "Something in there you want to show us?"

Nora nodded. "I'm glad you're here, Sara." She pulled out a laptop, opening it and then turning it so they could all see the screen. "I could use your insight. My office recently learned that an ancient Greek artifact may have been uncovered, and we need more information about it. That's why I came to see Harry."

Sara turned to Harry. "Do you have to go undercover?"

"I hope not," he said. "I'm busy."

"Whatever it is can wait," Nora said. "You won't want to let this opportunity pass."

He was intrigued despite himself. "What opportunity?"

"To find the truth behind what we've learned," Nora said. "It's a hell of a story."

Sara's arm brushed against Harry's as she leaned closer. Harry found himself doing the same. "We're listening," he said.

"My team works with agencies around the globe," Nora said. "Most are tied in some way to government entities in both public and private capacities. However, I would be remiss if I failed to cultivate sources in the world of antiquities theft."

"Which is part of what Harry does," Sara said. "He goes places you cannot."

Nora paused just long enough for Harry to notice. "Correct. One of my sources inside the antiquities black market heard rumors of a new find. An unusual piece, being chased by a very unusual man."

"Unusual how?" Harry asked.

"This man is rich, like most of the scumbags who buy stolen artifacts. He's also smart, which is why he's still free to pillage world cultures in more ways than one. But none of that stands out in my line of work. What does stand out is the way he is trying to acquire this artifact. The buyer offered a bounty for anyone who can locate the artifact and deliver it to him."

A spark of interest flickered in Harry's chest. "What sort of bounty?"

Nora seemed to sense it. "One I intend to be sure is never collected. By anyone."

"Are you talking about money?" Sara asked. "That's what motivates these men. Profit, or vanity."

"He's offered five million dollars," Nora said.

Harry sat back in his chair. "I thought you said this guy was smart. Offering that much cash is anything but. He'll have every yahoo in twenty countries chasing after his artifact, and all they'll do is get in each other's way. All you have to do is follow the trail of bodies and you'll find the artifact."

"He didn't offer an open contract to anyone who wants to chase the artifact. He solicited applications from people he trusts. There aren't many of them in the world, so from what I know he received only a handful of responses. I don't know who he selected, but I do know someone was, and now they're on the hunt."

"What are they searching for?" Sara asked. "Is it tied to Egypt? You said I might be able to help."

"I was thinking more of your general knowledge," Nora said. "This relic isn't Egyptian. I don't have the entire story, though I know it ties to ancient Greece." She pulled up an image on her computer screen. "This picture was taken a week ago in Turkey."

They were looking at the interior of a cave. Small rocks were strewn about the dirt floor, having fallen over the ages from the cave ceiling and walls. The camera flash extended only partway down the cave, and where the light stopped it looked like a black curtain had been drawn.

"This cave is dry," Sara said. "I can tell because there aren't any stalactites. There's little weathering on the stones. You can see how sharp they are. That tells me this is well protected from the elements."

"All correct," Nora said. "This is in the interior of Turkey, away from the coast."

Harry studied the image. What was he missing? "Doesn't look like much to me."

"Two months ago a pair of amateur spelunkers uncovered what appeared to be an ancient Greek tomb in this cave," Nora said. "The chamber where they found it had been sealed off by a rockfall, though I suspect the rocks were deliberately placed so as to conceal the chamber. The rocks hiding this chamber collapsed, which allowed the spelunkers to get inside. Here's what they found."

A low-quality snapshot appeared on her screen, one snapped by a cell phone in poor light. Rocks spilled out from the wall, covering the dirt floor and revealing a carved figure set back into the wall. The flat ground in front of it was a perfect place for people to gather, hidden from the outside world.

Sara grabbed the laptop. "A statue of a Greek warrior."

"A memorial to one," Nora said. "At least that's our best guess."

"Is there writing on the shield?" Sara asked, leaning closer. "Around the rim. Those appear to be letters."

"Unfortunately, this is the best resolution we could get. It's impossible to make them out."

"You can't get any more pictures?" Sara asked. "Why no..." Her voice trailed off. "Something bad happened in this cave."

Instead of responding Nora clicked a button and the picture advanced. Harry leaned in now. This shot was much clearer, a wide view of the cave's interior. A path had been cleared through the fallen rocks. Where before a muscled warrior had stood with shield and spear in hand, there was now only an empty hole. The entire statue had disappeared, but that wasn't the worst part. No, what grabbed Harry's eye were the bodies strewn across the floor. Four of them.

"These two were the ones who first found the memorial." Nora pointed to a pair of corpses. "These other two were members of the National Parks oversight body. Local men responsible for maintaining the national park in which this was found."

"This is in Turkey?" Sara asked.

"Yes. Near the city of Çanakkale."

"Oh my. Then this is Troy."

Harry lifted a hand. "Troy as in the Trojan War Troy? Where the Greeks sent in the Trojan horse? I thought that was all a myth."

Though it had been an actual city, in Greek mythology Troy was known as one combatant in the Trojan War pitting the Trojans against the Achaeans, or Greeks. The Trojan prince, Paris, had seduced Queen Helen, the most beautiful woman in the world and also the wife of Menelaus, King of Sparta. Queen Helen became Helen of Troy, the face that launched a thousand ships of Spartan warriors on a quest to retrieve their queen.

Immortalized in Homer's *Iliad*, Troy eventually fell when the Achaeans left a gigantic hollow wooden horse outside the gates of Troy and vanished. Believing it signaled surrender, the Trojans brought the horse inside their city walls, unaware it was filled with Greek soldiers. A raucous Trojan victory party ensued, and after most of the city was asleep the Greeks came out of the horse and captured the city.

"The same one," Nora said.

"Myth and fact can be quite close," Sara said. "How did you get this photo of the memorial if the people who took it are dead?"

"The spelunker who took it had emailed it to himself," Nora said. "We were able to access his emails."

A cold pit formed in Harry's stomach. Nora hadn't come here just for Sara's opinion. "What's so special about this statue that you've come to us?" he asked. "Turkey must be full of artifacts like this one."

"No, not like this. This isn't just any statue. And the man who we suspect stole it isn't just any man."

The pit in Harry's stomach doubled. He sat forward. "Who is he?"

Sara pushed Harry back in his chair. "First tell us about the statue. It looks to be Greek, and I would date it to at least a thousand years before Christ. That's the time period when the real city of Troy thrived."

"Our assessment as well," Nora said. "That it depicts a Greek warrior from the time when Troy was a vibrant city."

"Which suggests this Greek warrior would be a man of repute," Sara said. "So why would his memorial be hidden behind a wall of rocks?"

Nora tapped the table. "I'm working on that. What I'm concerned with now is what this memorial may lead to."

Harry's ears perked up. "There's more to it?"

"Perhaps." Nora sat back, leaving the carnage up on her screen as she spoke. "The investigation into these four murders is going nowhere. The local authorities have no idea who killed these men."

"And what do you know that they don't?"

"One of my informants heard that a major player in the black market recently acquired a new piece from Turkey. A Greek statue like the missing one. This man has the resources and utter disregard for human life to pull this off."

"Which isn't all that unusual," Harry said. "What has your eye here?"

Lines creased Nora's forehead. "The man who I suspect

orchestrated these murders makes his money handling financial affairs for people who cannot use banks or other traditional financial institutions. He manages the finances of terrorists, growing rich while enabling death and destruction to flourish. He is far from alone in this, but this man is one of the worst."

Sara's face was grim. "He may be paying terrorists to locate artifacts."

"That's my fear," Nora said. "We're late to the game."

Harry's gut was a ball of ice now. "You want to find the artifact before they do."

"And I know just the person to do it."

Of all the times to ask for his help. Harry opened his mouth to tell her no, but Nora cut him off. "I don't need an answer now. There's more to the story, information I can't share here. Not because of you," she said quickly to Sara. "Because there's someone who wants to meet with you. An attorney in the D.A.'s office. A man I'd very much like you to meet before you answer."

"What aren't you telling me?" Harry asked. Dangling pieces of information to bait him into a meet didn't sit well with him. He wasn't about to put his backside or Sara's on the line without knowing everything Nora did.

"Come to our offices and talk," Nora said. "That's it. I promise it will be worth your time."

Sara spoke up. "You're not running this operation, are you?"

"It's my operation," Nora said quickly. "But I'm part of a larger team for this one."

Harry looked at her with unease. There was more to this than Nora or Sara realized. He could feel it. "Who do you want us to meet?" Harry asked.

Nora hesitated. "An attorney who prosecutes antiquities crimes."

Sara jumped in. "Why would you ask Harry to go up against a man who may have terrorists at his disposal?"

"I'm asking Harry to listen," Nora said. She leveled her gaze at Sara. "If I ask him to go after the relic, I'll do it for one reason only. Because Harry is the best at what he does."

"My father was the best," Harry said. "I'm still learning." He reached for his beer, found it empty. "This collector. How rich are we talking here?" He had to ask, even though he already knew.

"Billions," Nora said. "Around eleven or so."

Harry dropped his head. *It had to be him.*

Sara wasn't buying it. "If you know he's funding terrorism, other governments know as well. He can't be that successful at hiding it."

"His money protects him. Though eleven billion will not be enough in the end." Nora tapped her screen and another image came up. "This is the man we suspect is chasing the relic and who authorized the deaths of the four people in that Turkish cave. He is an exiled Russian oligarch."

Harry looked up. His heart sank.

"Evgeny Smolov," Nora said. "Harry, you have a chance to do what entire governments and the new tsar of Russia can't. You have the skills to beat him at his own game."

Her laptop snapped shut and Nora stood. "My office. Tomorrow morning at ten. Both of you." Nora headed for the front door, pausing as she opened it. "I mean it, Harry. You're the only one who can stop him."

The door clicked shut behind her.

Chapter 5

Brooklyn

The head of the most powerful crime family in New York gripped the phone hard enough to shatter it.

Joey Morello kept his voice level. "My father always said I could count on you, Gio. You two go way back. To the early days."

"May he rest in peace, Joey. Your father was a saint." Gio Sabella spoke softly. "I swear we will find the pigs who killed him, and they will pay. My men have not stopped looking since it happened."

Wonderful. And you didn't answer my question. "I appreciate it, Gio. This won't be forgotten."

There were times to push, and times to pull back. Right now, Joey Morello was in no position to push anyone.

"You are your father's son, Joey. You will see this through."

Joey Morello had a real mess on his hands. He didn't need kind words.

"I need men I can count on," Joey said. "I'm hearing the families aren't as united as they were under my father. All five of us must stand together. We're stronger that way."

"We were strong for many years, Joey. Together. Have the times changed? I hope not, but I am only one man. First, we find who killed your father. Then, we talk about the future. A future where no one can question our strength."

The conniving old mobster wouldn't commit, and Joey would never ask him outright. Do that and he may as well give up hope of following his father as the leader of the five families. Nobody would hand him anything, son of Vincent Morello or not. Joey had to earn this. That's what Gio Sabella was saying between the lines. Figure out who killed your father, Joey. Show us you can handle this, then we'll talk about you sitting on the throne.

"Thank you, Gio. You've always been a true friend of our family."

"Let me tell you a story, Joey." The sound of a lighter clicking filled the phone. Joey could practically smell Gio Sabella's cigar as it caught fire. "Years ago your father ran a gaming house here in Brooklyn. It was his first big assignment, his chance to show the other families he could handle more. A couple of guys thought they could take advantage of this new house boss. Card sharps trying to cheat the house, make a fast buck."

Joey frowned. He'd never heard this one before.

"Three men were involved. They were frequent players, people we trusted. They used a system to signal each other what cards they had. Know that, and you can make a winning bet."

Gio chuckled. "They were smart, but Vincent was smarter. He saw what they were doing but didn't do anything, not at first. He let it go for a week to be sure. Once he was, he invited the three men in for a private game. The three show up and find Vincent with his crew waiting. Your father gave them a chance to admit to cheating, and if they did, Vincent would let them pay back what they stole on the condition that they never come back. One catch. Only the first guy to confess gets the deal."

"Did they?"

"One of them jumped on it. Admitted everything. Vincent gave him a week to pay back the money he'd wagered while cheating—and your father kept tight books, so he knew the amount to the penny—and told the guy to never come back. He agreed."

Joey had a feeling he knew what came next. "And the other two?"

"Nobody ever saw them again."

Vincent Morello. A soft-spoken man who had earned the respect of his peers the hard way. He had also turned them from adversaries into allies. Over time, Vincent Morello had shepherded the five organized families into a loose agreement to stop the infighting and stay out of each other's way. It had brought decades of prosperity to them all.

"Vincent Morello was the strongest man I ever knew," said Gio. "No one crossed him more than once. He was either the best friend or the worst enemy you could have. You know why so few people challenged Vincent? Because he was *strong*. We respected your father. We loved him. But we all, to a man, feared him. Nobody wanted Vincent Morello as their enemy."

The message was clear. Joey was Vincent's son. It remained to be seen if Joey could become his equal.

"It is my hope the families agree on a successor," Gio said. "You will be considered. Make certain when that happens no one can say Joey Morello is not strong enough to control our city."

"Thank you for the advice, my friend."

"You will not be the only person considered," Gio said. "There are other families who wish to be considered. When your father was alive, there was no question. He led us. Now that he is gone," Gio paused. "I cannot say what will happen."

Joey knew what would happen. They'd listen to Gio Sabella. If Gio said that Joey should replace his father as the leader of all the families in New York, the other family heads would grumble, but they'd go along with it. If Gio didn't support Joey, then there was no telling how many other families would look to take the lead. A continued peace between them all was no sure thing if that occurred.

"One more thing." Gio cleared his throat. "I hear the district attorney's office has been asking many questions about your business operation. An Irish man named Doyle."

"So I heard," Joey said. "I appreciate the warning. We will speak soon."

Joey ground his teeth as he hung up. *Focus, Joey.* Gio hadn't committed to supporting Joey in the coming weeks, but to be fair, Joey would play it the same if he was in Gio's shoes. Someone—and Joey had a good idea who—had murdered his father. Now Joey had to prove it, then exact his revenge. Do that, and Gio Sabella would have his back. Once Gio supported Joey the other family heads would fall in line. They listened to Gio, these men who would decide the next leader of the city's families.

The desk Joey sat behind had belonged to his father. A month earlier Joey couldn't imagine it being his. Now it was, along with the weight of a city. The entire Morello family was counting on him to maintain their position as the first family among equals. The day after his father was murdered Joey had unleashed every tool at his disposal to uncover the identity of the person, or persons, who had ordered the hit. Finding that person proved harder than he imagined.

The bomb that exploded under Vincent's restaurant table was meant for both father and son. Joey had narrowly escaped with his life. He'd searched high and low for those responsible, but all he had to show for his efforts were two names. A pair of recently hired waiters. Both names were fake.

"I'll find both of you," Joey had vowed. However, he had a sinking suspicion neither man would be seen by anyone again. If Joey had been the one who'd hired them, both would either be halfway around the world now or at the bottom of the Hudson River.

His cell phone buzzed. It was one of his men. "Yes?"

"It happened again."

Joey clenched his fist. "Where?" he asked.

"The social club. Another brick through the window with bullets tied to it."

"How many customers were there when it happened?"

"Packed house."

Joey slammed his fist on the desk. "Did you get a look at them?"

"No, boss."

"Tell our guests we caught them. Then don't answer any questions. Get out there and find them."

Joey laid his phone on the desk, then stood and walked to a bar across the room. His father wouldn't be happy if he was looking down now, but today had been hell and Joey needed a drink.

He polished off two fingers of bourbon in one go, then poured another. As the pleasant fire in his throat slowly faded, he swirled the amber liquid in his glass while a clock ticked on the wall. Each hour inched him closer to losing control of everything his father had made for his family. Someone had been throwing bricks with bullets tied to them through the windows of gambling houses and gentlemen's clubs run by the Morellos. Customers didn't come back, and the girls found other places to dance. All of this hit Joey's bottom line at a time when he could scarcely afford it. But that wasn't the worst part. No, what ate at him and churned his guts at night was that Joey knew exactly who was behind it all. Altin Cana. Head of the Cana family, and the one man crazy enough to take on Vincent Morello.

A degenerate Albanian who thought he was better than any Italian, Altin had scraped by for decades at the edges of Morello territory. Last year it had changed. Altin had broken the rules when he launched a guerilla assault on Vincent's empire, attacking in ways that made it impossible to prove to the other families that the Albanians were behind it.

Joey knew Altin had hired out-of-town hit men to try and kill him. He just couldn't prove it. That attack had left several of Joey's men dead, though he was unharmed. The assailants had all died, and none could be directly tied back to Altin. After that, the smaller affronts had escalated, Cana family members had begun openly running games and girls on Morello turf. Altin claimed he had nothing to do with it, that he punished any renegade men, but it was all lies. It only took a few incidents to scare off customers and affect business.

The most serious problem Joey faced now was the bricks and bullets through windows. He couldn't prove Altin was behind it all, but he'd bet his life on it. Toss in the unexplained police raids on other Morello properties, the ones where men could gamble, drink and spend time with friendly hostesses, and Joey had no doubt. Altin Cana had declared war on Vincent's empire. If Joey could prove Altin had done this, no mobster in the city would tolerate Altin's presence.

Joey sipped his bourbon. One of his men walked by the window, a bulletproof vest visible under his coat. Since Vincent's murder, security had been round-the-clock at the Morello headquarters in Brooklyn. This was a Morello neighborhood through and through, but Joey could take no chances.

And now the district attorney was taking an interest in Morello affairs. Gary Doyle, one of the D.A.'s top prosecutors, had recently started asking pointed questions about the Morello family. No one could tell him why, out of the blue, Gary Doyle wanted to know more about Joey Morello.

No one except Harry Fox. One of the few men he trusted unconditionally, and who now worked with the D. A.'s Anti-Trafficking Unit. Joey had been furious when Harry first suggested it, though after he listened to what Harry wanted to do, it made sense. Harry worked with the Anti-Trafficking Unit when the cops needed information. Otherwise, he kept his head down in the city, possibly because Harry fenced all his relics exclusively through Rose Leroux, the last person on earth who would sell Harry out to the cops. In exchange for Harry's assistance, the D.A.'s office didn't look too hard at what Harry did outside the city. Their version of making a deal with the devil. That, Joey understood. It was how the world worked.

Joey texted Harry asking for information about this Irish prosecutor named Gary in the D.A.'s office. Harry would come through for him. Just as Harry's father had come through for his.

The streetlights had come on by the time Joey finished his drink. He refilled his glass one more time and sat behind his father's desk. A picture of Vincent sat in one corner of it. Joey looked at the photo, and for the first time in his life, questioned whether he could do it. Vincent Morello had taken life by the neck and changed organized crime in New York. How could he ever follow that?

Chapter 6

A heavy stream of vehicles crawled down Jay Street. The season's first fallen leaves rode gusts of warm air to swirl around Harry's legs as he kept pace with the surprisingly sparse pedestrian traffic, Sara at his side. Not long ago the sidewalks would have been jammed. Now they were almost tolerable.

Harry led them to a coffee shop down the block from the district attorney's office. Their appointment with Nora wasn't for another half an hour, and Harry had something on his mind. Or rather his phone, to be precise. He needed an opinion from someone he could trust to be truthful. The person who fit that bill stood at his side.

They snagged an open table in the corner. "Why do you think Nora wouldn't tell us more about the cave?" Sara asked as she poured milk into her coffee. "The only reason I can come up with is she has something explosive."

Her dark eyes practically gleamed. For a professor of Egyptology who loved time spent in the field, there could be no better answer.

"Could be." Harry blew on his coffee. "Or maybe she knows I won't do it unless she puts the screws to me."

Sara raised an eyebrow. "Since when does Harry Fox turn down a relic hunt?"

"Since we made a connection between the Ramses statue outside Luxor and Mark Antony's crown." He tapped the amulet beneath his

55

shirt. "What I'm interested in now is finding whatever it was my father chased for so long. We're getting closer. Anything Nora Doyle wants me to find has been gathering dust for thousands of years. Another few weeks won't matter."

"Unless Evgeny Smolov finds it in those weeks."

"Don't make her arguments for her."

The only other conversation in the coffeehouse came from baristas taking orders. Most everyone around them had their heads buried in electronic devices, though Harry spotted a pair of actual books and one newspaper. He pulled out his own phone and set it on the table. He drank more coffee.

"We came here for a reason," Sara eventually said. "Want to tell me what it is?"

"How did you know?"

Sara laughed. "Harry, reading you is too easy."

He didn't like that. How was he supposed to be interesting if she could see right through him? "Lucky guess," he fired back. "But you're right. Joey texted me last night. I haven't responded yet." He twisted his phone so she could see the message.

"Do you know a prosecutor named Gary in the D.A.'s office?" she asked after reading the message. "Joey wants you to dig for information." Sara shook her head. "Please tell me you're not going to skulk around the D.A.'s offices. These people prosecute criminals, which is what you would be if you do what Joey is asking."

"I'm not going to look through their files. I have a better idea."

"What's that?"

"I'm going to ask Nora. She wants something from me? She can answer a few questions."

Sara tilted her head. "Questions, plural. But hold that thought: do you even need to ask? I doubt Nora will tell you anything. She's not the sort of person to share out of the goodness of her heart."

"I owe Joey a lot. If he wants me to ask, I'll ask."

Sara fell silent as a suited man walked past. "You said you have questions for Nora," she said when he had moved on. "What else do you have to ask Nora besides what Joey needs?"

Now it was Harry's turn to sit in silence. He did it for so long she reached out and touched his arm. "You don't have to tell me."

"It's fine."

Why the sudden reluctance? she wondered. It wasn't as though she would tell anyone. If he couldn't tell her what was on his mind, who could he tell?

"It's about my mother," he said after a few moments.

Sara didn't blink. "I had my suspicions."

"Really? You've been here for over a week and haven't mentioned it." Harry pulled her hand up and kissed it. "Thank you. I appreciate it more than you know."

Sara winked. "As I said. You're not hard to read."

"I'll work on it." More coffee, delaying it by another few seconds. "It's not easy to talk about. I hardly know what to think. For two decades I thought my mother was dead. Suddenly, I'm told she's not."

His entire life upended by one forgotten police report. For twenty years Fred Fox had told Harry that his mother died when he was young. "An accident," was all Fred ever told him, something to do with the river. Over time, Harry had learned to let it go. Maybe Dani Fox had committed suicide and Fred was ashamed. Or maybe he'd never got over losing his wife and couldn't talk about it. Either way, the story of her death had been a blank canvas that would never be completed.

Then Fred had died and Harry got swept up in replacing his father as Vincent Morello's antiquities hunter. The work was lucrative, dangerous, and exactly what Harry wanted to do. Fred had trained him in the dark arts of relic hunting for years, and Harry was the best man for the job.

As Harry's world changed, however, he was no longer content with letting the past alone. He had asked the city's biggest fence to look into it for him. See what she could find. If anyone could peel back the layers of history, it was Rose Leroux. She'd gotten her hands on the original police report of Dani Fox's death. A report that had been "lost" for years. Rose gave the file to Harry with a warning—she had no idea what it contained, and perhaps Harry would be wiser to leave the past alone. He said he'd think about it, then he'd opened the file. The report shook Harry's world. Dani Fox's body had been found on the banks of the Hudson River with no obvious signs of foul play. The medical examiner had conducted an autopsy, as per protocol, and a throwaway note in his report stated that the body wasn't his mother's. How did he know?

The dead woman had never given birth.

That bit of information told him one thing with absolute certainty. The woman whose body had washed up on the riverbank was not Harry's mother. How she'd been so readily misidentified was a mystery. Harry had his suspicions when he first started reading the report due to a missing detail. His mother had been unlike his father in many ways, but in one particular instance they were alike. An instance related to fashion, of all things.

Fred Fox never went anywhere without his amulet. Dani Fox had one nearly identical to it, a piece she wore almost all the time. The body police claimed to be Dani Fox did not have any notable jewelry on it. Certainly not a golden amulet. Had it been stolen? Perhaps, but Harry didn't think so. One thing Fred had made clear about Dani was how resourceful she'd been. Not the sort of woman to let anyone get the drop on her. If that amulet had been found on the corpse, Harry would have accepted it. But no amulet made him suspicious. Then he found out she never had children.

Now Harry wouldn't stop until he found the truth behind what had really happened to Dani Fox.

Harry looked at people walking past the coffee shop windows without seeing them. "I'm stuck. I can't find anything more about the woman misidentified as my mother—who she was or what happened to her."

"A person with access to law enforcement archives could help," Sara said. "It's logical. The question is do you want to know?"

"Wouldn't you?"

"I would."

"That's why I'll ask Nora to dig for anything she can find on the case. I have the names of every officer in the report. I'm hoping some of them are still around. I want to talk with the ones who are, and Nora can make that happen."

"She'll use this request as more leverage to get what she wants." A statement, not a question.

"Nora and whoever else she's in cahoots with need my skills. Why else would they ask us to come here for a secret meeting today? She's not the only one with leverage." Harry finished his coffee. "Scarcity of resources. Remember economics class?"

She smacked his arm. "You are also the least funny man I have ever known. Come on." Sara rose and displayed her watch. "We have a meeting."

They muscled through a crowd at the intersection, crossed the street, and stopped in front of a massive building that housed the District Attorney's Anti-Trafficking Unit. Harry pointed to a staircase that started at ground level and descended out of sight. A manned guard booth stood beside them. "That looks like the place. You have your passport?"

Sara headed straight for the booth and left Harry to catch up. His chest tightened a tiny bit when he realized there were two guards seated in the booth and two guards standing outside. All were armed.

"We are here for a meeting with Agent Doyle of the Anti-Trafficking Unit." Sara stopped in front of the window and held out her passport.

The seated guard stared at Sara, and not in the way most men did when they first met her. He did not take her passport before he looked at Harry. "And this man is with you?" A breath passed. "Ma'am."

"He is."

Still the guard didn't take her passport. "The reason for your visit?"

"As I said, sir. A meeting with Agent Doyle."

The guard offered her an unfriendly look. He finally took her passport. "You are not an American citizen." He consulted the Egyptian passport. "Sara."

"It's Ms. Hamed," she said icily. "My citizenship should be evident."

The guard looked up from her passport. He seemed to get the message. "One moment, Ms. Hamed." He confirmed Sara had an appointment, then went through the same drill with Harry before stepping out of the guard booth, looking down his nose at their passports.

"Proceed down those steps. Stop at the red door on your right and wait for the buzzer to sound. Walk inside, present your identification to the guard, then take the elevator to the Anti-Trafficking Unit. Floor twenty-seven."

He handed both passports to Sara. He did not wish them a good day.

Sara waited until they were safely out of hearing range before speaking. "Think it's because I'm a woman or because I don't have white skin?"

"The skin," Harry said. "Same reason he didn't like me. He probably doesn't like Nora either. Forget him."

The red door opened for them, they repeated the passport process, then an elevator whisked them to where Nora waited twenty-seven stories up. The last thing Harry did before the doors opened was confirm his amulet remained hidden under his shirt.

"Welcome." Nora Doyle stood waiting for them. "Follow me."

"We met a friendly guard outside," Sara said.

A dark cloud crossed Nora's face. "That has to be Mitch. Ignore him. He's a pig. The rest of the guards are wonderful. Mitch has a problem with anyone who doesn't look like him. He's also the union steward, so we pick our battles."

Prints of past district attorneys lined the walls. The nicest government carpet Harry had ever walked on cushioned his feet as

Nora led them into a reception room. A secretary rose from behind her desk.

"Good morning, Miss Doyle. He's ready for you."

"Good morning, Carla." Nora kept moving and stepped through the open door. A placard informed visitors whose office they were entering.

Executive Assistant District Attorney Gary Doyle.

Harry paused. The Gary who was investigating Joey. A golden opportunity may have fallen in his lap, but the surname caught Harry's eye. *Doyle?*

A voice rang out from the inner sanctum. "Nora. Good morning."

Sunlight poured through a window inside the office. It fell on the man who had spoken, now standing beside a gargantuan desk. Harry blinked. He had the most vibrantly red beard Harry had ever seen.

"Good morning, D.A. Doyle." Nora's response was terse, professional. "Harry Fox and Sara Hamed are here."

The D.A. extended a hand to Sara. "Dr. Hamed. Thank you for joining us." He turned to Harry. "Mr. Fox. It is a pleasure to meet you."

Harry had the distinct impression this man knew far more about Harry than his name.

"You as well, D.A. Doyle."

"Call me Gary." He gestured to a table near his desk, one with a stack of folders atop it. "Have a seat."

Only after they were all gathered around it did Gary join them. "You'll have to forgive Nora's vagueness. I instructed her that the only place where we could openly discuss this case is my office."

"Do you run the anti-trafficking team?" Harry asked.

"No," Nora said quickly. "I do."

"I am the legal consultant for their work," Gary replied. "Without Nora, there would be no anti-trafficking team."

"She's quite skilled," Harry said. "Forgive me, I really don't know how a D.A.'s office works."

Gary pointed across the room to a table covered with accordion folders. "Those are my other cases. I work on city and state matters, financial crimes, and certain community programs." He paused, his gaze turning back to Harry. "Along with organized crime."

Yep, this was the guy Joey wanted to know about. "That's a large caseload."

"We move quickly."

And that was all Joey would get. "I appreciate you inviting me here. Can you tell us what this is all about?"

Nora cut in. "It began with four dead bodies in a Turkish cave. You saw those photos."

"Two cave enthusiasts and two government employees," Harry said. "A statue was also involved."

"A memorial," Nora said. "Sara was correct."

Sara spoke up. "You wouldn't have asked us to come if it was a simple memorial. All we saw was a grainy picture of a statue. You clearly know more than that."

Nora looked at the stack of folders. She turned to Gary. "Where is it?"

"I was reviewing the file before they arrived." Gary walked to his desk and retrieved a file.

Harry looked to the wall behind Gary to a photo of a man with brilliant red hair, clearly Gary, standing between two women. Both had darker complexions, though one was lighter than the other. He squinted at the photo. At the younger woman, the mocha one who looked familiar.

"Hold on." Harry rose from his chair and stepped closer to the framed photo. "That's you." He pointed at the picture, then at Nora. "That's you in the photo."

Nora ran a hand through her hair. "Yes, that is me. With my mother and father."

Harry looked to Gary, then back to Nora. "Gary *Doyle*. You're—"

"—Nora's father." Gary couldn't keep the pride from his face. "She is the most wonderful, trying daughter a man could ask for."

"We are not here to discuss my family," Nora said tersely. She stuck a hand out to her father. "The photos, please?"

Harry couldn't let this go. "Why didn't you tell me you worked for your father?"

"Because I don't work for him. We are colleagues." Nora's words were delivered in an even, direct manner. Her body language was quite different. It told Harry in no uncertain terms he should stop asking questions, or he would regret it. "May we continue?"

Harry gestured at the file in Gary's hands. "You have my attention."

"Here is an enhancement of the image you saw earlier," Gary said. "It is the only picture of the statue we have."

Gary laid a blown-up image on the table. The resolution was terrible, yet revealing. "The figure is holding a shield," Harry said. "There's writing on it."

"I can't make it out." Sara grabbed the photo and held it close to her nose. "It's too grainy. Are you certain this is the only image of the shield?"

"Yes," Nora said. "However, that photo isn't the only lead we have in this case. You're correct, there's a reason I need Harry's assistance."

Harry looked from Sara to Gary. "Do you know where the statue is? If you can't read the inscription in this photo, you need to find the statue."

Nora shared a look with her father, one Harry couldn't read. "We suspect the statue is at one of Evgeny Smolov's residences. Our best bet is his estate in Windsor."

An estate Harry knew well. He looked at the ground and closed his eyes. *Think, Harry. What did you see?* It didn't take long to find it in the replay running through his head. "About how large is this statue?" he asked.

"Approximately eight feet," Nora said. "Why?"

The wooden box he'd seen in Evgeny's museum was a little bigger than that. Big enough to hold an eight-foot-tall statue. Perhaps a statue Evgeny meant to show off in the half-built display. "Small enough that he could move it out of the country easily."

"It would be simple for a man like Smolov to take the statue from Turkey to England." Nora tilted her head. "Do you have a thought?"

Damn Sara and Nora and anyone else who thought he was easy to read. "I'm thinking that breaking into a Russian oligarch's estate to possibly get a look at this statue is crazy. I hope that's not what you're asking me to do."

"We do not condone illegal activities," Gary said.

"Are you working with the British authorities?" Harry asked.

"That statue, if it's there, is protected by Smolov's British lawyers," Gary said. "We will never get access to his estate."

Sara raised a hand. "Again, you know more than you're telling us. Please stop wasting our time."

Gary Doyle looked at Nora and raised an eyebrow. "You were right."

"What does that mean?" Sara asked sharply.

"I told my father you are an intelligent, no-nonsense woman," Nora said. "It's why you're here today."

"That is one of the highest compliments my daughter can pay," Gary said. "I see she was correct. As are you, Dr. Hamed. We already know what is written on the shield."

Nora touched a file folder. "One of the men's bodies had a notebook on it when the authorities found him. Inside was a sketch of the statue, along with a copy of the writing on the shield."

Sara reached for the folder. "Are you certain he copied the writing from the shield?"

"Yes. If you look closely, you can see the first phrase along the top of the shield is most likely "*In honor of.*" This matches what's in the journal."

Harry started to read over Sara's shoulder. "These notes are in English," Harry said. "Who translated it?"

"A linguistics professor at NYU," Nora said. "I assure you it's accurate."

Sara shushed them both.

In honor of Aci Los, a warrior without equal, struck dead by Pari Zitis in the battle for Troy. Long may his memory live to remind the Trojans who now rules their city.

Aci Los lives forever through the prize he received from Mount Olympus. A gift from the gods for only the strongest Greek leader.

The Koraki will protect this prize to preserve the Greek city-states. Only the worthiest Greek leader may wield it. We will make it so.

Harry didn't speak when he finished reading. He waited. Finally, Sara looked up.

"The statue is more than a memorial," she said. "It's a *message.*"

"Why do you say that?" Gary asked.

Sara tapped the page. "Wait. Why is this word not translated from Greek?"

"*Koraki,*" Nora said. "It means—"

"—*raven.* I know. Why not translate it to English?"

"Because we weren't sure of its meaning," Nora said. "I'd like your thoughts."

Sara lifted a hand. "Let's start at the beginning. The statue honors Aci Los, a Greek warrior killed during an invasion of Troy." She paused. "War between the Trojans and Achaeans, or Greeks, was not uncommon. The Trojans lived in Troy, and the Achaeans, for the most part, lived in Sparta."

"As in King Leonidas?" Nora asked.

"Yes, though there were other Achaean city-states over the centuries. Sparta is the one most people remember. Troy and Greece had numerous documented skirmishes, though the most familiar is tied to Greek mythology. This conflict provides the subject material for Homer's *Iliad.*"

"A brief summary would be welcome," Gary said.

"The *Iliad* is an epic poem—not an historical truth—detailing events during the Trojan War, specifically during the ten-year siege of Troy by the Greeks. The events in the story take place over a few weeks near the end of the war but reference numerous past battles. The Olympian gods are heavily involved in parts, using humans as pawns in their inter-deity struggles."

"And this is where we get the Trojan horse legend," Gary said.

"Yes, though that isn't actually described in the poem. Homer's story tells about Helen of Sparta running off with, or being stolen by, the Trojan prince, Paris. Her husband, King Menelaus of Sparta, declared war on Troy and ultimately destroyed the city, though not until numerous princes and famous warriors on both sides died. Prince Hector of Troy and the Greek warriors Achilles and Patroclus are the most notable."

"The story is a myth," Harry said. "A legend. There's never been any real evidence that it documents actual events."

Sara held up the paper. "I'll reserve judgment until we learn more, but this text may be the first physical proof that Homer's story is grounded in fact."

Gary Doyle put his arms on the table. "A fascinating story, Dr. Hamed. I promise you any items we recover will be made available to you for study. But only after we exhaust all avenues of inquiry into our current focus."

Harry groaned silently. *Until we learn more, she says.* Sara was basically volunteering him for what could be a suicide mission. "We haven't agreed to anything yet," he said.

"You seem to be interested," Gary said.

"Back to the shield," Sara said quickly. "It talks of a battle between Trojan and Greek warriors. The Greeks eventually conquered Troy. *Aci Los* died in spite of possessing a *gift from the gods,* which could be anything. A physical object, or perhaps knowledge. It's hard to say."

"You and Harry have both told me that certainty is rare in your line of work," Nora said.

Harry couldn't disagree. "I do the best I can."

Nora gestured to the photos. "If you decide to follow this path, where will you go?"

"You must have your own ideas," Harry responded.

"Yes, but I'm not you."

Less than subtle, but it worked. He pointed to the image. "I'd start with the last portion. Where the *Koraki* talk about protecting the prize in Greek hands. This Aci Los warrior died, but his side won. The Greeks clearly place value on the prize he carried."

Sara jumped in. "Their goal is to keep it with the *worthiest Greek leader.*"

"The Koraki group, and it's unlikely to be just one person, have a single purpose. To preserve whatever it is they're talking about for the worthiest Greek leader to use."

Harry looked at each of them in turn. "Thousands of years have passed and we don't have the memorial to inspect. Which Greek leaders received the prize? Identifying who may have had it over time is critical. Look at the wrong leaders and we'll never pick up the Koraki trail."

"We need a list of Greek leaders," Gary said. "Did their culture have separate city-state rulers and military leaders, or was there an emperor ruling over everyone?"

Harry shook his head. "That's not how I'd go about it."

"Why not?"

"Ancient Greece was composed of city-states," Harry said. "Hundreds of them. The sheer number of leaders would take years to investigate. I doubt whoever Evgeny Smolov hired will take that long."

"What do you propose?" Gary asked.

Harry grabbed a pen from the table. He underlined one word on the sheet in front of him, then slid it over to Sara. "Agreed," she said.

"We let the Koraki narrow the search for us," Harry said. "Their goal was to keep this prize with Greek leaders." He flipped the page around so Gary and Nora could see what he'd underlined. *Koraki*. "We find them, we find our Greek leaders."

"Logical," Nora said. "How long will it take you to find them?"

Harry laughed. "Depends on how long you keep us here." He held Nora's gaze. "And it depends on whether or not I'm going to do it."

You couldn't measure it, but to Harry the office air suddenly chilled. Gary Doyle consulted his watch. Sara became engrossed in the photographs. Nora, however, looked right at him.

"I hope I can count on you," she said. "Follow this trail, beat Evgeny Smolov's man to the end, and you will help more people than you realize. He funds terrorists, Harry. They're the reason the three of us"—she indicated them both plus Sara—"get suspicious looks in airports. As I said, there aren't many people in the world who can do this. You can."

Harry looked over to find Sara watching him.

Gary Doyle spoke with the tone he likely used for closing arguments. "You know, Harry, she's right. No one can force you to do anything. However, I don't need to tell you many would say there's a right choice and a wrong choice here. I'll let you decide which is which."

Harry spread his arms out wide. "Sara and I are in the middle of something else right now."

"More important than stopping money flowing to terrorists?" Nora asked.

"It's personal," Harry fired back.

"I can help you," Sara said.

Her words knocked Harry off balance. "You know a lot more about Greek history than I do," he said.

"That's not exactly what I meant." Sara gestured to the Doyles. "Gary and Nora are working to stop people from stealing antiquities. Not merely stealing, but using them to fund global acts of violence. What these two are doing is vital. You must help them if you can."

Great. Now she was on their side. "What about our project?" he asked.

"We will continue to make progress while you work with Nora."

"We can't do that if I'm chasing a Greek legend."

"We can't. *I* can." She kept going before he could object. "I'll help you unravel Nora's Greek mystery. Together we can do this much faster. I can continue working on our other project while you're in the field."

The immediate objections rose in his throat, and there they stayed.

"It takes two people," was all he said. "You need someone to watch your back too."

"And what did you do before I came along?" she fired back. "It was the Harry Fox show. A solo act."

Lines creased his forehead. "This isn't a game, Sara. One misstep and you'll become part of the story."

"I will thank you not to underestimate me."

"What other project are you working on?" Nora asked.

"A private one." Harry looked at her and made it clear that was all she needed to know.

"I was going to offer to help," Nora said.

"Could we have a moment?" Sara asked. She looked to Gary, then Nora. "Alone?"

Gary took his cue from Nora, who stood without argument. She stopped with one foot out the door. "Remember, Harry. You're one of the good guys." A pause. "Unlike some of the people you're around every day."

Nora turned and left, Gary following behind her. The door closed to leave Sara and Harry alone. Sara tapped a finger on the photograph. "Nora is right," she said. "You can find this. We already know what to look for first."

"References to the Koraki," Harry said. "Specifically, any ties between this group and Greek leaders during times of trouble."

Sara couldn't have been happier. "That is exactly what I thought. The Greeks supposedly needed this prize to protect their culture. How do we narrow our search even further?"

"Find times when things don't look good for the Greeks." Harry fought to keep any enthusiasm out of his voice. It wasn't hard. "Identify their leader at the time, then search for Koraki references. If the group truly wanted to keep this prize for the Greek leader, they'd need to be close enough to ensure it was never lost."

"Give Nora a week," Sara said. "That will be enough time for me to confirm if there's anything to our Luxor theory."

"You think I can find a lost Greek relic in a week?"

"I know you can."

Darn Nora and Sara and their flattery. "Maybe I can. But right now I want to find the truth behind my father's amulet."

"And we will."

Harry's jaw tightened. Not long ago, Sara Hamed had been ready to leave him. He was a man who helped gangsters make money by stealing artifacts and selling them to the highest bidder. It didn't matter if that was the life he'd been born to, or if he was really a decent guy just trying to get by. Sara had wanted nothing to do with a man like that.

Then Nora Doyle had thrown him a lifeline. She'd hired him to be part of her anti-trafficking team. Harry Fox became her man on the inside, a real-life adventurer who rubbed shoulders with criminals, unraveled centuries-old mysteries and helped save cultural artifacts by risking his neck every day. The sort of man a certain Egyptologist could put on a pedestal. Harry had signed up without thinking twice. Now, it seemed, the bill had come due.

"You want to do it," Sara said. She tucked a strand of auburn hair behind one ear. "I can see it on your face."

She most definitely could not. "I *want* to go to Luxor."

"You're a good man, Harry. You'll do what's right. Which is let me help you by going to Luxor instead of you." She lifted an eyebrow. "Who knows? You might join me there in a few days."

"Even I'm not that good." He spent a long minute searching for a way out of this. Plenty of options came to mind, though none ended with him still being part of Nora's team or having Sara around. Harry looked up at the ceiling. *What would you say, Dad?*

Fred Fox would tell his son to play the hand he'd been dealt. Just as Fred himself had.

So be it. That would be his first demand. Nora would agree or he'd walk, no matter what.

"You'd better be careful," was all he said to Sara. Harry turned to the door. "We're ready," he called out.

Gary and Nora stepped back in. Gary had taken the ejection from his own office with grace. "Are there any concerns?" he asked.

"One," Harry said. "I need your help getting some information. This is non-negotiable."

"What sort of information?"

For years Harry had thought his mother was dead. That had all changed last month. "Information about a body found by the Hudson."

"When was this body found?"

"Around twenty years ago." Harry took a piece of paper from his pocket and handed it to Gary. "Those are the police report details. Dates, names, circumstances."

Gary studied the sheet. "Why do you want to know about this incident?"

"Because the dead person was identified as my mother."

Gary did not seem to pick up on the ambiguous turn of phrase. He remained perfectly still. "My condolences," he finally said. "Is there a problem with the report?"

Harry had debated about what to reveal. The more he thought about it, the easier it became. The veil of secrecy and deceit had hung over this case long enough.

"This report was 'lost' until an associate of mine managed to retrieve it."

"Who is this associate?" Gary asked.

"Someone with friends and influence," Harry said. "That's all I can say."

"I see. And your concerns with the report and the investigation?"

"The report says the police found my mother's body on the

riverbank. An autopsy note said the woman whose body they found had never given birth. That's a problem, because I wasn't adopted."

Gary Doyle walked slowly to his desk. He did not sit. "I see."

"If the person they found isn't my mother, who is it and what happened to my mother?" He aimed a finger between Nora's eyes. "You want my help? Get me those answers."

It was Gary who responded. "Agreed. I will do anything I can to help you."

Harry sighed. "Then we have a deal. Give us a day to start looking into the Greek statue. I'll contact you tomorrow with an update. And I want to know anything you learn about my mother's supposed death. Anything."

"I know a few people in police records who can help me. Quietly."

"Thank you."

A cloud shifted outside, letting sunlight once again fall through a window in Gary's office and onto Harry's arm to warm it. Harry didn't like pushing his amulet search onto Sara, yet when he stood from the table it wasn't the weight of a delayed investigation on his shoulders he felt. No, this was much different. An airiness, not of responsibilities unloaded, but of new hope. That he might actually learn the truth.

He and Sara were halfway to the door when Nora spoke. "There's one more piece of information we didn't share."

They stopped and turned. "About the Greek statue?" Sara asked.

"Yes. It's conjecture, and goodness knows you have enough of that in your work already." She flipped one of the photocopies over and wrote on the back of it, then lifted the sheet so Harry and Sara could see. She had written a name.

Aci Los.

"The man who died in spite of having the Greek prize was called *Aci Los.*" They both nodded, puzzled. "Ever heard of him?" Both said they hadn't. "You know how names can change over centuries. This one definitely has."

Nora wrote another name on the paper. "Remember, this is just a guess. But I bet you know him now."

She flipped the paper around. Harry's chest tightened. Everyone in the Western world knew that name.

Achilles.

Nora handed him the paper. "I look forward to your call tomorrow."

Chapter 7

Manhattan

The luxurious apartment was at the edge of a Manhattan neighborhood. Not too expensive, because the owner had no interest in impressing others, preferring the security of anonymity. Her personal safety couldn't be guaranteed in her line of work, though nobody could remember the last person who had raised a hand to Rose Leroux.

Likely because that guy was at the bottom of a river.

Her stiletto heels clicked on the marble floor. Rose poured a martini at her dining room bar, a cocktail that would be the envy of any bartender around the world. It was her fourth of the evening. Or was it the fifth? No matter. It was the best one yet. At least until she mixed another.

The city lights stretched in front of her. The towering buildings ran across the skyline like a castle wall. Rose dimmed the interior lights so the only thing obstructing her view was the reflected orange dot of her cigarette. The city lights were tiny dots representing millions of people, each living their own lives. Having those millions of people all around her helped keep Rose anonymous, or as much as she could be.

Rose Leroux was New York's biggest fence. If an item was not suitable for sale on the open market, the owner came to Rose. Why her? Because in a city where deals were made and lost on the back of connections, no one knew more people willing to pay top dollar for ill-gotten goods than Rose. It was said she could move the Statue of Liberty. For the right fee, of course.

The tip of her cigarette went supernova in the window as she took a deep, satisfying drag. Nothing was free. A lesson she'd learned a lifetime ago. A lesson, it seemed, that life was intent on teaching her again.

The doorbell jarred her out of her thoughts. Rose didn't turn around at the noise. She waited until the phone beside her rang. She pressed a button. "Who is it?"

Her security guard answered. "Stefan Rudovic."

Rose closed her eyes. Of all the people to show up unannounced. "Let him in. Be certain he is not armed."

"Right away, ma'am."

Rose turned the lights back up and returned to the bar. She needed another drink for this.

Her security guard appeared a minute later with a man trailing behind him. Her guard subjected the visitor to a second search for Rose's benefit, handling the smaller man a bit roughly. Rose appreciated it. She'd made it clear that Stefan Rudovic should now be treated with suspicion at all times. She never told them why, and they knew not to ask.

She waited until the frisk was completed. "Thank you," she said. The guard left. Stefan straightened his clothes, though the irritation on his face didn't reach his eyes.

Rose moved to light the fresh cigarette dangling from the stem of her long, black holder. "What brings you here?" she asked.

Stefan's forehead wrinkled. "You got a new lighter."

The flame hovered in mid-air. The ruby-red Zippo in her hand came alive under it, brilliant red flashes sparking in the light. "I did." She finished lighting her cigarette and set the lighter down. "Why did you come here unannounced?"

"Those are rubies." Stefan tilted his head. "Your lighter is covered in rubies."

Rose waved a hand at it. "Yes, those are rubies. What is so fascinating about my lighter?"

"You have had the same lighter for fifteen years," Stefan said. "Why get a new one?"

Because it's the color of blood, and it reminds me I should never trust anyone. Certainly not you.

Rose lifted a shoulder. "I like it."

Stefan blinked twice. He looked up from the lighter. "I came here to discuss business."

"Are you stealing for Altin Cana again?"

Anger crossed his face. "I've been retained by a third party to locate an item. I expect to find more items with it. Valuable ones. Items you will help me sell."

Rose took a drink. "Who is the third party?"

"I cannot say."

Ash fell from her cigarette. "Come now, Stefan. Do you think I won't find out?"

He didn't argue. Of course she would. Stefan leaned across the bar. She fought the urge to move away. "I am working with Evgeny Smolov."

Rose's heart beat faster. She soothed her nerves with a pull from the martini glass. "Interesting."

Her mind raced. Evgeny Smolov was a serious player in the market. He didn't always dive in, but when he did, money flew around like a hurricane. "What is he after?"

Stefan wagged a finger. "Why should I tell you?"

"You want me to help you move something? I need to know what it is. You can't walk through my door a month from now with a relic and expect me to get the best price. I have to prepare, contact potential buyers. Moving stolen antiquities isn't merely a business. It is a seduction."

"There may be several pieces," he said. "Ancient Greek. Evgeny is paying me to find a Greek artifact using this." Stefan held out his phone to display a statue holding a shield. "Evgeny believes the writing on this shield will lead to a great treasure."

"Where did he get the statue?"

"Turkey."

"Which was part of ancient Greece. That makes sense. When did he find it?"

"A few weeks ago."

Rose reached for the phone. "What does the shield say?"

Stefan pulled his phone out of reach. "That is not your concern."

"The less you tell me, the less money you'll make."

"I will tell you when I know more," he said.

Rose sat on a tall chair at her bar. "I hope you don't plan to swindle Evgeny Smolov."

"I do not want a bullet in my head. I want to be paid."

"How much is he offering?"

Stefan looked at her from under hooded eyes. "Five million," he finally said. "And I may keep any additional objects he does not want."

Smolov dealt only in the very best, Rose knew. He would throw away museum-worthy pieces if he didn't like them. "In that case, I agree. I'll help you move whatever you find." She jabbed her cigarette in Stefan's direction. "Provided Evgeny Smolov has no interest in them. He is not a man to cross." As though her opinion would keep Stefan from doing just that.

"Good," Stefan said.

He made no move to get up. "Is there anything else?" Rose asked. She looked at her watch. "I have plans." She didn't.

"The last time I was here you talked about my mother. I want to know more."

Rose forced herself to take a breath. Then a lungful of smoke, followed by a long pull on her martini. Only after her neck loosened did she speak. Softly. "The last time you were here is when Vincent Morello was murdered. By men you hired. You came here under false pretenses, but your true purpose was to use me as an alibi. If you were with me, you could not be killing Vincent Morello at the same time. You tricked me, Stefan. Nobody does that."

Stefan shrugged. "Now we have a secret together. No one will ever know."

"My life is in danger because of you." She pointed to the door. "If you have no other business to discuss, get out."

"I want to know more about my mother."

Rose stared at him, her face impassive. Why would she want to revisit the darkest period of her life? Memories she had buried under decades of anger and alcohol were meant to stay hidden, not be rehashed. Even if the person asking was the son of a woman who had been at her side for a time during those years. A son Rose had promised to protect. A boy who had now grown into a man she didn't recognize. A man who had betrayed her.

The thought appeared and was gone in an instant. Rose Leroux didn't do sentimental. She acted only in the service of reason, purpose. Tonight her reason was that fate had smiled on her. Stefan Rudovic wanted her help. Perhaps she could use that to hasten his undoing.

"Your mother did what was required to escape the Kosovo War, even though it meant leaving everything she knew behind. She agreed to smuggle drugs in exchange for tickets out of the Balkan region."

"The Yugoslavians would have killed us if she didn't. I remember."

"Your mother got you both safely to America. Then she had to pay her debt." Rose looked out the window at the sea of comforting lights. "She smuggled drugs into America for several months. Until one day another gang tried to steal the product. There was gunfire. Your mother died."

Her cigarette burned bright. "It was a tragedy," Rose said. "A terrible, avoidable tragedy."

A change had come over Stefan's face. For a few seconds he wasn't the hardened killer who had foolishly put her life at risk and provoked a gangland war in the city. He was the young boy she'd known so long ago.

"How do you know all of this?"

She wanted to tell him to piss off, that it was none of his business.

Only, that didn't serve her purpose. Talking to Stefan was the fastest way to get him to share what he knew about Smolov's artifact search with her. "Would you like a drink?" she asked.

"I cannot stay long."

"No one in New York knows my background. I prefer to keep it that way." She sighed. "I was born in France. My father sold arms to various factions in the Balkans. The region was constantly at war, so he had no shortage of buyers."

Her eyes narrowed. "It was not an easy life. My father knew money was the only sure path to safety in life. He taught me that lesson." The cigarette smoke in her throat turned sour. "And my father prospered. Yet there is one risk with such a north star; it inevitably makes you greedy." Her words slowed. "My father cheated an Albanian militia. He sold them guns that looked fine, but once in use they failed almost immediately. Many of the Albanian soldiers died because of it. Those who survived came after my father. We fled back to France, to a house in the French countryside, in a village where our family had ties no one knew of."

Rose no longer saw the city lights. Instead, memories of the small village took over, images of rolling fields, wandering sheep and the most delicious cheeses. "The Albanian soldiers could not find us, and we were happy. But it did not last." Rose crushed out her cigarette. "One evening a child knocked on our door. My father never let me answer when callers arrived, so I went to the back of the house. It was a local child, one we knew. My father was speaking with her when the back door flew open. I still remember his face."

It was the last time she ever saw him. "He was smiling at the girl. Her name was Sophie." Two men came through the rear entrance and grabbed me. My father ran toward me, but the men had guns. They forced him to sit in a chair and watch as they left with me."

"I am sorry."

Stefan's voice snapped her back. His dead eyes were too much like those of the men who had kidnapped her. The same emptiness behind them. "I was smuggled back to their country." She barked a laugh. "How appropriate. My first exposure to what built my fortune."

Her lighter burst to life and another cigarette caught. "They used me as leverage. My father was to provide discount guns, or I died. I lived for weeks at their base in Albania. I had food, books, even a radio. It was not horrible. Then one day I was told that my father had not given the soldiers what they demanded. I have no idea if this was true. That night I was given a backpack and sent in a car with a man and woman I did not know. We drove into Greece. At the border, the guards checked the man's and woman's bags, but not mine. I did not understand why at the time."

"They made you a drug mule."

"Yes. My bag was filled with drugs. What guard checks the pink bag of a child? Hundreds of times I crossed national borders, and never did the border guards search my bag."

"How does this involve my mother?"

Rose's mouth was open, ready to speak. She didn't continue, instead contemplating Stefan over her cigarette's ember. *You truly want to know. Good. I can use this.*

"That's enough for now," she said.

"What about my mother?"

Rose exhaled, a cloud of smoke enveloping Stefan. "My father died not long after I was taken. A car accident. I do not know exactly when it happened. For two years I moved their drugs across borders. Then I began to move people. A teenage girl would never traffic people, would she?" The humorless laugh again. "That is how I met your mother."

She waved a hand. "Enough for now. When will you know more about these artifacts you are chasing?"

Stefan had known Rose for a long time. He knew when not to press her. "Soon."

"You must tell me about them as you learn more. Information is how I identify and entice buyers. The more interested parties, the higher the price."

Stefan clearly didn't like it, but what choice did he have? "I will." He seemed to consider his next words carefully before speaking. "I spoke with a Greek historian. A man I trust. The shield's message is vague. This man believes it is only the starting point on a journey. The next step is in Greece. I am going there tomorrow."

Rose eyed him as coolly as she could. "Greece is a big country."

"I am going to the mountains."

The mountains? "I see," she said. "Keep me updated. As I have said, information is money in my world."

"I will be in touch." Stefan moved to the door. He stopped as the guard reappeared to escort him out, then turned and spoke over his shoulder. "When we talk again, you will tell me more about my mother."

"Business first," Rose said. "Then family."

Stefan disappeared through the door. Rose went to her desk and watched him on the surveillance cameras until he exited the front door and faded into the darkness. Only then did she pick up her phone and make a call.

Harry Fox answered on the first ring. "Good evening, Rose."

"Are you alone?" she asked. Harry said he was. "Listen closely. This is important."

Stefan Rudovic was once under her protection. Then he had used Rose for his alibi, drawing her into the deadly plot to murder Vincent Morello and replace him with Altin Cana. The past was over. Rose couldn't do anything to change the fact Stefan had betrayed her trust, had used her as an alibi to prove he hadn't killed Vincent Morello. She couldn't change it now. Now Rose would do anything in her power to ensure the next phase of Stefan's plan failed.

"I learned about a new artifact," Rose said. That was all she had to say to get Harry Fox interested. He was just like his father.

"You have my attention."

Rose relayed what she knew about the shield, including where it had been found and the message on it. "I know this is vague," Rose said.

"But there is a way to track it. Stefan Rudovic is traveling to Greece to search. Find him, and you find the trail."

She had baited the hook and Stefan took it. He may have crafted an airtight alibi for the night of Vincent Morello's murder. He was with Rose. Everyone trusted Rose, and if Stefan was with her, he couldn't have been killing Vincent at the same time. Rose knew this was a lie, that Stefan had orchestrated the bombing, but she couldn't reveal the truth without putting herself at risk too. If she told Joey Morello that Stefan had tricked her into serving as his alibi, had actually known about Vincent's death before it happened, Joey would naturally suspect her. He may never say it out loud, but Rose would now make him nervous. And the last person she wanted to be was one who made a mob boss nervous. Those people tended to disappear no matter who they were.

Now she had a chance to pay Stefan back for his treachery and also help Harry Fox along the way.

Harry worked for Joey. Joey Morello couldn't prove the Cana family killed his father, though he clearly suspected it. The two families were nearly at war, so offering Harry the chance to get one over on Stefan Rudovic would be impossible for Joey Morello to pass up. Rose reminded him of this.

"What is it with everyone using me for their dirty work?"

"What do you mean?" Rose asked.

"Forget it," Harry said. "Why are you telling me about this artifact? You're neutral. That's how you stay in business."

"I never forget a slight. That is all I will say." Rose could practically hear him thinking.

"Okay," Harry said. "You have your reasons."

"Are you interested?"

"I'm more than that," Harry said. "The truth is I was already looking for this artifact."

Rose Leroux was never caught off guard. At least that's what she told herself. "I see." She had nothing else to offer.

"I trust you, Rose. Perhaps to a fault. So what I'm about to say can't go anywhere. Understood?"

"I did not get where I am by betraying my friends."

He seemed to pick up on the *friends* part. She'd never called him that before. "I learned about the shield from the D.A.'s anti-trafficking team."

"The female agent you have dealt with before, I assume."

"Nora Doyle. That's the one." Harry offered a summary of where the statue had been found, who had died when it disappeared, and how Nora Doyle's team wanted Harry to find it before whoever Evgeny Smolov hired did. "Turns out I'm up against Stefan Rudovic," he said when he'd finished. "Why the hell did Smolov hire a Cana family stooge to find it?"

"Stefan is more than a stooge," Rose said. "Altin Cana has ties to unsavory financiers. I am not surprised he is acquainted with Smolov."

"Makes sense. There's one more thing you should know. I think I already saw this statue. Or at least the box it was in."

"How?"

"I was in Smolov's private museum earlier this week," Harry said. "Don't ask why. I'm pretty sure the statue was being readied for display. Did you recognize the warrior?"

"I did not have time to study the piece."

Harry waited for a breath. "I think it's Achilles."

"Achilles is a myth."

"That's what they said about King Arthur."

A fair point. Harry's adventures would have rewritten the history books if doing so wouldn't get him killed. "An artifact tied to Achilles would be invaluable."

"Why do you think Nora Doyle's team wants me to find it before Evgeny Smolov does?"

"To stop him from financing terror, of course." Rose tapped her ruby lighter on the bar. "Did you already know that Greece was the next location suggested on Achilles' shield?"

"I don't even want to find this relic. We were about to leave for Egypt when Nora Doyle knocked on my door."

"We?" *Ahh. His female counterpart.* "The Egyptologist is still here."

"Her name is Sara. She's helping me."

"With the Achilles angle?"

Harry took his time responding. "Do you remember my father's amulet?"

"How could I forget? He was entranced by it."

"It's not just an amulet. There's a story behind it, one tied to Cleopatra and Mark Antony. Sara and I are uncovering that story now. That's what we were doing when I was dragged into this new mess."

Rose had many questions. She chose the most important one. "Which search will you undertake now?"

"Both of them."

"Your father would be proud. And he would say to watch your back. Altin Cana's men do not adhere to the old rules." Perhaps Harry would read between the lines. "I will do what I can to assist you."

"Why?"

"I have my reasons."

She wished him luck and ended the call. Rose remained at the bar long after her drink was empty, looking out across the expanse of city lights stretching to the water. Harry Fox was as good as anyone she'd ever known, including his father. The question wasn't whether he could find the relic tied to Achilles. Harry would find it. What worried her was whether he could beat Stefan to it with Evgeny Smolov backing the Albanian. That pairing was a terrifying match. Two ruthless men who could not accept defeat, each for different reasons.

Rose caressed the ruby lighter. For years she had helped Stefan any way she could, an old promise not forgotten. Now she would aid Harry Fox. She had no idea if it would be enough.

Harry stood on his front porch after Rose clicked off. Of all the people to match wits against, of course it was a Cana man. Stefan Rudovic, who most guys in Joey's crew called a poor man's Harry Fox. Stefan had apparently wanted to get involved with the antiquities black market, though Harry had yet to hear of him finding or selling anything of note. The guy was an operator, albeit one who had worked his way up to Altin Cana's right hand. Dismissing him as a tough would be foolish.

Harry dialed Joey's number. "You alone?" Harry asked when Joey answered.

"Yes."

"You won't believe who Evgeny Smolov hired to find his Greek artifact."

Joey didn't, not at first. "Those Albanian scumbags do business with anyone," Joey said. "Including terrorists now. It's dangerous to compete with them, but you're up for it, and right now this is exactly what I need."

"What?"

"I need men I can trust. I'll be honest, Harry. The family is in a tough spot."

Harry didn't respond. This was family business—above his pay grade.

"The other family heads are hesitating," Joey said. "I asked for their support. Three told me privately they plan to acknowledge me as my father's replacement if the vote is unanimous. Gio Sabella isn't committing yet. The old man won't say anything until he knows what benefits him the most."

"Is that what he told you?"

"Not in so many words," Joey said. "He told me a story about my father. The story wasn't what he really said, though. He's too crafty for that. Gio isn't sure I'm strong enough to lead the families."

"You survived two assassination attempts in a year. You're Vincent Morello's son."

"Gio comes from a time when the families were at war. My father brought peace to the city by showing them they make more money working together than killing each other. He didn't do that by letting people push him around. People like Altin Cana."

Two teens on skateboards zipped past Harry's porch. He could hear them well after they vanished from sight. "I might be able to help."

Years ago Fred Fox had saved Vincent's life. Now maybe Harry could save Vincent's legacy. "Beating Stefan Rudovic to that relic would knock Altin Cana down a peg."

In truth, this was the last thing Harry wanted with the amulet search heating up. Antony and Cleopatra's secret was close enough he could feel it. Too bad the world had different plans. First Nora Doyle. Now Joey Morello. Harry rubbed a finger over the rough cement. He should get out of town, follow the amulet path with Sara. What did he care if Evgeny Smolov found a new artifact? Joey was his own man. He had to stand up to Altin Cana eventually.

That's what he should do.

"It would," Joey said. "You know anyone who can help me with that?"

Harry closed his eyes. *Yeah, I know a guy.* "I might. But he's not cheap."

Joey laughed long and hard. "You're worth it. Whatever you need, ask."

"It's not only me who needs supplies."

"I'm listening."

"Sara and I were looking into my dad's amulet," Harry said. Joey had seen it, both when Fred Fox was alive and on a few rare occasions when it slipped out of his shirt. Joey knew it held meaning for Harry, and he also knew not to ask. "We were going to Egypt to keep searching. At least until Nora Doyle showed up."

"Sara can keep up with you," Joey said. "She's still going, isn't she?"

"I tried to stop her."

"Don't be a fool," Joey said. "If she wants to go, let her. Just tell me what she needs."

"You have any contacts in Egypt?" Harry asked. Joey said he did. "Sara may need items that aren't readily available."

"I thought she didn't like guns."

"Not weapons. Tools. Climbing gear to start."

"I know a guy who can get anything you need," Joey said. "I'll get her the best."

As much as Harry wanted to stop her, he couldn't. What was Harry supposed to do, lie to her? Peddling half-truths and falsehoods had nearly ruined their relationship before it ever got started. Only Nora had saved him from that fate. "I'll tell her," Harry said. "It's her call."

"If she agrees, then we have a real chance to finally put Altin Cana in his place." Joey's voice lowered. "Knock him down first, then maybe prove he killed my father."

The fact Joey Morello had failed to find Vincent's killer meant whoever had done it wasn't just connected; they were smart. Two qualities you never wanted in an enemy. Two qualities Altin Cana possessed. "One step at a time," Harry said. "Life gets dangerous if you lose focus on what's in front of you."

"Did Fred say that?"

Harry laughed. "That one's mine."

"I'll write it down. And we'll find the bastards who killed my father. Count on it."

Harry had no doubt. "May as well call your Egyptian friend," he said. "There's no way Sara will pass up a chance like this."

"I will, and I'll pay for first class on her way over."

Chapter 8

Brooklyn

Harry's buzzing phone pulled him out of sleep. A message from Nora, returning the one he'd sent last night. He'd been purposefully cryptic, and now she was dogging him for clarity. Let her wait. He was still tired.

Rubbing sleep from his eyes, Harry turned to find Sara had vanished, rumpled sheets the only evidence she'd ever been there. She'd been nodding off at the table last night after he got off the phone with Joey, so Harry made her call it a night and leave her research books open where they lay. Both of them were asleep in seconds, though at some point Sara had snuck out and made her way downstairs. The rich scent of fresh coffee told Harry so.

He fired off a text to Nora saying he'd call her in two hours. He and Sara had to confirm their plans first. The only way this happened was if Sara wanted it to. If she said yes, Harry was in. Any doubts on her part and Nora had to wait, threats or no. Joey, well, he'd deal with Joey when the time came. Preferably after the amulet quest was finished.

Sara was seated at the table with her nose buried in a book. This time she was actually awake. "Grab a chair," she ordered. "I found a reference to the Koraki. I think it tells us where you need to go next."

Harry slid into a chair beside her, steaming mug in hand. He paused for a second to admire her. "You look great," he said.

"Flattery will get you nowhere," she fired back. "Now look here."

She flipped a massive book around for him to inspect. He peered at the dense text. The stuff was impenetrable. At least it was in English. "What is this?"

"The only review of a specific ancient Greek burial ground in Turkey I could find," Sara said. "Done by a Greek doctoral student."

"Should I be worried that the only information we have to go on comes from a grad student?"

"Quite the opposite," Sara said. "No one has ever had any interest in looking at this burial ground more closely. The most interesting part of this research to most people is a passing reference."

Harry raised an eyebrow. "You'll see," said Sara. "This archaeologist studied the contents of several dozen coffins found not far from where the statue of Aci Los was last seen."

"Did he find a reference to Aci Los or the Koraki?"

Sara shook her head. "No, and for that we should be grateful. Aci Los died at what was likely the true battle for Troy, though I believe it's a stretch to call it that. That battle occurred around 1100 B.C., while this graveyard dates to around 500 B.C."

"Six centuries later."

"Yes. Which is important given the Koraki reference I found came from a tomb in this graveyard." She flipped to the rear section of the book, an appendix containing photographs. Small, hard-to-see photographs of rusty armor and chipped swords. She tapped one of the murkier images. "This."

"It looks like a warrior's armor."

"It is." Sara pulled at a length of her auburn hair and twirled it around a finger. "Elegant armor, which matches the sword found in this grave. The sword had an inscription on it. It's translated here." Now she flipped back to the original page and tapped a line. "Recognize anything?"

"*The Koraki brought Greece's prize to King Leonidas's battle against the Persians. This sword will fight beside the prize for all Greeks.*"

Harry blinked, then read it again. "*Prize*. The prize the Koraki were guarding."

Sara frowned. "That's it? Nothing else jumps out?"

"I'm trying to stay cool." And he was. "I don't want to get too excited about the Leonidas reference until you tell me I'm not crazy."

"You're not crazy."

"Then holy smokes. This guy has a sword used in King Leonidas's last stand." Harry's chest tightened. "That's incredible."

"The Battle of Thermopylae," Sara said. "Where Leonidas and his Spartan warriors saved Greece."

"Sparta was Greek," Harry said. "A Greek city-state representing a direct line from the Trojans. If anyone needed the *prize*, it was Leonidas when Xerxes showed up. If this is the same prize, that is."

Sara had that look in her eyes, the one Harry could only describe as being truly *alive*. He loved it.

"It's the most logical explanation," she said. "Which in our world also makes it the most likely. The main issue I had was Leonidas and his three hundred were annihilated. They fought to the death. I cannot imagine this sword would make it from the battle back into Greek hands. As for a Greek soldier's body somehow coming back to where Troy stood? Seems impossible. It's several hundred miles by boat. Considerably more by land."

"Then how did the sword or this soldier get to Turkey?"

Sara lifted a shoulder. "Hard to say. I suspect the sword was a gift from the Spartans to the Koraki. Not all the Spartans under Leonidas died at Thermopylae. Most of the army was sent home when Leonidas realized he would lose. This man could have been among those told to leave, and he carried the sword with him."

"We'll likely never know the truth," Harry said. "And who cares? If this proves where I need to go next, I'm all for it." He took a sip of coffee. "Where do I go?"

"First, listen to who I think this warrior was. His remains show he had well-developed musculature, was quite tall for his era, and he suffered three separate wounds consistent with being cut by a sword or spear."

"He saw action."

"Yes. Unfortunately, there's no indication of his name."

Harry lifted his chin. "A destination?"

"The reverse side of the sword blade is also engraved. The etching appears to have been done by someone with little training."

"Like ancient graffiti."

"Graffiti with purpose." Sara indicated another paragraph in the book. "The etching is translated here."

Harry read aloud. *"Prize secure in shadow over Sparta beneath Ares' shrine."*

"I'm not certain what it means."

"You said you knew where I should go."

She wagged a finger. "I can give you an informed guess."

Great. He was about to traipse halfway around the world on a hunch.

"Follow my logic," she said. "Like many early military groups, the Koraki kept records on their weapons and armor. Why? Soldiers are transient. They move quickly and without notice. What are the two possessions they would never leave behind?"

"Their weapons and armor."

"Correct."

"In this warrior's time Sparta was a major city. What do we call the same city in modern Greece?"

"Laconia. It is smaller and built outside where the ancient city sat. A mountain range called Taygetus is nearby." Sara leaned closer. "When the sun is out, the shadow from the tallest peak shaded the ancient city. Care to guess the name of that peak?"

Hair rose on his forearms. "Mount Ares?"

"Right. Named after the Greek god of war. The fierce Spartan culture held Ares in high esteem. Little surprise they named a prominent geographic feature after him."

The story was plausible. Yet Harry had never once heard of the Koraki until a few days ago. The idea that this information had sat in plain sight for centuries without being noticed was remarkable.

"Okay, let's say I'm buying it." Harry drummed his fingers on the table. "Two questions. First, where is *Ares' shrine?*"

"The most likely location is on Mount Ares," she said. "Talk to the locals in Laconia. They are the best sources for this sort of knowledge. And wear comfortable shoes."

"Very funny." Now to the bad part. "Second question. Is the information you've gathered available to the general public?"

A look of discomfort crossed her face. "This research is, yes."

"Acknowledging your otherworldly research skills, it's possible we're not the only people making this connection. Smolov's team could find it."

"True, but it isn't easy. I found this research by using an internal university database. Someone else would need that same access. The database is limited to members of academic institutions and researchers."

"Which means there are thousands of people who could find this same lead if they knew what to look for."

She paused. "In theory, yes."

Harry's thoughts turned to the ceramic knuckledusters on his nightstand. His favorite accessory in a world where fighting fair was for suckers. "Then this next step could be dangerous."

"Isn't everything you do?"

"If we include dating you, then yes." She smacked his arm. "Easy," he shouted. "I'll spill my coffee. That's unforgiveable."

Her smile lit up the room. "Be careful with the insults. Planes fly to Germany every day."

"You're too smart to leave a prize like me." His grin faded. "I have a third question. Assuming I go to Greece, that means you're going to Egypt, right? Alone?"

She nearly scowled. "You think I can't handle myself?"

"I know you can. But you've always had a partner. If not me, Nora. This time it will be different. Just you, and who knows what you're up against."

"I'm going to Luxor. You need to worry about finding a shrine on Mount Ares. Let me worry about your father's amulet."

Any further discussion ended when a thunderous banging sounded on his front door. Flashes of a home invasion ran through Harry's mind. He ran to the umbrella stand beside the door. A stand empty of umbrellas, but containing one shotgun loaded with double-aught buckshot.

Sara knew about the invasion, and how it had impacted Harry's sense of safety at home. She also knew something else.

"Harry, intruders don't knock before they come in."

He paused, one hand on the shotgun. "I'd rather not take chances." He lifted the blinds on a nearby window. "We're good. I think."

Only once the booming knocking sounded again did Harry open the door. Nora Doyle stopped her assault on it.

Harry stood in place. "Why are you here?"

"I need an answer." She came in without waiting for an invitation. "Good morning, Sara."

Sara was always happy to see Nora. "Harry didn't say you were coming."

"Something came up," Nora said. "Harry, can you step outside with me?"

Sara turned back to her books as Harry followed Nora out to the sidewalk. "I said I'd text you," he said.

"We need an answer now." Nora's hands were on her hips, pulling her jacket open so her shoulder holster was visible. "Every hour you don't get out there is an hour Smolov's hired guns get closer to the relic. Once that happens, terrorists get what they need. You don't want that to happen, do you?"

"I don't care who has this relic," he said truthfully. "I planned to go to Egypt until you started banging on my door."

"Going to Egypt with Sara." Those five innocuous words dropped like iron. "You're lucky, Harry. She's a nice lady. You don't want to lose her."

His vision narrowed. "Blackmail again? I know she's still here because you covered for me."

"I'd say 'gave you a sheen of legitimacy where none existed,' but call it what you will." Nora lowered her voice. "You help me, I help you. That being said, I won't play this card again. I hope you decide being on my team is better than not being on it." Nora rubbed one eye. "I'm sorry I have to do this. It's not how I'd like to handle it."

Realization dawned. "Your father is pressuring you."

Birds flew about in the trees beside them, branches bouncing as they took flight and landed. "He's under tremendous pressure," she finally said. "The District Attorney."

"It's an election year." Harry shook his head. "The D.A. needs good press. Politicians are the worst species on the planet."

"My father is not a politician, but his boss is. My father cares about providing for his family."

"I'm sure your dad could get a sweet private gig if his boss isn't reelected."

"What if that's not what he wants? My father went into public service to help people." Nora waved a hand. "Enough about my family. Are you taking this assignment or not?"

"It's an official assignment?"

"You signed an agreement, remember? You're part of our team. Now act like it and say yes." She waited a beat. "Even if it's only for Sara."

Backed into a corner with no real choice. He shook his head again. "You really know how to hit below the belt."

"I'm doing the right thing. So are you. Is that a yes?"

"I'll do it."

"Excellent." Nora tapped his chest. "Now go tell Sara. She has a trip to plan."

Nora turned. "Not yet," Harry said. Nora stopped and looked back. "What have you found on my mother's case?"

"My father is looking into it," Nora said. "Quietly. The police don't like it when you suggest they messed up."

Don't *like* it? They misidentified a body. "Who cares? The cops should want to get it right."

"That's not how they look at it. Cops stick together, as they should."

"Even if the case is decades old? Most of those people have to be retired. Or dead."

Harry looked out the window as a city garbage truck roared past. The engine backfired, and he nearly jumped.

"I'm going to a benefit dinner tonight," Nora said. "Against my better judgment."

"What's a benefit dinner have to do with my mother's case?"

"It's a benefit for retired officers. Everyone involved with your mother's case is retired or close to it. Including a cop who I know will be at the benefit tonight. I'm going as my father's representative." She pulled a phone from her pocket. "Speaking of him. Hang on a second."

Harry kept one ear toward Nora as she took the call.

"I'm at Harry's," she said. "Yes, I remember. I'm covering for you." Silence while Gary Doyle must have been speaking. "Yes, tell Mom I'll wear it. You know I think it's too flashy and heavy. Yes, I know people like to talk about it. Got it. I'll tell you what Jess Barnes has to say."

Nora slipped the phone into her pocket. "Retired Detective Jessica Barnes is sitting at my table tonight."

"She was one of the detectives who investigated my mother's case," Harry said. "Her name is in the report."

"That's why I'm sitting next to her," Nora said. "To introduce myself, then to have a private word."

The emotions rising in Harry's chest were immediately tamped down. He couldn't easily find answers after this long, so he was forced to rely on Nora. He didn't like it one bit.

"Thank you for following up." That's all he could say. Nora

appeared to sense his struggle, for she turned and went inside. Harry followed her.

Sara had her nose buried in a book. "Everything okay?" she asked without looking up.

"We're good," Harry said. "Let Nora know what you need for Egypt." He looked to Nora. "That offer to help still stands, right?"

"It does," Nora said. "My father approved it."

Nora spoke as Sara got to work. "It would help if I knew why you're going to Egypt."

"Personal business," Harry fired back.

Nora lifted a hand. "Fine. Let me know what I can do for you. Now tell me where you're going in Greece, and why."

Harry pulled the book from Sara's hand and began the story. "A town called Laconia. People used to call it Sparta."

Chapter 9

Sparta, Greece

The cool air coming down from the mountains was like an elixir from heaven. Harry closed his eyes and breathed deeply. The scorching heat of the late Greek summer vanished as the Taygetus mountains grew taller in the windshield of his rented Land Rover, and as he now stood at the base of Mount Ares, it was hard to believe that scarcely twenty-four hours earlier he had been in his apartment after Nora had blackmailed him into coming here.

No, that wasn't quite the truth. Harry had willingly backed himself into a corner of Nora's choosing. Tree limbs heavy with foliage rustled all around him. He'd agreed to do this, and even though it led him to the Greek city of Laconia while Sara was travelling to Luxor, it felt right. The dirt beneath his boots, the sun warming his face. And the promise of an ancient relic ahead. It was exactly what he wanted.

A thought of his mother's case came and went. Worry about that later. Right now he was in a race against the man who had likely killed Vincent Morello and tried to kill Joey. And, lest he forget, who was bankrolled by an exiled Russian oligarch. Harry glanced skyward. *I hope you're enjoying this, Dad. I am.*

A new topographical map came out of his pocket, marked with a route provided by a very curious man he'd met earlier at a café in Laconia. How Harry had met that man was an adventure of its own.

On his drive from the airport to the foot of Mount Ares Harry stopped in Laconia, where he had found the local library and asked the librarian about anything on Mount Ares tied to the god for which it was named. A shrine would be best, he'd told her, though he'd take anything she had. The enthusiastic lady promptly dumped an overwhelming amount of material onto his table, information ranging from historical treatises on the origins of Greek gods to old newspaper articles detailing expeditions undertaken by the local boy scouts.

She was disappointed to realize he couldn't read a word of it. "Is there someone I can talk to?" Harry asked. "Do you know anyone who's explored the mountain?"

She tilted her head to one side, placing one finger on her lips. For a moment she was silent. "You could try Dimi. He loves the mountains."

"Who's Dimi?"

"Dimitrios Tzolis. He was our maintenance technician for decades. He retired last year. He spent every weekend walking this country, including most of the Taygetus range. I know he has been to the top of Mount Ares."

"Any idea where I can find him?"

The librarian pointed over Harry's shoulder. "At the café across the street. He's sitting at the front table right now drinking coffee and reading the paper. He does that every morning. Tell him I sent you."

Harry thanked her and booked it across the street. The man seated at the table looked to be made of beef jerky and snow-white hair, with very little else. His clothes looked capable of withstanding a hurricane, while the sinewy muscles beneath the thick coat of coarse hair covering his arms made it clear he could likely pick Harry up and throw him through the window. His sunglasses came off as Harry approached to reveal two dark eyes between slitted lids. They did not invite conversation.

"Dimitrios Tzolis?"

The man responded in a flurry of Greek. Harry played a hunch. "*No, ma io parlo italiano.*" No, but I speak Italian.

Dimi's impressive eyebrows lifted a fraction. "*Vedo.*" I see.

Most Greeks spoke multiple languages, and with Italy right across the Ionian Sea, Italian was a common one.

"Though my English is better," Harry said quickly. "My name is Harry Fox."

"Not an Italian name. Where are you from?"

"Brooklyn."

"Ah." Dimi sipped from the tiny cup on his table. It looked to contain tar. "How do you know my name?"

"The librarian sent me."

Dimi did not blink. "Do you know her?"

"We met ten minutes ago."

"She is my cousin's granddaughter."

"And she's a very nice young woman," Harry said.

"She is." Dimi nodded to a vacant chair. "Sit."

A waiter materialized, and Dimi looked at Harry expectantly. "I'll have what he's having," Harry said, pointing to Dimi's cup.

The waiter disappeared, and Harry began. "I heard you know Mount Ares better than any man in town." Dimi didn't dispute it. "Do you know of any shrines to the namesake?" Harry laid his map on the table. "I'm here on personal business."

"What business do you have with the mountain?"

"Personal."

Dimi sipped coffee. "I see." He didn't speak again until Harry's drink arrived. Harry sipped what turned out to most definitely be tar. "Delicious," he said.

"I have climbed the Taygetus range."

"I'm interested in Mount Ares," Harry said. "Have you ever seen a shrine to the god Ares?"

Dimi watched the empty street. He closed his eyes and folded his hands. Harry tried very hard to keep still, though the unexpected avalanche of caffeine hurtling through his system at that moment made it hard.

"I first climbed Mount Ares eighty years ago," Dimi finally said. "I was twelve."

Harry nearly knocked his cup over. "You're *ninety-two*?"

"How old do you think I am?"

"At least a hundred."

Dimi's lips curled up at the corner. "I like you. I will tell you two things. First, the mountain holds a unique story for anyone who climbs it. She is quiet, so you must pay attention to learn it. Let the rocks be your guide and you will find what you seek."

Harry had a pen in hand, hovering over the map. It stayed there. What the heck was Dimi telling him?

"Second, Ares wore a helmet."

"He's the god of war," Harry said. "A fight was never far."

"Follow his helmet." Dimi reached a wizened hand across the table and pulled Harry's map and pen over. He consulted the map for a moment, then drew a shape on it partway up the mountain and an *X* at the base. Only after Dimi returned the map could Harry see that the first shape was an elegantly outlined ancient battle helmet. The kind Achilles or Leonidas would have worn, with two cheekpieces protecting the face and a nose guard in between. A warrior's helmet.

"Look to where Ares watches," Dimi said.

"Thanks," Harry said, unsure how else to reply.

"You should go," Dimi said. "The mountain is taller than it looks."

Either this old guy was crazy, or he'd just given Harry valuable guidance. Only one way to find out. "I appreciate the help."

Dimi grabbed Harry's outstretched hand and pulled him closer with the force of a tank. "There are bears on the mountain."

"Bears?"

"Leave them alone. If you cross one, try bear repellent. I have been told it may work."

Holy smokes. "*May*? Where would I get bear repellent?"

"A city one hour away."

He didn't have time for that. Dimi let go of Harry's hand and sat back. "It is unlikely you will see one. They stay in their caves. Do not go into a cave."

Dimi turned and called for the waiter, and Harry had enough sense to get going, map in hand. He jogged to the car and headed for the area where Dimi had scratched an X on the map. What did Dimi mean about the helmet? And how was the mountain dangerous, other than the bears, and the obvious issue of hurting himself alone and far from help?

The cool wind had picked up by the time he parked at the mountain's base. He glanced at his watch. Dimi was right. Time to move. He didn't want to get stuck up there at night. He slipped on his backpack and took off. A gravel path led toward the tree line, though the ground underfoot turned to dirt when Harry crossed into the shade of towering evergreens. The bark on one was rough when he reached out to touch it. A gradual hill stretched ahead of him, sloping sharply upward as it veered to the right. A hiker appeared from the trees with a walking stick in hand. He offered a wave as he passed Harry, who returned the gesture, then put his head down and kept walking.

The sun was nearly overhead by the time he reached a small plateau several hundred feet up. Evergreen trees blocked most of the sky, and the only sign he passed was one at the base warning hikers to beware of wild animals. The sole animal outline pictured? A bear. He pushed aside thoughts of massive claws ripping him to shreds as he pulled the map out. Given most of his experience with maps involved the New York subway, it took him a few tries to locate where he was.

Harry's cell phone map was little help. It told him he was on the mountain and not much else. The device went into his pocket and Harry sent a silent request for protection to any deities in the area as he forged onward. Nearly an hour and he was barely halfway to the helmet. The path he followed was just wide enough for him to pass through in places, yet big enough for a car in others. If he knew what a goat path was he'd have called it that, and after one final half-run, half-climb up a horridly steep hill, he leapt up into a clearing and stopped.

The outline of a Spartan battle helmet was carved into the mountain.

At eye level, it was approximately the same dimensions that a real helmet would be. Faded, sure, but undoubtedly what Dimi had been describing. The image even faced the same way Dimi had drawn it, with the eye slots looking left.

What had Dimi said? *Follow his helmet.* The helmet of Ares. If a warrior was wearing that helmet, he'd be looking to the left. Harry followed the helmet's gaze. A trail pushed onward and upward. So would Harry.

The sun had reached its zenith as he began climbing again. Judging from the map he was roughly a third of the way up the mountain. That meant at least two more hours to get to the top. After that, he still had to get back down. Even he knew one of the fastest ways to kill yourself coming down a mountain was to do it in the dark. His pace accelerated.

The air cooled after another half hour. The scent of pine trees filled his nose, with no sounds other than his footsteps. Startled birds overhead vanished as he walked. The path wasn't exactly straight, but given his hopes were pinned on a nonagenarian's doodle Harry didn't worry too much. Keep climbing and don't miss any carvings. And watch out for bears.

After thirty minutes he came to a switchback. Blue skies stretched out overhead, the city of Laconia beneath them. And five feet in front of him the ground dropped off a sheer cliff. He leaned over. The tops of some very tall trees were a good twenty feet down. Harry pressed back against the cliff face. Then he noticed it.

Another helmet had been carved into the rock face. Facing left again, telling Harry to move ahead.

Hold on a second. The city was beneath them. If Mount Ares was the shrine casting its shadow over ancient Sparta, could this be what the sword meant? Sara had said as much to him before they parted ways, that the message could be factual. Perhaps the shrine symbolized Ares looking over Sparta and protecting the city, but was also factual in that you could actually see Sparta from the shrine. Harry looked above him to the mountain's peak. No, this wasn't the end. If the Spartans truly wanted Ares to watch over them, he would do so in fact as he did in myth: from on high.

A quick scan revealed nothing of interest other than the carving. Harry pushed onward. Up and around the trail led. Twice he hugged the rockface when the trail became a narrow ledge. He passed a large, open area with a rocky overhang that could offer shelter in the event of a storm. Good to have in his back pocket if the weather turned. He passed it, then turned and went back. Might as well test it out. The depression in the cliffside was big enough to shelter maybe a half-dozen people and their supplies. A good stopping point.

A bottle of water quenched his thirst before Harry kept going. He was halfway to the summit now, though one thought had occurred to him again and again during the walk: the peak of Mount Ares wasn't a curve, but more of a needle. It was unlikely you could stand at the top, which meant you couldn't build a shrine there even if you wanted to. Odds were a shrine wasn't at the top. Any shrines on the side of Mount Ares overlooking ancient Sparta would likely be about two-thirds of the way up, in a location where people could actually stand. Any higher up and you'd be sliding down on your backside.

This all ran through his head as he climbed. It was well into the afternoon when he stopped dead, the water bottle halfway to his lips. He stared at the mountainside twenty feet ahead. A black hole stared back. A cave mouth, yawning wide to swallow the sunlight.

Grass around the cave rustled in the breeze. In front of it, the grass didn't move because it had been trampled flat. Either by lots of little animals, or one very big one. The bark on a tree across from him had been scraped off, leaving an ugly scar of freshly exposed wood. His heart beat loudly enough to alert any monster inside as he crept past, trying to tiptoe at world record pace. Whatever beast had ripped that tree apart could do the same to Harry.

He raced past the cave mouth, all the while expecting a bear to leap out and grab him, though he made it across without incident. Keeping his head on a swivel for any living creatures, he jogged through towering trees that seemed to lean together above him, throwing shadows everywhere. Shadows in which forest predators could lie in wait for defenseless, scared prey to pass by. Harry reached into his pocket and slipped on the knuckledusters. Not totally defenseless.

He stopped in a small clearing and listened. No bears came crashing through the trees, so he pulled out the map. Less than a thousand feet of elevation remained to the top, though little more than half of that was fit for walking. The mountainside grew ever more sharply angled the higher he went. He stuffed the map back into his pocket and hefted his pack. Anything Dimi's helmets led to wouldn't be far now.

His shadow grew longer with each step. Harry glanced at his watch. He was now pushing his chances of getting back down before nightfall. Each breath seemed to come at a higher price, the air less fruitful up here. He wiped cold sweat from his forehead.

Harry looked up. A flood of spilled rocks lay across the narrow trail, blocking any easy way forward. Harry bent over and picked up one of the stones. He frowned. Why was one side flat and smooth? Unnatural. He grabbed another and found the same flat face on one side. This was no coincidence. An idea took root. *Could it be?*

He picked his way through the fallen rocks with care, always making sure of his footing before moving on. He was glad he did, for after a short climb the pile of rocks ended abruptly at the edge of a cliff. Gingerly, Harry craned his neck and looked over. A jumble of similar rocks lay strewn several hundred feet down. One more step and Harry would have followed them. He scrambled backwards as quickly as he dared, heart thudding, breath coming short, the hair on his arms standing up.

When he had regained his composure, he looked around him. Yes, his idea had been correct. This collapsed side of the wall had been a staircase. That was why so many of the rocks were flat on one side. They had once been steps, a way to ascend the hillside. Harry shielded his eyes and saw a flatter area some twenty feet overhead. Easy to get there with steps. But by climbing the remains of a wall—a flat wall, at that, from which the steps had naturally sheared off? Not so much. His gaze fell from the ruined wall to another pile of stones, about five feet high, at its base. He tilted his head to one side. *That's odd.*

Something about the pile didn't look natural. He stepped carefully over to it and pushed the top rock, which fell. Maybe it was just how they'd fallen. Or perhaps Dimitrios had stacked them and used it as a springboard to get up there. If so, he was the most agile old man on earth. Harry took a step up, lost his footing and tumbled down onto the bed of broken rocks. He cursed loud enough to be heard down in Laconia.

He tried again, this time with care. Clambering up, he gained a precarious foothold at the top, but even up here he couldn't reach the upper level, still a good ten feet overhead. He craned his neck and looked upward again. There was a small tree growing out of the hillside ten feet up. He'd have to get around it in order to get to the flat area. Now, if he could just somehow—*hold on.*

The tree was thick. Better yet, it was far enough up that if he could get on top of it, he might be able to get a handhold on the ground above and haul himself up. Only one problem: he couldn't jump high enough from his perch atop the rock pile to grab it. Even if he were on flat ground, he needed a good four feet of vertical leap to grab it. No chance of him turning into Michael Jordan, but he could pull an Edmund Hillary and out-think the mountain.

He reached into his pack for a length of nylon filament rope. Harry possessed a respectable knowledge of knots, so he tossed one end of the rope up and over the tree, caught the end, and then did it again. Knotting this same end into a loop, he passed the other end through and crafted a support rope to haul himself up. Two sharp pulls told him the tree would likely hold his weight.

He took a breath and started pulling himself up, hand over hand, his back muscles bulging as he moved up the mountainside and grabbed the tree with one hand, then the other. He didn't wait for his confidence to falter before reaching up to grab the lip above him. Another pullup and he was staring at level ground. Harry kicked himself up, holding the rope in one hand as he landed safely on the flat bluff.

He lay flat and took deep breaths, his chest pressed to the ground. He looked off into the distance. The ancient town of Sparta spread out below him. How much farther did this trail go? Scaling that wall had been no mean feat. His arm muscles protested as he pushed himself up onto an elbow and looked the other way—directly into a cave filled with darkness. He started, jumping away, nearly sending himself back over the bluff's edge. *Easy, Harry.* Fingers in the dirt, he kept still, searching for any sign of movement. A long-ago zoo visit flashed to mind, when he'd seen a bear climbing not only trees in its enclosure, but a vertical wall. No doubt a big enough bear could scale the same rockface he had. Perhaps it did so daily, coming to and from the dark cave now yawning in front of him.

Harry blinked once, twice. With difficulty, he tore his eyes from the empty cavemouth and looked above it. His eyes widened.

Another carved Spartan helmet stared back at him from the rock wall above the cave. As though it had been waiting thousands of years for him to arrive. No, not at *him*. Harry twisted his head. At the ancient town of Sparta below.

Prize secure in shadow over Sparta beneath Ares' shrine. The sword's message. A shadow over Sparta held the key to their search for Ares' shrine. It was on this mountain of the same name. Sparta bred warriors, men born to wear the helmet of Ares, a helmet that had guided Harry to this spot by instructing him to follow its gaze. Now this helmet which looked over Sparta. And perhaps it guarded the cave mouth as well. A final carving in homage to their patron god of war.

Harry's tongue was as dry as the rocky ground. Dimi had warned him about the bears. Could it be Dimi knew a bear lived in this cave? Was that why he'd never gone inside, why the cave remained unexplored? Any prize hidden inside was protected by a guard, one with claws and teeth and the unpredictable temperament to keep curious humans away. If they were smart enough to heed the warning signs, that is.

Harry pushed himself up. He took a step forward, then another, forcing his legs to move. A cloud shifted overhead, letting sunlight fall across the bluff and into the cavemouth. He stopped.

A massive, hairy bear's paw lay in the sunlight.

Harry couldn't say how long he stood there. His breath came in short, ragged gasps as he waited for the bear to move. He could jump, slide down the tree, hit the rocks running and race down the hill. If he didn't fall, snap an ankle, or look back, then maybe he could beat it. But right now, the bear lay still. Perhaps it was tired, Harry thought hopefully. Maybe it was asleep and wouldn't give chase. Or... *damn*... What if it had cubs up here and –

A flash of color caught his eye, a dazzling burst of fire that came alive when the sun hit it. A burst of red beneath the paw, so bright it could only be one thing. Blood. A pool of it.

The bear had just killed something.

Harry tilted his head. If the bear had killed its dinner there would be evidence of it. Bloody ground from the bear dragging its meal up here. He knelt, moving silently until he gained a better view.

There were footprints inside the cave.

Human prints in the dirt. Right at the edge of the cave. One set leading in, another leading out. Someone had been here. Someone might *still* be up here.

He waited. Only for a minute, until his brain caught up. He'd made enough noise clambering up here to wake the bear. Anyone else around would have heard him cursing when he fell. If someone was still here, they were lying in wait. A heat bloomed in his chest. The hell with them.

He stepped forward. The bear didn't move. Light glinted beside the pooled blood as he walked. Another silent step and it made sense. His stomach dropped.

Shell casings littered the ground. The blood wasn't from the bear's meal; it was from the animal itself. It had pooled all around the dead creature, leaking from a half-dozen holes in its carcass, including one between the eyes. Someone had shot the bear. A .357 Magnum, if Harry had to guess. Harry grabbed a rock and tossed it at the animal, ready to bolt if the thing moved. The rock hit it. Nothing happened. He tossed another rock, this one right at the bear's head. Another hit with no result. He crept closer and watched for any sign of life. The animal wasn't breathing, wasn't moving, wasn't alive.

This time the heat in his chest was a furnace. It had to be Stefan Rudovic. Somehow he'd beaten Harry here. How, he had no idea, though if that chump were still around he'd have blasted Harry to kingdom come by now. That's how Cana stooges operated. In the shadows, skulking around, afraid of a real fight. Stefan was here and gone. What had he taken with him?

He skirted the bear's corpse and pulled a flashlight from his pack. The powerful beam pushed away the darkness to reveal an interior large enough to drive a bus through. Rough walls on either side, going up to a rounded ceiling. Nothing suggested this was anything more than a bear's den. The cave bent slightly as he walked further in, the air much cooler on his skin. He turned a corner and paused. One large bear was dead behind him. That didn't mean there wasn't another back here.

Leaning around the corner, he noted two things. First, detritus suggesting the bear had bedded down against the rear wall, the safest place in the cave. Rocks had fallen from the cave wall in front of Harry and some lay strewn across the bear's bed. He shone his flashlight beam up to the spot they'd fallen from, then down to the rocks themselves. They appeared to have been in place for a long time, and then recently pulled down. His light played over the wall, and what he saw brought a sense of déjà vu. He'd seen this before. *The photos of the Aci Los statue.*

The fallen rocks in front of him had been pulled down from a man-made wall inside the cave. Tightly packed, secured with some sort of mortar, the stones had been cut to blend in with the cave wall so you could hardly see the wall unless you were right on top of it. Someone, and he had a pretty good idea who, had cut a hole in the cave wall, then resealed it so well that Harry might have missed it if half the stones hadn't been knocked down. A sputtering torch, back in the days of the Spartans, would have created nothing but shadows, effectively hiding the secret opening.

Harry looked around. A familiar carving was directly across from the opening, engraved on the opposite wall. A Spartan helmet, looking directly at the hidden opening.

What was inside? Picking his way through the fallen stones so as not to disturb them, he stepped through the opening. It was barely wide enough for two people. Judging from stray marks on the wall, Stefan Rudovic had used some sort of metal tool, and he'd done it not long ago. Harry stepped through the opening and into a lost world.

It was a hidden shrine. A place to worship Ares. A place of secrets, where only the chosen few would come. How did he know? The place was hardly big enough for a half-dozen people to stand in. The antechamber was natural, not man-made, the back wall scarcely ten paces from the opening. An empty pedestal stood against that wall, and behind it an inscription was carved into the wall. Not Greek letters. Latin. Harry's mouth was dry. He could read every word.

As below is above. Fallen King Leonidas and his three hundred saved Sparta. The prize of Greeks did not perish with him. Though peace reigns, it is through strength it will stay. Here we honor the memory of Leonidas, his heroism seen by the wounds on his helmet below.

War threatens us. To secure Greece's future, our prize traveled to Macedon to aid Greeks once again.

The final lines were written well below the first, the letters different from those above them. As though it had been carved into the wall much later.

Harry pulled out his cell phone and took a video of the interior of the temple, then several stills of the inscription. Only once that was done did he let his mind run. *Leonidas*. This antechamber honored the Spartan leader and his warriors, whose heroism had in no small way saved Western civilization. Goosebumps rose on his arms. He was standing in a memorial to one of the crucibles in which the fate of the world had been decided over two thousand years ago.

The beam from his flashlight fell on the pedestal. The empty pedestal, a chest-high carved square stone balanced atop two circular columns. He walked to it and leaned over the top stone. Centuries of dust had accumulated on most of it, though a circle in the middle remained clean. Something had sat here. A Spartan helmet, perhaps, once worn by a great king. A helmet that Stefan Rudovic had stolen.

The glow of his watch cast a soft green light on the ground. He glanced at the time and his nerves tightened. Twilight was approaching, bringing with it his last chance to descend the mountain without killing himself. This cave was big enough for more than one bear. If he got stuck on it after dark, he'd be nothing but a waiting meal for whichever large beast found him first.

He checked the antechamber one final time but found nothing else. How long had that helmet, and he was sure it had been a helmet, waited here? Harry turned and carefully made his way back to the exit, stopping to touch the dead bear as he passed. Still warm. He'd missed Stefan by half a day at most.

He descended the fallen staircase fast as he dared, looped his rope around the tree and slid to the stones below. Down he went, following the trail at speed. An hour passed, then two, the shadows around him growing longer by the minute. The sun setting behind Mount Ares brought a growing gloom as the mountain's shadow stretched further across ancient Sparta. As the air cooled and the darkness thickened, Harry tried and failed to focus on putting one foot in front of the other. His mind whirled with thoughts of the inscription on the antechamber's wall.

All signs indicated he had missed the helmet of Leonidas. The inscription told of how Leonidas and his men had saved Greece, then warned of a new threat to the Greek people. A threat to be dealt with in Macedonia.

The trees whizzed past as he hurtled down the mountain, blurry in the growing dark, their shade now uncomfortably cold as he ran. However, that cool air had nothing to do with the gooseflesh on his arms. *Macedonia*. An ancient Greek kingdom, a land of military and cultural might. Macedonians had shaped Western civilization for hundreds of years before Jesus was born. Among their many scholars and warriors, one stood above all. If any Greek leader had made proper use of the *prize* that had protected Greece through the ages, it was he.

Harry stumbled on a rock and regained his balance with difficulty, arms flailing. Breaking his neck running down the mountain was akin to serving the bears dinner on a platter. Get to the bottom first. Then unravel the mystery.

Harry raced out from the tree line with less than thirty minutes to go before the sun fully set. His car was still there. No one else was in sight. Hands on his knees, he gulped rich, filling air until his heartrate settled, then jumped into the car and raced back to town. Only after the door to his hotel room locked behind him did Harry pull out his phone. He peeked through the curtains, simultaneously wondering if the thin oxygen levels had made him loopy. If Stefan Rudovic wanted to kill Harry, he'd have waited for him on the mountain. So why was Harry peering up and down the street looking for the Cana man? If Stefan meant to ambush him it would have happened by now. This wasn't a trap, it was a race, one Harry had to win.

He dialed Rose Leroux's number. One thing he could always count on was Stefan's greed. The Albanian was in this for the profit, the power money bought. Stefan couldn't care less about the history behind it all. And that, Harry suspected, was a weakness he could exploit.

Rose answered and beat him to the punch. "I assume you have unpleasant news."

"Why do you say that?" Harry asked.

"My business provides information as well as money. I just discovered Stefan Rudovic has an artifact he wishes to move."

Of course. Before Harry could ask the question on his tongue, a nagging thought took hold, one he'd never quite voiced but which had circled the back of his mind for several days. He'd been running the Morello antiquities business, as it was, for over a year. Why had Rose only started warning him about Stefan now? It couldn't be the first time their paths had crossed to put Harry in peril. This was merely the first time Rose had warned him.

"One he found in Greece?"

"In a cave. I assume you've been there?"

"Yes. Earlier today. It appears Stefan had a close call with the wildlife."

"It is unfortunate for the bear. However, casualties are a hazard of your profession. What else did you see?"

Enough with her leading this discussion. "Tell me about the helmet."

She took a long second. "It is bronze, designed in the Thracian or Spartan style. Based on the condition, craftsmanship and provenance, I believe it is authentic."

"Is it damaged?"

"The previous owner would not have survived his wounds."

Leonidas. History told them he hadn't. "Do you really think it was worn at Thermopylae?"

"The owner's name was inscribed in Latin on the interior," Rose said. "I believe it belonged to King Leonidas. I already have a buyer."

Business never stopped. "What else can you tell me?"

"First I must know what you found."

Fair enough. "An empty antechamber. One that had been hidden for a very long time." He summarized following the Spartan helmet carvings up Mount Ares to the cave. "The antechamber resembled a memorial for King Leonidas."

"And on the wall?"

He recounted the inscription. "It's clear the path continues," Harry said. "Likely to Macedonia. But I can't be sure without the helmet. I could easily be missing a reference that changes everything."

"Which would send you in the wrong direction, while Stefan closes in on Evgeny Smolov's prize." Rose paused. There was the sound of a lighter flaring and tobacco crackling. She spoke after a long exhale. "Nothing inside the helmet contradicts the inscription. The cave is a memorial honoring King Leonidas. It also serves as a marker on the path the Koraki constructed."

"There's only one Macedonian the Koraki could possibly mean. The timing of Leonidas's death and his reign lines up with what the Koraki were doing."

More tobacco burned. Harry could picture the smoke swirling around Rose as she spoke. "Stefan made the same connection. Of all the men in history to find, there are none more successful. Hurry, but with caution. Men who dominated the globe do not reveal their secrets easily. Certainly not this Macedonian."

Chapter 10

Luxor, Egypt

The desert sky came alive at night. Sara stood on her hotel balcony overlooking the Nile. The floodlights illuminating the Luxor Temple faded quickly as they rose to the heavens and splashed over the endless desert surrounding it all. Over three thousand years ago people first put down roots on the banks of this lush river and built a town that grew to be the symbol of an empire. Unlike so much of Egyptian glory, Luxor was not a monument to the dead. Its temples were dedicated to the immortal power of pharaohs and kings, the unbroken lines that passed from king to king to make them gods among men, unquestioned leaders on earth. Countless pharaohs had come to the great Luxor Temple where crowning ceremonies took place. All around it lay a city of power that transcended the ages.

The evening air warmed Sara's face. The same winds her ancestors felt. She'd come to Egypt many times, for professional digs and personal travel, yet it never failed to move her. This was where she came from. Now, if she succeeded, it might also determine where she went next.

She left the balcony doors open as she walked back into her hotel room, taking a seat behind the small desk. Harry Fox's inherited amulet had brought her here. It had also done much more. The circular gold piece caused the chance meeting which intertwined their lives in a way she couldn't have fathomed one short year ago. Sara Hamed was drawn to the past; it was why she became an Egyptologist. Now the man who had caught her off guard and tempted her with the discovery of a lifetime had brought her back here to the land of her ancestors. Perhaps, if her adventure in Luxor went as planned, he would once again draw her back to America.

Sara shook her head. A year ago she'd never have believed it possible. Moving to America? Never. But that was before Harry, though, before she was drawn into a world where the past came alive, far differently than it ever had in a classroom. Harry's work with Nora Doyle's team was dedicated to making sure the bad guys didn't always win, and even though he crossed a few lines—more than a few, in fact—Harry stayed on the right side. Now Sara could help them and put her training to the best possible use. Would she cross an ocean to America for the chance to do it every day? More and more, she thought yes.

Their work mattered. The situation between Harry and her could wait. He wasn't pushing it, and she appreciated that. Enjoy the ride, she told herself. Figure out what it all meant later. Right now she had a statue to climb.

"First step, don't get arrested." Sara pulled up the surveillance photographs she'd taken earlier that day and shook her head. What Egyptologist took surveillance photographs? It wasn't like the mummies chased her. The first snapshot was of the remaining obelisk in front of the Luxor Temple. The obelisk the Ottomans hadn't given to the French. An old joke popped into her head, one not meant as humor. *Why are there pyramids in Egypt? They were too heavy for the British to steal and put in a museum.*

Thankfully this obelisk remained. Without it, she couldn't unravel the reason a message had been hidden inside Mark Antony's crown. To do that she had to somehow get to the top of a statue across from the obelisk and determine which of the thousands of inscriptions Antony and Cleopatra had left as part of this trail. Sara moved to the next picture. Dual statues of Ramses II, one on each side of the temple entrance. Both statues stood nearly forty feet tall, with nary a stair or handhold to be found.

She pulled up another shot, one with both the obelisk and statues in frame. One attribute stood out. There were people everywhere. Tourists, guards and state employees were all around the landmarks. Climbing the statue unnoticed would be impossible during the day. And forget being on top of Ramses long enough to figure out Antony and Cleopatra's message. She'd be spotted in seconds.

Outside, the sun had dropped almost entirely below the horizon. Night's curtain was falling, bringing cooler temperatures and calling to tourists and locals alike. Time to go home, to eat with families or enjoy Luxor's nightlife, which included experiencing the Luxor Temple under the stars. Strategically placed lighting turned the temple into an enchanting wonderland in the cool air with engaging guides, all of it open until late in the evening. A challenge, yes, but she knew the question to ask. What would Harry do?

He'd improvise. Play the hand he was dealt. For an academic like Sara, improvisation required research. Grabbing a cardigan and her handbag, she set off for the temple. She made a thorough canvassing of the grounds, with an eye toward identifying how best to subvert the Luxor's defenses. Her first break appeared in the form of near-disaster. A temple security guard. Sara had been standing near the base of the temple studying the powerful floodlights that illuminated it at night. A floodlight that also shined on the Ramses statue she needed to summit.

"Good evening," the guard had said.

Sara hadn't noticed him coming. She started as she turned and looked at the mustached man.

"Forgive me." The guard raised his hands and stood back. "I did not mean to startle you."

A quote from Harry's father spoke to her. *The best lies begin in truth.*

"I did not see you," Sara said. "Is anything wrong?"

"No," he said. "I only wanted to ask if you require assistance."

She tilted her head. "Assistance?"

The guard pointed to the light fixture that had transfixed her. "Most visitors are more interested in the temple than the lights. I thought perhaps you had a question." His smile beneath the salt-and-pepper mustache was genuine.

"Oh, the lights." Sara offered a shy grin. "They are quite interesting. I am an Egyptologist based in Germany." Very true. "I'm here for research." Mostly true. "These lights are so well-placed. I wanted to get a better idea of how they work, so we might use similar ones in a display at my university." Not in the same universe as true.

"You are a scholar?" The guard touched his hat. "I am happy to assist. What would you like to know?"

How I can avoid these massive lights and steal the ancient secret you don't know exists? The time for truth had passed. But how to get the answers?

Inspiration struck again. "Are the lights operated manually?"

The guard, whose nametag identified him as Mohamed, said they were not. Upon further questioning he described how they were controlled from a central location and each was individually powered. Mohamed helpfully pointed out the short stretch of protected wire protruding from the floodlight's rear. Wire that disappeared into the ground below.

"You must have quite a large team to keep this running."

"Actually, we have only two engineers on duty each shift." Mohamed talked about budget cuts and the parsimonious oversight committee who held the purse strings so tightly. Sara sent a quiet thanks to the penny-pinchers. Their frugality was her chance.

"I see a lot of guards on site," she said. "It must be expensive."

"The force is halved during night shift. No one wants to pay overtime, and there is much seniority, so everyone chooses day shift." He shrugged. "Myself included. I am too old to stay up late."

Half the guards, two engineers to run the whole temple, and nightfall.

"You are so helpful." Sara stuck her hand out. "I am in your debt."

She bid him good night and then wandered into the temple while

Mohamed continued his lethargic rounds. Once he was out of sight, Sara moved with purpose, snapping photos, finding sight lines, observing the other guards. A plan came together. She moved on from the temple so as not to draw the guards' interest. Instead, she took a stroll down the Avenue of Sphinxes, a massive and ancient road lined with stone sphinxes. Sara passed an occasional eye over the glyphs on each mythical creature, half-heartedly noting a few incredibly odd ones.

At last she made her way back to her hotel room. The entire time, her thoughts never strayed far from the plan taking shape. One that held up as she studied the photos on her laptop one more time. It could work. With help from a friend. Lucky for her she had two.

One was Nora Doyle. The other, Joey Morello. For what she had in mind there was only one correct choice. She dialed.

"Sara, are you okay?"

"I'm fine, Joey." She pulled at a strand of her hair. "Any word from Harry?"

"None yet," Joey said. "He only landed in Greece this morning. It could take a day or two for him to make progress."

"Right."

"You having any luck?"

"In fact, I am. I need your help."

"Anything."

She rattled off several items she needed. Joey didn't hesitate. "Let me make a call. I'll text you a photo of my man and the meeting details."

"How long do you think it will be?"

"For you? I'll have them tonight."

"Thanks, Joey." A thought hit her, cold and hard. "Joey, is it safe? For me to meet your associate, that is."

Joey's response was instant. "I'd never put you in danger," he said. "You're with Harry. Which means you're family. You can trust this man with your life."

That calmed her for a reason she didn't want to fully acknowledge.

Harry had never told her this outright, but Nora had. Joey Morello was connected. In every sense. He kept his promises.

"That means a lot," she said. "Harry's doing a good thing in Greece. This is my way to help him."

"Figure out the truth behind his father's amulet and he'll never let you go," Joey said. "Keep your phone nearby. I'll be in touch."

After they hung up, Sara dressed in black athletic pants and shirt, generic enough that no one would give her a second glance. Even if they did, her Egyptian heritage made it hard to pick her out. Exactly as she wanted. She tried to eat and found her appetite had vanished. Sixty minutes after she'd hung up with Joey, her phone pinged with a message from him. An address in Luxor. Sara was to be there in a half hour. A photo followed, along with the name of her contact. Omar.

She tied her shoes, grabbed her room key off the desk and headed out. One hand wandered to her back pocket as the door clicked shut behind her. The can of pepper spray was still there. Not much if things got sticky, but she'd promised Harry it would stay with her no matter what. Trained in kickboxing and self-defense, Sara needed only a step to get ahead of trouble. Shooting liquid fire into an assailant's eyes could buy her that step.

The revolving hotel door had scarcely spun behind her when Sara's phone vibrated. Her chest lifted when she saw who it was. "Harry?"

"Hey."

"You sound out of breath."

"I ran down a mountain."

She stopped under a blazing streetlight. "What mountain?"

"Mount Ares. Listen to this."

The world around her faded to nothing as Harry detailed his ascent, guided by the Spartan helmet carvings, his discovery of the bear carcass in a cave atop the mountain, and the hidden antechamber inside.

"Was it hidden the same way as the Turkish cave was?" she asked when he'd finished.

"Yes. It was way in the back with a stone wall hiding the entrance.

The bear was just bonus security. Unfortunately for it, Stefan brought a gun."

"You're certain it was Stefan Rudovic?"

"I'm sure."

"What was inside the antechamber?"

"An empty pedestal. There was something round on the pedestal for a long time. Stefan took it. And there was Latin writing on the wall." He read her the words from the inscription.

Her arms and legs tingled at what she heard. *King Leonidas and his three hundred. The wounds on his helmet.* "The helmet of Sparta's greatest leader. You nearly had it."

"Here's the most important part. The last line said *'our prize traveled to Macedon to aid Greece.'* I have an idea what that means."

Sara grabbed the lamppost for support. "Leonidas died in 480 B.C. The context of the message makes it clear the war had ended and the Greeks won. It could easily have been written a century later when he lived."

"You thinking about the same Macedonian I am?"

His name seemed to float on the air. "Alexander the Great. History's most acclaimed military commander." She pinched the bridge of her nose. "The circumstances and timeline fit. He was king of Macedonia, part of ancient Greece. He lived a century after Leonidas died at Thermopylae. Alexander spent his entire adult life at war. He never lost. If anyone had earned the Korakis' prize, it was him."

"I'm on it," Harry said. "If there's anything out there about the Koraki and Alexander, I'll find it. You wouldn't happen to know of any ties between them, would you?"

"Unfortunately, no." The burbling engine of a passing motorcycle jerked her to attention. "Harry, I'm sorry. I have to run. I'll call you."

He sounded almost excited for her. "Stay safe. If anything seems dangerous, don't do it. We can go back there together later."

She bit off a sharp retort. "We'll talk soon," she said. Sara slipped the phone into her pocket and kept moving. She'd nearly snapped at him that she didn't need him to protect her, thank you very much.

To her right side, Luxor Temple burned with the fire of gods. Sara turned away from it, down a street filled with restaurants and strolling tourists. The address Joey had given her was a law firm on prime corner real estate, well-lit and utterly empty. She stood under the awning and checked a street sign above. This was the right place. Where was Omar?

Her phone vibrated. She didn't recognize the number. "Hello?"

A man's voice. He spoke Arabic. "Is that you in the black clothes?"

Sara spun around. "Where are you?" she asked in the same language.

"Look across the street."

She turned and saw nothing but a darkened storefront. A grocery of some kind. "I don't see you."

"And now?"

Lights came on in the grocers, then flicked off and back on.

"Are you doing that?" she asked.

The lights blinked again in response. "Use the side door," Omar said. The line went dead.

Sara's gut told her this was a bad idea. She ignored it and crossed the street. A door opened on squeaking hinges to let a sliver of light spill out. All she could see was an arm holding it open, an arm covered by a dark sleeve. She walked to the light.

"Sara?"

Even though she'd been expecting it, the voice made her jump. It came from inside the building, the same voice she'd just heard on the phone. A head immediately followed it and peered around the door's edge. The first thing she noted was a dark, bushy beard. The second was that this man appeared to have no neck. It was lost in the bulk of his chest. "Are you Sara Hamed?"

"I am."

"I am Omar." He stepped out and beckoned her inside. "Hurry. We are supposed to be closed."

She walked into a storage room. Wooden boxes were stacked to chest height to form tight passageways. Sara followed Omar through the fire hazard to a metal door that stretched from floor to ceiling. A rush of frigid air washed over Sara when Omar opened it. He gestured for her to enter.

A single bulb burned in the ceiling. Omar closed the door behind them and pushed past her, nearly toppling a crate of eggs in the process. He bent down in front of stacked vegetable crates—mostly lettuce—and grunted as he slid them to one side. Another door was concealed behind the crates. Omar pushed it open and walked through. She put one hand on the pepper spray in her back pocket and followed him into the darkness.

She stepped into nothing. No light, no sound, no cold air. The only sound was her heart beating. The pepper spray came out of her pocket as a metal jangling sound filled the air. Sara tensed, her finger on the trigger.

Light blinded her. She covered her eyes with one hand, raising the spray with her other. Several long moments passed as she blinked rapidly, the room slowly coming into focus.

Omar stood in front of her, wide shoulders even more massive up close. His hand was on a lamp. The metal jangling had been the chain he pulled to turn it on. He looked down at the pepper spray in her hand. He looked up at her. "Your materials are in here."

They were in a much smaller room, the walls made of plywood and the floor of concrete. The walk-in cooler thrummed behind them. Sara had a feeling this room wasn't on any blueprints. She realized Omar was again looking at the pepper spray. "Forgive me," she said. The pepper spray disappeared into her pocket. "Nerves."

"You are a friend of Mr. Morello. You are safe with me." Omar pointed to the room's only furniture, a single metal table with two chairs pushed into it. Several items were on top of it. "Mr. Morello requested these items." He pointed to each in turn. "Climbing rope and gloves. Night-vision goggles. Infrared flashlight. Wire cutters. And a night-vision monocular for me."

Germany, where she lived now, was home to mountains that

challenged climbers of all skills. Sara had taken classes on how to climb, and though she was far from an expert, she could work her way up a moderately challenging cliff with little difficulty. "This is wonderful." She asked Omar to turn off the lights, then she slipped the night-vision goggles on. The darkened room came to life in shades of green, and when she flicked on the infrared flashlight the green world suddenly had a spotlight roaming it, bathing whatever it touched in a light nearly as bright as day, albeit in green, and crystal clear. She could use this to highlight specific locations on the obelisk and actually read them. No other light needed.

"How far does this flashlight reach?" Sara asked.

"Three hundred meters."

More than enough to reach from the Ramses statue to the obelisk. She took the goggles off and asked Omar to flip the light on again. "Do you have a bag?" she asked. He produced a simple black backpack into which everything slid neatly. She slipped it over her shoulders, cinched the straps, then jumped up and down. It stayed in place. "How much do I owe you?"

Omar raised a hand. "You are a friend of Mr. Morello. It is no charge."

"We won't forget this." Sara pointed at the rear door, the one they hadn't walked through. "Where does that go?"

"To my home. My wife and baby are asleep. Would you use the other door?"

The question came out of her mouth before she could think. "How old is your baby?"

All the muscles in Omar's shoulders relaxed. His thick beard parted to reveal a wide grin. "He is nearly one. A big baby, so strong and smart. He drinks milk like a lion."

"What's his name?"

"Azizi."

"*Precious*. A beautiful name."

"Yes, his name means precious." Omar put a hand on his heart. "He is the most precious thing in the world."

This burly man was central to her plans, the outlines of which Joey had shared with him. Minutes ago she'd nearly pepper sprayed him. Now she found herself questioning whether he should join her at all. "Omar, are you certain you're willing to help me? You don't have to."

"I will help you." He looked around the cooler. "If not me, who else will?"

He had her there. "Only if you're certain. Joey won't mind if you choose not to."

Omar put a hand on her shoulder. It was surprisingly gentle. "Mr. Morello's father was a great friend to my family. I owe him much." That quick grin flashed. "And why would I worry? It is easy to act like a crazy man."

"Thanks, Omar." She reached in and hugged him. His beard was like coarse fur on her cheek. Sara's arms didn't nearly encircle the man, and he didn't move, seemingly stuck in place. "Now," she took a step back. "What's the quickest route to the temple?"

"Follow me." Omar led her back through the storeroom and out to the street, where she fell into step beside him as they took several side streets Sara wouldn't have taken on her own. The few people walking there shied away from the burly Omar, which she found a bit amusing now that she knew his nature. A few more turns, and the majesty of Luxor Temple spread out before them. They passed gently waving palm trees and traversed the Avenue of Sphinxes until the temple stood directly in front of them. Floodlights illuminated stone walls nearly a hundred feet high. The surrounding temple grounds were open and somewhat empty. At least not as crowded as Sara imagined they'd be.

Omar leaned in close so only Sara could hear him. "Which one will you climb?"

"The one on the left. It faces the obelisk."

"Where do you want me to be?"

She pointed to the far side, well-lit and well away from her intended target. "Do you have your monocular?"

Omar lifted the device from inside his shirt. "It is ready."

"The statue is thirty-six feet high. I should be able to climb it in three minutes at most. Count to thirty when it gets dark and then start your show. And Omar." She touched his arm, pulling him closer. "Make sure everyone's looking at you."

His eyes were like tiny planets in the night. "I will not let you down."

"I know you won't." She took one last look at the path in front of her. "You go first. I'll follow."

Omar turned and moved with purpose down the avenue. Sara let him get a head start as she put on her climbing gloves and then followed. Most of the tourists were inside on guided tours, enjoying the dramatic lights and environment of the ancient temple at night. The faint voices of tour guides filtered out of the temple as she walked. Two visitors nearly ran headlong into her. Sara juked to one side and they jumped. "Excuse us," one said in English.

Sara responded in Arabic and kept walking. Her dark ensemble was working.

She passed the final pair of sphinxes and walked onto an expanse of dark sand that stretched to a row of floodlights set back twenty-one steps from the Ramses statue. She knew this because she'd counted them this morning. Looking left and right, she counted six security guards patrolling the front grounds and four times as many tourists. Sara pulled the wire cutters from her backpack and headed for the spotlight illuminating Ramses II, the pharaoh Antony and Cleopatra directed her to climb. Her entire body tingled. Slipping the night-vision goggles over her head and the infrared flashlight into a back pocket, she bent down and opened the cutters. A look across the row of floodlights found Omar in place. *Go time.*

Her blades cut through the wire with ease. Darkness fell across Ramses and the temple wall behind him, the night seeming to swallow everything in a flash. Sara jammed the cutters into her pack and took off at a run, her feet silent on the sand. Ten running steps brought her to the base of Ramses. She circled around back, grabbed hold of a convenient decorative outcropping and began climbing.

The first voices called out. No shouting yet, more questioning, but that could change at any second. Hand over hand, moving only when her feet were secure, Sara raced up the pharaoh's rear end in record time. She'd mapped out the climb beforehand, taken photos of each grip and rehearsed it in her head a hundred times. Halfway up she found the rock smoother than anticipated and her hand slipped. One foot hung in the air, leaving her dangling nearly twenty feet above the ground. A fall from this height on sand was nothing. Land on the sharp corner of Ramses' base and she was dead.

Sara nearly ripped her shoulder out of its socket as she hauled her entire weight up with one hand, scrabbling until she regained a grip. Shake it off, she told herself, and then kept climbing. Don't stop or the fear will catch up. On to the torso, then Ramses' broad back and shoulders. She could actually kneel on one shoulder, giving her a much-needed chance to catch her breath. Three deep gulps were all she allowed herself. Down below, several guards were now clustered around the damaged floodlight. One had a flashlight out to inspect it. No fuss yet.

Sara kept to the back side of Ramses' ceremonial headdress as she climbed onward, despite the front offering a much easier ascent. If by some miracle the guards fixed that floodlight while she was up here, this was over. Pulling herself up the last few feet of the headdress's wing-like sides, she stood and grabbed for the cylindrical cone at the very top. Her arm muscles screamed in protest at the final pullup that vaulted her to the top. Her chest heaved. Sweat trickled down her arms. She blinked through a drop falling down her face, then looked up. The obelisk stared back.

Raised voices calling in Arabic sounded in the night. The guard with a flashlight was gesturing, calling out that he'd found the problem. Sara pulled the goggles up from around her neck and put them on. Nothing. Precious seconds ticked away as she scrambled to power them on. Finally, they came to life, and she looked up to find the obelisk waiting for her, now bathed in an ethereal green glow. That's when the shouting started. Music to her ears.

"Help, please help me." A booming voice filled the air. "I cannot find my child."

Sara watched as the guards kneeling around the broken floodlight abandoned their efforts and made haste to the bearded man now shouting to the heavens. As agreed, Omar was putting on a show to get everyone's attention and keep it long enough for Sara to do her thing on the statue. She'd asked for one minute. He'd promised at least three.

"My child went this way." Omar hadn't told her his plan, so she was thrilled when he waited for all the guards to get close to him, only to run in the opposite direction from Sara's illicit climb. Ever the helpful crew, all of them followed. She pulled out her infrared light and brought the obelisk to life.

Hieroglyphs came into brilliant perspective under the light, as though she had a magnifying glass over them. She was supposed to look straight across, though at this distance it was impossible to tell which glyphs were at eye level. Sara made a guess, went two rows higher, and started reading.

The first row was an entreaty to Osiris. *Bring life to the grounds.* A plea for good harvests, one she'd seen many times before. The next row down was a tribute to Ramses, recounting a long-ago battle he'd won. Another tribute followed, then another. Her stomach twisted, and not from the height. There weren't many other lines to choose from. One ridge in the obelisk had nothing on it, and she skipped to the next line below to find another testament to Ramses' greatness. None of it helped her.

Sara leaned closer, willing the obelisk to give up its secret. She leaned too far. Her foot slipped and she fell forward, gashing her chin on the top of Ramses' headpiece. Hot pain flared when she touched her chin and found it wet. Sara grabbed the statue, cursing when her bloody hand couldn't find a grip. She knelt lower to balance herself. The guards were huddled around Omar at the far end, but her time was about done. She looked up.

There's writing under the ridge.

Hieroglyphs she hadn't seen. An entire row, obscured from her vantage point only a few feet higher moments ago, now visible under the obelisk's midpoint ridge. She read the first glyph and stopped breathing. *That's impossible.* She read it twice more; the glyphs did not change.

The future of Ptolemy is destined by the gods. Look ahead to the Greek sphinx. Dispatch it with the fate of Oedipus's scarlet eye.

Cleopatra was a member of the Ptolemaic dynasty, the Macedonian Greek royal dynasty that had ruled for centuries in ancient Egypt. Cleopatra was the future, ordained by the gods. The obelisk was referencing her—which was impossible because the obelisk had been built over a thousand years before Cleopatra was born. Unless she had added this line herself.

Outraged shouting grabbed her attention. Omar, yelling at the top of his lungs in Arabic. "Sara, come to me. The dawn is here!"

The dawn? What was—oh no. She looked down at the broken floodlight. Two men were around it, men who weren't security guards. They had to be the mechanical team. She ripped the night-vision goggles off, started climbing down—and her foot slipped. Stone scraped her fingers raw as her tenuous grip came loose. The sky filled her vision, the statue rushing past as she tumbled through darkness. She curled up, covering her head lest it bash off Ramses' unforgiving base, and then, an unending beat later, Sara crashed to the ground. Her vision blurred and one ankle burned with searing pain. Men shouted. Strong hands grabbed hold of her as the floodlight burst to life and she was lifted off the ground, locked in an iron grip.

Chapter 11

That rarest of English fall sights covered the Strait of Dover with brilliant light. The sun beamed down from a cloudless sky, practically unheard of in this nation of drizzle and gloom. Pleasure craft dotted the strait; small boats bobbed near the shore with jet skis buzzing around them, sunbathers lay on the beach and families strolled on the boardwalk. Many of the people there that day admired the massive yacht floating further offshore. Over two hundred feet long, the vessel was one of the largest private crafts in Britain, though if authorities cared to check, it was registered in the Cayman Islands to a shell corporation, which in turn was owned by several subsequent shell corporations of murky origin. At the end of this opaque path, if an enterprising detective ever managed to follow it, was found the true owner, one Evgeny Smolov.

If any of the beachgoers had failed to notice the yacht, they certainly noticed the helicopter that buzzed loudly overhead and landed on the boat's helipad. They may have assumed the helicopter carried a wealthy owner out to his yacht. None would likely have guessed the helicopter was in fact ferrying the three senior-most leaders of the Salafi Front. The United States Department of State designated this group as a terrorist organization for numerous crimes against humanity.

As three men exited his helicopter, Evgeny Smolov waited in his private office aboard his yacht, seated behind a monstrosity of a desk and sipping a glass of Dom Perignon. It wasn't yet noon, though given how much money he was about to make, Evgeny felt it was time to celebrate.

"*Marhaba.*" Evgeny welcomed his guests in Arabic as they were shown in by two of his security men. Three bearded men, all wearing the clothes of common vacationers. Chinos, polo shirts, no socks with their loafers. If you looked closely, you could see how uncomfortable they were. These men spent most of their time in traditional Arabic garb, flowing *thawbs* with *keffiyehs* atop their heads.

"*Marhaban bik.*" The man who responded was the shortest, the oldest, and the only one wearing long sleeves. Evgeny knew he did this to hide horrific scarring on each arm, a souvenir from an American Hellfire missile years ago. This man moved toward a chair in front of Evgeny's desk.

An arm thick with muscle stopped him. The arm belonged to Evgeny's chief of security, Maksim Mostovoy, former Spetsnaz SSO operative and a man you truly did not want to cross. He had defected with Evgeny and served the exiled oligarch with unflinching loyalty. Why? Evgeny had brought Maksim's family over to England, and Evgeny paid him well. Even though Maksim was a man he'd lured in part with money, Evgeny trusted him, for no one could outbid Evgeny Smolov.

Evgeny's guards held the three terrorists in place as they subjected each to an additional, intrusive search. The visitors glared at Evgeny as they suffered this indignity. He shrugged. *What am I to do?* In truth, he'd ordered his guards to do this; it was a sure way to throw them off. Angry men were not shrewd men. Any advantage helped in negotiations, and Evgeny intended to fleece these bastards.

After confirming the men had no weapons Maksim let them pass. Three men with murder in their eyes took seats across from Evgeny. Maksim and his counterpart stood at ease by the door.

"Was that necessary?" the long-sleeved leader spat. Rafiq Pasha had fought his perceived enemies for decades, everywhere from sandy deserts to dense urban streets. He'd been in a Salafi Front safe house several years ago in Afghanistan when an unmanned drone sent a missile through the window and brought the house down on top of them. Rafiq survived. His two brothers did not. That's why he was on Evgeny's boat today. Rafiq sought vengeance against the West. Against the enemies of Allah. Unfortunately for him, that cost money.

Evgeny couldn't care less what he wanted. What mattered was that Rafiq's personal crusade against the West required money, so the Afghani had come up with a way to pay for it. Lucky for Evgeny, Rafiq hadn't been able to locate much cash.

"Are you here to complain or to do business?" Evgeny asked.

Rafiq glanced over one shoulder at the two towering security guards. "Business."

"Excellent." Evgeny poured himself more champagne. "Would you care for some?" he asked, holding the bottle out. "I have several cases on board."

"We are not thirsty." Rafiq angled his head to the ground. "Your men forced me to leave my bags on the helicopter."

"So they could also be searched," Evgeny said. "It's not just you I don't trust. It's everyone." He glanced up. "And here they are, as promised."

Two additional guards walked through the door. Each clutched an oversized duffel bag, one of the men clearly straining under the weight. They set them on a sprawling conference table and left the room.

Evgeny stood. "What have you brought?"

Rafiq trailed Evgeny to the table. "Jewels and gold in this bag." He pointed to the heavy one, which he opened to reveal metal containers amid bricks of solid gold. "One hundred pounds troy."

Numbers whizzed in Evgeny's head. "About two point three million dollars. And in the metal boxes?"

Rafiq displayed tea-stained teeth. "Diamonds."

Which could be worth anywhere from nothing to millions. "I will have my jeweler appraise them."

Rafiq knew not to warn Evgeny not to cheat him. In this business, reputation was everything, and Evgeny had never cheated anyone. "How long will it take?" Rafiq asked.

Evgeny shrugged. "A few days. I will contact you. What is in the second bag?"

Rafiq opened it and removed two paintings. Evgeny lifted an eyebrow. He recognized the two post-impressionist works, both stolen from a Dutch museum a year earlier. They were worth up to ten million if sold at auction. On the black market, where Evgeny would have to move them, he'd get a fraction of that.

"Impressive," he told Rafiq. "Though not easy to liquidate."

"I need the money now," Rafiq fired back. "My work must continue."

Suicide bombs at shopping centers. "If you are unhappy with my services, find someone else to handle your finances."

Rafiq glowered at him. There wasn't anyone else in the world who could handle Rafiq's money as effectively as Evgeny did. Even criminal financiers were turning their backs on terrorists now, and none who still did business with people like Rafiq had anywhere near the capital Evgeny possessed. He had Rafiq over a barrel.

"You will have the money in two weeks."

"I need it now."

Evgeny turned from the table, looking out a window at the brilliant sea that stretched to the horizon. He made a show of thought. "I can advance you two million today. No more."

Rafiq's beard trembled. "The gold alone is worth more than two million."

"Not after my fees."

If the terrorist could have strangled Evgeny right there, he would have. Rafiq made do with several curses muttered in Arabic.

"There is no reason to say such things," Evgeny told him. "This is business. Two million now. The rest in two weeks."

Evgeny stuck out a hand. "Agreed," Rafiq said before he shook, scowling all the while. Evgeny held his hand well beyond when social norms dictated he should let go. "What will you do with it?" he asked.

Rafiq blinked several times. "That is not your concern."

"No. And yes. I will hold up my end, but only if you tell me what you plan."

Rafiq ripped his hand away and took a step back. Evgeny stepped closer, keeping him off balance. "You are on my boat, Rafiq. You have no weapons. Now, tell me what the money is for."

Rafiq was a remorseless killer. But when Evgeny looked at him like this, unblinking, Rafiq stood down.

"My cause is just, yet it also requires money. I cannot arm my men with prayer alone. This money will resupply our army."

"You are not attacking children?"

Rafiq looked puzzled. "Why would I do that?"

"You practice Wahhabism," Evgeny said. The fundamentalist movement often attracted the more puritan devotees of Islam, men who not only looked down on Western culture, but occasionally sought to destroy it. "So do Boko Haram. They kidnap and kill children."

Rafiq sneered through his beard. "Those fools. We are nothing like them. Sharing a religion does not make us the same."

"So tell me. Will you harm any children?"

"Would it matter if I did?"

Evgeny grabbed hold of Rafiq's bicep. "Yes."

"You have no say in what I do with my money. And why do you care?"

Evgeny kept the pressure on Rafiq's arm. "I have handled finances for many different organizations. I have few rules which cannot be broken. Do not steal from me. Do not lie to me. Do not use my money to harm children."

Rafiq finally answered. "I am not attacking children." He nearly fell backwards when Evgeny let go of him.

"Excellent," Evgeny said. "Then we have a deal."

Rafiq rubbed his arm. "Why does this concern you?"

"Because I have seen what my money can do. I will not let children be involved."

Rafiq had no interest in arguing. "I will expect the money in two weeks."

"It will be in the usual accounts." Evgeny gestured to the door. "My guards will see you to the helicopter."

As the door closed Evgeny moved to his desk and reached for the phone. One of his German clients would purchase the paintings, no questions asked, at whatever price Evgeny quoted. Evgeny's hand rested on the phone, his gaze falling to a framed picture on his desk. The only picture on a desk large enough to do snow angels on. A picture of a small boy and girl, both no more than seven. A little boy who would go on to great things. A little girl whose life had ended far too soon.

Evgeny blinked, his eyes focused on the photo. He reached out to it as though he could bring her back. It was the only photo he had of his sister, a snapshot taken when they were both children playing on a snowy day in the streets outside their little apartment. The two of them on a sled, Evgeny in front, his sister Irina in back. Irina loved that sled, and Evgeny loved that she did. Those were the simple days before it had all changed.

One week later that sled had been painted red with his sister's blood. Irina had been riding the sled alone that day, racing down the streets blocked off by city officials. Streets that cars couldn't drive on. Unless the cars were driven by officials of the Communist party, the few who had cars more powerful than lawnmowers and the gasoline to run them. Officials who paid no heed to rules for common Russians. Rules like traffic laws.

It didn't matter that the streets were closed. It didn't matter that the driver was drunk. He was a government minister. When Irina's sled came flying down the street, the minister's car was traveling in excess of eighty kilometers per hour. He never saw Irina or her sled until Irina's brains covered his windshield.

Of course, the officials had covered it up. The police suggested none-too-subtly that Evgeny's parents should accept the settlement offer—enough money to make their lives comfortable, and a full scholarship for their surviving son. If they didn't accept? The police shrugged, saying nothing. They didn't have to. Evgeny's parents were nobodies. The drunk driver, exactly the opposite.

Evgeny looked around at his opulent surroundings. An ostentatious yacht. A private helicopter. One hundred pounds of gold, boxes of diamonds and two world-class paintings. All of it paid for with his sister's blood.

Evgeny shook his head. He couldn't change the past. The only solution, an imperfect one at best, was looking ahead. Which for him involved boarding his returning helicopter and flying back to London. Business never stopped in his world. A deep rumbling reached his chest as the helicopter buzzed into view, having deposited Rafiq Pasha and his men back on shore.

"Maksim," Evgeny called out.

His chief of security appeared within seconds. "Yes, boss?"

"See to these containers." Evgeny waved at the gold bars, diamonds and rolled paintings as though they were groceries. "We are going to London."

Maksim and one of his team hurried off with the plunder. Evgeny followed, reaching into his pocket when his phone vibrated. It was Altin Cana's treasure hunter, the man named Stefan. "What have you found?" Evgeny asked.

"Proof I am on the right path," Stefan said.

Evgeny listened as Stefan briefed him about a forgotten mountain in Greece that loomed over the ghost of a legendary city. Mount Ares had once looked over Sparta, and it still stood as sentry for the memories of that distant civilization, nothing more than a historical footnote. Until Stefan Rudovic sat down at the bar in Laconia closest to Mount Ares. Stefan had bought enough beer to loosen old tongues, and the stories poured forth. Legends mostly, yet hidden in the boasts of daring climbs and embellished recounts of ancient battles, he'd found actual gold. One man told of the carvings on Mount Ares, the Spartan battle helmets that tied back to Leonidas himself. No one had proof, of course, but this was the sort of dusty, forgotten legend where truth could hide for a thousand years.

Stefan found the helmets, and he started climbing. A cave was found. Thankfully for Stefan, he had a gun. "A bear lived in the cave," Stefan said. "He nearly killed me."

Evgeny ignored him. "What did you find?"

"A hidden chamber with writing on the wall and a treasure inside. A piece of armor that belonged to King Leonidas. One of his greaves." Stefan recited the inscription on the wall. "I believe I know where to go next." He named another city, one not far away. "I am going there now. Though I may not be the only one on this trail."

"Who else could know?"

"A man who works for the Morello family."

"Vincent Morello? The old man is dead."

"Yes," Stefan said. "He is. They employ a man who handles artifacts. A treasure hunter. I suspect if he is not close behind me, he soon will be."

"Then handle him," Evgeny said. "There always are winners and losers in this business. People get hurt. Where is the armor?"

Stefan hesitated. "I sent it to my fence. She has a buyer."

"Fine." Evgeny didn't care about a hunk of metal that Leonidas may or may not have worn. He had a bigger prize in mind. "Eliminate any obstacles in your way—including this Morello man if he interferes."

Chapter 12

Pella, Greece

Mark Antony and Cleopatra had understood that the best place to hide what you didn't want to be found might be in plain sight. Apparently, the Koraki faithful dedicated to protecting Greece knew this as well. A piece of knowledge or an item of incredible value need not be hidden in a mountaintop cave. It could be stored out in the open where anyone could find it. The secret lay in making sure no one realized what they were looking at when they saw it.

Harry was on the streets of Pella looking at a structure that had stood for thousands of years. Sunglasses protected his eyes from the bright morning light. After surviving the harrowing descent of Mount Ares he had returned to his hotel to get some much-needed rest. On a whim he'd played a hunch, a long shot that didn't make much sense— until it did. An idea that perhaps Alexander's gargantuan ego may have served a greater purpose than simply inspiring him to conquer most of the world. The belief in his own immortality led Alexander to leave his mark in countless cities and countries. Alexandra, eventual capital of Egypt and home to the famed lighthouse. Raqqa, now infamous as the capital of ISIS during the Syrian Civil War. More than twenty others across Africa, Central and South Asia. He also funded the construction of temples not only where he conquered, but where he came from.

Including his home town of Pella. The capital city in Macedonia, a kingdom ruled by his father, Philip II. One of those temples to Pella still stood in an enduring testament to Macedonian engineering. The

Temple of Alexander, a monument to his might and home to hundreds of relics and artifacts tied to its namesake.

One of these was a contemporaneous account detailing Alexander's military prowess. The collection of scrolls was notable only for the fact each of them allegedly included first-hand accounts of several battles, though some of the content was at odds with what history knew had occurred, so while the scrolls were a source of pride for the Temple staff, they were not a reliable resource for historians.

The scent of coffee pulled Harry off the sidewalk and into a café. He emerged minutes later with a cup of the black nectar in hand. Three hours of sleep was all he'd managed after uncovering what had to be the link between the cave on Mount Ares and where the Koraki had spirited the *prize* of Greece next. A link that was evident for anyone in the world to find, if only they knew what to look for.

Now Harry did. A delicious, unwanted feeling of satisfaction threatened to fill his chest as he ascended the steps into the Temple. No, not yet. He pushed it away. There was so much that could go wrong. Starting with his entire theory. It was based on a hunch, after all. Even though it looked to have panned out, he had no way of knowing, nobody to bounce it off to find the holes in his logic. Harry pulled his phone out and frowned. Sara must be busy in Luxor. She hadn't returned his calls since last night. Not even when he offered a cryptic hint about turning the page in his adventure to reveal a new Koraki mystery.

Towering white marble columns fronted the temple, gleaming in the morning light. Orange construction fencing was visible around back. Harry purchased a ticket and looked up as he entered, the soaring ceiling giving the impression that the heavens above were not hidden from view, but were one with the building. Soft blue paint was visible in a few locations, while the intricate carvings of Greek mythological creatures and deities told stories that transcended time. It was a monument worthy of the man who had conquered the world, a room that promised much more to come.

He passed a gift shop selling yellow baseball caps. Canary yellow, like the plumage of a colorful peacock. Who would buy one of those? He passed on the headwear. The day's first guided tour was getting underway in the main hall. Harry stopped to get his bearings and listened to the enthusiastic guide kick it off.

"Welcome to the Temple of Alexander." She first spoke in Greek, then repeated her message in English. "Built to honor Pella's most famous son, Alexander the Great. Today you will learn about the origins of this cultural titan, his unstoppable march across the globe, and also look behind the curtain to discover who Alexander truly was. We will then move outside to view several of the burial grounds across Pella. Over one thousand tombs have been uncovered in the last two decades, including one right behind our Temple, which is currently being excavated."

On another day Harry might have been tempted to join. Today, though, he had his own secrets to reveal. Oh, and he also had to stay away from Stefan Rudovic, who had outwitted him on Mount Ares and would surely still be on the trail. Harry tossed his empty coffee cup in a waste receptacle and walked deeper into the temple to a spot where even the longest beams of morning light failed to penetrate. The temple was grand, tall and wide, but it was not excessively long. His long drive through the night wasn't only to stay ahead of Stefan. Harry needed an early start to stay ahead of the crowds.

The temple's repository for written material was a domed room ahead which included a series of scrolls written by one of Alexander's scribes, a man forgotten to history but who could hold the key. Unusually, this scribe had given a name to his accounts. *The Ravens of Alexander.*

The odd title was a footnote to what it contained. Summaries of Alexander's battles over time. Harry had never heard of the scrolls before last night, but he knew the temple existed in Alexander's hometown and it seemed a good place to start. He'd nearly fallen out of his chair when he discovered what the scrolls were called. He had tried to connect with Sara last night, though she remained out of reach, as elusive as the sleep he needed after a day on Mount Ares. Now the scrolls were laid out in front of him, twenty in all, one for each of the major battles Alexander had fought. Every single one of which had ended in victory.

Soft lights washed over the ancient scrolls. Each had its own display case, the sheets rolled flat and protected under temperature-controlled glass. Translations were below each scroll's case. For some reason the scrolls had not been digitally rendered for sharing online so the only option to view them in their original form was to visit Pella. For Harry, a stroke of good fortune.

He leaned over the closest scroll. The title page was first. With no one else in the room, the stone walls were like an echo chamber in which he could hear himself breathing. He leaned over the scroll. One word in the title grabbed his eye. *Koraki.*

The sounds echoing around him faded as he read the summary notes below. This scroll was estimated to have been written at least a decade after the oldest scroll. In fact, it was most likely created after Alexander's death in 323 B.C., when he had no successor and his empire was in turmoil. A time when Greece threatened to tear itself apart at the seams. A time when the *prize* of Greece was no longer needed in battle, for the Greeks made war amongst themselves.

This had to be it. Didn't it? He checked his phone and found nothing from Sara. He bit his lip. Harry had been doing this long before Sara crossed his path. He'd learned from one of the best. What would Fred Fox say? *Everything you need is right here.* Then he'd tap little Harry on the head. Believe in yourself. That's what Fred had truly meant.

He didn't need Sara. Not right now, anyway. What he needed to do was keep moving. With the entire room to himself, Harry moved to the next scroll and started reading methodically, one tiny line of text after another. No mention of ravens in this first scroll. Same with the next. Seventeen more followed, each with nothing showing ties to the Koraki, no hints his guess was correct. No matter. He hadn't expected to find any mentions in these papers. The *prize* was meant to preserve Greece, to aid the embattled nation's most valiant leaders in troubled times.

Harry stood over the final scroll. The shortest by far, it detailed Alexander's plans for invading of Arabia. During this planning phase Alexander fell ill and died, likely from typhoid fever. This scroll summarized Alexander's rapid deterioration and death in succinct fashion. Nothing about his mysterious tomb—undiscovered to this day—or the political machinations of potential successors that had ensued were mentioned.

The final lines of the scroll made Harry's throat tighten. Incongruent, opaque, but only if you didn't understand the context. Perhaps for the first time since this scroll was written, someone did.

Alexander is at rest. The raven has taken wing, taking the prize to where Alexander first drew breath. The protection of Greece flew to the throne of Persephone, following the tunnels from which Achilles warned Odysseus of Hades domain. Fear not, brave Grecian, for the raven began and landed at the altar of Alexander's birth.

A raven. What scholars had believed to be an odd spirit animal for Alexander was in fact nothing of the sort. It was a beacon, a waypoint left by the society dedicated to protecting Greece above all else. It was where the *prize* of Greece had flown after Alexander's death. The question was, to where?

Harry did not linger over the last scroll. A scan of the room found one other person inside now, one he hadn't notice walk in: a gray-haired woman leaning on a walker. She wasn't a threat, which didn't excuse his lapse. It could be Stefan Rudovic who walked in. An armed Stefan, carrying a gun he didn't mind using.

Visitors had not flocked into the Temple of Alexander during his reading session. The museum was still nearly empty, a handful of tourists barely outnumbering the staff beneath the towering ceilings on which Greek gods ran riot. Harry barely glanced at it, his eyes roving across every face as he made his way toward the cathedral, scrutinizing each wandering visitor as well as the custodian making his rounds. His gut instinct was to call Sara again. She hadn't called him back. Luxor was keeping her busy, he knew, but he couldn't wait. Why the cathedral? That's where the Koraki seemed to point him. To the *altar of Alexander's birth*.

Harry walked out and turned a corner, boots slapping up the marble steps into the long room of worship, down the central aisle past row upon row of pews. These wooden seats were newer additions, several hundred years old at best. The altar in front of him, atop a dais where the priests held court—that was original. An altar where an infant Alexander the Great had been introduced to the world, and which had been standing since the Koraki left their cryptic clues in a scroll for all the world to see.

Several steps up brought him to the dais. A name was inscribed in Greek across the altar's front. *Alexander III*.

Harry knelt, running his fingers over the worn marble. All of it one piece, no cracks or crevices to suggest a hidden alcove or chamber. This thing was huge. He could lie down in front of the altar, arms stretched overhead, and no one behind it could see him. Harry checked each side and came up empty. The entire altar was one big block of solid stone. He touched the amulet tucked beneath his shirt for luck and moved around back, eyes toward the cathedral entrance, wary of pursuit. Nothing but a tourist passing in one of those hideous yellow hats.

His foot caught. Harry stumbled, trying to catch himself, but something grabbed his other foot and he tumbled to the floor. A soft landing, for the floor back here was carpeted. Harry got to his feet and looked down to find the floor behind the altar was raised, creating a short platform on which the priests stood. Harry had tripped on it.

He stepped back. Something about this was wrong. The floor wasn't really carpeted. There was a heavy rug on the platform, a rug he'd dislodged. He knelt and tugged hard on it, sliding the rug to one side and discovering the platform wasn't a solid stone block. There was a lock on one side of it. Hinges gleamed on the other.

It's a door.

Why would there be a door back here? Priests didn't need an escape route. He turned on his phone's flashlight and knelt closer to the door. It was white marble, but not the exact same color as the floor or altar. It looked newer. Why did the museum add this?

He needed an answer. Who better to ask than the person responsible for keeping this rug clean?

Harry retraced his steps toward the entrance. The custodian had been right around this corner, pushing a cart, one piled with long-handled tools. Harry turned another corner and spotted a cart in the hallway just ahead. An elderly man stood behind it, attempting to balance a yellow sign on the floor.

"Excuse me?" Harry stopped behind the man and addressed him in heavily accented Greek. "Sir?"

The custodian turned with the look of someone who has been asked where the restroom is many times, yet never tires of answering. "Yes?" He actually smiled when he said it.

"I have a question," Harry said. May as well go for it. "I found a rug out of place behind the altar." The lie rolled smoothly off his tongue. "There's some type of door beneath it. It's fascinating."

The custodian's smile vanished. "I must fix the rug."

The custodian didn't say a word until he'd wheeled into the cathedral and his cart was parked near the altar. The man hopped up the dais steps faster than Harry expected. He looked down at the rug. "Someone must have tripped." He fixed the rug and said something in Greek Harry didn't catch.

"What was that?" Harry asked.

The custodian answered in English. "I said I fixed it."

"Right." Harry plowed on. "I noticed the door is new. It's not original."

That made the custodian chuckle. "No, it is not. They did not have such locks in Alexander's time."

"Why is it there now?"

"To cover another door. When the temple was built, a hidden opening was made in the floor where the priests stood. We do not know why."

Harry forced himself to take a long, slow breath. "Interesting. Any idea what it leads to?"

"What is underneath all old buildings in Pella," he said. "The sewers. We Greeks were one of the first cultures to use underground sewers."

The Korakis' message suddenly made sense, and Harry's gut instinct was vindicated. Sewers were tunnels located below ground. The Koraki mentioned tunnels and more. The line *from which Achilles warned Odysseus of Hades domain* fit as well. That was a reference to Homer's *Odyssey*.

In the story, Odysseus had summoned Achilles' soul and questioned him about life in the underworld, a land ruled by Hades. The Koraki had been literal, masking their true direction in a snippet from Homer's famous work. *Underworld* meant the sewers. Tunnels that ran under the Temple of Alexander.

"Thank you," Harry said.

"The sewers are interesting," the custodian said. "They are no longer used, which is lucky for the departed."

"The departed?"

"Those whose tombs are in them." The custodian shrugged. "I would not want to be buried in the sewers, but many were. New tombs are still being found in them."

"Like the one found this month?" Harry asked. "Behind the temple?"

"Yes. That one is not yet explored. Who knows what it contains?" The custodian was truly excited. "It will take a long time until we know."

"Why is that?"

"The sewers are dangerous. They are not steady." He stuck a hand out, wobbling it back and forth. "They can easily collapse. Only after careful inspection can digging begin."

Harry thanked the man for his time and turned away. Sewers ran beneath the temple. Sewers with tombs which had been around Alexander's time. The raven had taken flight with the Greek *prize,* and the bird may just have landed somewhere in the sewer tunnels underneath this temple. The underground, ruled by King Hades and his wife *Persephone.*

"One last question." Harry spun around toward the custodian once more. "Have you ever seen the old door behind this altar?"

The custodian leaned on his cart. "Yes. I helped put the new cover on it ten years ago."

"Was anything on the door? Any carvings or writing?"

The custodian angled his head. "Why do you ask?"

Harry tried very hard to appear less curious. "I like the carvings here," he lied smoothly. "I thought maybe there was one I hadn't seen."

The custodian bought it. "Yes, there is a carving on the door. I remember because it is not one I expected to see." He started pushing his cart. "The Greeks who created it must have loved birds. They carved a raven on the door."

Harry nearly ran out of the cathedral. "Thank you," he called over a shoulder. A raven carving. That's what the Koraki wanted their *learned Greek* to find and follow. A raven guiding him into the underworld, a vast collection of sewers hidden beneath Pella's streets. A network containing still-undiscovered tombs. Harry needed a flashlight and a distraction. He was following the raven.

The town had woken up since Harry had arrived. Not Brooklyn by any means, but cars now buzzed down the street and the sidewalks were filling with pedestrians. Harry walked quickly to his car to grab a flashlight, a Zippo lighter and a small crowbar from the trunk. He stuffed the crowbar in his waistband and went into the coffee shop again, this time coming out with a dozen copies of the morning newspaper stuffed in a paper shopping bag. He walked back toward the temple, skirting the front entrance and making for the orange construction fencing he'd spotted behind the temple on his way in. Fencing that kept tourists from tumbling headlong into a recently unearthed archaeological site.

The cathedral stood near the temple's rear wall. A paved walkway led alongside the temple, ending at a rear door. Harry counted his steps beyond the door to get an idea of how far he needed to travel once underground to get back to the cathedral and the altar above. The starting point marked by a carved raven.

Beyond the temple was an empty field. Oversized treads and tires had recently churned the earth leading to the circular area roped off by the orange fencing. A single trailer stood to one side. Clearly construction to install a road or foundation of some sort had started recently, with the project screeching to a halt when the ancient tomb was uncovered. If Pella was riddled with the tombs and tunnels of two millennia, it would not have been much of a shock that another tomb had been uncovered; what was more surprising was that any construction projects were ever completed.

The construction site was nearly deserted. A lone security guard stood watch at the "gate"—really only a pair of posts in the ground where the fencing wasn't attached. He had a tent for shade, a chair and a radio. A chain stretched between the two posts. The sign hanging from it read *Kamía Katapátisi.* No Trespassing.

Harry veered away from the guard. It took him one-hundred-ninety-nine steps to get from the rear wall to the guard's location, then roughly another forty steps to the center of the fenced area. Two-hundred forty, give or take a few. The guard paid him little mind, more interested in the paperback novel on his lap. The opened ground eventually turned to grassy fields, the sort through which people would enjoy a stroll.

Harry wandered in the general direction of the trailer, looping far around it until the guard was out of sight before turning back and running in a straight line until he could kneel by the trailer, hidden from view. He set the paper shopping bag holding the newspapers by the trailer, weighing it down with several stones. His Zippo lighter came out. Several handfuls of dry grass went into the bag. Harry frowned, moved the bag a bit farther from the trailer, then grabbed another handful of grass and flicked the lighter to life. Flame touched the grass, Harry shoved it into the bag, and then he hurried back the way he'd come and ran into the fields.

The first hints of smoke rose from his doomed bag by the time Harry turned around to watch the guard. Newspaper was thin and covered with cheap, dark ink. When burned it produced black, thick smoke as the flames burst to life and then died out a beat later. The stack of newspapers would produce a column of dark smoke. The smoke would linger long enough to look serious, and an attentive guard might think the trailer was on fire. The shock of an actual threat would get him out of his chair to investigate, taking him well away from the site. More importantly, the trailer would block his view of Harry running into the restricted area.

That was Harry's plan. Set the fire, distract the guard, get down into the hole. Safe? Not a bit. What looked like a ladder poked up from the excavation site. If it wasn't a ladder, at least he had something to grab hold of on his way down.

Harry strolled as though he had all the time in the world. The guard was fifty feet ahead and still engrossed in his book. Harry glanced behind him and saw the first plumes of thick, black smoke climbing above the trailer. Within seconds it turned into a stream, then blossomed further. The guard still didn't notice.

Harry hit the gas. "Fire!" Arms waving, feet stomping, he ran straight toward the guard and shouted in broken Greek. "A fire in the building!"

The guard looked up. Harry pointed, the book went flying, and the guard zoomed past him, grabbing at the radio on his belt. He shouted at Harry as he ran. "Get out of here!"

Harry pretended to run, though if the guard had looked back he would have found Harry heading for the gap in the fence before he ducked beneath the chain and ran in. The hole wasn't as big up close. He skidded to a halt; the guard was nowhere to be seen as black smoke continued to pour into the sky. The inferno wouldn't last long. As he'd hoped, a ladder poked up above the ground between a crude wooden brace erected to keep earth from collapsing into the opening. He leaned over. The ladder disappeared into darkness.

Shouting came from near the trailer. The pillar of smoke had tapered off as the guard appeared from around the trailer, radio pressed to his ear as he scanned the grounds. His yells had attracted a visitor sporting one of those yellow hats, now racing toward the trailer at speed. The crowbar pressed against his back as Harry jumped onto the ladder, rungs whizzing by his nose as he slid into the emptiness.

Chapter 13

Pella, Greece

The ground rushed up to meet him.

With a jaw-cracking *whack* Harry hit the dirt before he knew it was there, tumbling and getting a face-full of ladder for his trouble. Damn, that hurt. He felt around, resisting the urge to use his flashlight. If the guard had seen movement around the hole or suspected Harry was up to something, he'd come back, and the light down here would give Harry away. No, he had to get clear of the opening, which meant skirting the ladder, getting out of sight and running into the darkness.

The ground beneath him was stone, with lots of rounded bumps like a cobblestone street. The temple lay ahead, as did the altar, beneath which he expected to find the starting point on this journey through Hades' domain. By squinting against the dark he found the shadows ahead less dense than those to either side of him. Looking back, he found the same. Harry was in a tunnel. The sewers under Pella.

Forward it was. Moving by feel rather than sight, he counted off fifty steps straight ahead before stopping. The way ahead was impossible to discern. If the guard wanted to get to Harry now he'd have to slide down the ladder himself.

Satisfied he wouldn't be seen, Harry flicked on the light. He was in a stone tunnel, with smooth stones underfoot. Rocks had been carved into roughly square shapes and mortared in place to hold the ceiling up, rounded walls forming a tunnel for rain or waste water to drain through. Ahead he found more of the same. Another hundred-ninety paces should take him to the altar. Where the Korakis' path began.

He moved quickly, checking occasionally over his shoulder for any sign of pursuit. There were no side tunnels, no smudges of light overhead to suggest other exits. Fifty steps to go. Thirty steps. He could almost feel the countless tons of dirt and stone pressing down from above like a physical weight on his chest; he was in an impenetrable darkness where time stood still.

One final step and he was there. Harry looked up.

Nothing. One step after another, he moved on. *There.* Five steps beyond he spotted a square outline in the ceiling. Barely visible, even when he stood directly below it. A thin outline the exact size of the trap door he'd stumbled over. There was nothing else. No words, no images, nothing but an outline. Harry looked down.

A carved raven was nearly underfoot, its wings outstretched in flight.

A circular stone had been set here, bigger than any others and clearly meant to serve as a canvas for the carving. Intricately detailed, the bird was in mid-flight, its wings out and beak aimed ahead. Harry looked up. The bird was a message. Another beacon. The ravens of Alexander had taken flight and led him to this tunnel. He was meant to follow them further. Toward the *prize* of the Greeks.

A distant echo sounded behind him. Harry covered his light and ducked down, twisting to peer into the darkness but seeing nothing. No light, no sound, only darkness. Were his ears playing tricks on him? He counted to one hundred. Still nothing. The darkness was getting to him and he'd been down here ten minutes.

Silence returned as he got back on his feet and moved farther down the tunnel. The cylindrical sewer line was incredible. Thousands of years ago it had been hacked out of the ground with precision, the stone blocks still fitting snugly together in most places. A few had fallen underfoot, so between checking everywhere around him for another raven guidepost and dodging the occasional tripping hazard, he made slow progress as the sewer tunneled on. Eyes down, light circling around, he didn't realize what lay ahead until he nearly ran into it.

A cave-in. He stood in front of a small mountain of dirt and stone. The ceiling had partially collapsed, bringing down an entire side wall with it to block the tunnel. *No.* How could he get around this? He had no idea where he was standing in relation to ground level. He could be under a building, a hillside. Even the police station. Harry closed his eyes. What would his father do? He'd remind Harry there was never just one way. There was only the way Harry would make it happen. However he did it.

Okay, no problem. Count your steps back to the raven seal. Sewers run in straight lines. Count your steps, get topside, then start again at the altar and walk in a straight line. He'd worry about where it led later. Turning, he caught his foot and stumbled. The flashlight slipped loose, light bouncing everywhere. His chest caught for an instant but the light didn't break. Bending to scoop it up, his eyes turned to the cave-in. He stopped. *What's that?*

Rocks in one upper corner gleamed under the beam as though they were soaked with water. Which was impossible, because the sewer floor was dry. A massive amount of water would have to pour through here to reach the ceiling, which was a good ten feet from the floor. Any flow large enough to reach the ceiling would also be strong enough to push this cave-in out of the way. That hadn't happened. He stood still for a moment. He looked up. *Unless the water hadn't come down this pipe.*

Fallen stones rolled and twisted underfoot as he scrambled up the fallen pile of dirt and rock. The glistening rocks were at the top, in the far corner. He dug his feet in for balance, then reached out and touched where the rocks were shining. His fingers came back wet. He'd been right. This water wasn't coming from inside the tunnel; it had come from the ceiling, groundwater seeping down from above. Or perhaps they were under a house and a burst pipe had leaked through. It didn't matter. What did was that the rocks in this spot had been loosened by the water flow. This area wasn't as hard-packed as the others. He grabbed a rock from the top. It came free without trouble. He grabbed another, tossed it behind him. Then another.

Five minutes later he'd opened a hole large enough to poke his head through. Burying thoughts of the unstable ground overhead deciding now was a good time to collapse, he pushed his head and a shoulder through, aiming the light forward to find the tunnel stretching ahead, wide open once he got past this cave-in. Several massive stones had fallen from the wall here, big chunks still mortared together like concrete traffic barriers. He pulled stones and threw them until he could fit through. One arm first, then the other, he crawled through until his feet slid past and he was on the other side of the pile of rubble. The sewer stretched ahead, wide open.

Without warning, the rocks below him gave way. Harry careened down the slide, trying to roll and failing miserably until he crashed into one of the massive chunks at the bottom. It was not a soft landing. *Nice work, genius.* Break an ankle down here and he'd be lucky to get out alive.

The stone had fallen into a corner and he was partially underneath it. He twisted and pulled his way out, brushing himself off and loosing a few muttered curses at the world in general and his own clumsiness specifically before setting off down the tunnel. No more collapses were visible ahead. He was still counting steps should he have to turn back if one appeared.

Ninety-four steps later, he found another raven. This one had also been carved into the floor on a large, flat stone, identical to the first in all ways save one. This raven wasn't flying ahead. It was turned to look at the wall to his right.

He aimed his light at the wall. Dusty carved stones turned a dull black under it, the grit of centuries coming off when he rubbed a hand over the bottom row, checking each as far as he could reach on either side before moving up a row. Solid mortar bound the stones together. One stone looked to have been chipped at with a tool; he pulled and twisted with his crowbar to no avail. The stone must have naturally fallen apart. Another row, and another. He didn't skip any, afraid that whatever had been left as a marker may have faded to nothing.

His breaths came faster as he checked the upper rows. Sweaty palms left smears on the stones. Harry stood on his toes, reaching up with the flashlight in his mouth to help aim, rubbing each stone in turn. Nerves twisted his stomach. Had the Korakis' marker faded, or was he flat-out wrong?

Wait. Pain streaked up his fingers. A square stone above head height ripped into his skin as he rubbed it. He leaned back. The light nearly fell to the floor. A single word had been carved into the stone. *Koraki.*

Raven. The calling card was here. This raven was looking at its own name. What did it mean? He had a pretty good idea. The flashlight went down, propped on the ground. Both hands gripped the crowbar. Harry heaved, lunging at the wall with a grunt. Mortar flew, sparks flashed and the stone below where he'd aimed shattered. He snapped a quick photo of the inscribed rock as evidence before smashing another stone, then another. Each crumbled bit by bit under his assault. The stale air stung his lungs. Broken rocks crunched underfoot. His crowbar hummed against the wall, smashing over and over until dust coated his tongue and sweat beaded on his forehead, while his ears rang with the cacophony of destruction in this underground tomb.

Harry leaned back, gave one great swing and that did it. He broke through. The crowbar slid halfway into the wall and he stumbled forward, getting a face-full of sharp rock before yanking the bar back to bring a dinner-plate-sized chunk of wall down. The pain of it bouncing off his foot barely registered. There was an opening in the wall. A hole of utter blackness. He grabbed the flashlight, pulled himself up by grabbing onto the hole and promptly ripped another stone off. The next one held as he lifted himself nearly off the ground to get a better look. He aimed the light inside.

Metal flashed. A spark of muted light, off what he couldn't tell, but it was like he'd stuck his finger in a socket. He propped his light against a rock and redoubled his efforts. The crowbar nearly glowed red from his savage assault on the wall, all the pent-up nerves and doubts released in a barrage of strikes that brought stones down at a dizzying pace. The hole expanded, fine grit filling the air until one last blow brought down half the wall and left an opening big enough to climb through.

Panting, sweating, seeming to float on a cloud, Harry grabbed his light off the ground, clutched the crowbar tight, and stepped through. The square room pressed tightly in on him. No more than ten feet wide or deep, the second thing he noticed was how the walls were composed of different materials. Actual bricks, unlike the hewn stones of the sewer. This room hadn't been carved out as part of the sewer system. It had been cut to *join* the sewer from this side. Interesting, but it could wait.

A pedestal grabbed his eye first. It stood in the room's center, a simple stone column reaching waist-high. No carvings enhanced its beauty; there were no inscriptions cut into the stone. None was needed, for the object sitting atop it captivated all Harry's attention. A sword.

Harry slipped the crowbar into his waistband and circled the weapon without touching it. This was a *xiphos*, the double-edged sword used by ancient Greeks such as Alexander, meant to be wielded with one hand in close-quarters combat. The iron blade was two feet long. Scarcely any rust tinged the surface. This was an impossibly preserved specimen, thanks to it being stored in cool, dry air instead of buried underground. An ivory handle with gold inlay and rubies proclaimed this sword had not belonged to a common soldier. It was the sword of a general, a sword meant to inspire men as the owner wielded it from his horse, signaling to massed armies before battle. The sword of a general who had never tasted defeat.

Sara's voice intruded on his thoughts. *Document, document, document.* Harry knew she was right. He took a series of snapshots of the sword, both up close and from a few steps back to capture all angles. Only then did he reach out and touch it. He drew in a sharp breath. *Those are words.* What he had first taken for decorative scrollwork on the blade was in fact lettering. Ancient Greek words ran across the blade from point to hand guard. A message.

Our prize flies to the Athenian Temple of Alexander.

Deciphering that would have to wait. There could be more on the other side, so he grasped the smooth handle, sent out a silent prayer to any gods in the area to keep the sword intact and lifted. The weapon was surprisingly light, but more importantly, it held. Far from being fragile, the well-balanced sword flipped with ease in his grasp, the rubies sending flashes of light across the walls as he turned it to find more writing on the other side. He couldn't read any of it in this light.

A rock crashed down behind him. Harry spun, sword raised for battle. He found no enemy but his own nerves and a stone that rolled to a stop inside the chamber. It had fallen loose, a remnant of his digging. *Easy, Harry.* He turned and had just set the sword back on the pedestal when the back wall caught his eye. There was a hole in it. A hole in the back wall of a room made from bricks, not stone like the sewer. A hole that meant he'd been right and this room had been cut to meet the sewer, not to come *out from* the sewer. He stepped around the pedestal. This room wasn't the end. It could be the beginning.

Several bricks had come loose from the wall and fallen away from the hole. The bricks lay by his feet as he stood and ran a hand across the wall. This wasn't like the sewer wall in any way. The stones were precisely cut and tightly mortared, yet the construction wasn't nearly as solid. When he pressed his hand on the wall he could feel fissures in the mortar where it had crumbled. This was meant to hide the room he stood in from the other side, he realized, more of an illusion than a barrier. Something waited on the other side, a room or another passage, perhaps a relic. Only one way to find out. He stuck his flashlight in the hole, hoping to peer through and get an idea of what waited. All the light in the room where he stood vanished.

Or should have. He blinked in the gloom. Not absolute dark, but a murky gloom. His flashlight was in the small hole. He looked down. Why was there weak light by his feet?

He spun around. A new light flashed from the sewer and then another flashlight beam aimed at his face, painfully bright, as a voice broke the silence.

"Stay back." A man, speaking English.

"*Baja eso*," Harry responded in Spanish, telling the man to put his light down. "*No puedo ver.*" I can't see.

"Speak English," the man said. "I know who you are."

The blood in his veins went cold. That meant only one thing. The man shining a light in his face was the person Harry needed to stay one step ahead of. The man who had stolen his relic from an ancient Spartan cave. A man whose boss had probably killed Vincent Morello.

"Rudovic." Harry turned slightly, hiding his right arm. "You followed me here."

"I knew where to go." Stefan Rudovic stepped nimbly through the hole Harry had created. "You are lucky to find this room."

Harry's blood grew hot now. "Not lucky. Good. Better than you."

"No matter. I have the prize. You do not."

Harry took a step toward the sword.

"Stop moving." An unmistakable sound filled the room. The hammer cocking on a revolver. Stefan stepped closer and pulled his light back enough to reveal a revolver in one hand, the barrel aimed at Harry's chest.

Harry shuffled forward a step. "You planning on shooting me?"

"Maybe." Stefan's aim didn't waver. "I would not be upset."

"Real sporting of you. I'm unarmed."

"I do not care."

Harry managed to get hold of the crowbar without Stefan noticing. He gripped it hard, the bar behind his back. "Your boss doesn't want war with the Morellos. My guys know I'm here, and they know you've been following me. It won't take much for them to connect us if I go missing."

"The Morellos are now weak."

Harry got a half-step closer. The pedestal was between them. "Men with power don't pick fights. They're strong enough to avoid them.

Altin has been starting trouble with us. He's nervous about the Morello family."

Stefan sneered. "No one is nervous about Vincent. He is dead. He was careless. He let the wrong people get close."

The way he said it made Harry stop. Stefan looked pleased with himself. Too pleased. "What's that supposed to mean?"

"Vincent and Joey were not paying attention that night." Stefan shrugged. "Too bad for them."

"How do you know they weren't paying attention that night?" Harry asked. Nothing. "Did you have something to do with it?"

Stefan waited a long time. "Be careful, Harry Fox. You have no idea what happened."

Harry's mind whirled. Stefan didn't deny it. In fact, he seemed pleased with himself, like he was in on a joke Harry didn't know had been told. Stefan knew something. Something big. And if Harry got too close to the truth, odds were that gun would go off and Harry would be on the wrong end of it.

Time to throw gas on this fire. "You know who killed Vincent," Harry said. "So do I."

It was like a physical blow. Stefan took a half-step back, stepped on a rock and went off balance. Harry threw the hidden crowbar at Stefan's face and aimed his flashlight at Stefan's eyes as he dropped to one knee. Stefan fired. The gunshot thundered, Stefan grunted, then the soles of Stefan's feet were airborne as he fell on his backside. Harry launched himself at the fallen man. He still held his flashlight, the beam going outside the entrance hole to glint off a hunk of metal outside. The revolver. Stefan had dropped it. That's the last thing Harry saw before Stefan's foot lashed out and hit him square in the chest.

Harry was suspended in the air for an instant, the boot in his chest taking his breath away before another kick sent him spinning backward. The pedestal raked fire across his back when he crashed into it, the world jarred loose and his vision slipped sideways for a beat. He blinked. Stefan did some kind of ninja flip and got himself back on his feet faster than Harry could draw breath. The Albanian had Harry's crowbar in hand and murder in his eyes.

Harry twisted around the pedestal and stood. The metal bar whistled in the stale air as Stefan swung and missed, metal banging on stone and knocking something into Harry's arms. The sword. Harry didn't think as he grabbed the handle and held it up.

Stefan kept coming. Both men held flashlights in one hand as the Albanian lunged at Harry over the pedestal and tried to decapitate him with the crowbar. Harry parried the blow with the sword by pure luck. He'd never held a sword in his life. Now he went on the attack with one to save it. A cutting blow missed, and the follow-up slash was blocked by the pedestal in front of him. Damned thing. He would have taken a chunk out of Stefan's arm otherwise. Harry stepped back out of range as Stefan aimed his flashlight at Harry's eyes, the light painfully intense.

Stefan dodged the pedestal and pressed his advantage. Blow after blow came, the metal bar a cudgel banging again and again on Harry's sword, forcing him to circle the room as he retreated. Harry dodged a vicious swipe at his legs and Stefan stumbled, letting Harry get around him and level a cutting slash at Stefan's calves. The iron blade bit hard.

It hit the Albanian's legs and bounced off. The blade hadn't been sharpened in two thousand years. Any edge was long gone. Stefan's teeth flashed as he brought the crowbar around like a sledgehammer. Harry lifted the sword in desperation. Steel slammed against iron with a clang like a giant bell in the tiny room. Harry went down on one knee. His sword had held. Teeth gritted, he pushed back, holding Stefan at bay as the Albanian swung the crowbar again and tried to smash Harry to the ground. The sword blade nearly pressed against Harry's face as he struggled. In that moment, Stefan's light came up and Harry could make out an inscription on this side of the blade. Two words flashed in front of him. *Koraki Panoplia.*

Harry got a foothold and pushed back. He muscled Stefan back enough to get up, then twisted his sword so the crowbar slipped out of

Stefan's grasp and Stefan backed off.

It was a feint. Stefan lunged at Harry, swinging the crowbar like a baseball bat at Harry's shoulder, with enough force to crack bone and snap tendon. Harry lifted the sword to parry. Iron and steel collided again and, with a loud crack, the ancient iron finally gave in. Harry's sword stopped the blow and then snapped in half, leaving him with only a jeweled handle and no blade. Stefan shouted in triumph. Harry punched him in the nose.

The blow sent Stefan reeling. Back he went, into the pedestal off which he rebounded toward Harry just in time for a hook to the body and a right cross to the jaw. Stefan spun, his light went flying, and he twisted around to trip and fall back, arms windmilling until he staggered over the lip of the hole Harry had broken through and fell back into the sewer tunnel. The tunnel where his revolver had fallen.

Harry was trapped. A solid wall behind him, an armed Albanian in front. Instinctively, he turned and looked behind him, then squinted and looked closer. The wall wasn't quite solid. No, it was more of an illusion, meant to hide what was on the other side. Time to find out what that was. Harry backed up, lowered a shoulder, and charged, closing his eyes as the wall rushed up to meet him.

Brick and mortar exploded. Harry crashed into darkness, flashlight in one hand and a bejeweled sword handle in the other. His light revealed a stone floor as old as the sewers. Rock walls had been carved out of the stony ground; the ceiling was barely above his head when he stood. Shouts in a rough tongue sounded behind him. Stefan, yelling in his native language. Ignoring him, Harry looked ahead to find a rectangular outline in the stone. No, not stone. The wall ahead was brick, with what used to be a door in it. A door that was only partially bricked over. Partially because half the bricks had collapsed, revealing more bricks behind them. He darted over and pounded the second layer of bricks. Nothing. *I'm trapped.* Stefan would find his gun, come through the door and it would be over. All this for nothing, racing across the world only to be shot in an ancient sewer with a useless sword handle as the last thing he'd ever find.

He punched the wall and shouted in frustration. A brick fell out.

Harry grabbed the brick, hurled it through the opening behind him, then lowered his shoulder once more and charged. *This damn wall better give.*

Another explosion, this time in Harry's head. He could almost feel his brain rattle as he smashed into an unforgiving wall. It held, but just barely. Astonished, he saw that he'd actually caved it in, put a depression in a brick wall. He shook his head and pushed against it now, feet digging for purchase as he shoved against a seemingly immovable object—until it started to give. An inch at first, then two more, until, without warning, the wall stopped resisting and he fell through.

Harry landed on his hands and knees. Looking up, he saw that the walls were lined with wooden shelves. He dug his flashlight out of the debris and looked around. *These shelves have bones on them.*

Dozens of skeletons surrounded him, ancient bones bleached white under his flashlight. He was in a crypt. He turned to find a Harry-sized hole in the wall behind him, bones and wooden planks piled all around where he sat. A skull lay beside his hand, while another one next to it looked up at him with vacant eyes, grinning toothily. He'd burst through a clearly forgotten entrance into a tomb with dozens of bodies. He was surrounded now by what was left of them after hundreds of years underground. The room was reasonably orderly, suggesting someone had been down here and tidied up. Which meant there might be people above. People meant safety. Even Stefan Rudovic wouldn't shoot him with witnesses around.

Bones rattled and rolled as Harry got to his feet, dusted himself off and then plunged ahead to where another door waited, all wooden slats, though the handle was metal. He shoved the sword handle under an arm, grabbed the doorhandle and pulled. Faint light came from yet another door ahead. He ran through a second room decorated with the bones of more people long dead, more skeletons piled on shelves lining the walls. This door was also unlocked, and after passing through yet another room of bones he found stairs. Shouting came from deep in the crypt behind him.

Up the stairs he went. At the top he found a modern wooden door. It was unlocked. Harry opened it and rushed through. Two monks stood in the room he entered. A half-finished, empty coffin lay on the table between them with tools around it. The monks stared at him with open mouths.

Harry lifted a hand, the one with the sword handle. The jewels glinted blood-red.

"Hello," he said.

Chapter 14

Pella, Greece

Stefan emerged from the recently uncovered dig site looking like a zombie escaping the grave. Dust caked his face, dirt covered his clothes and the congealed blood trailing down his nose was nearly black. Two barely rusted pieces of iron were clutched in his hand. Another piece of shining steel was tucked under his shirt, fully reloaded. The dig security guard pointedly looked the other way as Stefan walked past him.

Stefan stopped beside the guard. "Did you see a man come out of here?" The guard had not. Stefan reached into his back pocket. "Here."

A bundle of euro notes landed in the guard's lap. "The other five thousand," Stefan said as the money disappeared. "Did you ever see me?"

"No."

"Good." Stefan took a step closer. "Do not change your story or I will find you."

The guard, who had just slipped half his annual earnings into a pocket, didn't even look at Stefan as he walked away. There were no security cameras here. No way for anyone to know Stefan had gone into that hole in the ground and come out with a broken sword. The guard was a smart man. He wouldn't bother Stefan.

Not that Stefan cared. He had what he came for. A sword, albeit in two pieces, broken when Harry Fox had barely avoided getting brained by a crowbar, but a sword that had had Harry's full attention when

162

Stefan found him, and it had ancient Greek writing on it. This sword must tell him where to find the treasure Evgeny Smolov wanted so badly. Why else would Harry have gone after it?

No one followed him through Pella. A few gave him strange looks or a wide berth, or both, on the sidewalk. He thought about looking for Harry Fox, even had an idea of which building the man could be in— there were only a few churches near the dig site—but dealing with Harry Fox could wait. Stefan was closer to fulfilling Altin Cana's mission, to putting the Morello family in their place. Finding Evgeny's treasure came first.

Stefan locked his hotel room door and sat at the desk. He put his revolver within reach, then laid the two halves of the broken sword in front of him. A towel wiped across his face came back smeared with grime. He didn't get up, didn't take a shower, didn't do anything but study the sword pieces. Writing ran along both sides of each piece. He couldn't read it, so he took a picture and sent it off to a linguistics expert he knew at a university in New York. A man who had no idea Stefan Rudovic was part of the mob. All he knew was Stefan paid in cash, and he paid well. An answer returned less than five minutes after Stefan sent the message.

Stefan read it twice, writing the translation down on a sheet of hotel stationery. Then he read it again.

Our prize flies to the Athenian Temple of Alexander.

That sentence came from one side. The other side of the blade had an even less helpful line.

Seek the raven armor.

Stefan had zero idea what that meant. Another five minutes passed while he researched. He sent a follow-up question to the linguist, who connected with one of his fellow faculty to provide an answer. A short back-and-forth later and a possible solution presented itself. Possible, not certain, though in this sort of search certainty was rare. Stefan ran a hand through the stubble on his chin. Evgeny Smolov wasn't paying for excuses. It wasn't far. Five hours if he drove fast, and if he was wrong at least he'd still be in the same country. He picked up his phone and texted the linguist, who said he would work round the clock if Stefan gave him a full day to investigate. The professor didn't need to know why he was searching for meaning in an ancient riddle that scarcely made sense. He only needed to find that meaning. And given Harry Fox no longer had the sword, Stefan could wait one more day for the right answer.

His phone buzzed. Stefan's muscles tightened. He cleared his throat and answered. "Yes, boss?"

"Did you find it?"

He'd learned long ago to bite his tongue. "No, but I am making progress."

"Progress does not finish the Morellos."

"I found a sword. Harry Fox was after it." Stefan recapped finding Harry Fox at the temple in Pella. He skipped the part about having little idea what to look for inside the temple. That didn't matter, because he'd let Harry find the prize for him. Stefan related how he had waited outside with a view of the entrance until Harry showed up. Stefan had donned a horrid yellow tourist hat to blend in and followed him to the cathedral. After that it was simple: watch Harry distract the archaeological site guard by setting a small fire, bribe and threaten that same guard for access, follow Harry inside, and then steal what Harry found.

Altin grunted when the tale ended. Stefan could picture him chewing on a cigar. "You missed a chance to kill him," Altin said. "No witnesses in a sewer."

"It was not worth the risk. I will have other chances."

"When will you find this piece for the Russian?"

Again Stefan bit his tongue. The Greek artifact Evgeny wanted had been hidden for two thousand years. No one even knew for certain it existed. How should he know? "As soon as possible," Stefan said.

"The Morellos look weak." A pause. "But not weak enough. I have Al Zurilli's ear. He will not support Joey Morello yet."

Traditionally, the families voted on their next *capo di tutti capa*, the "boss of all bosses." The vote had to be unanimous, or there was no new boss. Zurilli was one of the family leaders, and he had a vote. If Zurilli didn't support Joey, then he would never be the boss. That was good, but not good enough, because Al Zurilli wasn't guaranteed to support Altin Cana, and Altin wanted to be the boss.

"What about Gio Sabella?" Stefan asked. "I do not think he will support Joey either."

"He is a bastard. Gio wants Joey to give him a reason to support him. Gio and Vincent Morello were too close. It will take more than the five million I paid Al Zurilli to change his mind."

"A more permanent solution."

"It is possible," Altin said. "Making Harry Fox look like a fool will help. If you get a shot, take it. He is a Morello at heart. The world needs less of them."

Stefan said he would and hung up. Sunlight falling through a slit in the window curtains hit his revolver, making the dull metal come alive for an instant. He got up and closed the curtains, then sat back down. The revolver drew his attention once more. It was an old gun, reliable but limited to six shots. The thing was heavy as a brick. Nothing like the tactical sidearms he carried in Brooklyn, though given he'd had to purchase this from a friend of a friend on short notice, it would do. Perhaps it was fate. Altin Cana had never given him explicit instructions to take out Harry Fox until today. In fact, he had never been directly told to take out any Morello, though Altin had made it clear he wouldn't mind if Vincent Morello met an untimely demise. Stefan took advantage of the chance to clear Altin's path to the top, and his ambition would be rewarded. A gamble, yes, but power was never given. It was taken.

Assertiveness had got him here. There was no reason to stop now. He picked up the phone and called an old friend. Or at least someone who had once been his friend. A question had been circling in his head since he'd spotted Harry Fox. Was Harry really that good that he'd been able to discover that this convoluted path ran through Pella? Or did he have help? Stefan wasn't sure.

Rose Leroux always answered her phone. "Hello, Stefan."

"Have you sold my Greek armor?"

"Several buyers have expressed interest. Multiple bidders increase the selling price. Have patience, Stefan. It is a virtue."

So is loyalty. "Good. I have another piece for you to move. Similar to the armor." He detailed the sword, mentioning the writing but not that he'd had it translated. "The same buyers might want this too."

"I will let them know." A lighter scraped and the sound of tobacco catching fire crackled over the phone. "Your trip to Greece is proving productive."

"It is."

Silence. "Are you finished collecting?" Rose eventually asked.

"Not yet."

"I see. Should I expect more items to sell? Larger packages of related artifacts often bring greater returns."

Perhaps she truly was interested in maximizing profit. Or she could be asking for another reason, one not in his interests. Rose was a businesswoman interested in profit. Additional relics to sell would pique her interest—and perhaps loosen her tongue. "I hope so. More Greek artifacts. I am not sure what they will be. My next stop is Athens."

"Athens is filled with ancient treasures," Rose said. "Though the authorities are everywhere. Obtaining items is not a challenge."

"I know where to look. They do not."

"Impressive. I assume your new sword helped?" He said it did. "Be cautious. You cannot spend your money in a Greek jail."

He waited. She didn't ask where he was going. *Maybe I'm wrong.* A part of him hoped so, wanted Rose to be the neutral fence he'd once believed she was. A woman ready to help him when he needed it, a woman he could trust. He knew that was before he had used that trust against her and made Rose the unwitting alibi he needed in the plan that killed Vincent Morello.

"The sword suggests there is another prize waiting in the Temple of Alexander in Athens," he said, breaking the silence.

"Alexander was fond of leaving monuments to his own greatness in every notable city. Another relic tied to him will be quite valuable."

"I do not know if this next relic is tied to him." He didn't say *if it even exists*. Two in a row had proven real. This third would be as well. It had to be.

"When are you going?"

"I will be there tonight."

"Good luck."

That's all she said. Rose didn't press, didn't ask for specifics. She had enough to send Harry on his way if that was her intent, but if so, she wasn't overplaying her hand. Exactly how he would expect her to handle it. If she really was helping Harry Fox. Perhaps she wasn't.

Stefan frowned. *Assume the worst of everyone.* That's what Altin did. That's what he would do too. "I have a question for you," he said. "You met my mother when you were smuggling people into America. She brought me to America and had to pay off her debt, but she was killed."

Rose hesitated a long time. "Yes," she finally said.

"I came here with my mother." He was too little to remember it. "What happened between when we arrived and when she died in the shootout? Did you ever talk to her?"

"Yes. She was forced to smuggle drugs, as I had been."

"When did you meet her?"

"You do not want to hear about this."

A strange feeling took hold in his chest. He actually wanted to know, needed to. For the first time in his life the chance to learn more was actually at hand. "Yes, I do. Tell me."

She laughed, though there was nothing humorous in it. "As you wish. I met your mother for the first time in Albania." The crackling of burning tobacco preceded a long exhale. "The same time I first met you."

"Why were you in Albania?"

"To smuggle you and your mother into America."

Stefan actually stood up. "*You* brought us there?"

"I had no choice. I was being held captive by the gang, not unlike your mother. I even had to purchase diapers on the black market for you. The most expensive ones in history. We came across the Canadian border in the back of a truck after putting ashore with a fisherman on our payroll. The gang established New York as your mother's base of operations due to the existing Albanian population. She was able to assimilate with little trouble. As did you."

Stefan had no recollection of it. "Then you left us in the city."

"Not quite. Your mother was a survivor." Another long pull on the cigarette. "And one who faced the same path as me. For a number of reasons, I chose to help her."

The ghost of anger materialized in his chest. "How? She died in a gun battle. Your help did not save her."

"No, but I saved you. That was my promise to her. Your mother knew her life had little value to her captors. You, however, were an anomaly. The gang did not know what to do with a baby, one whose mother earned them significant profits."

"And those profits would stop if I was harmed."

"You were her leverage as well as theirs. So you were protected. To a point. That is where I stepped in. My promise to your mother was that I would protect you if anything happened to her."

Memories of his time being fostered by an elderly pair of Albanian immigrants came flooding back. "How did you protect me? I lived with friends of my mothers from the old country until they died. Then I was on my own."

"Who do you think provided the money for you to live with them?" Rose asked. "Did you ever want for anything?"

He had not. "After they died I was on my own. Until I met Altin."

"You were never on your own. The next family who cared for you received the same payments. I also made them aware of what would happen should you be mistreated in any way."

Another Albanian couple, kindly people he'd spent most of his teen years ignoring or running away from. In truth, they were better than he deserved. Stefan's voice was uncommonly soft when he responded. "Why did you never tell me?"

"So you could grow into your own man." Bitterness tinged her words. "Whatever that came to be."

Altin Cana had taught him many things. One of the most important was to always look ahead. The past was for cowards, no matter how painful it was to turn the page. "I chose my path," he said. "Thank you for your help."

"I did it for your mother," she said.

Whatever had taken hold of him at her revelation passed. Rose had failed his mother. Watching over him was not enough to make up for it. "Nothing will change what happened. I have to look forward. To a future where Altin Cana is the king of New York."

"Everyone makes choices. Each brings a consequence." Another pull on her cigarette. "Not all can be foreseen."

With luck, one consequence of this dive into his family history would be Harry Fox's death in Athens—if it turned out Rose was channeling information to Harry, and that information brought Harry to Athens, where Stefan would be waiting. If she wasn't and Harry didn't show, Stefan would deal with him later. "Notify your buyers of a new item for sale. I will send pictures."

Rose said she would. "If you can find it in yourself, consider what I said. Every decision has a consequence. Your mother would tell you to be cautious, Stefan. Everything she sacrificed was for you."

His stomach tightened for a breath. "My mother would want me to survive. I am doing a fine job so far."

"You involved me in your schemes without my permission. I can never forgive that, but I promised your mother I would try to help you in any way I can. Heed my advice."

"I would not be where I am if I did. My future will be what I make it. No one else."

He clicked off and looked out his window. Pella didn't stretch into the distance so much as fade to nothing outside the city limits. A small city, once great, now forgotten. A city that had once stood atop the ancient world, now an afterthought, nothing but dust and memories. His future would be much the same if he didn't take this chance. Stefan had paved the way for Altin Cana to control the city, securing his own opportunity to join Altin along the way, an opportunity he could solidify. All he had to do was beat Harry Fox. If Harry didn't survive this race, so be it.

He sent off pictures of the sword to Rose, packed his bags, and walked out to his car. Rose Leroux had the bait. Now he needed Harry Fox to take it. Stefan would be waiting if he did.

Chapter 15

Luxor

Sara floated on air, suspended in a darkness so absolute she couldn't see her hands or feet. She heard nothing at all and had no feeling as she lay with arms out and legs together. It was like floating in the depths of the ocean, far below the surface, no light or noise to disturb her, all weight gone and no power to move. She gritted her teeth, blinked against the dark, and then the world came rushing back.

Light assaulted her eyes as they cracked open. She tried to raise a hand against it but found her arms wouldn't move. A shadow filled her vision. A shadow in the form of a person.

"Do not move."

A man's voice, harsh and close. She struggled, twisting to gain her freedom, pushing against whatever bound her arms against her sides. Hot pain erupted in her ankle and Sara cried out.

"Stop moving." Strong hands took hold of her. Strong, but gentle. "You hit your head. Try not to move."

I know that voice. A name rushed out of the depths of her memory. "Omar," she said.

"Yes."

The strong hands let her go, and Sara's vision slowly cleared, her pupils constricting until Omar's face came into view. He reached out and touched a tender spot on her head. "Does your head hurt?" he asked. "You hit the statue when you fell."

Luxor. Ramses II. Her ascent on the ancient statue came rushing

171

back. Along with the terrifying feeling of slipping during her descent and plunging to the ground. Rough, powerful hands had grabbed her. The temple guards? "What happened?"

"You fell," Omar said again. "I distracted the guards, as you asked, when they were about to turn the light back on. I saw you fall right at that moment."

The strong hands. Not guards. *Omar.* "You tried to catch me," she said.

"Yes. I carried you away. No one noticed." He pointed beside her. "I have your equipment."

For the first time she realized the softness beneath her was a cot. Her night-vision equipment was on the table beside her. "The guards didn't see me?"

"I brought you to my store," he said. "This is a room I do not tell people about. You are safe here."

Her ankle barked and she winced. "I twisted my ankle."

"Let me see it." She started to sit up and her head spun. "Slowly," Omar said.

Her headache was already subsiding. She sat up, blinking to clear away the dark spots that flashed in her vision. A few deep breaths and the wooziness faded. "I didn't hit it very hard," she said, probing the tender area. "It's sore. Not bleeding."

"That is good." Omar lifted the sheet that had covered her, which Sara had thought were bindings. "May I touch your ankle?"

Her shoes were still on. Sara pulled her pant leg up to reveal the first hints of purple already forming along the bottom of her leg. Her ankle had swollen, though she was able to flex her toes and could rotate her foot each direction. Painful, but not broken. "I think it's only sprained."

Omar said nothing as he poked and prodded, watching her face to see where it hurt. "I was trained as a medic in the army," he said. "Can you stand?"

She accepted his proffered hand and lifted herself off the cot. Ligaments shouted in protest when she put weight on it, but they held.

"Yes," she said through gritted teeth.

"Good. It is not broken. I will wrap it. That will keep the swelling down."

She didn't ask why Omar had a military field medic's kit on hand. A new one. He wrapped her ankle expertly, tight enough so that when he finished, she was able to walk gingerly around the room. "Take two of these." He held out two pills. "Aspirin."

"Make it three," she said, then dry swallowed them all. "Thanks."

"You should rest for the day."

Her head snapped up. "Day? Did I sleep all night?"

"Yes. It is now the morning after your fall."

The ache in her ankle vanished as everything came rushing back. A message inscribed on the obelisk. A message that shouldn't exist. Yet she had seen it in the darkness, through the night-vision goggles. A message from Mark Antony and Cleopatra.

"I need a pen and paper."

Omar jumped up without question and retrieved both. She pushed her night-vision gear aside and wrote from memory, recalling words she would never forget. "This is what I saw on the obelisk," she told him. "The obelisk this is written on was built over a thousand years before Cleopatra's reign. She was the final member of the Ptolemaic dynasty, which began with Ptolemy I in 300 B.C. and ended with Cleopatra's suicide in 30 B.C." Sara pointed to the first sentence. "Ptolemy didn't exist when this obelisk was built."

"The message was somehow added later," Omar said.

"That's the only explanation—that another inscription was scraped off the obelisk and this replaced it. Only a few people could have done this. Luxor was a central Egyptian city. This obelisk is outside the front gates. No one could have climbed it without being noticed. So, this change was made with official approval. Who could give that?"

Omar let her answer the rhetorical question.

"Only a supreme ruler," Sara said.

"A pharaoh." Omar nodded at her.

"Cleopatra. That's who I believe ordered this. She had the obelisk altered into another marker on her path. One she wanted only a certain person to follow."

"Who is that?" Omar asked.

"Right now we aren't certain. A person well-versed in Greek and Egyptian history who had access to levels of society that most did not. A person who could understand what was truly being said in a message such as this."

"An educated man," Omar said. "Or woman." He pointed to the last line she'd written. "Oedipus."

Sara stared at him. Omar was no simple shopkeeper, it seemed. "A king from Greek myth," she said. "A prince who killed his father and married his mother, then blinded himself when he realized what he'd done. But I've never heard the myth refer to a *scarlet eye*."

"The color could reference blood."

"Which would tie back to the second line," she said. "*Look ahead to the Greek sphinx.* Is that literal or figurative?" She looked at Omar. "How well do you know the grounds around Luxor?"

"I know every stone," he said. "Why would Cleopatra talk about a Greek sphinx and myth? She was a pharaoh. Such a powerful woman determines her own destiny. They do not leave their fate to others."

"Cleopatra and Antony knew war produced winners and losers, and no matter how well-prepared she was, she knew that the loser could be her. I believe she wrote this as an insurance policy, in case there came a time when she wasn't in power and couldn't choose for herself, couldn't guide whoever was meant to locate this message on the correct path. So she laid out a path stretching from an amulet to the obelisk. That's what I know so far. Now we must find the Greek sphinx."

Omar didn't ask what she meant about an amulet. "What can I do to help?"

"You have done enough."

"You are Mr. Morello's friend, so you are my friend." Omar touched his chest. "I will help you."

Sara reached over and touched his shoulder. "Thank you, Omar. You saved my life. Some men would say that was kindness enough."

"It is my pleasure."

"Now about this message," Sara said. "What could this mean if it is literal, and Cleopatra wants us to *look ahead?* Assuming it's literal and the message wants you to be in front of the temple, tell me anything that comes to mind when you think of a Greek sphinx."

Lines furrowed Omar's brow. "There are many sphinx carvings inside the temple. I am not sure where to look first."

He was right, Sara knew. Thousands of glyphs decorated the temple, both inside and out. Doubtless hundreds of them were sphinxes. Figuring out where to start from the obelisk message alone was impossible. "Perhaps there are certain sphinxes of note inside the temple. Ones we should look to first, which have been studied before for a reason. Do any come to mind?" It was a stretch and she knew it.

"Inside the temple?" Omar shook his head. "None."

Her throat tightened. "Are there any scholars you know in the area? I could consult with them."

"Yes, but there is another option. I do not know any sphinxes inside the temple to study first. But I do know of many outside."

"We must find one, not many." She tilted her head. "What do you mean by outside?"

"Most sphinxes in Luxor are outside the temple. You have seen them."

Sara leaned back and looked at the ceiling. *Of course.* She snapped her fingers. "The Avenue of Sphinxes. Of course." She'd walked down the avenue only yesterday. A nearly two-mile walkway connecting the Temple of Luxor to Karnak Temple. Nearly one thousand sphinxes flanked either side. A massive renovation, completed only last year, had restored many of the statues to their former glory. "I need to go to the avenue."

"You are injured," Omar said. "The avenue is long."

She tested her ankle and found the pain had dulled. "Those pills are working. So is your wrapping. I'll be fine. I have to check those sphinxes."

Between the two of them it would still take half a day to cover the sphinxes, and then what? If they were successful, another project awaited. One that almost certainly would run afoul of the authorities who kept watch over the national treasures. "I need to call Harry. Nora promised she would help if she could."

"Who is Nora?"

"A friend." Sara rummaged among the night-vision equipment. "Where's my phone?"

Omar reached into his pocket. "I am sorry, Miss Sara. It broke when you fell."

She tapped the shattered screen, but the device resisted any attempts at powering it on. "Is there anywhere to buy a new one?" she asked.

"Yes, if that is what you want. I could also get one that no one will know is yours."

Anonymity was a valued commodity for many people, including Omar. Sara would be wise to take the hint. "I would appreciate that."

Omar rose and vanished into the depths of his store. Sara watched him go, her mouth slightly open. "Thanks," she said, though he had already gone. The broken phone in her hand reflected every color of the spectrum as she studied it. Green, blue, yellow. And red.

She stood from the chair. "Omar, get back here."

Her bearded host rumbled back into the cramped room in a flash. "What is wrong, Miss Sara?"

"The Avenue of Sphinxes." She pointed to her eyes. "Many of the sphinxes were decorated with carvings, colors and indentations for stones. They were restored last year, correct?" Omar said she was, that there had been a massive project. "Some of the sphinxes had colored eyes." A forgotten journal article jumped into her head. "Restoration specialists identified specks of pigment where paint had worn off. Any colors they found were restored to the original state. Several had blue eyes, or black eyes, even green ones."

"I have seen these as well," Omar said.

"One of the sphinxes stood out from the others. It had unique eyes. The only red eyes I saw on the entire avenue."

"Were the eyes bleeding?"

Sara shook her head. "I don't think the Oedipus reference ties directly to the story. The myth is important because it comes from Greece, the same mythology Cleopatra has referenced before, stories an educated Greek in her time would know. Red is the important part of the story. Red eyes. I only saw one pair of them."

"There are hundreds of sphinxes on the avenue," Omar said. "There could be more."

"Or there could only be one. I need to find out. That's why I need a new phone. I have to call a police officer. Harry works with her."

Omar's face darkened as though a cloud had passed over it. Then the sun came through, though it took a long second. "I see," he finally said. "Harry and the police have an agreement."

Not how she'd phrase it, but fine. "Yes. Harry does work that others can't."

"Yes, he does. Mr. Morello speaks highly of him." Omar held up a hand. "One moment, Miss Sara. I will return."

She turned back to the paper in front of her. The scrawled message wasn't so mystifying now. At least, she didn't think it was. The *scarlet eye* was Cleopatra telling her to look for a sphinx with red eyes. That cleared up the second part. She bit her lip. How in the world did you dispatch a stone carving?

"Here is your phone."

Sara started. Omar had returned to her side on silent feet. "Thank you." Only after she took the phone did she actually think. "How did you get this so quickly?"

"Extra phones help in my work."

He didn't offer anything further and Sara didn't ask. "Lucky for me," she said.

The phone was completely charged and brand new. No calls, no texts, nothing at all was stored in the phone's memory. The phrase that came to mind was *burner phone*. A slight thrill tingled in her veins. She enjoyed it for a beat, then punched in Harry's number.

"Hello?" Suspicion in his tone. The sound of a car engine in the background.

"It's me."

"New number?"

"It's a long story. Can you talk?" He said he could. "I have news."

He listened silently as she detailed reconning the Temple, meeting Omar, climbing Ramses and finding a coded missive on the obelisk. She mentioned the broken phone, but not how it had happened. "I saw one sphinx on the avenue with red eyes," she told him. "Omar and I are going out tonight to investigate."

"Call Nora," Harry said. "She promised to help. Make her deliver. And nice work. You make a fine treasure hunter."

"What makes you think I need Nora's help?" Forget that she intended to call Nora. Coming from Harry, she couldn't help but hear a different message: that she couldn't do it.

"I don't think you need help. I know what you're doing is illegal. Having her on your side any way you can is smart. Not a sign of weakness."

"Perhaps." That was all she'd give him. "I'll call her shortly." Or perhaps she'd forget.

"I have a few more minutes before I get to Athens. If you'd like, we can talk through your plans."

"Athens? That's all the way across the country from Pella. Why Athens?" Oh. She didn't give him a chance to answer. "You found something in Sparta." She reverted to the ancient moniker. "What did you find?"

As Harry relayed his adventure, she struggled to process it all. A nonagenarian spelunker, Spartan helmet carvings leading to a missing relic and then a hidden antechamber in the sewers of ancient Sparta concealing a sword possibly belonging to Alexander the Great, with flying bullets and a swordfight mixed in. Sara ran through it again in her head after he stopped speaking. Harry had done it without her. That was infuriating, but what mattered is he was safe. Move on. "What's next?"

"There was a message on one side of the sword that said *'Our prize flies to the Athenian Temple of Alexander.'* Alexander loved to build temples to remind everyone he was a big deal. I plan to find a Koraki reference tied to armor in Athens. Not sure what comes after that."

"Shouldn't you call the police?" Sara asked. "That man tried to kill you."

"And tell them what? That I was shot at and then had a sword fight in an ancient sewer after breaking into an active archaeological dig site?"

She opened her mouth. She closed it.

"Read me the inscription again," Harry said. "That's the important part. Nora and Gary Doyle can pound salt for a minute. Our amulet search comes first."

Our amulet search. The stewing, somewhat contrived resentment bubbling in her stomach simmered down. Not Harry's amulet search. Ours.

She read from her notes. "'The future of Ptolemy is destined by the gods. Look ahead to the Greek sphinx. Dispatch it with the fate of Oedipus's scarlet eye.'"

"Cleopatra is part of the Ptolemaic dynasty. No surprise she believed herself favored by the gods."

Sara couldn't help but jump in. "The *Greek sphinx* refers to the Avenue of Sphinxes, which connects Luxor's two temples. When I looked out from the temple entrance, the avenue is directly ahead. Cleopatra's ancestors hail from Greece, giving her a Greek identity in no small part. I think she altered a sphinx on the avenue to conceal her true intent."

"Don't forget Greek sphinxes are female," Harry said. "She's sly. There could be two red-eyed sphinxes out there. If one of them is female, that's where I'd look."

Of course. How could she have missed that? "Another layer to conceal her message," Sara said. "A distinction only a classically educated person would understand. Greek sphinxes are female. Egyptian sphinxes are male."

"Which leaves the final line. I'd agree *scarlet eye* means we need to find a red eye. It's the most direct and logical explanation for this. And it's straightforward, which makes me think there's a twist coming."

"One tied to the Oedipus myth," Sara said. "Which, again, only an educated person would know."

"Oedipus stabbed himself in the eyes. He didn't die, which is what *dispatch* suggests, but don't get hung up on that. Focus on the stabbing part."

"I cannot stab a stone statue."

"Not literally. What if this sphinx doesn't have an inscription on it? Putting a marker on her path in such a public place means Cleopatra has to conceal the message. One way is making it look like anything but an important message. That's when you hide it in plain sight."

"A common phrase or saying that no one will interpret the proper way. Unless they know to look for it."

"Which is what I hope you're dealing with here. That's preferable."

"Why do you say that?"

"Because you're one of the smartest people I know," Harry said. "A cerebral challenge doesn't stand a chance against you. Plus they're usually a lot safer. The physical ones tend to be dangerous."

"Fair enough." She bit her lip. "But just to be clear, I may need to perform some sort of physical exercise to reveal the truth behind Cleopatra's sphinx reference."

"How big are the eyes on those sphinx statues?"

"The size of a large coin. An American silver dollar."

"Take a stick with you. One no bigger around than a silver dollar."

"A wooden stick? What good could that do?"

"Call it a hunch."

"Do better than that."

"Oedipus didn't *dispatch* his eyes without tools. He used a knife. I think a wooden stick should do nicely for you, if I'm on the right track."

"It could be a mechanism. Hidden in plain sight, the same as a veiled message. This could be both a literal and a figurative message."

"Now you're talking," Harry said. "What's underneath the avenue of sphinxes?"

"Nothing, as far as I know."

"Good. That tells me that if there is anything down there, no one's found it yet. Cleopatra could have created a hiding spot below the avenue. One accessed through a hidden door that's activated by pushing a hidden button. A button, let's say, that looks like an eye on a Greek sphinx statue."

"Use the stick to push the button." Hardly plausible, yet incredibly logical. The sort of device that could have survived undetected for two millennia. She was partly thrilled at his intuition and a tiny bit perturbed she hadn't thought of it first. "I'll take a stick."

"Good."

"Be careful in Athens," she said. "It can be dangerous."

"I'd tell you the same," Harry said. "Except I'm not worried. You'll solve it. Whatever *it* is." His voice dropped a note. "I wish I was there."

"Stay positive," she said, her chest growing light. "You will finish Nora's quest soon. Do that, then come meet me to find the end of your father's amulet trail. We will do it together."

"We will," Harry said. "Keep your eyes open. Relic hunts tend to get more dangerous near the end. Don't let your guard down."

His words rang in her ears as she clicked off. Yes, she'd been successful so far, though not without a healthy dose of luck and help from Omar. He walked into the room a minute later. Sara stood and made a circle with her thumb and forefinger.

"I need a walking stick," she said. "Roughly this big around."

Chapter 16

Athens

The heart of Athens had beat strongly for over two thousand years. Horses and chariots had turned to Teslas and helicopters, hurricanes and armies had churned the dirt and soaked it with the blood of change, yet still Athens endured. Time had passed countless cities by in those years, but not Athens. The birthplace of Western civilization refused to yield. Millions of Greeks still called it home, a city where the past and present had settled into an uneasy truce, past and future locked in an eternal struggle to claim Athens as their own. It was, in short, a city where history was made.

The Aegean Sea shimmered with liquid fire as the last sunlight trickled out of the sky. Harry veered in and out of traffic, a silent clock counting down in his head as his own voice filled the car. Nora Doyle was on the other end of the call, and right now he was making her wish she wasn't. He hadn't come this far to be lied to.

"What do you mean you can't?" Harry pounded the wheel. "You promised any help I needed. That's why I took the job."

"I promised all the help I could *provide*," Nora shot back. "I can't send a team into Athens to help you now."

"Why not? More important relics to find?"

"Not more important. Just more. My team is stretched too thin as it is. Even if I could spare the manpower, which I can't, sending them to Greece would take weeks of negotiation with the local authorities. We work for the *Manhattan* district attorney's office, not the Athens one."

"Tell your father to step in. He's the assistant D.A. Guys like that love throwing their weight around."

"He already did. Where do you think I got the money to pay for your expedition? You need equipment? Ask and you'll have it."

"Did you forget what just happened to me in Pella? I got lucky. Next time a crowbar won't cut it against a sword and revolver."

"Don't ask for a gun," Nora said. "There are some laws even I can't get around."

"Guns are for people who aren't smart enough to figure things out," Harry said. "I don't want a gun."

"Did you come up with that one?" Nora asked.

"Wrong Fox," he said. "My father did. He had plenty of good advice." *Not that I always took it.*

"Then put your thinking cap on and figure out where they have raven armor in the Athens' Temple of Alexander, and do it before Stefan Rudovic does. Better yet, convince him to come back to New York and my father will arrest him."

"For trying to kill me in Athens? I thought your jurisdiction didn't extend here."

"He'll make something up. He's an attorney, remember? He'll find a charge."

Harry's life would be a lot simpler if he could make that happen. "I'll take a rain check on that one."

"It's not only my father," Nora said. "I already tried to convince him to give you more assistance."

"You just told me I was on my own."

"I didn't say that."

"Not in so many words."

"It's more than my father." Their conversation pointedly tacked in the direction she chose. "I asked him to let me come with you. If it were only us making decisions, I'd be on a plane to Greece. You're lucky. You're in the field, actually finding artifacts *before* they're stolen, not trying to chase them down months or years after the fact with little to go on other than coerced confessions and conjecture."

Who was this person and what had they done with Nora? "Don't forget getting shot at."

"Experiencing the thrill of the chase." He actually laughed when she said it. "And I am glad you are safe," she said quickly. "If I could be there, I would."

"He's your father," Harry said. "Daughters are meant to manipulate fathers, not the other way round. Do it."

"The problem is that Gary is my father. Not my mother."

He darted through a red light and horns blared. "Don't tell me she works for the D.A. too."

"No. She's married to my father, which means he works for her. There is zero chance she would tolerate him sending me into the field in this situation."

"You mean where you could be killed."

"Yes."

"But I'm acceptable as cannon fodder."

"Get your head out of your ass and think for a second." Her sharp words buried the retort in his throat. "I work in the real world, the same as you. We each have limitations to deal with whether we like them or not. In order for me to do this job, I have to work for my father. Nothing will change that. And that means having my mother involved."

"By involved you mean telling him what to do."

"She would leave him if he ever lied to her about my involvement," Nora said. "That is a risk my father would never take."

Harry couldn't relate. A part of him he'd never talk about envied her. "She's only looking out for you," he conceded.

"My mother is protective of me. More than most mothers, and I realize that is saying a lot. I don't know why. All I can guess is something happened to her a long time ago, and that's merely a guess. If I'm correct she never talks about it and has never told my father."

Nora's words were hard to catch now, as though the phone had fallen away from her mouth and she didn't notice. "Whatever it is, she keeps it to herself. She's good at that in a way I'll never be. But regardless, I cannot send a team to help you."

The last sentence was much clearer. Cold and sharp like an icicle in Harry's back, one he never saw and didn't expect. "I'll find the relic. Then I'm going to help Sara."

"What is it you want to find so badly you sent her?"

"A private matter." That was all she needed to know. "I'm getting into Athens. I'll call once I figure this out."

He clicked off without waiting for a response. Forget Nora, hiding behind her mother's worry and her father's influence in New York while he was over here risking his neck. For all he knew Stefan was already on his tail again. He had the sword, and if the guy was sharp enough to find him in Pella, he could find Harry in Athens. Harry blinked, and the image of Stefan's revolver was on the back of his eyelids.

Athens' Temple of Alexander was located on the northern slope of the Acropolis, away from the Parthenon and other more famous structures on the southern side, and far less public. Yes, it was notable for the ties to Alexander, but tourists came for other sites, including the Acropolis Museum at the foot of the hill, which contained most of the site's artifacts. The Temple of Alexander still stood, but Alexander would have been less than thrilled to learn it had become an afterthought.

Harry, on the other hand, was grateful. He parked on a quiet street a half-mile from the Temple. He walked two blocks in the wrong direction, ran one more, then stopped in the darkest doorway he could find. Headlights painted the road as one car passed. It did not slow down. He waited, all small breaths and stillness as he counted to one hundred. Nobody came past, no Albanian gangsters moving through the twilight searching for him, no random cars cruising by, slowing at each alley. It looked like he was alone. Right now, that was good enough. Finish this hunt and get to Egypt.

Nora and Gary Doyle had roped him into this. His jaw tightened as he retraced his steps, passing his car and finding nobody of concern in the vicinity.

The Temple of Alexander rose on a hillside in front of him. Marble columns stretched toward the sky, the classical Greek symmetry imposing with its squared angles and slanted roof. While the stony hillside doubled as the structure's back wall, the temple was built as an open-air concept with no walls on three sides. A long chapel filled one side of the structure, while the other consisted of an open assembly hall sporting an elevated speaker's platform where scholars had once gathered for discourse. The dozens of circular columns were unadorned, yet majestic. Harry's tension went from his jaw to his stomach. There were no decorations on the columns or friezes at roof level to make his search easier. This also meant he had fewer options.

A statue of Alexander stood to one side of the temple. As though people needed a reminder of who had built the place. Alexander sat atop a towering steed, sword pointing to the sky, his mouth open in a battle cry. Harry closed his eyes for an instant and could almost hear the terrifying cacophony of armies readying for battle behind a leader who never lost. A terrifying sight, though one most of Alexander's opponents experienced only once. Carved letters ran across the front. *REX MORTUUS ES. The king is dead.*

Harry ran on to where long steps fronted the temple. An inscription ran across the uppermost step. Harry flicked on his flashlight and found it to be Latin. *SALVETE OMNES ALEXANDER. All hail Alexander.* The conquering hero had made sure anyone who walked into his temple remembered to pay homage, at least for that instant.

A stone road ran in front of the temple. Harry checked both ways and found it empty before crossing, jogging up the steps to duck beneath a linked chain that drooped from pillar to pillar. A sign posted at the entrance told Harry the temple was *CLOSED* in four different languages, three of which he read. He slipped past it and into the temple.

The last remnants of daylight had faded. In a temple of white marble open to the world, it hardly mattered. Moonlight brought the interior to life; long shadows pushed away from the almost iridescent glow radiating from each column, stone and block. The floor reflected light to guide his way, while faint emergency lighting told visitors that exits were located in any direction except straight ahead, where the hillside waited. He looked left and right. No one else was here, no sound filled the cavernous interior; there was nothing at all to worry him as he approached the first statue.

The temple contained dozens of them. Several of Alexander, of course, but also of Zeus and Ares, Aphrodite and Athena. Statues of both gods and Alexander stood in the chapel, though only the gods of Olympus watched over the assembly hall, ready to strike down any scholars who questioned their place in the world. Where to start? He needed to find armor, but gods were mostly immortal, rendering armor superfluous. Harry turned toward the chapel.

Light suddenly swept across the interior. He dropped to the floor, the marble cool on his cheek. Headlights from a car that stopped outside the front entrance and for some reason turned to shine them inside. Harry risked a look. The driver had pulled onto the long sidewalk fronting the temple. Harry crawled until a column stood between him and the headlights, then peered around with his head at ground level.

A man stood in shadow in the main entrance. He hadn't crossed the linked chain, merely walked up to it. A flashlight blazed to life in his hand, strong enough to make Harry wince. The light flashed across the interior, left to right, then aiming right at Harry. He closed his eyes. No one shouted. When he opened them the light had moved on, now shining on the gods across the temple. It swept back, and Harry kept his eyes down.

The light stopped near him. He kept still, head down, fighting the rising panic and the urge to flee. He could run in any direction, head into the winding streets and take refuge in a doorway. Forget this chase. Nora Doyle could come find the raven armor herself.

The world darkened again. He looked up as the man who stood outside turned and put his face in profile, the moon as good as daylight. It wasn't Stefan Rudovic. It was a security officer, one with a small vehicle sporting a flashing light on top. The man walked back to his small car, tugged on the brim of his cap, the sort that only security officers and steamboat captains wore, and then ducked inside. The engine whined, and the only security guard who seemed to care about this lonely temple disappeared.

Harry ran to the chapel. It was open to the elements, with pillars along all four sides but no roof overhead. Exterior stairs led out to the street on one side, stairs which all visitors had to ascend to enter. The chapel stood as it had since the Ancient Greeks built it so long ago in this building meant to serve as the center of social discourse. He'd be in plain sight if anybody walked by outside.

He didn't dare use his flashlight any more than necessary, but thankfully it had a low setting, one that couldn't be seen from outside the temple. The rectangular chapel had no pews, only an altar with Alexander's name carved across the front and statues around the perimeter, all Greek gods—except two. A pair of seemingly identical statues stood on either side of the altar. Statues of Alexander wearing ceremonial robes. A crown rested atop each head.

Harry moved toward the most exposed statue first, the one closest to the exterior steps. He didn't need a flashlight to inspect it, not with the full moon. He stopped in front of the statue and looked up at Alexander. If the statue were to be believed, Alexander had stood north of seven feet tall. He'd have to climb up on the thing to get a look at that crown. But first, the robes—and that's what they were. Plain robes, rich and full like those of an important man, but utterly devoid of anything helpful. The same for Alexander's sandaled feet. No armor to speak of, not even on the scroll he grasped in one hand. Everything was blank. Thinking light thoughts, Harry grabbed Alexander by the neck, hauled himself up level with the statue's head, and peered inside the crown.

Curly hair. The statue actually had curly hair inside the crown, intricately carved and no help at all. Harry dropped down and fortunately the head didn't break off. He stepped around the altar and found that the second statue looked almost identical. Almost. This Alexander had the same robes, same sandals, but the scroll was in his other hand and the crown was larger. Much larger, with tall points that looked like perfect handholds.

A quick check confirmed he was still alone. Harry hoisted himself up, and once again found nothing but darkness on Alexander's head. The moonlight didn't quite reach the interior of the bigger crown. Out came the flashlight, which he held between his teeth so he could shield it with his free hand. He flicked it on, blinked at the sudden brightness, then stared at more curly hair. Harry swore. It came out as gibberish, and he flicked the flashlight off by accident.

A bang shattered the stillness. He jerked around toward the noise, and the sudden movement proved too much for Alexander's crown. The point Harry was grasping broke off, sending him flailing down to crash onto the marble floor with a resounding thud.

Brain scrambled, eyes almost rotating in their sockets, he lay still, listening, and waited for his vision to clear. No footsteps pounded the marble floor. What had that bang been? A car backfiring several blocks off, or maybe a distant crash, he told himself. The open chapel played havoc with the acoustics, making it impossible to tell where the sound had come from. No matter. He was still alone, and if the *Koraki* had left anything behind, it wasn't here. Harry got gingerly to his feet, set the broken piece of statue at the base, sent out a silent apology to any Greek gods in the area and set to work checking each of the statues surrounding the chapel in turn. None offered anything remotely approaching armor or a clue of any sort. The chapel was a bust. He turned and went into the assembly hall.

The columns in here offered protection from anyone who might be looking for him, so he kept close to them as he moved toward the opposite side where the raised stage and open discussion area waited. Along with the Greek gods whose sanctuary he had defiled. Terrible gods who played with the lives of men as though tossing dice, including one god who tossed thunderbolts when angered. He'd be worried if he truly believed in any of that nonsense.

He never saw the waist-high pedestal before he slammed into it and bounced off. The first thing he did was curse. The second was reach out and grab a trident before it fell off the block and smashed into a million pieces.

As he fumbled around in the dark, the underwater weapon nearly slipped from his grasp twice before he snatched it, just inches from the floor. Why in the world did they have an artifact like this out here? Crafted of stone and leather, it was well balanced and a true work of art—so why leave it out here in the open for anyone to knock over? The leather was smooth in his hands. Far too smooth to be authentic. Harry took a step back and found a placard on the pedestal explaining this was a replica of an original piece, now stored in the museum. That made sense. Not to mention that he could actually hold the thing in his hand. It had to be hollow, the stonework manufactured as a thin covering with metal support inside. It was heavy, sure, but if the weapon were solid stone he'd never be able to hold it like this.

He touched the trident's stone tips. They were *sharp*. Setting it back in a likely brand-new position, he skirted the pedestal and headed with care toward the assembly hall, passing several other display pedestals sporting other reproductions of artifacts. A replica stone shield, which he checked for any sign of ravens and found none. Another replica sword, this one allegedly belonging to Alexander as well. No luck with raven references here either. The others were less lethal objects that gave no guidance, so it was with a growing sense of unease that he cleared one last column and found himself looking up at a massive, terrifying sea god.

Poseidon, owner of the biggest beard Harry had ever seen, was armed with a trident taller than Harry. The next column down had Ares, the god of war, followed by Athena, Apollo and others. Zeus took place of honor behind the raised speaker's platform. All gods, none wearing armor. Harry clenched his hands into fists, his throat suddenly dry. *Where else can I look?*

An inscription ran across the bottom of Zeus's statue. *IN HONOREM ALEXANDRI.*

"In honor of Alexander," Harry said to the air. The words made him stop. In honor of? That's what you said about a man who was living. A man who equated himself with a god, a man who could bestow patronage on those who flattered him. A different inscription flashed across his mind. One he'd seen minutes ago. Again, he spoke aloud. "The king is dead."

A sudden glint of light caught Harry's eye and he spun around to see moonlight flashing off a piece of metal clasped in a man's hand, a man who had stepped out from behind a column with a gun aimed at Harry's chest. The barrel loomed large even from twenty feet away.

"Don't move."

Harry growled. "Stefan."

The Cana man kept walking toward Harry, the pistol out. "Where is it?"

"Where is what?" Harry asked.

"The next—"

Stefan fired as Harry dove away, the pistol making a sound like a firecracker going off, sharp and short. *Not the revolver,* Harry thought as he hit the ground and rolled. *He missed.* Stefan fired again. The bullet sparked as it ricocheted off the ground, searing Harry's vision for a beat. Harry rolled until a column was between him and Stefan, then stood and ran to another one.

Footsteps pounded behind him. Harry kept moving, headed toward the chapel. He couldn't run out the front, not with that long sidewalk there. Stefan would gun him down in seconds. Use the columns, stay hidden, keep moving. Another shot cracked and chips of marble erupted a foot from Harry's head. He ducked and moved. Into the main hall now, where he nearly ran into one of the pedestals again. A spin move took him around it and further in, the trident he'd saved from destruction appearing ahead. Inspiration struck like a lightning bolt from Zeus. He grabbed the trident and ducked beside the pedestal, crouching low.

Stefan came at a fast clip, his gun leading the way. Harry slipped further out of sight, back so far that only Stefan's footsteps told him when to attack. Gripping the trident in both hands, he lashed out at ground level, aiming to take Stefan's legs out from under him.

He was a beat too soon. The trident missed by inches, sending Stefan tumbling back and crashing down. The gun came up and Harry stabbed at it with the trident, sending the weapon spinning. Harry stabbed again, missing Stefan as the Albanian man rolled away and knocked against his gun. It clattered away out of reach on the marble floor, like a hockey puck gliding on ice, and disappeared into the darkness. Harry made the mistake of watching it go.

Stefan's fist smashed into his stomach. Harry dropped the trident and doubled over. Years of sparring experience with Joey Morello in Brooklyn gyms kicked in. He lifted his arms to block an unseen blow, juked to one side, then went back fast at Stefan with his eyes open and a right jab leading the way. He got inside Stefan's guard and the shot landed. Stefan fell back, stunned, then backed up further when Harry's left hook caught him flush, knocking him back into a pedestal to his rear. Stefan flipped up and over the stone square, out of sight.

He reappeared in an instant. Harry couldn't really see because this pedestal had the sword on it, a sword now in Stefan's hands. Harry snatched at the trident lying behind him, but before he realized what was happening Stefan was racing toward him, an ancient replica Greek sword held in front of him. Harry brandished the trident. Fake stone clashed with fake stone, some of it chipped, and the two of them were locked in combat.

Harry stepped back out of range. He jabbed at Stefan, who feinted and tried to get inside the reach of Harry's longer weapon. Harry quick-stepped back and jabbed at Stefan again, forcing the Albanian back toward the assembly hall. Once, twice their weapons clashed, each time forcing Stefan back. Harry tried to run the man through, a man who would kill him for this prize of Achilles, if it even existed. Right now it didn't matter. Only survival did. Live through this and get to Egypt.

Harry jabbed. Stefan took another step back. A step too far. His foot came down awkwardly on the edge of a column, the square base tripping him up so his weight came down on the ankle in all the wrong places. An audible *snap* made Harry's gut churn.

Stefan cried out as though the trident had run him through. Arms flailing, he fell back into the assembly hall, where the disdainful gods watched over this foolish mortal whose screams filled the air, bouncing off the marble walls and echoing into the night. Harry didn't think, he didn't hesitate. He moved on Stefan with his trident up and ready to skewer him.

They both saw it at the same time: Stefan's gun, lying on the stone floor, now within arm's reach. Stefan grabbed for it and Harry turned and ran. A gunshot cracked, the bullet whistling wide. Harry gained the nearest column and darted around it, racing for the front exit as Stefan Rudovic shouted in pain or frustration; Harry couldn't tell. He did know that next scream. Pain, the sound a man makes when he tries to put weight on a shattered ankle.

Columns flew past as Harry took a winding route out of the temple, his breath coming fast, body tensed for the next shot. It never came. The open entrance area stretched ahead of him—basically a shooting gallery now—with the city beyond. Harry stopped at the last column before he'd be exposed. Had Stefan managed to hobble closer? Even on one leg there was a good chance he could pick Harry off before he made it to safety. His gaze fell to the statue of Alexander on his horse outside the entrance. A statue he'd raced past earlier. A statue he didn't want Stefan to know mattered.

He forced himself to take deep breaths. And he listened. Instead of the sound of an injured man growing louder as he struggled to get in position for a shot, Harry heard different noises. The growls of an injured man trying not to scream. They grew progressively fainter. Stefan wasn't coming after Harry. He was running *away*.

Why would he do that with Harry so close? Only one answer made sense: Stefan didn't want to get caught. One of the relic hunter's commandments. *Thou shalt never get caught.* It's what he would do faced with the same situation. Run now, live to chase another day. Plus, with all the noise from their battle, it wouldn't be long before the authorities showed up.

Harry bolted from his hiding spot, skidded to a halt near the statue and kept low. The first sirens sounded in the distance. Harry assumed that the guard he'd seen earlier had raised the alarm. Stefan's gunfire would have alerted him to trouble, but pinpointing where it had come from would be tough. The neighborhood was an obvious choice—who shot up a vacant temple, after all? Maybe it would buy him a few seconds.

Harry stepped back, closed his eyes. *Focus.* Get this right and get it now. He opened his eyes and looked up at Alexander the Great astride a rearing war horse, both forelegs in the air with Alexander seated on its back. The warrior king looked into the distance, a crown circling his head and a sword held out to one side, his cape flowing perpendicular to the ground as though lifted by the wind. An armored top covered him to mid-thigh, short-sleeved with supplemental protection around the chest and shoulders. No greaves protected his legs; he wore leather-string sandals on his feet. Harry grabbed hold of the sword and pulled himself onto the base. This sword looked an awful lot like the one from the Pella sewer.

He thought again about the inscription across the front of the statue: *The king is dead.* A tribute to a man who would never see it, which was completely out of place here. All the other monuments to Alexander meant to flatter the king, to remind him of how important this temple was and as such, why he should support it. Even though he had built it himself, the city caretakers would have sought patronage by promising new statues. And of course, once Alexander died, his money stopped flowing. No one paid for new statues to old emperors. Unless they had a good reason.

And what better reason than to leave a marker for your hidden trail in plain sight? Harry stood on the pedestal and peered at the armor on Alexander's chest. The moon backlit the statue, giving him no clear view, so he took a risk and flicked on his flashlight. The breath caught in his throat as he leaned closer. Something was engraved on the right side of Alexander's chest. Faint, filled with grime and difficult to see, but it was there. He rubbed embedded dirt from the thin lines and revealed a miracle.

A raven, with a long beak and wings folded together. The sword's message had been true. This was raven armor. *Koraki* armor. But what did it mean?

Another siren burst to life in the distance, faint and far away, but growing louder as he studied the engraving. Ducking under Alexander's outstretched arm brought him to the rear side of the armor, which was utterly blank. No engravings, no carvings, nothing at all. Back to the front of the statue, where he tried to lean over and look between Alexander and the horse's mane. Had it been actual hair he could have slipped through, but this mane was stone and Harry nearly lodged himself tight. Only by slipping under the horse's raised forelegs could he access the other side.

The sirens grew louder. Harry looked over a shoulder and noted faint blue lights on the far-off neighborhood buildings. Flickering lights, the kind atop police cars. He turned back to the statue and nearly dropped his flashlight. There was writing on the left side of Alexander's chest armor. Two words, one atop the other, six letters each. Both words were the same, and they sent a bolt of cold ice up his spine.

Koraki. Written twice, one word directly atop the other. Two ravens? None of the earlier clues made mention of dual birds. One hand on a foreleg, he searched the rest of the armor for any other clues. Nothing on the shirt, and nothing anywhere else. The blue lights grew brighter as he searched, with only one part of the statue left to inspect.

The crown.

It was worth a shot. Vaulting onto the horse's flank brought him to eye level with the crown. A simple ring, points on top and no decoration. He held the flashlight in one hand while he grabbed the front of the crown with his other for support.

His fingers scraped across a defect. A perfectly cut and vertical defect. An impossibly straight cut. Harry scrambled around front and found twelve tiny, perfectly carved letters across the front half of Alexander's crown, the same letters that were carved twice on his breastplate. *Koraki.*

Wait. Perfectly carved, but not aligned. Whereas the words on his chest were directly atop each other, these were not. The *A-K-I* on the top word stuck out from the edge of the lower word, hanging in space on its own. That misalignment extended to the bottom word, which had *K-O-R* with nothing above it. The words were three letters off on each side.

A purposeful mistake. The kind of error a sculptor intended to be seen, but not understood, not unless you were part of the group that made it. A group hiding secrets in plain sight. A true raven on Alexander's breastplate looked across his chest at two aligned words. The same words that didn't match up on his crown.

Blaring sirens now filled the air. He had seconds left to jump down and make his way to the safe anonymity of the neighborhood, where he would blend into the shadows. Harry looked around anxiously. Getting himself arrested meant he'd never get to Luxor, couldn't help Sara. Harry adjusted his grip as he looked toward where the police cars would soon appear. Without thinking, he grasped a point on Alexander's crown. A perfect handhold. As though it had been designed for it.

Could it be? This was his last shot. Time was up. He shoved the flashlight in his pocket, grabbed two points on the crown for leverage and twisted with everything he had.

Nothing moved. Teeth gritted, he pulled again. Still nothing. A bead of sweat ran down his forehead before he realized. *I'm pulling the wrong way.* If he wanted to align the words on the crown to look like they did on the breastplate he had to move them left, not right. The power of a man cursing his own stupidity put force into his aching muscles and he twisted the crown again, tried to rip it right off Alexander's stony head.

It moved. The top half twisted as he pulled until the two words aligned atop each other. Ancient levers ground, metal shrieked, and when Harry looked down the raven engraving on Alexander's chest had parted to reveal a hidden chamber. An opening skillfully hidden along the edges of the carved bird, one you couldn't see and would never know existed if you hadn't followed the clues. An object lay inside, hidden in shadow.

Headlights lit the buildings to one side. Harry grabbed the chamber's contents before twisting the crown back to its original position, relief flooding him as the chamber door swung shut again. The best crimes were ones nobody knew had happened. He leapt down and ran toward his car as police headlights washed over the statue. Now he could see a string of cars coming down the hill and stopping in front of the temple. Their lights never quite caught up with the man running for his life, a man with an ancient Greek mystery tucked under his arm.

Chapter 17

Luxor

The walking stick clicked with each step. Sara moved down the Avenue of the Sphinxes feeling as though every eye was on her. Foot traffic was sparse in this late hour, most people either in for the night or finishing their visits at the Luxor and Karnak temples. She had the nearly two-mile-long avenue to herself, more or less. Only one person was in sight.

Omar stood several hundred yards distant in the middle of the avenue. Ground-level spotlights illuminated each sphinx at night, though the main avenue had only running lights like those on an airplane aisleway. The dark kaftan he wore stretched from neck to ankle and helped him slide between the shadows. Sara knew he was there but could barely see him until he pulled a cell phone from his pocket and called her.

"There is no one this way," Omar said when she answered.

"Same here." She looked away from Omar, toward the distant lights of Karnak. If anybody was out there, she couldn't see them. "I'm going for it."

"I will call you if anyone comes near."

She thanked him and clicked off. Adrenaline hit, the stones under her feet seeming to electrify, making her float instead of walk. A sphinx in front of her demanded attention, drawing her to it. One of hundreds lining the stone walkway, not all that different from any other sphinx in sight. Except in one way. This sphinx had red eyes. It was one of only two sphinxes on the entire avenue with eyes that color, and of those two, the only female.

Dispatch it with the fate of Oedipus's scarlet eye, Antony and Cleopatra had told her. In the heat of the day she and Omar had checked each statue on this route, finding only two with red eyes, one of them female.

They had spent the evening in preparation. Omar acquired a walking stick and resisted any attempt to keep him away from an evening that promised trouble.

"I need you to be my lookout," Sara said. "The avenue has much less traffic at night, correct?" He said it did. "Then we go at night, right before the temples close. That way we will not look suspicious out on the avenue and we will likely be alone." That would at least offer some protection for her while she inspected the sphinx.

A cool desert breeze flitted through her hair. She took one last look at Omar, who was busy scanning for trouble like a reliable lookout should. Her feet moved without instruction from her brain until she found herself standing in front of the red-eyed sphinx, walking stick in hand, black clothes shielding her from view in the night. Its head rose not far above hers. Dipping down to one knee, she stretched black tape across the spotlight on this sphinx to create further shadows. Cloaked in the night, her walking stick found the first red eye, resting on it; the stick was slightly smaller in diameter than the eye. She leaned on it, slowly at first, then putting her weight into it.

Nothing. Her leg muscles stretched taut as she pushed harder, all her strength on it now as she pushed. She put her shoulder into it, her shoes slipping in the sand that had blown across the stone walkway. It felt gritty on her tongue and she could feel it crunching between her teeth. The eye didn't budge. She pulled back and stabbed the eye, once, twice, the sounds like gunshots in the night.

Her phone buzzed. She looked up to find Omar waving frantically and pressed answer. "Is someone coming?" she asked, breathing hard.

"What are you doing? The noise is too much."

"I got carried away."

"No one is coming, but if you make so much noise again, they may."

"Got it." She clicked off, shoving the phone back in her pocket. One eye down, one to go. This next one had better work. She put the point of her walking stick against the second eye and pushed with everything she had. It nearly cost Sara her front teeth when the stick slipped off and she went face-first into the stone sphinx, smacking off it and falling to one knee as the stick clattered away. She grabbed it, touching her lip to find it wet, the salty taste of blood in her mouth. Arabic curses she couldn't recall learning spewed from her lips.

She drew back, muscles taut and ready to spring, and then jammed the stick against the second red eye as though the sphinx were racing in to bite her head off. The stick smacked home and she fell forward, nearly impaling herself on the wood. The wind flew from her lungs. She'd missed again. Cursing, pulling on the stick, she closed her eyes, leaned back and pulled with everything she had, but the stick wouldn't budge.

It's stuck. That's impossible. The near-rage filling her kept rational thought at bay for a long moment. Only when she opened her eyes did she realize what had happened. The stick hadn't missed and become stuck. *It was buried in the eye.* Half the stick was now inside the lion's head because the eye had given way.

The ground rumbled. For an instant she felt weightless, untethered to the stones beneath her. In the darkness behind the sphinx a shadow rose, a blot against the endless desert sky. The sphinx's tail rose into the air as she watched.

The stones stopped shaking and the tail went still. She stood statue-like, all the years of academic research failing her, the admonitions to believe only evidence, only what you could confirm. Well, she'd just seen a stone statue come to life. That took a second to process. Sara ran a dry tongue over her lips. It had happened. Holy crap.

Focus. She shook her head and moved. Her theory was correct. Correction: their theory. She and Harry had unraveled Cleopatra's message, found what others had missed for thousands of years. What came next?

Omar appeared at her side as she ran around the sphinx statue. "Did you know it would do this?" he asked, indicating the raised tail.

"No." A flashlight came out of her pocket and its beam cut through the night. An opening behind the sphinx had appeared, one the tail had covered so well it was impossible to know it existed. It revealed rough steps cut out of the desert floor descending to the underworld. Sara turned to Omar. "I'm going down. You don't have to wait for me."

Omar, it seemed, knew better than to argue. "I will be up here in the shadows. I do not believe the tail will be noticed in the dark."

"I won't be long."

Sara descended the steps, Omar's sandaled feet the last sight she had before going underground. The sphinx's base had been hollowed out and this passage cut into the ground. Ten large steps brought her to a level floor; a sheer stone wall lay several steps ahead. Passageways stretched out on either side. The sphinxes to the right and left of her red-eyed statue concealed hidden chambers, it seemed; the entire area was a rectangular room. A pedestal stood at the end of the hallway to her right. An identical pedestal stood at the far end to her left. Both were empty. Arches separated the three different areas beneath each sphinx, though the entire space was open.

A chamber hidden for thousands of years built by a woman who bent history to her will. All here, laid out in front of Sara with nothing to stop her from exploring at will. That thought made the hairs on her arms stand up.

Somehow this looked too open. Too easy. The internal alarm she'd developed since meeting Harry Fox blared at full volume. Cleopatra wouldn't leave her prizes unprotected down here. Her light played over the walls. There had to be another marker, an indicator of where to go. Dust motes glittered as she shined the light back and forth, into one section of the room and then the other. The pedestals had her attention, drawing her gaze, so it was several long seconds before she realized what was odd. The arches supporting the ceiling had writing on them. Not Greek. Ancient Egyptian glyphs.

Glyphs that a tenured Egyptologist could read. Finally, a break. Still cautious, she knelt and studied the floor before taking a step. It looked safe; no lines or marks to indicate a trap. Which, if the trap builder was any good, wouldn't be easy to spot. The arches were too far away and the writing too small for her to decipher from here. She had to risk it to get there. But which way? The spaces on either side looked identical, separated by arches with writing she couldn't quite make out and empty pedestals that promised more. Luxor lay to her right. Karnak to her left. Cleopatra's message had been in Luxor, so she went right. Stick with what had worked so far.

The ground held as she reached the arch. Egyptian glyphs ran across the top of it, glyphs she recognized. A single line. Sara tilted her head and the language of her ancestors came alive, Cleopatra speaking to her across the centuries.

The sah of Khons holds the path.

Connections unspooled in her mind in a flash. *Sah* was how ancient Egyptians referred to bodies that had undergone mummification, and *Khons* was a male name from Cleopatra's time. A man named Khons must have been mummified, she reasoned, and his remains held the secret behind how to continue along this path. One problem: there were no mummies in sight.

Sara lifted her face and fought the urge to scream. Her mouth hung open when she found the answer right above her head, carved on the underside of the arch. A carving of the night sky. A full moon amid stars dotted the arch, intricately carved so she recognized it immediately. She'd seen those stars before. They were in the constellation Orion. The ancient Egyptians had been fascinated by stars, naming some of their gods in honor of the various constellations. Orion had inspired one of their most important gods, known as the "Father of the Gods" in the Old Kingdom. All this ran through her head at the same time the bottom fell out of her stomach.

The god's name was *Sah*. The same word that could also mean mummy, depending on how it was used. Did an actual mummy wait for her, or was she meant to view this through the lens of the stars overhead? Her stomach churned at the thought, for in Egyptian burial rooms, security was not taken lightly. Cleopatra would not have left this secret unguarded.

Sara did the only rational thing. She stopped moving and started thinking. The inscription across this archway referenced a man named Khons, specifically his mummy, indicating that his wrapped remains held the truth. However, the arch also contained an image of Orion in the night sky, a constellation that had so moved Egyptian priests they'd named a god after it. Named him *Sah* and placed him at the top of the pecking order as gods went, one step below deities such as Osiris and Ra.

So was she looking for the mummified remains of a man named *Khons*, or was she overthinking this and the message referenced the god *Sah*??

Sara aimed her light down the hall toward the other arch. Perhaps she didn't have all the information she needed. Checking the floor and finding nothing to suggest it had traps waiting to kill her, she made it to the second arch and stopped. The same inscription had been carved across the face of this one as well. *The sah of Khons holds the path.* Identical stars were on the underside, a clear depiction of Orion. There was only one difference. Instead of the moon, this arch had a sun cut into it. A sun surrounded by the same stars. Stars that couldn't normally be seen in daylight, though such depictions weren't unheard of. These were gods, after all. Accuracy about celestial visibility wasn't a necessity.

Why the difference?

The challenge here was having knowledge along with a deep understanding of all relevant cultures. Egyptian was the culture of choice here, her specialty, and one clear solution jumped out from the others. Ancient Egyptians had worshipped quite a few gods, but the most important?

Ra. The sun deity ruled all parts of the world, from the sky to the earth and down to the underworld. Ra created all forms of life, including humans, who allegedly came from Ra's tears and sweat. On the other hand, the moon was worshipped as the nightly replacement for the sun, a placeholder to keep the cosmos aligned until Ra returned each morning.

The sun had ruled all in ancient Egypt. Not unlike the woman who had created this trail, whose secret began with Harry's amulet and ended at parts unknown. So the sun was Sara's obvious choice. Decades of experience told her to follow her gut. Above all, she believed in herself. The answers she sought lay through the archway with a sun on it.

She took one step through the archway, holding her breath, peering between slitted eyes, and stopped. The floor didn't quake, the walls didn't collapse. Her gaze immediately went to the empty pedestal. Now she could see there was writing on top of it, glyphs carved into the stone that she hadn't been able to see from outside the arch. She took another step toward it.

That was one step too far. Now the ground shook. She jumped and her foot caught on something as holes opened in the walls before massive poles shot out. Poles with spear tips on the end of them. One *cracked* into Sara's head, sending her world spinning as she twisted, tossed up and flipped around while her flashlight flew away. The last thing she saw before darkness consumed her was the bronze tip of a metal spear slicing for her throat.

Chapter 18

Athens

A monitor beeped at the bedside. Nurses and doctors passed in an endless, quiet parade outside the hospital room door, none of them looking inside the room at the man lying on the bed, a fiberglass cast on one ankle. The patient had hobbled into their hospital claiming to have fallen and then driven himself to the hospital. The nurses believed he had driven himself. They did not believe he had fallen.

Stefan Rudovic did not care what they believed. All he cared about was not getting arrested. He'd been in surgery for several hours to repair his broken ankle and kept telling the medical staff he had a flight to catch soon. Yes, they said, he could leave in a day. No, he wouldn't walk without the cast any time soon. He should be able to run again, eventually, though when the weather turned chances were he'd feel it for the rest of his life.

That was the second-worst part. Sitting in his hospital bed, watching television in a language he didn't understand with his only associates thousands of miles away—that was what ate at Stefan. There was a chance he'd have to feel this pain of failure for the rest of his life. A permanent reminder of when he'd lost to Harry Fox. The stony mask Stefan used to keep the world at bay cracked for an instant. He vowed again that he would do whatever it took to make Altin Cana the boss of all bosses in New York. The next step would be toppling Joey Morello. Getting rid of Joey's antiquities hunter would make that happen all the faster, for no one would support a new leader who couldn't protect his men. It didn't matter if he was Vincent Morello's son or not.

Stefan re-read the last text message from Altin. *Progress?* That's all it said. Altin had sent it earlier that morning, not long after Stefan awoke from surgery. His boss had no idea about the broken ankle, about the fight with Harry Fox or that Stefan was now out of the game. Altin wouldn't care about that. He only cared about results. Stefan bit his lip. Altin only promoted men who got results. Stefan had to be one of those men. He texted Altin back and assured him things were in hand.

His phone lit up with an incoming call. A blocked number. Stefan put the device to his ear and connected the call. "Yes?"

"It is me."

Stefan's body tensed. No mistaking that Russian-accented English. "Yes, sir."

Evgeny Smolov got right to it. "Have you found it?"

"No, sir. I am getting closer." Stefan closed his eyes, rubbing a hand over his furrowed brow. Why now? Of all the times for Smolov to call for an update.

"How much longer?"

Stefan lied with ease. "It is hard to say. I would guess a week." He'd be lucky to be in a walking boot within a week. Finding Smolov's Greek treasure was out of the question, and of course, he couldn't tell Smolov the truth. Do that and their arrangement would end, taking with it any chance of fulfilling Altin Cana's desire to put the Morellos in their place.

"Good. I will be in touch." The call disconnected as Evgeny clicked off.

Stefan lowered the phone to his lap. He stared at the wall in front of him, a chart explaining who his nurse was and when he needed his next dose of medicine. He didn't actually see any of it. All he could see was Altin Cana's face when he learned Stefan had failed. A face that might turn to another man to fill his shoes, someone who wouldn't disappoint him.

The ankle pain flashed like fire. Teeth gritted, clenching the phone so hard it might break, Stefan wanted to shout loud enough to break the windows. He was helpless, unable to accomplish what mattered. Once the pain passed, he opened his eyes and looked at the wall-mounted television where a BBC news anchor reported on the new Taliban government in Afghanistan.

Stefan's jaw unclenched. The pain in his ankle vanished. A forgotten name flashed into his head. One he had forgotten on purpose. But that was before his broken ankle. Before he'd lost to Harry Fox. Now he didn't have the luxury of forgetting. He looked down at his phone and tapped the screen.

The list of contacts in Stefan's phone was short on names and long on apparently random words. To anyone else in the world they made no sense, though to Stefan they were crystal clear. Need an untraceable weapon on short notice in New York? Call *LAWN CARE*. Have an artifact that Rose Leroux can fence? *MOVING COMPANY*. Only a very few of the numbers in this phone made Stefan think twice before dialing them. His finger hovered over one of them. A number he had never used before, for if there was anyone in the world who made him hesitate, made him consider whether there was another option, this was that person.

He reached for a drink on the table beside him and accidentally put pressure on his injured leg. His ankle screamed, the pain making him bite his lips. The hell with Harry Fox. He deserved what was coming. Stefan punched in the number. A number stored under the word *BEIRUT*.

"*Min hadha?*"

The harsh Arabic was so low Stefan nearly missed it. *Who is this?* Stefan responded in Arabic as well. "*Sadiq min albanya.*" A friend from Albania.

"*Salam Alaikum.*" Peace be upon you.

Stefan wished the man peace as well. "*Wa Alaykum as-salam.*"

This was the man he'd met once before, in Altin Cana's smoke-filled office. A man Altin treated with respect. The man's eyes had been narrow cuts in a weathered face, a face leathered from years under the desert sun. The man's beard had glistened even in the half-light of Altin's office. His eyes were dark pools offering nothing at all. The man's name was Rafiq. Stefan had, for the first time in a long while, been frightened. Rafiq had been traveling through New York for reasons Stefan didn't know, and Altin had provided him with money for his travels. It had something to do with an imam they both knew, one who had convinced Altin to help this brother in faith.

A doctor passed Stefan's open door. Stefan continued in Arabic so no one walking past would likely understand. "I have an opportunity."

Rafiq hesitated. "I am busy."

"It comes with great reward."

No hesitation now. "I am listening."

A simplified tale spilled forth from Stefan's mouth, one heavy with the promise of money, a sure way to get Rafiq's attention, for Rafiq headed what most Westerners would call a terrorist cell. His base of operations? Beirut. A city where anything, including death, could be had at wholesale prices. Providing this service could be lucrative, but death was a business, and being in business cost money. Rafiq's terrorist enterprise—the Salafi Front—was always looking for new funding in light of the ever-expanding international sanctions against certain countries that supported his efforts. The money Stefan offered would keep him in business for a long time.

"Why do you want this piece of junk?" Rafiq asked.

"It is valuable."

"You do not know if it exists."

"Is it worth two million to find out?" A forty percent cut of Evgeny's payment, more than fair considering Stefan provided all the intelligence. All Rafiq had to do was activate his network and follow one man. "Follow the man. He will lead you to the prize."

"Is he connected?" Rafiq asked.

Perceptive of him. Rafiq had clearly fought and survived enough battles to understand the importance of who he went up against. "Harry Fox works for the Morello family."

"The family who controls New York."

"*Controlled.* The old man is dead. His son is weak. Do not worry about the Morello family. They are on the way out."

"Are you using me to hurry that change?"

No use denying it. "If you succeed and it hurts the Morellos, then I am happy. But that is not the focus. I only care about the prize."

"Is it gold or jewels?"

"That is for me to worry about. Do you want the money?"

"If I find jewels, it will cost you more than two million."

"If you find it and think you have been underpaid, I will reconsider. But do not play games with me, Rafiq." This sort of man respected strength. Stefan would show him what strength sounded like, even from this hospital bed. "I will treat you fairly. As one man of the true faith to another." He paused, letting Rafiq chew on that. "There is one other benefit to your quest."

"What are you talking about?"

"Harry Fox is a nonbeliever. He comes from Pakistan, yet he is an apostate."

To men like Rafiq there was nothing worse than someone who renounced their Islamic faith. Certain Islamic jurisdictions called for the death penalty for that crime.

"Death to all nonbelievers."

The conviction in Rafiq's words made Stefan smile with satisfaction. In truth he doubted if Harry Fox had ever been a Muslim, and he wasn't entirely sure about the Pakistani connection either. No matter. Harry looked like he had Pakistani blood, and once Rafiq had dealt out righteous vengeance it would be a moot point. As long as he could sell the man on it now.

"There is one other part of the deal."

"It will cost you."

"No. You will do this for free."

"You are no man to give me orders," Rafiq growled.

"This is a gift. I need Harry Fox to disappear."

Rafiq was silent for a long while. "Can you not handle this yourself?"

Stefan bit his tongue. "You are a resourceful man. It is important he does not return to America after his search ends."

"I see." Rafiq's voice lightened. "This is personal for you." Stefan's silence confirmed it. "Then I will do it," Rafiq said. "For a fellow believer. The apostate will meet his end. *Inshallah*."

"*Inshallah*," Stefan said. If Allah wills it.

"When will you pay me?"

"As soon as you have the prize," Stefan said. "I trust that is not a problem?"

Stefan was counting on Rafiq's ambition here. Even a self-righteous killer needed money. For what Stefan offered, Rafiq would fall in line.

"It is not," Rafiq said. "Do not try to cross me, Stefan Rudovic. If you do, it will be the end of you and your family."

I have no family, you fool. "Have faith, brother. This will be a great victory for us all. Here is what you need to find Harry Fox—"

"I already have what I need," Rafiq said quickly. "Go in peace, brother. I will contact you in one week. By then, it will be done."

The line went dead. Stefan leaned back into the unforgiving pillow on his bed, the ache in his ankle easing for the first time all day. Harry Fox had bested him for the last time.

Chapter 19

Athens

Sunlight pierced his eyes with razor sharpness. Harry threw an arm up to cover them, rolling to one side and pulling the covers over his head to get away from the horrid light slipping through a crack in the hotel window curtains. The warm embrace of sleep surrounded him, a cottony gauze wrapping each thought and pulling him back into unconsciousness.

His eyes flew open. *Sunlight.* He shot out of bed, tripped on the covers and tumbled down, bouncing off the hotel room's desk as he fell to land back on the bed, where he'd started. Adrenaline was better than ice water at getting him awake. He looked toward the windows at a line of sunlight falling between the two thick curtains. The sun was up.

He cursed loudly. The last thing he remembered was sitting on the hotel bed, mind racing but body ready to collapse, swearing he only needed to close his eyes for a second. Now it was morning. He'd been asleep for hours.

"Where is it?" He twisted and turned, heart in his throat. *Stop.* Harry leaned over and looked under the bed. His bag was still there, where he'd left it last night. Only after checking that the door was securely bolted did he unzip the bag and remove the object he'd taken from inside Alexander's statue. A bronze box, tinged blue with age, with a carved raven on the top. The etching was intricate, with detailed wings so life-like it seemed the bird could take flight, though it was the eyes that arrested him. They were blue of the most brilliant color, for each had been dotted with a stunning sapphire.

The hinges squealed madly when he opened the lid of the box. Inside was a small stone tablet with Greek writing on it. Incongruous with the delicate blue-eyed bird, yet perhaps practicality that drove the *Koraki*. What better than stone to survive the elements for ages? He set the box aside and read the carved script once more, working feverishly to translate it using an app on his phone.

You have proven your worth, brave Grecian. The prize you seek was safely stored in Athens for centuries, though now our culture faces terrible danger across the sea to the Eastern capital. The king of Greeks and Romans must repel the conqueror's force. Once his mission ends, the path to our prize will be found in an altar atop the Pammakaristos.

His phone buzzed. He glanced at the screen and frowned. What did Nora want? Against his better judgment, he answered. "Yes?"

"Where are you?"

"Still in Athens."

"Where in Athens?"

"A hotel."

She sighed. "Which hotel, Harry? I need a name."

"You checking my expenses? What does it matter?"

"Because I'm in Athens. I landed thirty minutes ago."

He nearly dropped the tablet. "You're *here*?"

"Yes. Try to keep up. Now where are you?"

Any thoughts about the ancient Greek prize evaporated. "You were in New York last night. I talked to you."

"Now I'm in Athens. I took a red-eye. Tell me where your hotel is or I swear I'll hunt you down and make you regret it."

He glanced at the pad of hotel stationery and rattled off the name and address. "Why did you come here?"

"I'll tell you when I see you," she said. "Don't leave."

She hung up, accomplishing the impressive task of leaving him with more pressing questions than deciphering the stone tablet in his hand. Nora in Athens. That made no sense. Her father had forbidden her to come, and Nora was the last person he'd pick to make trouble for her father. Was she telling him the truth? His thoughts went whizzing down a half-dozen different routes as he tried to figure out why she'd come. None of them ended well for Harry. He should leave, get out of here and tell her to leave him alone to clean up the mess they'd dragged him in to.

Yet he didn't stand, didn't pack his bag. Why not? Because the idea of having her in Athens was, and he truly hated to admit it, slightly comforting.

He nearly smacked himself on the cheek. *Get with it, Harry.* All your life Fred showed you how to do it alone, how to succeed without anyone's help. Fred Fox had done it alone, and so had Harry, until Sara. Except in Britain. And Egypt. And then in Iraq, and then in Britain again. Couldn't forget that one.

The truth hit him in slow motion. Over this past year things had changed. Harry Fox might be the Morello family relic hunter, but he definitely wasn't a one-man operation any longer. He'd gone from working solo to liaising with the city authorities and consorting in several ways with a respected German Egyptologist. Heady company for a man who until last year hadn't trusted a person in the world not named Morello.

He would have laughed if he'd had the energy. What had Fred told him? Life changes when you're not looking. Enjoy the ride.

He touched the amulet around his neck. *I will, Dad.* And nothing would make him happier than figuring out what this tablet actually meant. Decipher that and he was one step closer to Egypt, to where he should have been all along. Working with Sara to unravel the only mystery that mattered. The stone tablet went back into his bag, which looped over a shoulder. It had been in darkness for nearly two thousand years. It could wait until he got a cup of coffee.

Minutes later he was back in the room, on his way to being properly caffeinated and studying the tablet now lying on a table. The Koraki had proven to be masters of writing between the lines. Words on the page were often a cover for other meaning. This message, though, seemed straightforward. Perhaps too much so.

"It's meant for the same person," he said to the room at large. "The *brave Grecian.*" The second time that phrase had appeared. The message's second sentence offered greater insight into the Korakis' motivations. The Greek prize remained in Athens for centuries after Alexander's death, which coincided with a time period when Greek culture experienced relative stability, the successors of ancient Greece and Alexander expanding their influence in terms of both culture and land acquisition across Europe, subsisting through the Dark Ages as well as could be expected. The Koraki meant to preserve the idea of Greece, their shining beacon of progress in stormy times.

An idea that had been under threat when they wrote this template. Where did the threat exist? Across the sea, in the Eastern capital. That part made sense. Go east from Athens and you quickly hit the Aegean Sea. Beyond that, an *Eastern capital* where the Greek culture faced a *terrible danger.* Harry didn't need a map to decipher this part.

Greece had been annexed by Rome two hundred years before the Common Era. The Romans knew a good thing when they saw it, so they let the Greeks continue on largely unimpeded, looking to Greek philosophy, culture and excellence in science with respect. Greek and Rome became intertwined, each culture assimilating aspects of the other over the centuries, likely much to the chagrin of the Koraki. Or at least that was what Harry would have suspected—until now.

The Roman empire expanded to such a great extent that in the third century it was necessary to have two separate but equal centers of power, one in the East and another in the West. This gave birth to the modern concepts of the Eastern and Western Roman Empires, though Romans at the time would have told you the sprawling empire was a single entity with two coequal leadership posts. The seat of Western power sat in Rome. The Eastern Roman Empire—also called the Byzantine Empire—had its capital city across the Aegean, in one of history's most storied cities. Constantinople.

"This is talking about Istanbul," Harry said. The great city named by Constantine the Great, a man with no shortage of hubris, was at one time the largest and wealthiest city in Europe, the most well-defended and revered collection of brick and mortar in the world. Of course, times change, and one city encapsulated that better than nearly any other. Istanbul.

Once the most important city in Europe and Asia, the city's fortunes had followed those of the region and Istanbul was now struggling to define itself in the battle being waged by numerous ideological factions, the strife and turmoil of which threatened to drag Istanbul into the past instead of propelling it through the future.

"Who's this king they're talking about?" *The king of Greeks and Romans.* The hotel walls did not offer guidance. Harry had loads of experience with ancient Rome, but once you got past the collapse of the Western Empire, his expertise dimmed. This was a good question for Sara. He felt a stab of something close to concern in his chest. He hadn't told her about what he'd found. She wasn't going to be happy. He checked his phone and realized she still hadn't called him. The concern amplified. Was she okay?

His phone buzzed. Nora. "Hello?"

"I'm here." Loud bangs came from his door. "Open up."

The Nora standing outside his door when he pulled it open did not look like a woman who'd just caught the red-eye from New York. She pushed past him without waiting for an invitation. "Close it," she called over her shoulder. "Tell me what you found."

"How do you know I found anything?" He was stunned, but not so much he was giving away information for free. He hadn't told her about the tablet yet.

She pointed to his hand. "If you want to keep a secret, don't walk around holding it."

He looked down to find the tablet clenched in one hand. He hadn't even realized he still had it. "Oh." That was all he could offer. "This."

"What is it?" Nora sat at the table he'd been using. She picked up his coffee cup, removed the lid and took a long drink. "That is *delicious*."

"They sell it across the street." He sat down across from her and set the tablet down on the table, face down. "Yes, I found something. No, I won't tell you about it until you start talking."

Her eyes were on the tablet as she waved a hand. "Talk about what?"

As though he were crazy for asking anything. "Why are you here?"

Nora looked at him for a long time before she answered. "Two reasons. One, you nearly got yourself killed."

"Which time?"

She lifted an eyebrow. "In that sewer."

Harry shrugged. "That was nothing. At least I had a sword that time. Last night was worse."

"When you found that." She pointed to the tablet. "What happened?"

"Evgeny Smolov's man happened—again. The same one as before, except this time he had an automatic. I had a stone trident."

The normally implacable Nora Doyle visibly started. "A *what?*"

"Trident. Three sharp points. Poseidon carries it around under the sea. That sort of trident. It's what I used last night to fend off the shooter." Harry glared at her. "Did I mention he had a gun?"

To her credit, she recovered quickly. "I'm glad you survived." He let the statement hang until curiosity got the better of her. "How did you do it?"

"The same way I've survived for this long. Being clever." He might as well be honest. "And a bit lucky. I think he broke an ankle when we were fighting. He didn't come after me."

"Did the police arrive? Gunfire wouldn't go unnoticed."

"They did. I think he limped away before they found him."

"So Smolov's man is out of the game," she said. "Bad break for him—no pun intended. A lucky one for you. But everyone's luck runs out eventually. That's why I'm here."

"You think I need your help? You're the one who blackmailed me into chasing this." He waved the tablet at her. "Don't act like you're doing me a favor now."

"We already covered this," she said. "Nobody's blameless here. We both got something we wanted, and it cost both of us."

"Lying didn't cost you anything."

"To Sara?" she fired back. "I lied to Sara and told her you were working for me when in fact you were stealing historical relics for a crime lord." Nora lifted her hands before he could argue. "I'm not here to judge you. It's in the past. You want to rehash it, do it on someone else's time. I'm not in the mood."

She had a point, loath as he was to admit it. Without Nora's help, the life Harry had today wouldn't exist. "Fine," he said. "What's the second reason?"

"I'm jealous."

"Of me?" What could possibly be attractive about running around Greece getting shot at?

"Of what you are doing," she said. "I spend most of my time behind a desk or on the phone. Field work is the exception. You, on the other hand, are always in the action."

"You may not feel that way after you get shot at."

"I may not." She leaned forward, reaching across the table for the tablet. She didn't actually touch it. "What I do know is seeing this makes it all worth it. You found the next step here in Athens. You're making history, Harry. That's what I'm jealous of."

She was right, of course. He tended to skip past the good parts when nearly getting killed was involved. "Fine. You want in on the action. Why now?"

"You sounded like you could use the help. And I can also tell how much it means to you that this ends quickly." She tapped a finger on the table. "I don't know what Sara is searching for. I do know it means a lot to you as well. The sooner I help you finish the chase, the faster you can get on with what clearly matters most to you."

He appreciated the sentiment. Funny how she skipped past the fact *she* was the reason Harry was in Greece rather than in Egypt. "You want to help me? Fine." He paused. "You weren't bad in Iran."

A hint of a grin crossed her face. "That was a good time."

Harry, Sara and Nora had ended up jumping off the side of a mountain to stay alive during that adventure. He laughed. "It was."

"There's another matter," Nora said. "My father has no idea I'm here. I only told him I was going out of town for a few days. I didn't say where."

"He won't be happy."

"No, which is why he won't find out." Nora took another drink of Harry's coffee. "This is my operation, so I'm doing what has to be done."

"I've done fine so far on my own," he pointed out.

"This isn't about a lack of faith in you," she said. "I would never have hired you if I didn't think you were capable. It's about owning the operation. I put your neck out there. I made this happen. I need you to believe I'm behind this all the way, to see I'm fully committed to you succeeding. I'm here to prove I have your back."

It was, hands down, the nicest thing she had ever said to him. "That's pretty awesome of you," he said. "Thanks."

Nora looked past Harry, toward the crack in the curtains through which daylight fell. "It's not only you," she said. "There's also a family dynamic at play here. If you couldn't tell, my father is a high achiever. He puts his mind to a task or goal and makes it happen, no matter what."

"You don't get to his place in the world by letting life push you around."

"Because my father runs the team, not everyone thinks I made it to my role on merit alone." Her mouth tightened. "I've worked twice as hard to get half as far as everyone else in the department." She aimed a finger at him as though it were loaded. "That is not a complaint."

He lifted a hand. "Got it."

"People think my father gave me this job." She laughed without humor. "Nothing could be further from the truth. I started as an intern and worked my way up. My work has produced the most convictions and recovered the largest number of cultural artifacts by both dollar and number. I deserve this job."

"I think you're an excellent agent," Harry said. "But it sounds like some people don't think so. You know what I say?" She looked up, actual interest in her eyes. "The hell with them. They're probably jealous. Just keep getting results."

"Thank you. You're correct; there are people in my department who don't agree. Those conviction and recovery rates I mentioned? Mine are twice what the next closest agent has. *Two times* as many."

"Let me guess who's saying favoritism played a role. Those guys."

"Correct." She reached for his coffee again and found it empty. "It's not only my last name. My mother is involved."

The mother Nora had mentioned in passing. "I thought she didn't work for the department?"

"She doesn't, unless you count her being my father's boss in every way. He worships her. Which means that when my mother tells him to make sure I'm never in any danger, he listens. I have to battle her as much as the resentment for being my father's daughter."

"You said your mother had a troubled past."

"As far as I know." Nora kept her eyes on the window, looking somewhere far beyond this room. "She never talks about it, not even to my father."

"Did she get into trouble?"

"No. Her secret is dark. Traumatic. She is one of the most intelligent women I know, yet this hounds her every day. Whatever it is makes her overly protective of me. Which I know sounds quite normal, but this is different. The thought of anything happening to me is a nightmare for her."

Harry refused to acknowledge the weight in his chest, keeping his eyes on the table. This gaping wound was more than he could handle right now. "Sounds complicated."

"It is." Nora snapped back to the hotel room. "Forgive me. This is clearly a hard subject for you." Harry waved a hand to show it was no big deal. Nora wasn't deterred. "I mean that. I'm sorry."

"Forget about it."

"I spoke with Detective Barnes."

The detective who'd investigated his mother's death. "What did she say?"

"Not much," Nora said. "I got the impression she didn't want to say much of anything. But don't worry. When I explained who was asking, she agreed to speak with you after you get back."

Harry had a million questions. Nora wouldn't have any answers. "Thank you."

"We're a team, remember?"

Nora had proven it. "We are. Now, do you want to see the tablet?"

"Sure." He flipped it over so she could read the script. Or at least see it. "What language is it?"

"Greek."

"Can you read it?"

"Pretty well." He translated for her, then read it again. "Any thoughts?"

"I think I'm grateful you're here." Was that a hint of new respect in her voice? Hard to say. "What does it mean?"

He ran through his theory of how it referenced Constantinople, a city across the Aegean Sea from Greece. "I have a guess who *the king of Greeks and Romans* is. The way he's described and the fact they reference the *Eastern* capital tell me this man led the Eastern Roman Empire long after the Western Empire fell in the fifth century. The Eastern Empire, or Byzantine Empire, lasted much longer. It didn't fall until the mid-fifteenth century when the Ottoman Army captured the capital city. The Ottomans were led by a sultan named Mehmed II." He pointed to one word on the tablet. "Also known as Mehmed the Conqueror."

"*The conqueror's force,*" Nora said. "It makes sense." She was swept up in it, leaning over the table, her almond eyes coming alive. Exuberant.

"What is this about a *grave?*"

"Plan B," Harry said. "I think they're telling whoever follows this that if the Byzantines fell, the next marker would be in *an altar atop the Pammakaristos.*"

"Which is?"

Harry shrugged. "No idea. That's what I was working on when you barged in."

"How do we know where to look?"

"Pammakaristos means superior, or almighty. It's a religious reference."

"We need to find a church," Nora said. "That isn't helpful without a location." She snapped her fingers. "Who is the Greek leader in this scenario? First was Leonidas. Then Alexander. Now who?"

"Constantine the Eleventh. The last Byzantine emperor."

"I assume it did not end well for him."

"He died fighting the sultan's troops at Constantinople. The last vestiges of the Roman empire died with him."

"Perhaps the Greek prize from Achilles is not as powerful as they thought."

"I'll tell you when we find it."

"Do you think we will find the next marker in Constantinople?"

Harry said he did. "We'll start with churches. I haven't had a chance to dig into that part yet."

A mutual silence fell over them. Nora studied the tablet, seemingly intent on divining its secrets despite being unable to read it. Harry's elbows found the table; he rested his chin in his hands and watched her until she looked up. "What will your father do if he finds out you're here?"

"I have no idea. There's an excellent chance I'll be reprimanded. Perhaps worse."

"You're risking a lot to come here. Why?"

Her eyes narrowed. "To help you. I had a long time to think about what you said, how this assignment conflicts with something quite personal to you. It's an assignment we forced on you, though when you report to a superior, that's how it happens. I realized that if we're ever going to be an effective team you need to trust me. The fastest way to make that happen was to show you I'm serious about our partnership. Flying here to help seemed to be a good way of doing that."

She couldn't have known that was the question that had been circling in his head these past few minutes. Why? Nora had everything, yet here she was, putting her career in jeopardy. For him. Of course, if this panned out and they recovered the relic or artifact, then it looked good for her. Success made people forgive a lot. It's possible Gary Doyle might never find out she'd come. Personally, Harry doubted that, and Nora likely did too. Gary was sharp, and when he learned his daughter had disobeyed him, Nora would pay. Despite that, here she was.

The last bit of reticence in him gave way. "I need to tell you something. About the man who tried to kill me twice."

Her lips pursed. "Go on."

"His name is Stefan Rudovic."

Recognition dawned on her face. "He works for Altin Cana. And now he's working for Smolov?"

Harry had suspected she'd know Stefan's name. "Stefan is an occasional artifacts trafficker, full-time pain in my ass. He picked up Smolov's contract to find this artifact. He made it to the cave in Sparta before I did, then we crossed paths in Pella."

"How did he find you here?"

"He's not stupid. Stefan ended up with the sword after I got away. I was able to decipher the message from a picture I took of it before he showed up. I suspect he did the same and waited for me here. Stefan would rather let someone else do the hard work, then snatch what he wants when it's easier."

"He's after a relic for Evgeny Smolov, not fulfilling a hit on you. Why try to kill you?"

Harry didn't need to think about that. "I work for the Morello family. Altin Cana has been pushing on the Morello turf since Vincent died." Harry's brow furrowed. "I know they had a role in it; I just don't have proof. If one of Altin's men can beat one of Joey's at his own game, it makes Joey look bad. Almost as bad as he would if Stefan Rudovic killed me."

"Nobody supports a gangster who can't protect his people," Nora said. "Joey Morello won't ever replace his father if that happens."

"Perceptive," Harry said. "Though I prefer the term *leader* over gangster."

"Fine. Leader."

"You still want to help me now that you know everything?"

"You're not only part of the Morello crew. You're part of mine." Nora pointed at herself. "This Rudovic character has one more enemy than he realizes. Me."

For the first time since Nora Doyle had tried to recruit him into her service last year, a feeling of solidarity swelled in Harry's chest. Not much, and not too warm—he'd seen too much of life to make that mistake. But this was as real as he'd let it be. Nora was on his side. For now.

"Glad to hear it." He grabbed his phone. "I need to call Sara and give her an update."

"And get one from her."

Harry lifted a shoulder as though the thought hadn't occurred to him. He dialed her new number, pressed the phone to his ear, then frowned when it went straight to voicemail. "She must be busy," he said. "I'll try her again after we check in."

"Check in?"

"At the airport." He stood and grabbed his already-packed bag. "We're going to Istanbul."

Chapter 20

Luxor

Sara was weightless, hanging in a void between life and death. Absolute blackness surrounded her, penned her in like a physical weight she could hardly bear, so heavy and complete it was hard to breathe, impossible to move. She drifted in the void as though the universe had ceased to exist.

She tried to look around. Pain erupted as she smacked the back of her head against something solid. She cursed and it all came back to her. The hidden staircase. A moon and a sun. The world collapsing around her. Her last thoughts had been jumbled by a bronze fist smacking her in the head. After that it all faded.

Her body was stuck, her shirt somehow pinned in place so she couldn't move. She closed her eyes, took a deep breath. Panicking solved nothing. *Think.*

She opened her eyes and immediately things improved. A light appeared at the edge of her vision. Small, oblong, it gleamed in the darkness beneath her. *My flashlight.* She'd dropped it when the walls opened and spears flew out. She was still here, suspended above the floor and unable to move much. Not completely stuck, though. It was her shirt holding her up, the weight of her body making it tough to move. It was like a clothes hanger had been run through the shoulders of her shirt and someone had strung her out to dry. Her eyes slowly adjusted to the darkness and she carefully turned her head.

A wooden pole ran partway across her shoulders. Another kept her legs up, tangling them together so she couldn't move and keeping her suspended in the air. Sara twisted. She turned. Then she flailed like crazy until fabric tore and gravity took hold, pulling her down. She bounced off wooden poles like a Plinko chip until she crashed face-first onto the stone floor. The flashlight was off to her side. A stripe of darkness bisected the faint illumination, arrow-straight. She kept still and took inventory.

Her fingers and toes didn't hurt when she wiggled them. Both legs moved, though one shin barked in pain from an unknown injury. The rest of her torso seemed intact. She stood, hit the top of her head on something immobile and shouted Egyptian obscenities loud enough to wake Ra himself. What was above her? She reached up and touched an oblong piece of wood. Smooth, carved, straight as an arrow. This had to be what came out of the wall and smacked her jaw. She moved toward the fallen light and found another wooden pole in her way, which she had to clamber over before finally grabbing hold of the flashlight. Sara lay down on her back, aimed the light up, and gasped.

Six wooden spears had shot out of each side wall. Metal points glinted at the end of each one. Bronze, hammered to spear tips and deadly sharp. One of them had grazed her when she sprang the trap, likely via a pressure mechanism activated when she crossed the threshold into this room. A room with a sun on the archway fronting it. The central feature of Egyptian religion, inspiration for their foremost god and one of the main reasons, along with the river Nile, that life existed in this area. Yet this sun had nearly killed her.

She must have missed something. The room with a moon above the door had seemed a clear one to avoid, as the moon had little importance for the Egyptian religion. The Egyptian and Greek faiths, the two halves of Cleopatra. Factor in Mark Antony's Roman heritage and his worship of Sol, the Roman sun deity, and the sun room trying to kill her made no sense—it should have been safe in here. Yet here she was, having just missed being skewered by sheer luck. Her assessment had been wrong and it had nearly killed her. She had to figure out what had gone wrong, because next time a spear could end up running through her chest instead of her shirt.

It wasn't the first time she'd been wrong with a historical assessment, so she did what usually worked to find the error and started at the beginning. *The sah of Khons holds the path.* Sah meant mummy, Khons was a male name, and the path led to Antony and Cleopatra's next marker. Simple, yet deceptively so, for she had chosen the wrong celestial body. Why was the room with a moon carved on the archway the correct answer, and not the room with a sun?

Think it through, consider the angles. She closed her eyes and a new option jumped to mind. *Khons.*

It wasn't merely a common male name. It was the alternate spelling for an Egyptian god. *Khonsu,* the moon god. She'd missed it. *That's what you get for hurrying.*

The message wasn't telling her to find a man named *Khons.* She had to find a mummy somehow related to the moon, to *Khonsu,* the Egyptian god. What better place than in a chamber marked by a moon?

It was the work of several minutes to extricate herself from the spear-filled room. Sara slipped over and slithered under the room-length spears, which had shot out of a wall on either side and smashed into their opposite walls. She could have been a piece of Swiss cheese right now. Perhaps *Khons* was watching over her, ready to share his secrets with a fellow Egyptian, one he deemed worthy. She smirked. *You're just damn lucky is all. Don't push it.*

The passageway between rooms echoed with her footsteps. Bright light parted the darkness, bringing the carved moon to life as she stood beneath it. This decoration was identical in every way to the one that had nearly killed her, except it featured a moon instead of the sun. She got to one knee and checked the stone floor ahead. No obvious cuts or marks to show the floor had any traps waiting, though she'd thought the sun room had been safe and look how that worked out.

Crawling ahead, she reached into the room, ready to pull back if danger lurked. Her hand did not trip any ancient wires. She touched the stone floor right where her foot would hit if she walked in. Still nothing. A moment's pause, then she banged the floor, hit it hard, as though she'd crossed the threshold. No spears. A long minute spent thinking of other ways to test for traps yielded nothing.

"Time to move." Her words bounced off the stone walls, surprisingly comforting in this potential tomb. Up she stood, teeth gritted, and stomped into the room as though it owed her money.

She did not die. So aggressive was her approach that she nearly collided with the pedestal in the room's center. Stone walls surrounded her, constructed of carved stone blocks, smooth and bare and fitted so tightly together she couldn't squeeze a finger between them. All this she checked twice before looking to the pedestal in front of her. A circular stone column rose from a square plinth four feet on each side. The flat stone on top was bare. No relics on display, nothing left behind by Antony or Cleopatra. At least, no physical objects.

Sara drew in a sharp breath when she stood next to the pedestal. *Another moon.* The pedestal may have been empty, but a scene was carved into the top of it. A moon identical to what was on the archway. Ten Roman numerals ran in a circle around the top of the pedestal, the numbers one through ten. The moon was inside this circle, directly beneath the *I*. A single line of Egyptian glyphs ran beneath the circle of numbers, at the very bottom of the flat stone.

The one true Queen will protect you. All others offer doom.

Sara read the glyphs out loud. What did that mean? The one true queen had to be Cleopatra. Who were these *all others*? What other queens could be involved, and why did they bring doom?

She reached out and touched the carvings. Her nail caught as she ran it over the flat surface. Leaning over, she brushed away the dust that had settled into the razor-thin line running beneath the numbers and above the moon. *This top is made of two pieces.* Once the dust came out it was clear. The flat top was not a single stone, but two pieces fitted together, like a watch face.

She stepped back. A watch turned. Is that what this was, a puzzle?

The moon wasn't merely a carved outline, but a chunk of stone that had been cut out. Almost as though it was meant to be used as a handhold. A place to grip if you wanted to turn the smaller interior circle and move the moon to another number. She grabbed it and twisted slightly. The stone moved.

This is a puzzle. Another layer of security to test whether whoever followed this path was worthy. In that case, the question was what did Antony and Cleopatra demand their chosen follower know? The one true queen must be Cleopatra, yet that wasn't the answer. It had something to do with numbers that only one worthy of this path would know. What about Cleopatra was tied to numbers and would be known only by someone faithful to her cause?

Sara closed her eyes. For some reason an image of an old textbook sprang to mind, one she'd used when she studied Cleopatra's dynasty as an undergraduate. The page she recalled showed Cleopatra's lineage, a family tree of the Ptolemaic dynasty stretching from Alexander the Great's time until Cleopatra's death after her forces were defeated by Emperor Octavian. Cleopatra was not the first queen to bear that name. Far from it. Six others in her dynasty had had the name before her, including her mother.

Cleopatra's full name was Cleopatra VII Philopater. The *seventh*. One of the numerals on this stone was seven. She was the seventh of her name, a fact that an educated Greek following her trail should know. Could that be the answer?

Her near-death experience in the chamber's other room flashed back. Sara stepped back from the pedestal and checked the walls again. She hadn't seen the hidden spears in the other room. They had been concealed behind perfectly carved circles in the walls, and she could see the same type of etched lines in this room as well. This puzzle was more than a test. It was a death trap for any other than the worthiest.

A year ago Sara would never have considered moving this moon. Egyptologists worked at safe digs and in the classroom. They didn't put their lives at risk in the field. At least she thought they didn't. The Sara

Hamed standing in this chamber was nothing like that woman from a year ago, a time before Harry Fox had opened her eyes to another world, one that frightened her beyond measure yet drew her further in every day. A world she was now part of. Sara believed in herself and she'd do whatever it took to help Harry uncover the truth behind his father's amulet.

She marched back to the pedestal, grabbed the moon, and twisted. The carving slid around silently until it stopped on *VII*. She waited, teeth clenched and muscles tense. Nothing happened.

Then the central circle she had twisted receded into the pedestal, dropping down to the sound of ancient gears grinding, weights shifting behind the stone walls that, this time, did not fire spears to cut her in half. The circle stopped falling and the floor began to rumble. She stepped back as the wall in front of her moved. A section fell open to reveal a hidden doorway. The rumbling stopped. Sara peered into the darkness of this new door, aiming her light inside. She was looking into an antechamber.

Rows of scrolls on an ancient bookcase lined its rear wall. She counted twenty-four in total, five to a row except for the top shelf, which held four. The scrolls stood vertically, each of them held up by a circular holder bolted to the wall. Interesting. She'd never seen a storage setup like this in all her years in academia. That thought set off an alarm bell in her head as she reached for the nearest scroll, ready to pull it off the shelf to reveal the contents. Her hand paused inches away, then she pulled it back.

Letters had been carved above each scroll. Greek letters. The Greek alphabet, twenty-four letters. Her flashlight played over the bookcase as she took a step back. Another row of letters had been carved above the bookshelf. Latin letters, which together made two words. *Rex Meus.*

"My king," Sara said without thinking. In Latin, no less. Why have a Latin phrase running across the top of a bookshelf with decidedly Egyptian scrolls marked by Greek letters? Only one answer made sense. This was a true test of the *learned Greek* meant to follow this trail. Only by having a foothold in all three cultures could you unravel the truth behind this bookcase. She frowned. Whatever that was.

The other walls around her were bare. The bookcase was all this room offered. Why the Greek letters? They tied in some way to the phrase on the top. *My King.*

Who was *My King?* Marcus Antonius, of course. She reached for the scroll beneath the Greek letter for *M.* Her fingers collided with something solid. She tried again, not accepting what her senses told her. The scroll wasn't made of papyrus. It was *metal.* Intricately carved, incredibly thin, but the tiny imperfections rippling under her fingertips weren't the fibers of a papyrus plant but rather etchings on the metal. These were sculptures, not scrolls, each one attached to the holder because they were all one piece. Her fingers closed around the scroll, and then she realized.

These were levers. A way to answer the question posed above them. She took hold of the *M* scroll and pulled on it.

It didn't move. She tried again, still nothing. *I'm wrong?* The thought was so foreign to her she almost laughed. Of course she could be wrong. She grabbed the scroll with both hands and leaned back, putting all her weight into it, but was still unable to budge it. What about twisting it like a doorhandle? No luck. Pulling didn't work; twisting didn't, either. Only one other option. She pushed on the scroll with all her weight.

Metal shrieked on stone as the scroll's holder receded into the wall. A dull *thunk* came from behind the wall. Success. These scrolls *were* levers, meant to be pushed in a certain sequence to solve this riddle. A sequence she knew.

The *A* scroll shouted in protest when she jammed it into the wall. A deadly trap might be waiting for any missteps, but she was in her element now, matching wits with a long-dead queen and being found worthy. The scrolls marked as *R, C* and *U* all followed suit, all bringing ominous noises from behind the wall. She didn't hesitate in front of the *S* scroll, the final one, leaning on it and hanging on tight. It gave way as a thunderous *boom* sounded, like massive tumblers on an oversized combination lock falling into place. The wall in front of her shuddered and her teeth vibrated as she held onto the scroll. Sara leapt back to avoid being smacked aside as the bookcase swung out from the wall like a door opening.

A black hole waited behind the bookcase. Sara took a step forward. Sparks flashed in the darkness. She leapt to one side, out of the line of fire of whatever horrid trap was waiting to send her to meet Osiris in the underworld. Her back pressed to the side wall as the flashing stopped, replaced by the flickering light of torches. Their warm, soft glow played at the edges of her flashlight beam, which she flicked off to reveal what shouldn't be. Actual torchlight coming from a room that hadn't been opened for two thousand years.

Sara kept her light off as she turned back and peered around the corner where the bookcase had stood just moments ago before it pivoted out. An elaborate series of weights and counterweights were behind it, and these had shifted when she pushed the scrolls to spell *Marcus*. The noises she'd heard were blocks dropping into holes cut into the door's rear. If she had pushed any out of order, the blocks would have traveled down the wrong path and become lodged, blocking any other seekers from getting through. Enter one letter incorrectly and the doorway became locked forever.

Ingenious. She marveled at the intricate security measure for all of two seconds before turning back to the previously hidden room.

Torches lining the walls burst to life inside the newly-revealed chamber, some sort of ancient ignition device setting them aflame. A single pedestal stood in the center of the room. A circular object rested on top. Sara tilted her head. *A shield.* And not just any shield. It was made of gold, and there was writing on it.

The knowledge of our founder will protect the dynasty. Honor him by seeking knowledge at his feet in the Great Caesareum. CSIIAH

The Great Caesareum was an ancient temple from Cleopatra's time in the city of Alexandria. Whatever Cleopatra wished her learned Greek audience to find could be found there. Which was the problem.

Rising sea levels had claimed the building. The ruins of it were now underwater in Alexandria's port. This didn't look good.

She shook her head. *Stop it.* Don't assume. Investigate, then decide based on the facts. So what if the building was nothing but a memory? That didn't mean she was out of luck.

The *founder* could only be Pharaoh Ptolemy Soter, first pharaoh of the Ptolemaic dynasty. Sara had to honor Ptolemy by seeking knowledge at his feet in a building that no longer existed. The line couldn't be literal, as Ptolemy had died hundreds of years before this was written, and while his tomb had never been located, he had almost certainly been buried in the royal necropolis in Alexandria. He had definitely not been buried in the Great Caesareum. Given that, the only way to seek knowledge *at his feet* in that building was if a depiction of Ptolemy existed.

The torchlight glowing in this room suddenly felt a bit warmer, for now it all made sense. The Great Caesareum had vanished. That didn't mean what it contained was gone too. She knew this because last year she had been part of a select group of Egyptologists invited to tour the nation's newest museum, the flagship institution meant to showcase the best of Egypt's unrivaled cultural heritage and redefine what it meant to walk through history. The Grand Egyptian Museum, situated just outside of Cairo and set to open next month. One of the artifacts she'd seen among the thousands on display? A statue of Ptolemy Soter originally found in the Great Caesareum.

And where does one *seek knowledge*? Usually, one looked in a book. This statue of Ptolemy stood out in Sara's mind because the pharaoh had been doing something rather odd for a man who had ordained himself a walking god. He'd been reading a book, or scroll. That's what Cleopatra wanted her *learned Greek* to do. Read the scroll in Ptolemy's hands.

Sara glanced at her watch. She'd been down here a long time. Far too long. Omar had no idea whether she was still alive or not. Sara turned back and headed for the exit to bring him up to speed, then connect with Harry. Whatever he was doing to chase Evgeny Smolov's relic would have to wait. The truth behind his father's amulet was closer than ever.

Only one question ran through her head as she hustled back to the surface. What did *CSILAH* mean?

Chapter 21

Beirut

Tendrils of smoke curled around the ceiling, the still air of Beirut doing little to move it on this oven-like summer day despite the open windows. Rafiq Pasha stared at one of the cell phones on the table in front of him, waiting for it to ring. He didn't move except to lift his cigarette, didn't blink when the thick white smoke streamed from his nose like dragon's breath and then filled his eyes as it twisted skyward. Rafiq was the worst kind of man you could have for an enemy. A patient one.

His network stretched across the globe. Brothers in arms in the crusade to preserve their culture, dedicated to stopping the degenerate Westerners from spreading their immoral lifestyle and corrupting those who sought to live as Allah had decreed. These brothers thought Rafiq to be one of them, motivated by the same passionate hatred of everything that did not align with their beliefs. They wanted to cleanse the world of nonbelievers, one bullet or bomb at a time.

Rafiq's motivation was far simpler. He wanted revenge for the deaths of his two brothers, incinerated when an American missile had crashed through the roof of their house in Afghanistan years ago. Revenge for the father he barely remembered, killed by Afghan mujahideen insurgents in his native land during the Soviet–Afghan War.

The tip of his cigarette glowed bright orange. Rafiq's family had lived in a village in the vast and often desolate Afghan countryside. A simple existence, one without modern comforts or perils. His earliest memories were of retrieving water from the village well with his mother, of collecting chicken eggs and herding goats. And of sitting at his father's side, listening to the strongest and most intelligent man in the world read from the dozens of books he owned. Rafiq's father had been the village's only teacher, and Rafiq recalled sitting at his father's side as he told fantastic stories of faraway lands or revealed the mysteries of how numbers could be used to unlock the universe's secrets. Rafiq had learned that mathematics and a good narrative could change the world.

That had all changed when war erupted. One day, mujahideen had arrived without warning, searching for supposed Soviet sympathizers. Rafiq had no idea whether any had existed in his village. He had no idea what mujahideen were until much later. All he knew was that the armed militants had appeared at one edge of the village minutes before a small company of Soviet and Afghan government troops came from the other.

The battle that ensued had lasted only minutes. The mujahideen had been overrun, driven from the village in a rout. However, those minutes had changed Rafiq's life forever. He and the other village children had been in their schoolhouse, listening to his father, the school's sole instructor, lecture on mathematics. When the troops arrived, the instructor had herded his charges into the one-room school's underground storage area. He told them to stay put, promising to return once it was safe. Then he left.

The students all obeyed, save one. Rafiq snuck out when the shooting started. He was afraid, yes, but his concern for the man who had shown him the world was greater. From his vantage point, he saw their teacher standing in front of the school's door, barring anyone from coming inside. His back had been to Rafiq when a mujahid's bullets tore through his chest. Rafiq saw him fall, heard the mujahid curse in his native Farsi as he ran back to his companions and they raced through the village. He didn't see anything else until the battle was over. He couldn't, not through the tears in his eyes as he lay beside his murdered father in the entrance to the school where he taught.

One of the cell phones buzzed. Rafiq blinked away the memory. He smashed out his cigarette in an ashtray, snatched the phone, connected the call and listened. "*Takraran*," he said. *Again.* The caller repeated the information and Rafiq hung up. He picked up another phone from the table and punched in a number. "I have it," he said when a man answered. "Come now."

Rafiq lit another cigarette and looked out the dusty window of his second-floor apartment. He did not live here. If anyone was inclined to check, they would be unable to prove Rafiq Pasha had any connection to this address. His ownership was buried under a web of false identities and anonymous companies, along with a healthy dose of bribery for good measure. This rundown apartment in a fading section of Beirut was Rafiq's operations center.

Minutes later a pair of men stood outside the door. He watched them through a camera mounted across the hall, then checked their faces up close through the doorbell camera. He knew them, had run operations good and bad with them over the years, but he still checked every time. He'd live longer that way.

He pressed a button on his phone and the door buzzed open. Omid came through first, Noor second. They joined Rafiq around the table. He waited until both had lit cigarettes before speaking.

"I have his location."

They all came from the same region in Afghanistan. There used to be many more of them. Now it was down to three.

"When do we go?" Omid asked.

"Tonight."

"Where?"

"Istanbul," Rafiq said. "Harry Fox is on a flight there now. I have a man waiting at the airport to watch him when he lands."

Noor pulled the cigarette from his mouth and blew smoke toward the ceiling. The hand holding it had three fingers. "Are we to kill him there?"

Rafiq had told Omid and Noor only that he had a job lined up, one that carried little risk. Rafiq was the operational mastermind, the one who called the shots in their organization, and the other two didn't mind that one bit. Rafiq was smarter than them. Listen to him and they'd live longer.

"Not there. Only after we acquire the artifact."

"What is it?"

"I am not certain," Rafiq said. "It is a Greek artifact. Perhaps a weapon."

"How do we know when he has it?" Noor asked.

"We listen before we move in," Rafiq said. "That is why all of us must go." If it had been a simple hit, Rafiq would have sent Omid. He was the most aggressive, the quickest to a fight. Noor, on the other hand, was patient. The sort of man who built bombs to kill his enemies. Also the sort of man who could mis-wire a bomb and lose two fingers because of it.

"The artifact must be valuable," Noor said. "More than any we have dealt with before."

Rafiq's team had trafficked their share of antiquities over the years to fund operations. "Yes," Rafiq said. "This is not a jug pulled from a cave. It is much more."

"Does this Fox man have friends?" Omid asked.

"Yes," Rafiq said. "He is with the Morello family in New York."

Both Noor and Omid paused. "Vincent Morello," Noor finally said. "He was a big man. Is this wise?"

"Vincent Morello is dead," Rafiq said. "And he is not the only man in New York." No need to get into the details with these two on who had hired them. Altin Cana's war with the Morello heir was none of their business. All Rafiq cared about was the money. "The Morello reach does not extend to Beirut," he said. "We are fine."

Noor and Omid smoked. They asked no more questions.

"Pack lightly," Rafiq said. "Our contacts in Istanbul will supply what we need."

All three of them crushed out their cigarettes in the ashtray. Noor and Omid stood and watched Rafiq expectantly.

"Be back here within the hour," Rafiq said.

Chapter 22

Istanbul

It took nearly two hours for Harry and Nora to clear customs after landing in Istanbul. Once they were admitted into the country, Harry went to get a rental car while Nora stood in a corner making calls. Having seen how glacially the Greeks moved, he told her to settle in for a long wait. To his surprise the rental car agency moved at light speed, getting him a car and sending him back out the door in under ten minutes. It was, mildly put, miraculous. He walked out into the terminal and spotted Nora standing down the hallway with a phone pressed to her ear. Her back was toward him as he approached.

"Hold on," Nora said into the phone. "I have to put you on speaker."

Gary Doyle's voice filled the air. "Did you speak with Harry Fox?"

"Yes," Nora said. "He's making progress."

"Tell him to move faster," Gary said. "I'm under a lot of pressure."

"I know," Nora said. "He's moving as quickly as he can. It's a dangerous assignment."

"Keep working him," Gary said. "He's an asset. Assets are expendable."

Harry stood frozen in place, five feet behind Nora. She did not turn around as she spoke.

"I understand," she said. "He is a good man. We need him."

"There are plenty of treasure hunters in the world," Gary said.

"I've been doing this long enough to know," Nora said. "There's only one Harry Fox."

"If he's so good at what he does, he needs to prove it. I can't risk you having to get involved if he fails. There's only one of you, Nora."

"Is this my mother or my father?"

"It's both of us," Gary said. "Remember, keep on Harry Fox. If you decide he's not cut out for this, get rid of him. We'll find someone else." Nora didn't respond. An announcement sounded over the airport loudspeakers behind them. "Where are you?" Gary asked Nora. "It sounds like an airport."

"Headed into the subway," she said quickly. "I'll be in touch."

Nora clicked off, shoved her personal phone in her pocket, and turned around. She spotted Harry and one hand went to her chest. "Harry."

It took him a second to find his voice. "An asset." He stood in place, unblinking. Why was he so surprised? "That's all I am. An *expendable* asset." He touched the amulet hidden beneath his shirt without realizing it. An amulet Nora had never seen. One he certainly wouldn't tell her about now. "Does he know what I stopped doing to come here?"

"No," Nora said matter-of-factly. "You won't tell me. What is it?"

He sputtered for a second. "None of your business," he finally said. "But it was far more important than this. I'm a pawn to you guys. Disposable. Replaceable. What was all that nonsense about actually needing me? You could get any chump to do this." He glared at her. "That's all I am. A chump you railroaded into doing this."

"Harry, we have a partnership now."

"Don't lie. I heard what Gary said."

"Don't hold my father's methods against me. He's doing what he must to protect the world's cultural heritage, the same as me. The same as us. None of us are perfect."

Harry didn't respond. The righteous wave of anger that consumed him at what Gary had said began to recede a tad. Nora wasn't right, not by a long shot. But this was business. Fred Fox had told him time and again to keep the personal separate from the business. This business required a clear head to stay alive. The kind of head you didn't have when it was personal.

"You're not giving me a fair shake." Nora tapped her chest. "Am I Gary Doyle?"

Harry shook his head. "No."

"He's my father and my boss, but he's not me. Do you consider me short-sighted or unintelligent?"

"Not usually."

"Very funny. I'm neither, yet I'm sticking my neck out for you. Maybe I shouldn't put my entire career at risk to fly over here and help a supposedly expendable asset instead of letting him take his own chances. The thing is, I don't consider you expendable." Now she stepped closer and touched his chest. She missed the amulet by inches. "You're part of the team. My team. We look out for each other. We don't hang each other out to dry."

A past shouting match with Nora about this very subject came to mind. "Not anymore," he said.

She pursed her lips. "Fair enough. Not anymore. We stick together. You are part of the team and I believe in you. I know you can find this artifact first. I'm here because it's getting dangerous and I can't let anything bad happen to you."

What she said made sense, but it by no means convinced him. Only one thing would do that. Had done it. The fact she was saying this in person. Plus, he knew a little bit about having to work in your father's shadow. It wasn't easy. "Okay."

She leaned back as though a strong wind had hit her. "What?"

"Okay. I believe you." Harry waved a hand to encompass their surroundings. "When people show me who they are, I believe them. You came here without permission to help me. You showed me who you are, and I believe you."

"Oh." She bit the inside of her lip. "Good."

"Some of what your father said had to be related to what your mother thinks," Harry said. "How she's worried about you all the time."

"Without a doubt." Nora picked up her small bag. "Let's go."

The center of Istanbul was thirty miles from the airport. Nora drove while Harry finished his research on their destination. Nora drove with the comfortable rhythm of a native New Yorker, which is to say she kept the pedal on the floor and blasted her horn at anyone who didn't follow suit. This far from home, anything familiar brought him comfort. Including having a madwoman at the wheel. Every taxi driver in the city would be proud.

"It all checks out," he said. "I think we're in the right place."

She started to ask a question when his phone buzzed. "It's Joey," he said. "I gotta take this." He connected the call. "Hello?"

"Where are you?" Joey asked. "I can't keep track."

"Driving into Istanbul, Turkey."

"What time is it there?"

"Afternoon."

"You okay?" Harry said he was. "Good."

The way Joey said it meant anything but. "What's wrong?" Harry asked.

Joey let out a long breath. "That Albanian chump is pushing onto our turf again. Someone hit two of our houses this week." The Morellos maintained private houses of chance where those averse to taxation and the rule of law in general paid for the privilege of gambling and purchasing accompaniment without fear of prosecution. Harry was constantly surprised at how many people wanted to be part of it. "We're still looking for the guys who did it."

"If it was Altin he probably hired out-of-towners." Going after Joey's operations so blatantly would likely cost him the support of the other family leaders, and he clearly had designs on filling the throne vacated by Vincent Morello. He'd bring in unfamiliar faces and pay them through cutouts so even if they got caught, they couldn't be tied back to Altin with any certainty.

"Probably," Joey said. "I gotta find these guys either way. I need to send a message."

Harry almost pitied whoever was dumb or desperate enough to do this. Their problems would be very bad for the very short time they remained alive if Joey caught them. "You will. And don't worry, I'm taking care of business on my end."

"Why Istanbul?" Joey asked. "Not a place I'd want to visit."

"It's beautiful. Like other pretty things, it can be dangerous. I won't stay longer than I have to. I need to check out a church. The Pammakaristos Church. It's Greek Orthodox."

"Heresy."

Harry chuckled. "That's what your father would say."

"Keep me in the loop," Joey said.

Harry said he would and clicked off as the city came into view ahead. "The church is open all night," he told Nora as he punched an address into the GPS system. "Access won't be an issue."

"I'm more concerned about the altar atop it," Nora said. "This Mehmed person conquered Constantinople. Why would he leave a Christian church standing?"

"The Ottoman Empire didn't force conversion to Islam when it conquered other lands. Mehmed let Christians and Jews continue to worship their gods, and he even gave them protection under his laws. Provided they paid an annual tax, of course."

"Smart."

"So were the Koraki. The Hagia Sophia is a mosque today, but it used to be a Christian church. Until Mehmed showed up. He converted it to a mosque because it was the biggest religious structure in the city."

Nora tapped the wheel. "Which is why the Koraki didn't pre-emptively plan to hide their prize there. If their side lost, that building wasn't long for Christianity."

"It makes more sense that they hid their prize in the Pammakaristos

Church. A very nice church, but not the nicest. Better chance that Mehmed leaves it alone, which coincidentally keeps their secret safe."

Lines creased Nora's forehead. "Why place the altar *atop* it? People don't worship on roofs."

Harry shrugged. "It could be a decorative altar. Maybe it's in a private room on the top floor. Or it could be a painting or decoration near the ceiling. We're looking for anything like that."

"It has to be accessible."

"I'd imagine so. The Koraki didn't have mountaineering equipment to hang from ceilings. Let's hope we can at least get to it."

They fell silent as Istanbul surrounded them. Modern skyscrapers stood in front of them, while all manner of buildings crowded on either side, some hundreds of years old, others built last month. It was the reality of Europe's largest city, a place home to more citizens than London and Berlin combined, bigger even than Moscow. The traffic felt like home as they alternately raced and crawled toward Pammakaristos Church under a gray sky, the sun nothing but a hazy memory far above.

"It's just ahead," Harry said when they neared. "What the heck is all that?"

The church sat on a large plot of land well back from streets that surrounded it on three sides. A metal fence protected the grounds, though the front gate was open. A large plaza in front of the church had a fountain in the middle. Throngs of people packed the plaza around it.

"Looks like a festival," Nora said.

"Take this left," Harry said. "We need to park away from here. I don't want to be stuck in this mess if we have to get out of here in a hurry."

Twenty minutes later they parked a good distance away, the highway not far beyond. The best they could hope for in a city this size. Harry and Nora walked single file like experienced city dwellers, Harry leading the way through the crowd with his shoulder, Nora right on his back to help push. Signs indicated the crowds were here for a festival, one replete with costumes, food vendors, musicians and all the other entrepreneurial entertainers who gathered at such events. The scent of grilled meats and fried everything called out for Harry's attention as he shoved his way to the entrance gate of Pammakaristos, where they purchased two tickets for the museum and were promptly admitted.

"Why the museum?" Nora asked. "You said that it was attached to the church."

"I want these in case anyone questions us," he said. "I'm not interested in the museum. I want to start at the top."

"You mean the roof."

"That's right. The very top."

Maintained grass stretched on either side of a stone walkway that brought them to a side door. A Turkish flag fluttered on a flagpole. Roses splashed dark red color across the monochrome sandstone foundation walls and creeping vines climbed a wall. Harry spotted no security of any sort. Darkness enveloped them as they passed beneath a rounded archway and into the church.

Rough stone walls that had never seen paint stretched on either side. White stone, which made the most of what little light fell through stained glass windows overhead. The ceiling quickly rose two stories as they passed from the entrance hall into a side chapel that would have been the envy of many churches a thousand years ago. The pounding racket of several thousand festival-goers outside faded to mere rumbles.

"Quiet in here," Harry said. It was an understatement. They were the only two people in this side chapel, though the soft echo of footsteps and murmured voices could be heard ahead in the main chapel. Exposed stone and mortar laid hundreds of years ago gave the walls a medieval look, more like a fortress than a church, capable of withstanding direct hits from siege engines. Decorative arches ran along the second level of this side room, with spotlights aimed at the ceiling and walls to bring ancient saints to life. Paintings in brilliant reds and greens jumped off the walls and ceiling as Harry moved with purpose toward the main chapel.

Three domes rose far above inside the spacious main chapel. Each had a magnificent painting in it, worn in places where time had claimed its due, though each was no less stunning despite missing a few spots. Two images of Jesus dazzled Harry's eye as he looked up. "The gold coloring is incredible."

"I believe it's gold leaf," Nora said. "Nothing else could be so bright. There is a window up there to let light in. That's why it's so bright."

A handful of worshippers were seated in pews facing the altar, while a sole priest lit candles along one far wall. Harry pulled Nora close and whispered as they walked toward the main altar. Harry dropped a few coins into the offering box with extra force so they rattled loud enough for the priest to hear. The holy man looked up at Harry at the sound. Harry nodded at him, a gesture the priest returned.

"See that door?" Harry asked under his breath.

Nora looked over his shoulder to a wooden door set into the wall. "Think it's a staircase going up?"

"That's where I'd put one," he said. "There's a window in the wall above them. I bet those are offices of some sort. Get up there, then you can access the roof outside."

"I doubt we're allowed to go up there."

"This isn't America. You don't have to obey the law."

"I was more worried about the priest," Nora said. "We can't get in the door without him noticing."

"I'll take care of him." Harry led her away from the priest and toward the door, looking at the golden images overhead as though entranced. Once they stood in front of the possible access door he moved to stand between the priest and Nora, getting as big as a guy his size could. "Is that door open?" he asked her.

Nora twisted the handle. "It is."

"You go inside while I'm talking to the priest," Harry said. "Text me if that staircase leads up. I only need to get to the second floor. I'll find a way to the roof from there."

"How are you going to get through the door?"

Harry winked. "I'll think of something. Now look alive. It's game time."

Harry turned and made his way toward the priest, passing between pews and massive silver candleholders. The priest was hard at work lighting an endless number of candles when Harry stood beside him and cleared his throat.

The priest turned to Harry. "*Merhaba.*"

Harry didn't speak a word of Turkish. "English?" he asked.

"Of course," the priest said smoothly. "May I help you?"

"Your church is beautiful," Harry said. "I have a question about a story I heard." Might as well ask the best possible source in the city while he could. "A legend about an altar on the church roof. Have you ever heard of anything like that?"

The priest's eyes sparked with joy. "I have. A fantastic story. And a true one."

Harry couldn't help himself. "For real?"

The priest nodded. "Centuries ago the Christian leaders feared they might lose control of the city to invaders. If that happened, they worried the invaders would turn this church into a place for worshipping a different religion." He stopped short of saying 'Islam.' "The church leaders wanted God to always know this was a house of Christian worship above all. To do that, they built an altar on top of the building. If the city fell and this building was lost, God would always know that it truly was a place to worship Him."

"How so?" Harry asked.

The priest smiled. "Because when He looked down from heaven, He would see an altar in His honor and know this was a church of God."

"The church leaders actually built an altar on the roof?"

"A decorative one," the priest said. "It exists, but it is a symbol. Of God's enduring power."

"You don't have services up there."

"No," the priest said. "It is far too hot during the day."

"How interesting." Harry inclined his head. "Thank you."

Harry turned and headed for the door. His phone buzzed with an incoming message. *Come up. Roof access. I left the door ajar.* He slipped the device back in his pocket. This couldn't get much better. First the rooftop altar confirmed, now Nora had found an access point. All he needed was for the priest to turn around and he'd slip through the door.

Another worshipper had come in while Harry was chatting with the priest, a bearded man who paid Harry no mind as he crossed the room. The man had one hand raised toward the image of Christ above the altar, murmuring prayers silently. Harry walked behind the man and noted the raised hand had only three fingers.

The door Harry wanted to sneak through was a good distance from the priest, who was now bent over a table trying to re-light his candles. Harry put his back to the wall and took hold of the door handle, standing in front of it to hide his actions. He waited until no one was looking, then opened the door and slid through, quickly pushing it shut on silent hinges until the latch caught with a snick. He ran up the stairs two at a time and nearly plowed over Nora at the top.

She lifted a finger to her lips. "I think we're alone," she whispered, her breath warm on his ear. "But be quiet."

"Where's the roof access?"

She waved at him to follow as she walked on, away from the main chapel and back toward the side one. "There is another staircase back here," she said. "It leads to the roof."

They passed several darkened doorways on the way. Offices, all empty, all filled to bursting with the detritus that accumulates over a thousand or so years. A green sign with *CIKIS* glowed faintly over a closed door. A solid door of the exterior sort, not another office door. Harry didn't have to speak Turkish to understand the little running man glowing green on the sign. "This is an exit."

"I knew you were smart," Nora said. "It's not alarmed."

"How do you know?"

Warm air and a wave of noise rushed into the hallway when she pushed the door open. "I tried it."

Harry pulled her through after him and shut the door. "This festival isn't helping matters. Too many people around to spot us."

From where they stood the roof line kept them hidden from people on the streets below, but if they moved closer to the edge they'd be in plain sight. "We need to climb that ladder." Harry pointed to a metal ladder bolted to the building's side that led to the topmost roof. "There's an altar up there." He recounted what the priest had told him.

"A useful priest," Nora said. "But climbing the ladder will expose us to anyone below who looks up here."

"We'll have to take the chance. Once we get up it, we'll be high enough that no one can see us."

Nora didn't move. "When do you want to go?"

"Right now." He grabbed her hand and pulled her against the wall, then sidled toward the ladder with his back close to the stones. "I'll go first. Climb as fast as you can."

He didn't give either of them time to second-guess, grabbing hold of the metal ladder, swinging around to face it and going up it at speed in full view of anyone who happened to look up from the festival. He slithered over the top edge, staying as low as he could, and had barely got to his feet before Nora came flying over and nearly landed on top of him. No shouts of alarm rang out from the crowd below.

"I think we're safe," Nora said. Her breath came quickly.

Harry wasn't listening. "There it is."

It looked as though a stone block had fallen from the sky to land on the Pammakaristos Church roof. It could have been placed there by the hand of God. It might have been, considering how big the thing was. They stood atop the church roof, looking at the altar and a towering window behind it.

"I suspect the altar was deliberately put in front of this window," Nora said. She leaned over the block. "What's that behind it?"

The altar came above Harry's waist. It was made of a darker stone than the church's interior, rough and unfinished. No decorations adorned any part of it. Harry walked around the altar, and it was wide, easily eight feet from end to end. He found nothing at all.

A low block of stone was behind the altar, of the same width but only six inches high. Were this an actual chapel it would serve to let worshippers at the far back see the priest in action. "That's a stand for the priest," Harry told Nora, "So that people at the back of the congregation can see them. Not that there would ever be a service up here." Up here, though, where there would never be a service, it seemed out of place. "It's odd," he said. "Which tells me one thing."

"What's that?"

"We need to look at this, not the altar. If you see something that's out of place, look harder. It's probably here for a reason."

He didn't need to add that the altar itself was completely bare and of no help. "The tablet said *the path of our prize will be found in an altar atop the Pammakaristos*. Here's the altar." His hand thumped off the stone. "It's blank. No writing, no lines, just one giant lump of stone. But this platform isn't. Look here."

He knelt down and pulled out his phone. "See this?" He aimed the phone's light at the floor, where the platform touched the roof. "What's that look like to you?"

Nora bumped him aside as she got lower. "Carvings." Her words came fast. "Carvings of animals."

Harry nodded. "And religious symbols. I see crosses, a crown of thorns, and the ichthys—the little thing that looks like a fish which represents Jesus."

"I know what it is."

"Right." Harry pointed at another one. "And birds. This looks like a dove."

He stopped talking, waiting to see if she caught it. Nora didn't take long.

"Look at this bird." She pointed to the platform's side. "The symbols run around the front edge and they don't repeat. There's no order. But this bird is different from the other. It's not a dove." She got down on her hands and knees, face inches from the low stone. "Harry, it's a—"

"—raven," Harry finished. "No doubt about it. Now what in the world is a raven doing on a religious altar?"

"It's a marker," she said. "The Koraki put this here."

"That's what I think," Harry said. "If I had to guess, I bet they paid the church leaders to put this altar up here with one request: this altar goes up here and never comes down."

"Why would the church agree?"

Harry shrugged. "Who knows? Maybe the Koraki had connections in the church and one of their men ordered this to happen. Said it was God's will or something. Could be they just threw money at the church and said this strange altar was part of the deal. The church has certainly dealt with its share of oddballs over the years. It wouldn't be all that crazy."

"The raven isn't on the altar. The message specifically said *in an altar*. Think that matters?"

"Nope. Watch."

The platform was directly behind the altar. The front part of the platform was perhaps two feet behind the altar and had images carved all along the face of it. Pretty, but it made no sense because nobody could see them. Why put carvings, even rough ones, in a tight spot where no one could appreciate them? A dove, two crosses, and this raven. Harry wouldn't waste his time with all these carvings unless they had a purpose, and he had a pretty good idea what that purpose was. To hide something in plain sight.

He pulled his foot back and kicked the platform as hard as he dared. Kicked the raven with a toe-crunching *smack*, hard enough to make Harry fire a string of colorful words into the air and for Nora to grab his shoulder.

"What are you doing?" she asked. "You're going to break your foot."

"I might have." His words came through gritted teeth. "It worked." She followed his outstretched finger and looked down.

A small panel had opened in the altar. "The raven image is a lever. Force it in and it opens that panel. Look."

The raven image had recessed into the platform; the bird actually carved on a separate piece of stone from the rest of the platform. The separate stone had been so well set it was impossible to notice. He'd played a hunch, a feeling in his gut that came from years in the field.

"Is there anything in it?" Harry asked as he rubbed his aching foot.

Nora was aghast. "You want me to look in there? What if it's a trap?"

His foot hurt. The real treasure he wanted to chase was in Egypt. Harry didn't have time for this. "No one puts a trap on the relic now. Those come before you find it." He knelt down, stuck his hand in the opening, and shouted.

"What is it?" Nora yelled.

He couldn't help himself. "Just kidding." She thumped him with two well-deserved punches. "Easy," he said. "There's something in here. And it's *heavy*."

It was metal, no doubt. Smooth but pointy. He grabbed hold of it and slid it out of the darkness. Every nerve in his body lit up. "Holy smokes."

He was staring at a golden crown. A half circle of dull yellow, like a medieval beanie that would have covered the king's head. Rubies and emeralds dotted the surface. One ruby the size of a quarter was at the top, sticking up like the pompom on an impossibly expensive tossle cap. The entire piece weighed around ten pounds, he guessed.

"That is incredible." Nora spoke through the hand covering her mouth. "It's real."

"There's more." He handed the crown to Nora, then reached into the chamber again and pulled out a braided golden necklace dotted with emeralds and sapphires, which he gave to Nora. As she shifted to take it, a length of something brown fell out from inside the crown.

"What's this?" He scooped it up. "It's a folded sheet of vellum." He flipped it around and now something metallic fell out from inside this new find. "And a key."

He turned over the vellum; there was a large red blot of sealing wax holding it together. It was folded rather than rolled, and when he pulled back one edge, dark ink was visible. "There's writing on it," he said.

"What does it say?"

"No idea." The folded vellum disappeared inside his shirt, the key into his pocket. "And we're not reading it up here. Come on."

They'd been exposed too long already. Harry pointed to the crown in Nora's arms. "Hang on to that, and put the necklace around your neck."

"You're stealing this stuff?"

"Only until I know I don't need it to follow this path. Then I'll give it back. Trust me, I don't want the Turkish version of you hunting me down."

"But whose crown is this?"

"I'd say Constantine the Eleventh, the last Byzantine emperor. He died defending Constantinople against an Ottoman invasion. That's the challenge the Koraki talked about Greek culture facing in their message in Athens. The Eastern Roman Empire traced its roots to Greece. This wasn't just the last stand of the Roman Empire. It was the last battle for an entire region of Greek culture. Now put that crown away and let's move."

She looped the necklace over her head and tightened her grip on the crown. He closed the hidden panel and the raven carving popped back out into its former position. Back to the ladder they went. Harry went down first, Nora behind him. They ducked down at the bottom of the ladder and Harry surveyed the festival crowd. His body tensed. "Damn. Somebody saw us."

Only his hold on her arm kept Nora from standing. "How do you know?"

"Because those are cops walking into the church."

A trio of uniformed officers pushed their way through the church's front gates as he spoke. The lead officer looked up at them, raised an arm, and shouted.

"Follow me." Harry pulled Nora out of sight and back toward the door leading inside. But instead of going in, he raced past it.

"Where are we going?" Nora asked, looking over her shoulder at the door. "Is there another way in?"

"Beats me," he said. "We're going down the back wall. There are only three cops and they'll all be inside. There should be a fire escape or something like it back here."

As luck would have it, he was correct. Unfortunately, it was the sort of folding fire escape with counterweights that made a godawful racket when lowered. It would save your life at the same time it saved you notifying the fire department you needed them, because everyone in a half-mile radius would know you'd unleashed the metal monstrosity.

"There is no chance the cops don't hear that," Nora said.

Harry cursed. "Yeah, I know. Follow me."

He raced back to the doorway and stuck his head through. "I can hear them in the main chapel already."

"They'll send two men up here to look for us." Nora spoke as though there were no other options. "The third will stay at ground level in case we slip past the first two. He'll be calling for backup now."

"We need another way out." Nora started to speak. Harry lifted a finger to quiet her. He needed to *think*. This wasn't the first time he'd been in a tight spot. What did his father tell him? Don't panic. That helps nothing. Take a breath and think.

"The flagpole." Harry snapped his fingers. "That's our way out."

"Excuse me?"

Harry led her back past the door and out onto the second-level roof until they looked out at the flagpole near the front entrance. A pole

Harry recalled passing on the way in that wasn't too far from the building. "It's less than ten feet away. We're not even twenty feet up. Jump out, grab the pole, and shimmy your way down."

"That's crazy."

"Would you rather explain to Gary what you're doing in Istanbul?"

Her eyes were lethal. "This is not how your treasure hunting normally goes. Thanks for leaving me no choice."

Harry shrugged as though to say *Welcome to the life*. Nora looked out at the crowd of thousands. "We're in full view of half a million people up here."

"Who cares? Nobody's looking at us. Come on."

"You go first. I have no idea if that pole will hold."

"Fine with me." Harry took a second to gauge his jump, stepped back, then sprinted until he ran out of roof and leapt. The pole was closer than it looked. He crashed into it, his vision blurred, and he nearly bounced off before getting an arm around the metal pole and clinging tight. He didn't waste time sliding to the ground, which he hit with a bang that jarred his teeth. "Don't smash into it," he called up. "Easy jump and hold tight. I'll grab you if you fall."

Nora tossed the crown down and he snatched it out of the air. She took one step back, squared her shoulders, and jumped. Unlike his clang-and-bang route down, she gracefully grabbed hold of the pole and shimmied down as though she were a firefighter.

"Smooth," Harry said when she was on the ground. "Hide this."

She took the crown back and it disappeared inside her shirt. They were halfway to the church gates when the first flashing lights appeared off to one side of the grounds, though the crowds kept the police cars from getting any closer. Harry ducked his head and accelerated. The archway at the front gate covered them before the police could get out of their car for a proper look around the property. Harry looked over his shoulder and up to where they'd been just moments ago. The roof door had just started to open when he stepped to the gate, Nora right behind him. They hit the crowd and immediately stopped. No matter.

The cops couldn't see them from here. The last thing Harry saw before they melted into the crowd was a single worshipper walking out of the church's front door. The man locked eyes with Harry, who held his gaze for a second and then moved on. It was only the three-fingered man from inside.

He grabbed Nora's hand and kept her close. "We made it."

Chapter 23

Istanbul

Thirty minutes of pushing and dodging through the crowds of Istanbul brought Harry and Nora to a quiet café. Harry chose a table in the back, checked there was a rear exit—there was—then ordered two coffees and a couple of sandwiches. Relic hunting, in his experience, made a person hungry.

Nora didn't touch her sandwich. "Harry, this crown is incredible." She had the crown in a plastic shopping bag, out of sight. "I can't even guess how much it's worth."

"Try priceless," he said between bites. "It's a national treasure. Same with the necklace."

Nora touched the necklace hidden under her shirt. "It's heavy. And I can't travel with this. There's no way customs will believe this is my necklace."

"We're not taking it out of the country if we can help it," he said. "First we figure out what the next step is. Then we give that stuff back." He pulled the folded vellum paper out of his shirt pocket, along with the key. "I don't think we'll need either treasure. This piece of paper and the key seem more promising."

They were seated alone back here. Harry slipped a table knife under the sealed wax and wiggled until it broke free. Thick and well-oiled, the folded vellum had held up well. It protested as he unfolded it to reveal elegant, flowing script running across the page. Harry pushed the top end of the sheet toward Nora. "Hold this down so I can read it."

But Nora didn't grab it. She was busy digging in her pocket for her phone, which was buzzing. "It's my father," she said, looking at the screen. "I can't ignore him."

Harry tried to tell her she was an adult and could ignore anyone she pleased, but Nora connected the call anyway. "Hello," she said.

"Nora." The volume on her phone was loud enough that Harry could hear every word. Gary Doyle spoke in his best prosecutor's voice. "Where are you?"

To her credit, Nora stalled. "Why do you ask?"

"Your phone location shows as Istanbul, Turkey. Is that correct?"

"You're tracking me?"

"I'm not only your boss, I'm your father. I'll track your phone if I deem it necessary."

Anger of cataclysmic proportions contorted Nora's face. She didn't let it reach her words. "Yes, boss. I'm in Istanbul."

"You didn't request a vacation."

"This is related to an ongoing investigation."

"No travel was approved."

"Send me a bill."

A sigh came through the phone. "Are you with Harry Fox?"

"He's right here."

Harry motioned for her to put the call on speaker. She did, turning the volume down low so Gary's voice didn't escape their table. "Hi, Gary."

"Harry. I hope your investigation is proceeding accordingly."

"Do you? I'm just an expendable asset, remember?"

A longer sigh this time. "I see Nora has been in your company longer than I realized."

"She didn't know you were going to be so honest about how replaceable I am," Harry said. "She didn't rat you out. I overheard your phone conversation at the airport."

"Please forgive my earlier comments," Gary said. "I let my emotion get the best of me."

"Hard for a bum treasure hunter like me to understand that, Gary. There are plenty of jokers who can chase relics. Not the brightest group in the world, or else we wouldn't be so easy to replace."

"If you're quite finished, Mr. Fox."

Harry wasn't, but there was a time and place to pick a fight. "For now."

"Good. Then perhaps we can get back to the business at hand?"

"I'm listening."

"Thank you," Gary said. "First, I apologize. What I said was unfair and inaccurate. It came from a place of concern. Nora is my only child. Her mother and I adore her. The thought of her being harmed warps my professional demeanor."

"So you're not all bad."

"That is one way to look at it. Second, you are a valued member of the team. Never more so than now."

"Why's that?"

"You are in a foreign country with my daughter. Your unique combination of skills and experience are assets I cannot hope to duplicate. While she is entirely capable, the world is a dangerous place, and her best chance of coming home unscathed rests in having you as an ally. I hope she can count on you. I hope we both can."

"I can handle myself," Nora fired back.

"This ill-conceived and poorly planned trip suggests otherwise. And you'll note I didn't say you *can't* handle yourself. I know you can. I also know Harry Fox is one of the best in the world at what he does, which includes staying alive while recovering cultural artifacts under difficult circumstances. I'm ordering you to listen to what he says."

If Gary Doyle was trying to get on Harry's good side, he was doing a heck of a job. "She's fine," Harry said. "Nora can handle herself." Harry mouthed *Should I tell him about Iran?*

Nora's fiery glare made it clear he should not. "I chose to come here," she said. "The mission is dangerous. Harry is on his own. You wouldn't let one of your team get in over their head, would you?" She raised a hand when he started to protest. *Just go with it.*

"I would not." Gary fell silent, as though considering the entire ordeal. "Harry, did you require her assistance?"

"I didn't ask for it," he said honestly.

"I'm sure you didn't," Gary said. "How did Nora acquit herself?"

"Like a professional," Harry said. "She's good in the field."

"Which is what worries me. I do not want this to become a habit."

"We can't rely on Harry for everything," Nora said.

"No, but he's the expert in this area. We have to trust him." His words got harder. "And we do trust him. I do. You do. As you said, he's part of the team. How much progress have you made?"

"I think we're near the end," Harry said. "We recovered another message, but we haven't had a chance to review it yet."

"Why not?"

Harry paused. "The circumstances of the recovery did not permit a review."

"Is there anything I should know about?" Gary asked. "That is part of the reason I'm upset with you, Nora. While I appreciate you helping a teammate, you have to consider the larger picture. If a member of the D.A.'s office were found to be working outside their jurisdiction without the local government's knowledge it would be a black mark for my office. I'm not only worried about you, Nora. This is also about our office."

The fact Nora didn't respond told Harry plenty. Gary Doyle was right and Nora knew it. Yet she'd still come. To help him. "Nora has been an asset here in Turkey," Harry said. "From what I can see now, I should be fine to handle the rest alone."

Nora kicked him under the table. "Good," Gary said. "Because it's time to follow orders, Nora. You traveled to Turkey without my knowledge. However, given Harry's assertion you provided valuable services, we can let this go. I expect you to be on the next flight back to New York. That's an order."

She grumbled something along the lines of "Fine."

"Excellent," Gary said. "Harry, is there anything you need for your search?"

"I need to know what else you learned about my mother's case."

"Did you speak with Detective Barnes?"

"No. We're connecting once I get back to New York."

"She is the best source to answer your questions," Gary said. "Once you meet with her, tell me what else you want to know and I will do everything in my power to find it. But it would be counterproductive to search without specific guidance from Detective Barnes. There are millions of case files in the NYPD database. Narrowing down what you are looking for is the only way to find answers."

"What if I don't find this Greek artifact before Smolov does?"

"I will still help you," Gary said. "I honor my word."

This was the best he could hope for. Answers would have to wait. "That's fair," he said. "I'll be in touch if I need anything."

"Nora, I expect to see you tomorrow."

Nora said she would follow orders before hanging up. "That wasn't necessary," she said to Harry. "Telling my father you can do the rest alone."

"He's right," Harry said. "You getting caught over here wouldn't help. Go back to New York and help me from there."

Her colorful language let him know exactly how she felt. "What are we going to do about this?" Nora lifted the necklace from inside her shirt. "It's massive. It's bigger than the one my mother wears for special occasions."

Gary Doyle must have splurged for a serious necklace. "We take it back to the church."

Her eyes got huge. "What? We'll be arrested on the spot."

"Not you. Me. I'll drop it off in a box along with the crown before I leave town. Which will be after you." He tapped his wrist. "You'd better get a ticket home. Gary isn't joking around."

"Show me the paper before I go," Nora said. "Please. I have to be in an office tomorrow. I want to know what we found."

Harry looked around the café. "Fine," he said. "But let's do it somewhere else. We've been here long enough. There's a guy in here who looks jumpy."

Nora didn't turn around. "Do you recognize him?"

"No," Harry said. "He's just fidgety is all. It's making me nervous. Come on."

He threw some coins on the table and they slipped out the back door. Harry waited at the alley's mouth for a long minute to see if the fidgeting man came out. They stood near a bearded Middle Eastern man who paid them no mind at all, chain-smoking as he spoke rapid-fire Arabic into a phone too quietly for Harry to make out. The man had long sleeves on even in the heat. Harry noted a tinge of discoloration on the skin below his wrists.

"That guy didn't follow us," Harry said. "We passed a park on the way here. Let's find a bench there."

Five minutes later they were alone in a city park, sitting on a bench beneath the shade of a bushy cypress tree. Harry kept the vellum sheet out of view and watched the pedestrians walking by. Nobody grabbed his eye.

"I have to go," Nora said. "Any day now."

"Patience. You can't rush things in this profession. At least, not all the time." He counted to a hundred, slowly. "I don't see any familiar faces. I think we're good."

Out came the vellum sheet. Harry held it gently as a window into the past unfolded on his lap. "It's Greek," Harry said.

"What does it say?"

"No idea. My Greek is terrible."

"Then how are we going to read it?"

The phone in his pocket buzzed. He saw who was calling and a grin creased his face, his heart beating a little faster. "Here's the person who can help." He connected the call. "Are you okay?" he asked.

"I'm fine," Sara said. "You won't believe what I found."

"I'm here with Nora," Harry said. "And do we have a story for you too."

"Nora's there? Where are you?"

"Istanbul," Harry said. "Nora has to go soon so I'll make this fast." He recapped their trip from Athens to Istanbul, deciphering the admittedly straightforward message regarding a tomb atop Pammakaristos Church. He glossed over their escape down the flagpole. "I was just trying to decipher Greek on the fly," Harry said. "I'm glad you called."

"What trouble did you have in Athens?" Sara asked. "You skipped over that quickly."

The woman was perceptive. "You could say that." Harry recounted his trident fight and one-sided shootout with Stefan Rudovic. "That ankle put him out of this hunt for good."

"Nora, would you please smack him for me?" Sara asked. Harry didn't have time to dodge before her palm loudly whacked his arm. "Thank you," Sara said. "That's for nearly getting yourself killed."

"It sounds like you might actually care about me," he said, rubbing his shoulder.

"Don't flatter yourself," Sara said. "I can't believe you let Stefan get that close."

Harry swore Nora covered her mouth to hide a laugh.

"Regardless, I'm happy you're alive. Send me a picture of this message so I can translate it."

"Where are you now?" Harry asked as he sent the photo off. "I haven't heard anything from you recently."

"Omar and I have been busy."

Harry's head snapped up. "Joey's friend Omar?"

"He's a saint," Sara said. "Without him I'd likely be in jail."

"I'm listening."

"It can wait," Sara said. "Oh my. This is amazing."

"Can you read it?" Nora asked.

"Yes." Sara's words were soft as she translated. Harry's and Nora's heads nearly touched when they leaned over to hear it.

The last Greek king is gone, lost in a valiant defense of his crown. We retrieved it from the battlefield, along with his royal chain. One day it will again show the world a true Greek king. Though our future appears dim, we Koraki know Greece will return.

The prize of our greatest warrior is resting in his home where he sits with the gods. Look to what Zeus's seat touches when Helios first drives across the sky. Beware, for only a true Greek versed in our storied past may possess the prize. Hades waits for any others who trespass on these sacred grounds.

"We were right," Harry said. "The prize followed Greek leaders or kings. Constantine was the last in their line, and he died fighting the Ottomans."

"Does it say anything about a key?" Nora asked.

"Nothing," Sara said. "Why?"

Harry told her about the key he'd found. "You should keep that," Sara said. "Return the necklace and crown."

Harry assured her they would. "The Koraki thought Greece would return to its former glory. They left the prize for their ancestors to find."

"What do you mean by return?"

"Their *idea* of Greece," Harry said. "They wanted to protect their culture, the people. It wouldn't be exactly the same, but Greece would still be alive."

"I get it," Nora said. "But no one ever found it. Why not?"

"Hard to say," Harry said.

"Perhaps the prize we're chasing is actually a weapon of war that's no longer useful," Sara said. "It's safe to say *Aki Los* is the greatest Greek warrior. A name that likely changed over the centuries."

"Achilles." Harry rubbed a thumb on his chin. "His prize finally returned to his home. Where he sits with the gods."

"Where would that be?" Nora asked.

"The Greek gods lived on Mount Olympus," Sara said. "That's where we'll find their prize."

Nora lifted a hand. "Hold on. Those are myths, legends. You're telling me there's an actual Mount Olympus?"

Harry nodded. "A mountain that helped form their entire myth structure. Greeks believed their world was ruled by the Olympians, twelve gods and goddesses who lived on Mount Olympus. They were the major deities representing various aspects of the physical world, and their squabbles impacted normal people. They weren't exactly nice."

Sara jumped in. "Zeus was their king. He ruled from the highest point on Mount Olympus. Zeus's seat is supposedly on the mountain's highest peak."

Harry turned to Nora. "Helios was the sun god. He drove a chariot across the sky each day to bring light to the world. We need to be on Mount Olympus at dawn to see where the shadow from Zeus's seat hits on the mountain."

"I found a location on the western side of the mountain known as Achilles' Bowl. It's a depression halfway up the mountain where legend says Achilles learned to fight."

"How much do you want to bet the shadow hits in that area?" Harry asked. "The sun rises in the east."

"The closest airport is in Thessaloniki," Sara said. "I can be there tonight."

"What about your search?" he asked.

"I can pause for a few days," she said. "I'll update you on what I found in Greece."

One look at Nora's face made it clear she wanted to know more. "What can I do?"

"Help me get this crown and necklace back to the church," Harry said. "A plain cardboard box should do the trick. Sara, I'll meet you at the airport tonight."

Sara promised to send him her flight information and clicked off. Harry and Nora stood, walking first in a direction away from their destination, then abruptly doubling back. "I don't see anyone following us," Harry said after a few minutes. "We passed a package store along the way. Let's get a box and drop this back at the church. The local cops should be gone by now."

They stopped at an intersection, safely anonymous in the pedestrian crowd.

"Be careful, Harry. We're working together. That means we have each other's backs."

"I know," Harry said. "Your coming here meant a lot."

"It better have." She rolled her eyes. "Nearly cost me my job."

"You're too valuable to be fired."

"I hope so," she said. "If you need anything in Greece, call me."

Harry started walking when the light turned. "Just make sure Detective Barnes will talk with me. That's the most important thing you can do." He turned and looked her in the eyes. "It's the most important thing anyone could do for me."

Chapter 24

Litochoro, Greece

Night's purple blanket stretched across the Greek countryside. Patches of light dotted the coast as Harry and Sara thundered from Thessaloniki to Litochoro. It was well past midnight. At that late hour the only rental car available had been a gas-guzzling Land Rover. It wasn't a black Range Rover, which was all Sara cared about. Last time he and Sara were chasing a relic they'd nearly been killed by one of those vehicles, so she had sworn to avoid them forever.

Harry had snatched several hours of much-needed sleep on the flight from Istanbul. Sara apparently had not, for she told him she needed to "close her eyes" when they got in the car. Since then she hadn't moved. She hadn't even shared what had happened in Luxor yet, and he hadn't asked. Harry touched the gold piece around his neck: he could wait an hour more to unravel the secret it contained.

The car shook as Harry veered out of his lane and ran over rumble strips alongside the highway. Sara jerked awake. "Where are we?" she asked, her voice thick with sleep.

Harry pulled back onto the highway. "We're almost to Litochoro." The town sat near Mount Olympus's base and was where most climbing expeditions began. "It's three in the morning. We have a few hours before the sun comes up."

Sara rubbed her eyes. "Where's the coffee?"

Harry pulled out one of the iced coffee bottles he'd purchased from a vending machine. "Hope you like it cold."

She drank half the bottle in one go. "Thanks."

"So what did you find in Luxor?"

Her eyes lit up in the dark car. "Try to keep up. First, I climbed the statue of Ramses outside Luxor Temple. Across from it at eye level were a row of glyphs I couldn't see from the ground." She recounted the instructions related to the *Greek sphinx* and *the fate of Oedipus's scarlet eye*. "Remember that Greek sphinxes are female, not male. Earlier, when I walked the Avenue of the Sphinxes, I saw two statues with the eyes painted red. Only one was female. I rammed my stick in its eye."

Harry had been right. The eye, she told him, had turned out to be a release mechanism that revealed a series of hidden rooms under the avenue. One room was booby-trapped, while the other held a vault with a golden shield pointing to a specific location. Unfortunately, the *Great Caesareum* had been lost to a changing climate. However, history couldn't lose Ptolemy Soter so easily: they still had a chance in the new Grand Egyptian Museum. What waited for them was uncertain. And what to make of *CSILAH*?

"Should I be worried about you taking my job?" Harry joked.

"You aren't exactly slacking in your search." Sara then demanded a recounting of his adventure atop Pammakaristos Church. One item held her interest more than the others. "Why the key?" she asked. "We're going to a mountain. There won't be any doors waiting that no one has found yet, right?"

Harry looked at the key sitting between them in a cupholder. It somewhat resembled a skeleton key from Victorian times. The teeth on it were curved, not straight, and the piece was made of bronze. "Doors come in all shapes and sizes," Harry said.

They fell silent as the brooding peaks of Mount Olympus darkened the early morning sky ahead, the snow-capped peaks shining as though electrified under the fading moonlight. Harry followed signs for the town of Litochoro, aiming for a flat expanse outside the town limits that offered an unimpeded view of the mountain's western face and the area where Zeus's seat should cast its shadow. The area known as Achilles' Bowl would be visible. If Zeus's shadow touched it, they had a destination.

"Achilles' Bowl isn't for casual hikers." Sara had her phone out. "Aside from the challenging terrain, there are wolves and jackals in the area."

"That's not terrible news."

"How so?"

"Wolves and jackals keep humans away. Fewer people around means there's a better chance that anything to be found there hasn't been."

"It's your optimistic nature I find so appealing," Sara said. "At least when it comes to finding relics."

Harry touched the knuckledusters in his pocket. It was a miracle he still had them after so many flights. Perhaps if a wolf happened by he could punch it on the nose. He nearly laughed at the thought. *Try that and I'll be in the market for gloves with fewer than five fingers.*

"Lucky for you I planned ahead." Sara reached around and dug through the small bag she'd brought from Egypt. "I checked my bag to avoid a security search." Sara pulled out a canister. "Pepper spray."

"If it works on humans, I bet it works on wildlife." Harry stuck his fist out for a bump. "Nice work. We're here."

The Land Rover's tires crunched gravel as he pulled into an empty parking area. "Sunrise is in about fifteen minutes," Harry said.

They sat watching as Helios brought his horses to attention and began journeying toward the horizon. Red snuck into the purple coloring and the first rays crept up the face of Mount Olympus. He got out and leaned against the car's hood, watching the shadows fade as the new day announced itself. It also brought their answer.

Sara's words were breathless in the cool dawn air. "There's the shadow from Mytikas, the highest peak. Where Zeus sits."

A dagger of shadow thrust into the heart of Achilles' Bowl. Sara snapped several photos with her phone. "That area looks open," she said. "Drive as close as you can to the base and let's start climbing."

Harry jumped back into the Land Rover and fired up the engine. He headed directly toward the mountain, eventually finding a parking lot several hundred yards from the base. Theirs was the only car in sight when they jumped out and marched for the trailhead.

The cold air deep in the mountain's shadows snaked up his pantleg. Harry pushed the pace, Sara matching him stride for stride as they ascended a relatively flat portion in short order. Half an hour into their journey the morning chill had burned off and Harry stopped walking. They had reached an intersection on the trail. Or rather, a turn, with only one way to go. The marked trail led to their left. A suspect-looking path led off to the right, toward Achilles' Bowl.

Sara studied a map taken from a visitor's station at the base. The trail on the right was the more direct route, taking them along a ridgeline and through expanses of green chaparral and thick patches of trees. "We can get to the Bowl by taking the left path," Sara said. "But it's a longer way. Going right is faster, but we have to take the ridgeline and hope the trail holds out."

Harry pointed right, at what could generously be called a game path. "You call that a trail? I'm not a mountain goat."

"Taking the longer route will be easier, but I expect it will add at least two hours to our journey."

Harry looked down the trail behind them. "We haven't seen anyone today. Stefan Rudovic is probably still in a hospital or on crutches. He's not climbing any mountains." She bit her lip and looked toward the marked trail. "Besides, where do you think we'll find wolves or jackals? Not near a marked path. It's when you go into the wilderness that the trouble starts."

"Agreed," Sara said. "We go left."

They stayed on the marked path. Twenty minutes later a switchback gave Harry a good view of the parking lot below. Several cars were now parked near theirs, including a sport utility vehicle even bigger than their Land Rover. At least Harry wasn't the only doofus driving an oversized beast. This new one looked like it could withstand a grenade blast.

Harry and Sara continued the walk mostly in silence. Occasionally they stopped for a drink of water, and each time Harry turned an ear back toward the path behind them. Twice he caught sounds that seemed out of place, as though someone or something were nearby. Twice he waited, telling Sara to remain quiet. Twice the sounds never amounted to anything. After the second time Sara let him know how she felt.

"Enough with the worrying," she said. "Four people know where we are. Gary and Nora Doyle and the two of us. We're safe." She reached up and re-tied her hair behind her head. "In truth, I'd prefer if there were others around here. More people make more noise, which keeps wild animals away."

She was right. That still didn't quell the nagging feeling in his gut, a feeling he couldn't quite describe. He'd learned to trust those feelings. He'd also learned when to keep his mouth shut. No need to pick a fight with the only person he trusted in a thousand miles. "You're right," he said. "I'm just on edge."

She grabbed his arm. "So am I. And I'm glad you're here with me." She hugged him once, tightly. "Now let's get moving. We're almost there."

Almost there meant another half hour's walk. A helicopter buzzed low overhead as they crested a rise and Sara put her hand up. "We're here." She double-checked the location on her phone. "The first shadow from Mytikas landed down there." Sara pointed into the natural depression ahead of them, an inverted curve that resembled a sweeping bowl cut out of the ground, as though this area were designed to collect rainwater. "This is Achilles' Bowl. We have to cross over the lowest portion and come up the far side."

"There are no trails," Harry said. "And lots of trees between us and where that shadow was."

"Then we'd better get moving."

Sara skirted the first copse of trees until she found a rough trail, a path better suited for a mountain bike than hiking shoes. Thick tree trunks stood alongside narrower, younger trees as they pushed into the cool shade of the thick, green canopy. The woods deadened any sound, the thick foliage a blanket that softened their footsteps and made it seem as though they were the only people on the mountain.

Harry stopped after a few minutes and lifted his hand. "Do you hear that?" he asked.

"No."

They resumed walking. The ground began to descend beneath their feet, forcing them to slow down to avoid slipping down the hillside. Harry picked up a stout stick and began banging it off anything he could reach: tree trunks, the ground, leaves overhead.

"If you think someone is following us, you certainly aren't making it hard on them."

"It's noise to keep the animals away," Harry said.

Sara grabbed a branch of her own and started making a ruckus to match. She also pulled out the pepper spray and held it ready. Down they walked until the ground leveled out. There were more shadows than sun here. The hair on Harry's arms rose.

"It's cold down here," he said. "Walk faster."

Sara didn't argue. They crossed the bottom of Achilles' Bowl at speed. The trees thinned out briefly, only the tallest of them reaching high overhead to blot out the sun.

On they walked until the ground sloped up again. Harry's calves burned with the effort; he and Sara kept pushing the pace until they reached a nearly vertical shelf on the mountainside. A ledge stretched horizontally above them, just out of reach when Harry stretched up to grab it.

"Come here," he said. "I'll boost you up."

Harry laced his hands together to form a step for Sara. She grabbed his shoulder, stepped onto his hands and pushed herself up as he lifted, arms and legs straining to drive her skyward until she could grab the flat ground above. "I have it," she called out. He kept pushing, lifting her up until suddenly her weight disappeared. Sara hauled herself over the lip above and out of sight.

"You okay?" he called out. He put a hand against the shelf, breathing hard as he looked up. He nearly jumped back when her head popped into view.

"It's flat up here," she said. "Come on."

The edge in her voice got his motor running. Sara reached down; he grabbed her hand, then hauled himself up, feet scrabbling on the tiny ledge's face until he flew up and over the edge to land in an undignified heap. They got to their feet, dusting themselves off.

"This is incredible," Sara said. "It's exactly where the shadow touched."

They stood on a flat area seemingly cut out of the mountainside. A mountainside that now resembled a wall more than a hill. "The trees hide this flat area," Sara said. "It's a natural cliff. If I wanted to hide something, this would be a good place to do it."

"One problem," Harry said. "That's basically a wall in front of us. Where could you hide anything?"

"It's not a flat wall," Sara said. She pointed to where different sections of the cliff face jutted out. Portions looked to have been plopped down next to each other like massive building blocks laid by giants. Or perhaps more like a row of uneven teeth. Either way, she was correct.

"These *look* natural," Sara said. "That doesn't mean they haven't been altered."

The rock face might be uneven, but it still looked like a big, solid wall to Harry. "What are you talking about?"

"Look closely. The Koraki used nature to conceal their secrets in the open. Check each crack and crevice on this wall."

"It's two hundred feet long."

"Then get started." Sara walked off to the left. "You start on the far side. Meet me in the center."

Harry set off to the right. Moss and small bushes grew out of the vertical crevices that nature had carved into the rockface. The mountainside was not so steep it couldn't be climbed if you made it past the first ten or so feet. The lowest portion facing them, however, was nearly vertical. Shadows hid the innermost cracks from view, the dark areas damp and cool to the touch. He ripped out patches of moss bigger than his arm, along with a few small bushes, but found nothing more interesting than bugs. He even tugged on the rock face where he could get a good handhold, as though he could rip the wall down through sheer force. Shockingly, it didn't budge.

Sara's voice rang out. "Find anything?"

"Bugs, trees, dirt." Harry wiped his hands on his pants. Sara didn't respond. "That would be a no."

"Come look at this," she called.

He stepped back from the wall and looked her way. "Why are you in the middle? There's no way you checked that whole side."

"There are lines in the rock."

She had his attention. He hurried over and stood beside her. "Where?"

"Here." Sara pointed at a series of cracks in the rock. "They're fairly straight."

They were. "What's the big deal?"

"I thought they looked *too* straight, plus they're parallel, and look at the one on top." She pointed at a pair of parallel lines roughly ten feet apart. Another line across the top seemed to connect them. "What does this look like?"

It took him a second. She waited. Harry blinked, and it hit him. "A door. It looks like the outline of a door."

"Right," Sara said. "The lines are unnaturally straight. And look at the moss." She grabbed a handful of the velvety green turf. "Moss grows in the shade. Look at every natural outcropping. Most of them

274

don't have any growing. Why is the horizontal line on this part of the cliff the only one with moss growing in it?"

Harry shrugged. "Beats me."

"Because the horizontal line isn't *natural*."

"These lines were cut into the rock," Harry said. "That's why the moss is growing out of them." Harry frowned. "I guess you could cut a door in here." He stopped, one hand halfway to the amulet beneath his shirt. "Hold on. If this is a doorway, that means one thing for certain."

"There's an opening behind it," Sara said, finishing the thought for him. "The cliff face isn't solid."

His mind jumped to warp speed. "The moss." He grabbed a handful and ripped it off. "It hides whatever is underneath." Harry reached into his pocket. "Like a keyhole."

"Pull all the moss off." Sara jumped to work, ripping the green carpet off in long strips as Harry did the same. Dirt caked his fingers and stuck to his arms as he tore anything green off the rock face. Nothing jumped out even when all the moss lay in heaps at his feet, so he attacked the dirt stuck on the wall, digging until his fingers hit rock below. Halfway down the interior of one vertical line he nearly severed a finger.

His cursing reached Zeus on high. "Are you okay?" Sara asked as she ran over and grabbed his arm. "What happened?"

"My finger caught in a hole." He swore a few more times. "I almost ripped it off."

"Let me see." Sara grabbed his hand, brushed the dirt off and looked at it closely. It throbbed with every touch and he told her so. "Stop whining. It's not even broken." She pushed his hand away. "Where exactly did you hurt it?"

"Here." Dirt crumbled as he poked and prodded. His finger disappeared into the mountainside. "My finger almost broke off in this hole."

Sara pushed him aside and ripped at the dirt until the hole was exposed. She stepped back. "That's about the size of the key."

"You think we're in the right place?" he asked.

"Yes. Where's the key?"

"I don't *think* we're in the right place." Harry reached up to where the ghost of an image had caught his eye. An outline, hidden beneath a thin layer of rich earth, at eye level on the same crack in the rocks where he'd nearly lost his finger. "I *know* we are. Look."

He brushed aside the last bit of dirt. Sara gasped. "A raven," she said.

"The same image as the one on Alexander's armor in Athens. There was a hidden chamber in the statue."

"I remember." Sara took a breath, collecting herself. "Give me that key." Harry handed it over. "This looks like a keyhole," Sara said. The careful academic Harry had met in Germany last year had changed. Now she was a true field agent. "Let's see if it fits."

Sara held the bronze key in front of the dark hole. Without hesitation, she pushed it in, gently at first, then leaning on it when it resisted. Metal scraped on stone until she stumbled forward as the key jammed into the hole. "It fits," she said.

"You made it fit," Harry said. "Hope it's not broken."

She twisted the key. It held. "Should it turn?" she asked. He nodded. She twisted again. Nothing. "I think I can twist harder, but I don't want to break it."

"Go slow." Harry valued his life, and as such did not offer to help her.

Sara gritted her teeth and leaned into the key. Her foot slipped as she pushed, skidding on the dirt and moss they'd pulled off the stone and hitting Harry's foot. He grabbed her before she fell. "Are you okay?" he asked.

"It turned." She pulled herself free from his grasp. The key was now sticking out horizontally. "It twist—"

The crash of ancient rocks shifting cut her off. First a groaning scrape, as though one tectonic plate had nudged past another, then a noise like massive boulders grinding against each other, rocks as big as buildings scraping and pushing on each other. The wall in front of them trembled.

"Get back," Harry shouted. He grabbed Sara's arm and pulled her away, back to the edge where they'd climbed over. The wall shook as they backpedaled, rumbling as massive stones shifted behind the wall with a rattle he felt deep in his chest. The doorway Sara claimed existed actually moved, twitching at first, then sliding back from left to right, an entire section of the solid stone cliff face moving to one side to reveal an opening cut from the stone. It was an actual, honest-to-goodness doorway, and Sara had opened it.

Sara's voice was low. "I told you."

He stood there, grasping for words. "I did not see that coming," he finally said.

Sara ripped her arm away from his. "Look," she said, running to the opened door. "Rollers. The slab was on a set of rollers. I bet there's a counterweight back here." Sara stuck her head inside the dark opening.

"Wait." Harry ran over and grabbed her arm again. "There could be traps."

She jumped back. "Right, traps. Good point."

They stood next to each other as cool air flowed out from the darkness in front of them. Five feet wide and twice as tall, the door to the cavern stood open like a portal to the unknown. Harry pulled a flashlight out and flicked it on. He took a step back. "That's not good."

Three skeletons were sprawled on the ground. Corroded swords lay between their bones, rags of cloth draped over ribcages; three pairs of ratty leather boots had leg bones sticking out of them. Sara aimed her own light on the macabre scene. "You were right about the traps."

Long spears jutted out from all three corpses. "I hope there aren't any more spears," Sara said. "Look at the holes in the walls. You can see where they shot out of."

Harry had noticed the round openings on either side. "One way to find out. Come on." Harry reached into the cave opening and waved his hand, quickly pulling it back. Nothing. "I didn't think it would be that easy." He knelt down and played his light over the floor. "It's dirt, not stone. There aren't any pressure traps here."

"What's that?" Sara pointed to their left, just inside the opening. "It looks like writing."

It was. Letters had been carved into the cave wall beside them, a waist-high series of Greek words, etched into the stone. "I can barely read any Greek," Harry said.

"Good thing I'm here. Listen to this." Sara read the passage aloud, her voice echoing in the cave.

Welcome, wise Greek. You have proven yourself as you seek the prize of our greatest warrior. Beware, for you must be worthy of this final path. Use the gift of Prometheus only where the gold eagle sat on Zeus's throne to show the path.

"Great, another test." Harry touched his amulet.

"We're in this together," Sara said. "You can tell from their clothing and weaponry that these men weren't Greek. The swords are all wrong."

"They clearly didn't know their Greek mythology."

Sara smiled grimly. "Go on. Impress me."

"Prometheus stole fire from the gods and gave it to humans." Harry leaned in a fraction, but not too far. "There are torches on either wall of this cave. We're supposed to light one side, not both."

"Agreed," Sara said. "The question is, which side?"

Harry couldn't spot any scorch marks or other indications to show which one the unfortunate skeletons had lit. "Maybe they never even tried to light one," he said before she could respond. "They walked in and set off the spear trap."

"That was my guess too," Sara said. "These men didn't know about Zeus's throne. A golden eagle with ruby eyes stood at the right arm of his throne. The eagle was a symbol for Zeus, and a reminder to all the other gods of his power."

"We need to light the torch on the right." Harry thought for a second. "Or pull it out of the holder. It's bolted in to the wall. There could be a trip switch to activate the spears. If there are any left, that is."

"You want to take that chance?" Sara asked. Harry said he didn't. "Grab the torch."

"I brought a lighter," Harry said. He pulled a disposable one out of his pocket, one he'd purchased at the airport.

"Don't light it yet," Sara said. "First try to pull the torch out."

The torch was in a stone sconce attached to the wall. Harry reached into the opening and grabbed the torch with both hands. He pulled. It didn't come out. He put one hand on the bottom and shoved it upward. Without warning the torch took off like a rocket and shot up in the air. Harry grabbed the sconce so he wouldn't fall, reached out and snatched at the torch, but the sconce gave way under his weight and he missed.

The sconce shifted under his weight. Harry grabbed the torch off the floor and then jumped back as the walls rumbled. A grinding noise came from behind them, the sound of more weight shifting in a manner they couldn't see.

"Look at the walls." Sara stepped into the darkness and aimed her light to one side. "The holes in them are closing."

The holes closed as he watched. "You were right," Harry said. "Pulling the torch deactivated the trap."

He moved farther into the cave now and they began to walk together. Harry led the way, but they didn't make it far.

"Do you hear that?" Sara asked a few steps later. "It sounds like an echo."

"Stop." Harry aimed his light ahead. The darkness swallowed it, seeming to pull his beam from the air. He glanced back over his shoulder. The entrance seemed to have shrunk in half, though they were hardly into the cave. "Do you see it?"

Sara's light joined his. "See what?"

"Nothing. I don't see any ground at all. Don't move."

One step, then another. That's all it took.

"There's a cliff ahead of us," Harry said. "That's what's echoing. Our voices are falling off a cliff."

The ground disappeared not twenty feet in front of them. Vanished, actually falling off a cliff, which Harry wasn't surprised to find. Not when their voices had started out by echoing as though they were in a valley. Same concept, except they were at the top. The bottom of the void in front of them sounded a long way down.

"It's a natural fault in the ground," Harry said. "There's no way this is man-made."

"How do we get across?" Sara asked. "I can't see the far end."

"Maybe it's hidden in the dark and we can actually jump it."

He truly doubted that, but he doubted the Koraki wouldn't lead them here only to have their chase end like this. His gut proved correct once more when they stood at the edge of the cliff. "Over there," Harry said, aiming his flashlight over the gap. "See it?"

Sara turned to her right, looking where he pointed. "A bridge."

Braided rope lines stretched out across the void. Four of them: two handrails to grab hold of, and two more lines holding wooden boards for walking on. Boards with plenty of space between them.

Harry played his light over the bridge. "Hold on," he said. "That's more than one bridge. It splits partway over the chasm."

The bridge wasn't a straight line, but a Y shape, with the single walkway stretching from their side into the distance. Twenty feet out it split off in two directions, both leading to a far edge that he could barely make out at the edge of his light's range. "I see the other side," Harry said. "All we have to do is cross that bridge."

"Why the split?" Sara said. "Why two options for crossing?"

She knelt down and grabbed a small rock by her feet, then tossed it into the void. Harry counted less than two seconds before it landed.

"That's not bad," Sara said. "Less than two seconds. Can we jump down?"

"Not a chance." A nearly-forgotten fact surfaced in his memory.

"Acceleration of falling objects is roughly the same for anything you drop. Gravity makes things fall about thirty-two feet per second. That rock took a second and a half to land. That means the ground is over thirty feet below. Fall thirty feet onto stone and you're not getting up."

Sara glared at him as though it were his fault. "Then we cross the bridge," she said. "It's our only choice."

"How do we do that safely?"

She grabbed his arm and moved his flashlight beam so it hit the stone wall beside where the bridge started. "By solving that."

He'd missed the block of text written on the wall. He gave the cliff's edge a wide berth as he walked closer. "Greek again," he said when he stood in front of it. "What does it say?"

Follow the path of Olympians, walking with only the true number who reside above. The false number leads to Hades.

"We're already at Mount Olympus," Harry said. "This is where the Olympians live. It has to be their path."

"The Olympians lived *above* this, on top of the mountain." Sara looked at the ceiling as though it would provide answers. "I'm not clear what *number* this passage references."

Sara began talking to herself, ignoring Harry as she tried to understand the riddle. He wasn't listening. A thought buzzed at the edge of his mind, one he couldn't quite grasp but he'd bet a dollar was important. Her mumbled speculations filled the air. Harry closed his eyes, reaching for the idea he couldn't quite grasp. *The Olympians. Their path.* No, that wasn't it. What had set his inner alarm off? *True number, false number. Hades.*

He opened his eyes. He looked at the bridge. "That's it."

"What's it?" Sara asked, annoyance in her voice.

"The *true number.*" He grabbed her shoulders. "Do you remember when we were talking about Antony's crown?"

"What does Mark Antony's crown have to do with the Olympians?"

"Everything. When I was researching Greek myths to try and understand what the crown meant, I read an article about the Olympians. I never knew Hades wasn't an Olympian. He was Zeus's brother, but he wasn't one of them."

"Hades didn't live on Olympus. He was the god of the underworld. That's why."

"Exactly. He doesn't count."

"I don't understand."

"Most people would count Hades as an Olympian, which would make thirteen in total. This path is meant for a *learned Greek*. We're not Greek, but we are fairly well-versed in their history." He paused. "A learned Greek would know there are only twelve Olympians, not thirteen. Which is important."

"I'm still waiting to learn why."

He pointed at the bridge. "That's why. The bridge splits into two paths. One of them is safe. The question is which one. The Koraki wouldn't have put this note on the wall unless it mattered, and they wouldn't have made a strange bridge like this without good reason. This bridge and the message are a test. We still have to prove our worth."

"By solving their riddle," Sara said. She put her hands on her hips. "What's the solution?"

"It's in the bridge planks. Look how far apart they are. You almost have to jump from one to the next."

"You think some of the boards are meant to break?" Sara said. "You can't stop once you jump."

"Good luck hanging on to the rope railings long enough to get across," Harry said. "One broken board and you're toast." He caught her evil eye. "Count the boards on each side," he said quickly. "Both cover the same distance. Why don't they have the same number of boards?"

She did. "One has twelve. The other has thirteen." Her mouth fell open as understanding dawned. "The *true number*. Twelve Olympians, not thirteen."

"Hence the reference to Hades," Harry said. "He's the one most people who know about Greek history would lump in with the Olympians. They'd be wrong. There are only twelve. I think the side with twelve steps is the safe one. The other will send you on a short trip to meet Hades."

"How certain are you?"

What had Fred Fox told him? Lots of things, but one stuck out now. "The past is never certain."

"Did your father say that?"

Harry nodded. "I'm not certain I'm right, but I'm pretty sure, and there comes a time in every chase when that's the best you can hope for. I'd never get anywhere if I didn't trust my gut once in a while." He looked down. The spaces between each stepping board yawned as wide as the chasm they spanned. "Which could get me to the bottom of this pit."

"Nothing like positive thinking."

"Or it could get us across. At the very least it will get *you* across. I'm going first. If it holds, you follow. If I fall and it's still up, take the other bridge."

Sara took hold of his arm. "Harry, we don't have to do this. We can tell Nora whatever is over there is gone. She's not going to come check, and if that Russian ever gets his hands on this Achilles relic, so be it."

Harry laughed. "I know you too well. You want to know what's on the other side of this bridge as badly as I do. We didn't come all this way to turn back."

She tried to argue, but the words never made it past her lips. "Perhaps," she finally said. "I still think it's crazy."

"Unlike what other part of what we do?" He pulled her close and hugged her tight. "I'll be fine."

He turned and started walking. The first board held when he stepped on it, as did the second. Each step was as far as he could stretch his legs; the boards were a good four feet apart. Sara would have to almost jump from one to the next. The rope moorings swayed as he moved, forcing him to pause on each step and wait for stillness. Ten steps brought him to where the road forked. The chasm ended abruptly ahead in a flat floor just like what lay behind him. The left path had twelve steps. Right, thirteen.

The braided rope was rough under his hands. He peered at the ropes on each side. No evidence of a sabotage or weakness presented itself.

"Left it is," Harry said to himself. He grabbed the rope as tightly as he could. Maybe if it broke he could hang on and drag himself back to safety, try the other path. He took a half-step toward the board ahead and laughed. No way he could hang on if it broke. He was done for.

Harry looked over his shoulder. Sara stood at the cliff's edge, hands clasped at her chin, eyes shining in the light.

Get moving. He stretched a foot out and leapt into the abyss.

The bridge rattled when his foot landed. He grabbed the rope and leapt to the next board. The wood creaked under the stress with a sound like gunshots, ricocheting off the stone walls. He closed his eyes. The board held.

"I'm good," he called back.

"Hold on tight," Sara said. "Any one of the boards could be a trap."

"Thanks for that." Not what he needed right now. "Don't step out until I know it's safe," he called back. He didn't wait for a response.

Another leap; the boards seemed to be even farther apart this time. Again the board held. His palms burned from clasping the rope so tightly, but he vaulted twice more without falling. The bridge swayed like mad, but didn't break.

Harry kept going. Six down now, six to go. He settled into a careful rhythm: leap and stop, leap and stop, keep your balance at all times. He paused on board eleven and looked back. "I told you I was right."

"Keep moving."

"Yeah, yeah," he said under his breath. "Let a guy celebrate."

Every sound echoed off the walls. The twelfth and final board stood between him and flat ground. Harry waited a beat until the bridge stopped moving and went for it. Harry took one last step and was on solid ground. He turned and waved, but Sara was already on her way and joined him moments later.

A sudden roar filled the cave.

"What's that?" Sara asked in alarm.

"I think it's a helicopter."

"It sounds like thunder. Must have flown low over the mountain."

"I suggest we don't wait to find out why it's here."

The ground rose ahead of them, sloping up and to the right as they moved deeper into the cliffside. Harry ascended a gentle rise and found what they had been searching for all along.

"This is incredible," Harry said. "The Koraki weren't joking around."

They stood on the edge of a roughly circular cave. It looked to be about sixty feet in diameter. The cave roof was perhaps thirty feet overhead. Torches lined the walls at head height and encircled the entire room. Some sort of wire or string connected them all. Harry took all this in with a glance. That was all he could spare, for what waited in the room's center demanded attention.

A pit had been carved into the floor—or gouged, judging from the rough toolmarks at the lip. The cave's floor had been cut away until only a ring of earth remained at its edge, circling the pit and giving little room for error if you stumbled. An oily-looking liquid of some sort filled the pit nearly to the brim.

A platform rose from the pit's center, no more than five feet across. It stood exactly in the middle of the pit, a single pole holding it aloft. A pedestal stood in the center of it. A row of square columns rose above the surface of the oily liquid like a series of stepping-stones from the lip of the pit out to the platform. Ten steps in all, each one a bit higher than the last, until the final step stood within easy reach of the platform.

Sara squinted across the surface of the viscous liquid. "Those look like spikes sticking up out of the water."

"They are spikes," Harry said. "Sharp ones. And I don't think that's water."

"Hang on." Harry grabbed Sara's hand and extended one leg over the pit, flashlight clamped in his teeth. He reached down and dipped the toe of his boot in the liquid. It came back sticky. "It's oil."

"Nice touch," said Sara. "Spikes in a pit filled with oil."

Harry lifted his light and shone it on the platform, where three objects glinted. "Yup. They're here to protect those."

"That's a shield," Sara said, indicating the first object.

"That's what the Koraki protected for so long," Harry said. "Greek's greatest treasure."

"There is a helmet beside it. And a chest plate."

Sure enough, a helmet rested beside the shield, and a sculpted metal chest plate sat beside it. The helmet was designed with ear pieces to protect the sides of the warrior's face, while the ridged top covered his head. The front was open to allow for a wide field of vision. A curved piece jutting from the top would have proudly displayed a plume of feathers or fur, making the warrior seem larger than life as he ran down his enemies.

The chest plate was a single piece of hammered metal that covered the entire torso, front and back. Sculpted pectoral and abdominal muscles added to the already fearsome effect.

"Do you think that's Achilles' armor?" Harry asked. "The actual warrior?"

"It appears to be from the correct time period," Sara said. "However, I can't tell until I inspect it. Which would require walking up those stairs." She pointed at the columns sunk into the oil.

They were small steps, yes, but nothing they couldn't manage. Sara's tone made it clear she had little interest in doing so.

Harry didn't like it. "Something's off about this. It's too simple. After all these riddles and traps, a balance test? I don't buy it."

"There are steps behind it as well." Sara pulled him around the circular pathway until he could see. "The same number and style of steps lead away from the platform to the far side of the cave. Why?"

"I bet we find our answer on that." He pointed to a carving on the cave wall adjacent to the entrance. He'd walked right past it. "The Koraki can't make anything easy."

"They're protecting what they believe is one of the most important pieces of Greek history ever created. Would you make it easy?"

No, he would not. That didn't mean he had to like this last hurdle.

"Greek again," Harry said when they stood in front of the engraved words. "You're up."

Sara opened her mouth as a faint *boom* filled the cave. "What was that?" she asked.

"Quiet." Harry turned an ear toward the entrance. "These acoustics are terrible. I can't tell how far away it is."

"Why does that matter?"

"Because it sort of sounded like a gunshot." She actually jumped an inch or two. "Easy." Harry grabbed her arm. "I'm not sure. It could have been a plane flying over, or that helicopter again, or maybe a rock slide miles away. I really don't know."

"Who would have a gun up here? These mountains are for climbing and hiking, not hunting."

"And I'm guessing some of those climbers and hikers carry sidearms in case they run across wolves or jackals. Get between one of those and her cubs and you'll be sorry you don't have a gun." All of these were plausible explanations, of course. Panicking would only get them killed. "It's a long way off, whatever it was." Probably.

"If you're sure."

He wasn't. "What does this Greek text say?" Harry asked, trying to refocus.

The academic puzzle of deciphering ancient Greek seemed to distract Sara. She leaned over to study the carving. "The first line is quite clear. We are to light the torches."

"Are you sure? That's a pool of oil. One wrong ember or spark and that pool turns into a roaring fire."

"Listen." She ran her finger underneath the carved words and translated.

Channel Prometheus to reveal the path to Greece's prize. Only then may you follow the path of Theseus to retrieve it. Beware the Minotaur who is always at your back, as Ariadne warned. Turning to face him will lead across the Styx.

"Prometheus stole fire back from the gods and gave it to man," Harry said. "You're right: we have to light something on fire."

Sara pointed to the closest torch. "Those are set far enough back from the oil that they *should* be safe to light. It also makes no sense for the Koraki to create a death trap. This path is meant to reward the worthy, not kill them."

Harry pulled out his lighter. "It'll take a few minutes to light them all."

"Stop." Sara pointed at the closest torch. "Start with that one and then step back. I think the Koraki made this easier than you believe. Look at the wall." She pointed to the lines between the torches that he'd noticed when they'd first entered.

"Right," he said. "What the heck are those for, do you suppose?"

"I have a hunch. Light the first one and watch."

The flint made a scraping sound as he flicked the lighter on and stepped up to the closest torch. Rushes jutted from it, and they must have been soaked in creosote or oil because moments after his flame touched them the torch burst to life. Harry winced at the heat, stepping back to Sara's side. She grabbed his arm and pointed.

"Watch."

Sparks flared, accelerant popped and the wall caught fire. The line Harry spotted was actually a channel carved into the stone, connecting each torch in line. More flammable material had been stuffed into the walls to create an automatic lighting system, the first torch setting it off so that flame raced around the room at a dizzying pace, lighting each torch in turn until a dozen torches washed away the darkness. Shadows danced on the curved ceiling and across the floor. Torchlight reflected brilliantly off the oil pool and glinted off the sharp points of the spikes sticking up out of the liquid. Spikes to impale anyone who fell from the steps or platform.

Harry looked around. "Impressive. Now to get through the maze."

"Labyrinth," Sara said. "Are you familiar with the legend of Theseus?"

"He killed the Minotaur," Harry said. "There was a woman involved. A princess, if memory serves."

"Princess Ariadne. Daughter of King Minos, who made Theseus's people send him boys and girls each year to be devoured by the Minotaur. Theseus volunteered to go kill the Minotaur and stop his people being killed, but Ariadne fell in love with Theseus and told him how to navigate the labyrinth. He killed the Minotaur and managed to escape."

"This message tells us not to face the Minotaur, which apparently requires turning around. Seems like looking back is a bad idea."

Sara shook her head. "There are several different versions of the myth. I only know the main one well, which is what I just recapped."

That didn't make sense. The Koraki weren't trying to trick anyone. Their concern was that only a properly educated Greek could retrieve the prize. A Greek committed to using whatever power these objects possessed, real or perceived, to do one thing. Protect the *idea* of Greece. There were only so many people who could get here who could also be counted on to act a certain way. The Koraki wouldn't jeopardize their success by pinning it on some little-known variant of a legend.

"No, your legend is the correct one." He told her why and she agreed. "We have to avoid crossing the river Styx. Do that and you're in the underworld, which means you're dead. How do we avoid that? By not turning to face the Minotaur."

They looked around the cave in the increased light from the torches. The walls were bare of any decoration save the torches and the instructions.

"I don't see a Minotaur," Sara said.

He needed to check the other side. They could be missing something. "Stay here." He made a fast circuit of the room. "The steps on the far side are identical to the ones on this side. That's important."

"Why?"

"Because my gut says so." He really had no idea. Having two identical sets of steps was meant to say something, it was a clue about how to survive this room. But how? "Give me a second."

Sara looked back toward the distant entrance. "I don't know how many we have. We have to get back before dark."

Get back.

"That's it." He turned and grabbed Sara, lifting her off the ground and scaring her so much she nearly kicked him into the oil pit.

"What's wrong with you?" She clutched at his arm when he stumbled. "Don't scare me like that."

"You're right." His entire body was alight with the familiar thrill, the sheer joy of hunting down treasures from the past and actually succeeding. "It's about getting *back*."

"Stop blabbering and explain yourself."

Torches flickered and shadows danced. "The Minotaur was always at Theseus's back. The princess warned him. He eventually fought it, but navigating the labyrinth kept the beast behind him. That's what makes the final line make sense. The Koraki are saying we *can't turn around*. We can't face him."

Sara had spent too many years dissecting legends in a classroom to stop asking questions now. "What does it matter if you turn around?"

"There are two sets of steps up to that platform. The first row that I walk up could have pressure sensors of some sort under them. My body weight could trip a lever or counterweight that makes going back down them unsafe."

Sara looked doubtful. "Which requires you to use the second set of steps? I suppose it's possible. But what if you're wrong? There's no way you can jump from the platform if the second set of steps is unsafe. It's too far."

"Then I'll throw you the artifacts and figure it out."

Her arms shot out wide. "Figure it out? If you get stuck on that platform, if you even survive that long, then I'm stranded here on the edge of the pit with no way to save you if I can't go back the way we came." Torchlight blazed in her eyes. "And we have to assume the torches will set this oil alight if you run afoul of the Korakis' directions."

"You're the most capable woman I've ever met," Harry said. "You'll get out of here."

"That is the dumbest, most selfish statement I have ever heard."

Yeesh. So much for the compliment. "It makes sense," Harry said. "You have a better idea?"

"I do. Walk away from here, tell Nora and Gary Doyle we didn't find anything, then go to Cairo."

The most sensible, practical thing he'd heard so far in this quest. "I can't do that."

"Why not?" Sara practically yelled. "You'd rather die?"

Harry touched the amulet under his shirt. "It's what I do, Sara. You know that." If Fred Fox could speak to Harry now, he'd say the same thing. Tell Harry to stay back, stay safe, that he believed in him. Then Fred would climb those steps. "You've known that for a long time."

Her voice was soft. "I have."

"Take this." Harry reached under his shirt and pulled the amulet over his head. "You might need it."

Sara's mouth opened in surprise. Never in his life had he handed the amulet to another person. She knew that, and when he pressed the warm metal into her hand she couldn't respond.

He took full advantage. "Stay clear of the oil. You're probably right about the fire part."

Harry turned and put one foot out onto the first step. Sara said something to him but he didn't hear it. The air went still. Tiny rocks crackled like wildfire under his feet. All his weight went on the step in one smooth motion. Harry's heart threatened to smash his ribs apart.

Nothing happened. No flames, no spears, nothing but an ache in his chest until he remembered to breathe. "It's solid." Harry turned back to look at Sara. "Feels great."

"What are you waiting for? There is no guarantee it will stay that way."

A great point. One more step, then another. The rising columns were an easy stride apart and at last he was on the last one, level with the final platform holding the Koraki prize. He didn't look at the spikes below him on all sides before stepping across the short gap. The platform held solid.

"Describe the artifacts for me," Sara said. "Are they authentic?"

So much for the heartfelt concern. Harry leaned over the round shield and flicked on his flashlight, the beam glinting brightly on its polished metal. Metal bolts held the layers together. Several deep grooves ran across the decorations, straight lines to deflect blows. Not grooves, but more like cuts. The sort a sword might make. "I think so. The shield is bronze laid over wood and leather." He turned to look at the other two items. "The chest plate is also bronze and leather. The helmet is bronze."

"All correct for the period. Is there anything else?"

He leaned over the pedestal and checked all around. "Nothing else." An urge that hit him the moment he stepped up here finally won out. Harry spun the shield around, slipped his hands through two straps on the rear and hefted the armor. "This thing is *heavy*. Whoever used this was strong as hell." His shoulder strained with the effort of holding the shield up and moving it around. Blocking spear thrusts and sword blows would be exhausting. He set the shield back down and grabbed the chest plate. It had been crafted for a man who stood well north of six feet. "Same with this. The pec muscles on here aren't just for show."

A slash mark across the front of the chest plate had been smoothed down, leaving a ghost of a cut across the metal. The helmet was pristine. This was a warrior's armor. "Aci Los was a big, strong guy. The sort of guy who leads armies."

Sara didn't respond.

"I might have to wear this gear to get it out and carry it down the mountain," he said. The stuff was that heavy. If he slipped the chest plate over his head and wore the helmet, he could manage getting out of here. Unless he fell in the oil pit. Then he'd drown, no question, after being skewered. "Will I damage anything by wearing it?"

Still no response. "Can you hear me?" he asked as he grabbed the chest plate and slipped it over his head. Harry turned and looked over a shoulder.

Four men looked back at him. One swarthy man had a hand over Sara's mouth and a gun to her head. A man who looked familiar. That's when Harry realized the hand covering her mouth had only three fingers.

Chapter 25

Mount Olympus

"Put down my armor."

A pale man stepped into full view. No taller than Harry, clad in outdoor clothes clearly brand-new, he stared at Harry with flat eyes in an unremarkable face. A face known across the globe, not for movie-star good looks, but for his wallet. Evgeny Smolov held the world in his fist. And Harry Fox had already stolen from him once.

Harry bluffed. "Who are you?"

Smolov looked at him as though he were daft. "You know my name. Everyone knows my name."

"Humor me."

"I am Evgeny. You are Harry Fox. The man who stole a crown from me."

Harry's legs nearly went out from under him. *How does he know?*

"This stuff isn't yours," Harry said. "I found it, so it's mine."

"And now you will give it to me." Evgeny looked to Sara. "I do not want to involve your woman. Give me the artifacts and you both may go."

Harry didn't bother asking what would happen if he didn't. The three-fingered man pressed the gun more tightly against Sara's head and scowled as Harry looked his way. Harry turned his gaze to the two other men on the platform and narrowed his eyes. At least one of the guys had been in Istanbul, smoking on the street. "How long have you been following me?"

The other man, clad in a long-sleeved shirt, sneered at Harry. "Longer than you know." By the way the other two Middle Eastern men looked at him, this guy was clearly their leader. Long-sleeves turned toward the one with three fingers. "Shoot her. I will get the artifacts."

"No," Evgeny said. "Rafiq, bloodshed is bad for business. He will be reasonable."

So long-sleeves was called Rafiq. "You can have this stuff," Harry said. "Let Sara go."

The man with three fingers holding Sara grumbled. Rafiq growled at him in Arabic. "Close your mouth, Noor."

Torchlight glinted off Evgeny's incredibly white teeth. "A good choice."

Three-fingered man was Noor. Harry paused. "How do I know you won't kill me? You think I stole a crown from you. Which I didn't. You're going to shoot me anyway."

"I don't think," Evgeny said. "I know. Once I learned who put my first man in the hospital, I checked the security footage again. A gut feeling. It was you, Harry Fox. And if you give me the crown back, you have my word I will not shoot you." Evgeny waved his hand around. "It is not as though you have a choice."

"Fine. I'm coming down."

He looked uneasily toward the second set of steps, then turned back to the armor. Like he'd told Sara, he wasn't going to try to walk down those steps off-balance. Harry stuck the helmet on his head. Someone in Evgeny's group grumbled, but he ignored them and hefted the shield onto an arm. He rounded the pedestal and stepped to the descending pillars behind it without thinking. Getting Sara away from those lunatics with guns was all that mattered. Do that, and he and Sara could figure the rest of it out later. Maybe Smolov was telling the truth. Maybe he wasn't. Either way, he had control of the other three men and was Harry and Sara's best chance at getting out of this cave alive.

His foot was off the tallest platform and halfway to the first step before he remembered. *This might be a trap.* Well, only one way to find out. And it wasn't like he had much choice right now.

He put his full weight on the pillar, then paused. Nothing happened. Harry almost smiled.

A voice boomed from behind him. "He is getting away. Stop him!"

Ice filled Harry's gut. He turned and waved his hand. "I'm coming down," he shouted. "I have to come down these rear steps. Stay back!"

Sara yelled much the same as the third man under Smolov's command ran onto the set of steps leading toward the platform. He hadn't made it to the second pillar when the walls began shaking.

A grinding noise filled the air as hidden gears began turning. The pillar beneath Harry's feet shook back and forth, blurring his vision and nearly sending him toppling into the spiked pit. He jumped to the next step as flames erupted from the walls. Holes opened above each burning torch and dark liquid shot out, streaming over the circular walkway and into the oily pit. Harry made it to the third shaking step before the oil gushing from the walls caught fire. Now a dozen flamethrowers were alight and aimed at the pit.

Harry hit the second-last step as it began to collapse under him. He leapt, hurling himself to safety between two jets of flame as a chilling scream filled the air. It lasted a half second and was abruptly cut off. *So much for that guy.*

The flames were all around him. Harry clattered into the wall, his leap barely carrying him over the now-vanished last pillar. He lifted the shield to cover his head and ran around the edge of the room toward Sara and the men. The steps leading up to the platform had disappeared. A conflagration where the second step had been was all that remained of the thug who'd run up the steps and unwittingly set off the final trap.

Evgeny Smolov led the charge back outside. Sara ran behind him, Noor trying to keep hold of her and failing as he gave chase. Only Rafiq watched Harry circle the room for a moment longer.

The heat from liquid fire pouring across the upraised shield singed

Harry's face as he waved an arm at Rafiq. "Get out of here!" he yelled.

Rafiq finally listened, disappearing through the entrance door seconds before Harry. Out they ran as the walls behind them cracked and crumbled. Harry made it into the next room as a massive boulder fell from above and landed in the spiked lake. Burning oil splashed across the floor, licking at Harry's heels and turning the room into an inferno that would burn for ages. Harry stopped beyond the burning oil and banged the shield off the floor to get the worst of the oil off. Incredibly, it had saved him from anything worse than a minor sear.

Evgeny reached the bridge just ahead of Sara. It rattled and shook as the Russian oligarch tottered across it, clinging to the rope handrails as he ran. Sara had put some distance between her and Noor and was only a step behind Evgeny, following right on his backside. Noor hesitated, staring uneasily at the bouncing bridge, and then veered to the left fork, which wasn't flopping around quite as much.

The side of the bridge that had thirteen steps.

Harry ran on. He didn't say a word.

Noor didn't make it past step one. The very first board cracked under his weight. A cry sounded, fading down into the abyss before cutting off.

Rafiq had been headed for the same fate, but seeing his partner drop like a stone, he stopped and turned to the side of the bridge with twelve steps. Evgeny and Sara had already safely crossed, but the planks still bucked and bounced. Rafiq hesitated. Harry did not. He barreled at Rafiq, shield lowered to knock him into the pit ahead. Rafiq must have heard him coming. He slipped aside to let Harry pass, following only after Harry was a few steps out onto the safe fork of the bridge.

Oh well. Harry didn't slow, didn't think, he just ran until he was back in the room with the spears waiting to blast them from either side. He did note with relief that the torch he'd pulled down to deactivate the trap remained in place as he went at full speed through the room. Brilliant sunlight beckoned ahead, too bright for his eyes after the darkness of the cave. On he ran toward it, muscles burning with the weight of the Greek armor pressing on him until at last he burst into the light outside the cave. And promptly tripped.

The bronze armor threw off his balance as he tried to hit the brakes. One second he was hurtling along; the next he was airborne, his feet tangled around each other. The ground came up to meet him, hard, as he crashed down, twisting and turning and rolling as the world spun. Something hard smacked off his helmet with a deafening gong before he came to a standstill, lying in a heap in the dirt.

Harry lay still. He wasn't dead, but it sure felt like he was close. Everything hurt. His chest. His legs. The dusty air caked in his dry throat as he gasped for breath. A baseball-sized rock beside him explained the ringing in his ears—and probably why he'd tripped. *Your armor works, Aci Los. Thanks.*

"Get up."

Rafiq had survived. Worse than that, he had hold of Sara once more, his pistol once again pressed against her head.

"Hold on." It took a bit of effort and a good amount of swearing, but Harry clambered to his feet, the armor like an anchor keeping him down. He briefly wondered if the shield was bulletproof.

"Nice work." Evgeny Smolov sounded genuinely impressed as he dusted himself off a few feet away from Harry. "You saved my armor."

"Thanks." Harry arched his back, to the dismay of several vertebrae. "This stuff is heavy."

Rafiq jerked his gun at Harry. "Take it off."

"No problem." Harry dumped the shield on the ground. Before he could remove the chest plate and helmet, Evgeny came over and grabbed the shield, lifting it easily with his massive hands. Harry set the helmet and chest plate at Evgeny's feet and stepped back. He looked at Rafiq and glared. "Let her go."

Sara stumbled as Rafiq shoved her toward him. Harry caught her, but didn't pull her close. Sara was too proud for that. "You okay?" he asked.

"I'm fine." She turned and gave Rafiq a murderous look. "Bullies like him are all talk."

Maybe not the best thing to say right now, but Harry ignored it. "We'll be leaving now," he said to Evgeny. "Good luck with your museum. I'll mail you the crown."

"Don't move." Rafiq took a step toward them. He looked only at Sara. "You are *kafir*."

"A nonbeliever?" Sara's eyes narrowed. "You have no idea who I am."

Rafiq moved another step closer. "Women must obey the laws of Allah. You walk in public with your head uncovered, consort with men who are not your husband." He spat at the ground. "You are unworthy."

Harry looked at Evgeny. The shield still had his attention. "We're leaving now."

Evgeny didn't respond. Rafiq kept talking, switching to Arabic. "*'ant last layqan lileaysh.*"

Harry started. *You are not fit to live.* He grabbed Sara's arm. "Time to go."

Sara wasn't having any of it. "You are a sad little man. Distorting religion to hide your weakness. Go away," she replied in Arabic.

Harry understood every word of it. Her gumption made him proud. It also scared him to death. "Stop it," he whispered under his breath. "That's a gun he's holding."

Too late. "You dare speak to me with disrespect?" long-sleeves said, this time in English. "I could kill you now. You are the enemy. Allah has told me to wage *jihad* against the nonbelievers. You do not believe."

Harry stepped in front of Sara and glared at him. "You got what you want. It's over, and I'm doing you a favor. You have no idea who will come after you if we die."

Rafiq spat again. "You protect her?" He scowled. "Is this woman your sister?"

Harry started. He was too shocked to respond. *Sister?* Across from them Evgeny looked up from inspecting the helmet. "What did you say?" he said to Rafiq, straightening and fixing him with that flat stare.

Rafiq ignored him. "I see now," he said as he raised the pistol, aiming at Harry's chest. "She is yours, either by blood or an unholy alliance. It does not matter."

"Run." Harry shoved Sara as hard as he could. She stumbled toward the tree line as Harry's feet dug into the dirt. This wasn't something his father had taught him. This was a Morello lesson. Run from a knife. Run *at* a gun. It was your only chance.

Rafiq was ten feet from him. His gun was up, aimed at Harry's chest, too close to miss. Harry dove at Rafiq, twisting in the air like Superman. There was the bark of a gunshot, and in the same instant, Rafiq dropped to the ground as though crushed by Zeus's thunderbolt. Harry's arms closed on nothing at all and he tumbled to the dirt, rolling to break his fall. Puzzled, he looked up. Rafiq lay a few feet away from him. Half of his skull was missing.

Harry twisted around to see Evgeny Smolov holding a pistol at arm's length. It was trained on the corpse beside Harry.

"Harry!" Sara ran over to him and knelt beside him. "Are you okay?"

Harry could only nod. She helped him to his feet, then they both spun around to look at Evgeny. The Russian billionaire put his gun in a pocket and picked the helmet up. He didn't acknowledge them at all.

Sara found her voice first. "Why?" she asked.

Evgeny still didn't look up. "Are you his sister? I don't think you are."

"I'm not."

Evgeny nodded. He kept looking at the helmet.

Harry wasn't about to waste another chance. "We're going to leave now."

"One moment," Evgeny said. "First you steal from me. Now I save your life. You owe me, Harry Fox."

Hard to argue with that. "Yeah, I do. I promise you'll get the crown back."

Evgeny tilted his head, seeming to look inside Harry, not at him.

"You are good at the relic hunting business. Very good."

Harry couldn't help himself. "I'm the best."

"I have a passion for antiquities. My collection is among the best in the world. What you saw in England is only a small part of it."

"It was very nice," Harry said guardedly.

"It is the best." Evgeny smiled, those white teeth flashing. "But it will get better. Finding new relics and treasures is not easy. It requires a very specialized skill."

"You're richer than a god," Harry said. "You can get the best relic hunters."

Evgeny's eyes gleamed in the sunlight. "I know."

His meaning slammed into Harry like a tsunami. "Hold on." The ground, so recently unsteady beneath his feet, seemed to shift once more. "You want to *hire* me?"

"I pay very well."

Harry's mouth opened. It closed. Evgeny appeared to be used to this sort of reaction and let it play out.

"I work for the police," Harry said. "Part-time."

"And the rest of the time you work for a gangster." Evgeny shrugged. "What is the difference? Police, gangsters, men like me. I am sorry to spoil this for you, but we are all the same. Anyone who thinks otherwise is a fool."

Harry had seen just enough of the world to know Evgeny spoke the truth. His gut told him to go with it, for two facts were indisputable. One, Evgeny Smolov could be his best friend in the world. Two, you didn't say no to men like him.

Only one question made sense. "How?"

"I will call you when I need you," Evgeny said. "Stay with the Morello son. Help the police if you like. I only look for the very best. When I find it, I will call you." Evgeny walked over, his eyes level with Harry's as he slapped a hand on Harry's shoulder. It may as well have been the hand of Zeus. "Trust me. Your boss will approve. If he does not, tell him to call me. We will make a deal."

He had no doubt Joey Morello would approve. Connecting with a man like Evgeny Smolov was something that couldn't be purchased. You had to earn it. And if Joey was on Evgeny's good side, that meant Altin Cana wasn't.

Harry met Evgeny's gaze. "You take care of your friends, don't you?"

"Yes," he said. "Unless you betray me. Then you die."

The best he could hope for. "It's a deal." Harry stuck his hand out. It disappeared into Evgeny's.

"Good. Now put the armor on. It is a long walk to my car." He lifted the helmet and set it on his head. The sunlight glinted off it as he turned toward the path. "I will wear this. I like it."

Epilogue

An angular glass pyramid sparkled under the desert sun. Acres of polished granite and flagstone walkways surrounded the world's largest archaeological museum, a testament to the architectural genius Egyptians had demonstrated for thousands of years. Construction workers in yellow hardhats milled about the grounds. while seemingly hundreds of both traditionally dressed and besuited Egyptians weaved between the ongoing construction zones toward the entrances.

A chill ran down Harry's spine. Two days ago he and Sara had nearly been killed on a Greek mountain. Now they stood outside the Grand Egyptian Museum, on the verge of unraveling the greatest mystery of them all. At least to Harry. He touched the amulet hanging once again beneath his shirt, the amulet Sara had kept safe for him in the fiery cave. Perhaps it had kept both of them safe. *I wish you were here, Dad.*

"Ready?" Sara didn't look away from the museum's soaring façade when she asked. "My colleague is expecting us."

One of Sara's former university classmates was a director at the museum, and she had been more than happy to escort Sara and her guest on a private tour of the collection. Such personal excursions with professional colleagues were encouraged, given the museum's grand opening was less than two weeks away. Sara's promise to publish a naturally glowing review of Egypt's new flagship museum had vaulted them to the top of the list. Sara's colleague hadn't questioned her interest in starting their tour with the statue of Ptolemy Soter. Egyptologists all had their unique interests.

They stopped near the spot on the plaza that Sara's friend had specified. "Did you speak with Joey?" she asked Harry.

"I did. He's thrilled."

Joey Morello had been more than thrilled to learn Harry was in Evgeny Smolov's good graces. Aligning the Morello family with a man like Evgeny Smolov made sense for all the right reasons. New York might be one of the biggest cities in the world, and the Morellos were at the top of the food chain, but Joey Morello had nothing on Evgeny. The man had his hands in more deals than Jimmy Hoffa ever dreamed of. Joey was already planning for how their two operations might collaborate for mutual profitability. No matter what, it all started with Harry. Anything Harry needed, he would have it. Including time to unravel the truth behind his father's amulet.

Gary Doyle, on the other hand, was less than thrilled to learn Smolov had acquired the Achilles artifacts. Harry and Sara had connected for a video conference before leaving Greece on their way to Egypt. Gary had grumbled when Harry reported what had happened, though his tune quickly changed when he understood it was Harry's life or the artifact. "We are running a marathon," he'd said. "Not the hundred-meter dash. There will be other criminals to undermine. Quite soon, I'd imagine. I hope we can count on you in the future."

As though Harry had a choice. "I'll see what I can do," he'd replied.

Gary frowned. He was smart enough not to argue. "I'm happy you are uninjured. You as well, Dr. Hamed. Your services are invaluable."

Gary couldn't have known it, but that cemented Harry in Sara's eyes. She'd been through one adventure after another with him, yet only when he showed his true colors as a legitimate protector of antiquities had she fully accepted him. Having a man like Gary Doyle counting on Harry put him above reproach. Even if his protector status was truly part-time.

After Gary had logged off, Nora had assured Harry she'd make sure her father understood Harry was for emergency use only. "At the risk of inflating your ego, your skills are unique. This is an equal partnership."

"That's quite enough," Sara said. "He's difficult enough as it is."

Later, Nora had called him with one last piece of information: confirmation that Stefan Rudovic had been treated in an Athens hospital for a fractured ankle. His whereabouts were currently unknown.

"Keep your eyes open," Nora said. "I doubt Stefan is a man to forget what happened."

"He's not, and I always do."

"Where are you going now?" Nora asked. She'd tried to sound casual and failed miserably.

"To an airport," Harry had told her. "You know how to reach me." He'd clicked off before she could ask anything further. This adventure was private.

Sara touched Harry's shoulder, jolting him back to the present. "There she is." Sara raised her voice and waved. "Engy, over here."

A woman clad in well-used dig clothes pushed through ever-moving people toward them. "Sara, it's so good to see you." Engy Tarek had her curly hair pulled back into a ponytail, and the boots on her feet spoke of long hours out in the open. A woman of the field.

"You as well." Sara released Engy from an embrace. "This is Harry Fox."

Engy's grip was firm when Harry took her hand. "A pleasure to meet you, Harry."

"Likewise," he said. "Busy around here today."

Engy shook her head. "You have no idea. We open our doors in two weeks. You'd think after ten years things would be in order."

"Coming through!"

Two men pushing a stack of pallets on wheels barged through the crowd, inattentive bystanders be damned. Harry dodged out of the way just in time. Engy didn't blink as the men missed her by inches.

"It's a busy time," she said, then rubbed her hands together. "Now, let's go see your statue."

Engy led them through a wide set of double doors cut into the side of the stunning glass façade. Panels designed in the shape of pyramids wowed guests as they entered, though they were nothing compared to what waited on the other side. An atrium big enough to land planes in welcomed them to the desert's newest attraction. Spotlights high overhead dazzled as they shined on polished floors. Sunlight poured through skylights, while the ceiling rippled in sharp waves overhead like dominoes in mid-fall. A towering statue of a long-dead pharaoh looked down on them from its spot in the middle of the grand entrance hall.

"Pretty neat, isn't it?"

Harry looked away from the glorious sight to find Engy watching him. "Magnificent," he said.

"Thank you. Most people have the same reaction." She pointed to a hallway as wide as the Champs-Élysées. "This way."

Engy's credentials whisked them past not one, but two different checkpoints manned by armed guards. People in fluorescent yellow vests roamed like ants all around them. Engy didn't bat an eye at the chaos. "What about Ptolemy Soter has your interest?" she asked as they turned down another imposing hallway. "Are you researching for a publication?"

"It's more of a personal visit, to be honest." Sara put her hand on Engy's arm. "For both Harry and me. I hope you understand."

"Of course." If Engy wanted to hear more, she did an excellent job of hiding it. "We're nearly there."

Another turn brought them into a quieter part of the museum, though 'quieter' meant only that the closest construction worker was thirty yards away instead of ten. Several men in security uniforms with pistols on their hips patrolled the area.

"Do you have security issues?" Sara asked.

"Not anymore," Engy said. "The last people to try and steal anything from the museum were given twenty-year sentences. That put a stop to any inside looting. These guards are here to stop visitors from taking pictures. The museum board wants every exhibit to be a surprise." Engy led them around one final turn and stopped. "Here he is."

Ptolemy Soter stood ten feet tall, not including his pedestal, and of course he did not deign to look at the subjects before him. His vacant eyes stared into the distance. A rectangular beard jutted out from his chin, framed by the traditional headdress that flowed down onto his chest. He did not wear a shirt, sporting only a wrapped garment covering him from waist to knees. Both arms were bent at the elbow as he held an open book in front of him.

"Quite impressive, isn't he?" Engy said. "This statue of Ptolemy Soter was originally housed in the Great Caesareum in Alexandria. However, rising sea levels claimed the building, and it was only recently that the artifacts inside the structure were recovered. This statue is one of the jewels from that find, and we're fortunate to have it here." She looked at Sara from the corner of her eye. "Though I'm sure you know that already."

"Yes," Sara said. "But thank you."

Sara looked toward Harry, so Engy did the same. She didn't seem to be sure why.

Harry was staring at a maroon velvet rope that kept guests several feet back from the statue. "Are we allowed to get closer?" he asked.

Engy winked. "I think I can help with that." She unhooked one end of the rope and let it drop. "Go ahead. My only request is that you not touch the statue."

Harry forced himself to take slow, measured steps until he stood beside it. The book it held was above eye level by a foot or so. Sara joined him at the base. "I can't see the book," he said, standing on his tiptoes.

"I thought that would be the case." Sara turned to Engy. "Would you be offended if we did something unorthodox?"

Engy smiled. "Not at all."

Sara looked at Harry. "Put me on your shoulders."

He blinked. "What?"

"Boost me up."

No one seemed to notice as the slender Egyptologist clambered onto Harry's shoulders. Harry took careful steps until Sara said she could see the open book, bracing his legs to keep her steady.

Engy was more curious than uncomfortable about what had just transpired. "I could have sent you an image of the book's contents," she said. "It would be no problem."

"We had to come here in person," Sara said. "And I couldn't miss a chance to see you again."

Engy clearly had her doubts. "I see," she said.

Harry held tight to Sara's legs. "What do you see?" he asked.

"Writing."

"Can you read it?"

"Of course. The glyphs are from the same time period as what I found in Luxor. Now be quiet."

He waited. Laborers and scholars moved around in a messy, concerted dance of preparation. None spared them more than a passing glance, their muted conversation covering the mutterings of Sara coming from above as she translated. Engy watched, one elbow in the opposite palm, chin in her hand.

"The first line is identical to the one on the Luxor statue," Sara said.

"Exactly the same?"

"Yes."

His body felt electrified. "That means we're correct. This statue is the next marker."

"It's more than that," Sara said, and she began reading.

The knowledge of our founder will protect the dynasty. Honor him by seeking knowledge at his feet in the Great Caesareum.

You are the future and have proven your worth. Look down to what you received from us that covers your hearts. The gift of gold and faience to AH led you here.

Now read the gift of CSII and use what you have learned to find the most valuable treasure of them all.

Harry nearly dropped her. "Did you say faience? As in the blue ceramic material?"

"I did."

"Does it say anything else?" She said it didn't, and, task complete, asked to be set down again. Harry grabbed her shoulders. "There's only one place we've seen faience."

She was staring at his chest. Harry reached into his shirt and pulled out the amulet. Engy stepped closer, her eyebrows raised.

"Right here," Harry said. "My amulet."

"The only amulet we have," Sara said. "Ptolemy's book is suggesting there are two. One that belonged to *AH* and another belonging to *CSII*. Which I think I can now explain."

"The same letters from inside Antony's crown," Harry said. "*CSIIAH*."

Sara turned to Engy. "Who do you know with those initials? Think Mark Antony and Cleopatra."

Engy's face lit up in an instant. "My goodness. Of course. Alexander Helios and Cleopatra Selene II."

Lines creased Harry's forehead. "Who are you guys talking about?"

"Mark Antony and Cleopatra's twins," Sara said. "Their children. That's who this trail was for. They left a hidden path for their children to follow."

"I have quite a few questions," Engy said. "They can wait."

Harry took a deep breath and pushed away the fire burning inside him. "There's something you should know. I never told anyone else about it."

"About your amulet?" Sara asked.

"About *either* amulet."

Now Sara took a step back. "Hold on. You *knew* there are two of these?"

"I never thought it mattered," Harry said. "My amulet drove this chase. It also captured my father's attention and was the one mystery he never solved. I never suspected this was about more than his amulet. That's why I never said anything, even to you."

"About what, Harry?"

All Harry could think about was the file waiting for him back in Brooklyn. A file he understood, only now, might contain the truth behind more than he'd ever imagined. "About my mother's amulet. She had one too. An amulet that resembled my father's."

"Only *resembled*?" Sara asked.

Harry nodded. "Same material and shape. The only differences were the engravings." He touched the glyphs carved into his amulet. "My mother's amulet had different glyphs. That's what we need now. We have to find my mother's amulet, and I know where to start looking."

THE END

Author's Note

In Greek mythology, Achilles is the greatest of all Greek warriors, a (perhaps *the*) hero of the Trojan War, and the protagonist in Homer's epic poem *Iliad*. This mighty warrior's tragic arc represents a vital truth for all of humanity: none of us is invincible, no matter how much power we possess. Achilles was virtually undefeatable on the battlefield, at least until an arrow struck the only unprotected spot on his body, his heel. This story reminds us all that no one can win all the time, be it at work, in sport, on the battlefield or at home. Eventually our time comes, and in knowing that, we should all strive to remain vigilant and humble while appreciating every experience we have. At least that's what I get out of the story—perhaps you will find other lessons, which is the beauty of Homer's work.

Such a powerful character proved irresistible as I was drafting Harry's fourth adventure. Despite his roots in myth, not everything in this tale about Achilles' armor is fiction. In fact, quite a bit is truthful, as you'll see below.

It is true estimates of the literacy rate in ancient Egypt suggest one to five percent of Egyptians *(Chapter 2)* were literate, though this figure represents the entire kingdom across multiple time periods. The true figure varied depending on location. For instance, written documents recovered from a village garbage dump suggest that nearly all men in the village were literate. As this cache of material included tens of thousands of documents, the total male population was likely in the thousands. As for women, scholars are not certain if they wrote their own letters or dictated them to men (which opens an entirely different avenue of inquiry). As the evidence pertains to literacy rates, this indicates that the truth regarding literacy rates is much more complex.

The Trojan War is an epic poem, not historical fact *(Chapter 6)*. The *Iliad* focuses on a four-day stretch in the tenth year of the siege of Troy, and while the epic poem is undoubtedly fiction, archaeological evidence suggests that it is possible the Trojan War is rooted in fact. The current body of research suggests a large battle occurred at Troy sometime around 1100 B.C., which is three centuries before the *Iliad* was written. Could this large battle have been what Homer claims is the Trojan War?

Ancient Greeks were a warring bunch, which means there are any number of real-life sieges and battles which may have served as the factual base for a story which ultimately grew into a full-fledged fictional war. The city of Troy existed, and at least nine different iterations of the city have been identified. Warfare, natural disaster, migration and economic upheaval all caused Troy's fortunes to fall and eventually rise again over thousands of years. The truth is no one really knows if the Trojan War occurred, and though there is little evidence to suggest Homer's depiction is factual, it is most likely true that his story is based on a real conflict of some sort.

Aci Los *(Chapter 6)* is a character I created for this story, as is Pari Zitis. The latter was intentionally meant to mimic Paris from Greek mythology, who fatally shoots Achilles in the heel with an arrow, a shot which is why we all have a tendon named for a hero from Greek myth.

Sparta is a city located in the administrative region of Greece called Laconia. While Mount Taygetus of the Taygetus mountain range is the range's highest peak and is located near the ancient town, it is not so close that the mountain's shadow would cover the town. Also, the Mount Ares Harry must investigate does not exist, but is a creation of mine used for story purposes. However, I cannot confirm or deny the existence of any helmet carvings which may be located on a mountain in the range.

When Sara risks life and limb to gain a perch from which to view the obelisk outside Luxor *(Chapter 10)*, she finds a strange message from long after the obelisk was built. Should you find yourself in Luxor, please do not try to climb any of the statues. One reason is that if you do, you won't find the hidden writing I mention, mainly because it doesn't exist, but also because there are no ridges on the obelisk, which is actually smooth the entire way up. The other aspects of Luxor as I describe them, though, are accurate.

The same idea holds true if you find yourself in Pella, Greece. While the Temple of Alexander *(Chapter 12)* is based on other well-known Greek and Roman-era temples, there is no temple dedicated to Alexander in Pella. Alexander may have been one of history's greatest generals, but he did not deign to leave his stamp on Pella in such a way. However, Pella truly is where Alexander was born, and I can recommend a wonderful museum dedicated to the archeological finds in this city—of which there are many—as an excellent place to spend an afternoon learning about Pella's most famous son. The Archaeological Museum of Pella holds many treasures, and perhaps some secrets as well. Should you try to locate the sewer system underneath Pella you will be unlucky, as none exists, though the reference to Achilles in the *Odyssey* where Achilles warns Odysseus of Hades domain is truly found in the story.

In the same vein as Pella, I also created the Temple of Alexander in Athens. It does not exist, though the statue described out front does, in the Greek town of Thessaloniki. In one of the more famous statues of Alexander, he is depicted mounted on his horse Bucephalus, and they stand overlooking the Thermaic Gulf. Investigative readers will be hard-pressed to locate a Karaki reference on this statue, but as for hidden compartments, I never discount those entirely.

The Pammakaristos Church in Istanbul *(Chapter 22)* is much as described, though I altered the layout of the outlying lawn and surrounding streets to fit this story. The streets around this church are much narrower than described, and there is no open plaza in front. The church itself dates from around the eleventh century, and today is part mosque, part museum, having been converted from a church in 1592 by the Ottoman Sultan Murad III.

When Harry and Sara climb Mount Olympus *Chapter 24)* on the final step of their quest, they go to a place tied to Achilles to locate his armor. While Mount Olympus is tied to countless legends, there is no geographic feature called Achilles' Bowl *(Chapter 24)* on the mountain, as I created it for the story.

One of the final tests Harry and Sara must pass to prove their worth relates to the myth of Theseus battling the Minotaur. It is true that versions of the myth say Theseus had to walk forward in the Labyrinth, never left or right, and he will find the beast. I did not read any versions stating this was so he did not turn his back on the Minotaur, but instead so that he did not get lost. The idea of facing ahead was my invention. In the myth, Theseus unrolls a ball of string as he walks so he can eventually get back out.

Grand Egyptian Museum *(Epilogue)* will be one of the world's foremost when—or *if*—it opens in November 2022. Construction on the massive complex began in 2012 and continued through the chaos of the Egyptian Revolution. Once completed, it will be the largest archaeological museum in the world. The statue of Ptolemy Soter I use to house the novel's final clue about Harry's amulet is not one of the many treasures inside the museum. The two people referenced inside the statue's book, though, are real. Alexander Helios and Cleopatra Selene II were twins, the children of Mark Antony and Cleopatra. Of all the historical figures I researched to date for the Harry Fox stories, Cleopatra Selene II is one of the most fascinating. More will be discussed about her in the next novel, but I heartily recommend reading about this incredible woman if you have a few minutes. Her journey from the pinnacle of the world to abject ruin and back again is fascinating.

Thank you for joining me on this journey, and I look forward to sharing more of Harry's adventures with you soon.

Andrew Clawson

September 2022

Excerpt from *The Pagan Hammer*

Visit Andrew's website for more information and purchase details.

andrewclawson.com

Chapter 1

Oslo, Norway

The cops were coming. Harry knew, because he'd called them.

The police would be here any minute. A black market antiquities deal was going down. One man planned to buy two recently-stolen Viking artifacts from another, but the buyer had a secret. His name was Harry Fox, and he wanted to get caught. Or at least he wanted the seller to. Harry had another plan, and if it didn't work he'd be inside a Norwegian prison for a long time. Harry exhaled, his breath barely clouding the cool air. This would work. It had to.

Boats left no wake as they glided across the pristine waters of the Oslofjord. Fishing trawlers, pleasure craft, tour boats and even kayaks dotted the glassy surface, so many in places it was hard to keep track of them all. A good place to get lost, if you were of a mind. And Harry certainly was. He just had to stay one step ahead of everyone else to get there.

The man appeared from around a corner. His collar was turned up against the chill. One hand clutched at a backpack slung over his shoulder. The other was buried in a coat pocket. A man Harry knew had no qualms about double-crossing one of the most dangerous men in Europe. A man like that was unpredictable. Dangerous. Harry touched the knuckledusters in one pocket. Ceramic, light, and the only weapon he had. It would have to be enough.

The man stopped just out of reach across from Harry. *"Hast du das*

Spiel der Yankees gesehen?" Did you see the Yankees game?

"Zusätzliche Innings. Harter Verlust." Extra innings. Tough loss.

The agreed upon code. One Harry chose, same as he chose German as the language. His command of the language was weak, but considering he didn't speak a word of a word of Norwegian it was the best he could do.

The men stood there, neither moving. It was the first time Harry had laid eyes on him. A man who stole from his boss to make a quick buck. Or a hundred thousand of them, in this case. A man who wasn't afraid when he should have been. That wasn't the sort of man Harry liked to do business with. If only he'd listen to his own advice.

"Do you have it?" Harry asked, switching to English.

"Yes." The man's eyes only landed on Harry for an instant. He looked every direction, unable to focus. His weight shifted back and forth.

Harry took an invisible step back. "Let me see them."

The man he knew as Jan finally looked at him. A fake name, the most common in Norway. Jan wasn't happy. "No. Too many people."

Enough to provide perfect cover in Harry's opinion. "Fine. Over there." Harry inclined his head toward a vacant bench. "Sit beside me and open the case." He turned and headed for the bench without giving Jan a chance to argue. Jan wanted his money? Harry needed to see the merchandise.

Greed proved a powerful motivator. Harry's backside barely touched the cold seat before Jan joined him. "This is not smart," Jan said.

"Asking me to give you a hundred grand without seeing the artifacts isn't smart," Harry said. "Quit wasting time."

Jan grumbled something in his native tongue Harry was glad he didn't understand. The backpack unzipped to reveal a rolled blanket. Jan dug through his pack until an object came into view. "Satisfied?" he asked.

Harry couldn't respond. Incredible. Decorative gold and silver bands covered with runic writing encircled the metal piece. A Viking drinking horn. One of the most impressive examples Harry had ever seen. He tried and failed to decipher any of the runes inscribed on the precious metal before Jan covered it again.

"Enough," Jan said.

Harry looked up. Dozens of people walked along the harbor, drinking coffee, admiring the opera house, enjoying the clear skies. Sunlight reflected off the Oslofjord waters. No one paid them any mind. "Show me the other one," Harry said. "Now."

Jan didn't put up much of a fight. He dug through the pack again until a second horn emerged. Gold and silver like the other, though the runes on this one were different. That's what Harry wanted to see. He had to be sure. "Very nice," Harry said.

The horn disappeared. "The money." Jan still couldn't keep his eyes on Harry.

"It's right here." Harry pulled an envelope from his pocket. A big one. Jan nearly jumped off the bench when it landed in his lap. "Go ahead and count it."

Jan finally paid attention. The flap of the envelope opened to reveal ten stacks of fresh hundred dollar bills. Ten grand in each times ten stacks. A hundred grand.

Harry reached into his pocket. Slowly, as though he had all day. He pressed a certain spot on the phone and a text message fired off. One he'd typed up several minutes ago which told an already alerted Norwegian detective the artifacts deal was going down outside the opera house. It even said what Harry was wearing. A bright blue coat. That was important.

"Don't follow me," Harry said. He grabbed one of the backpack's straps and pulled.

The bag didn't move. "I will not," Jan said. "But you are not leaving."

Harry tugged on the bag again. "What's the matter with you? We don't need a scene here."

Jan kept an iron grip on the pack. Harry's money had disappeared into the pack. "Do not argue," Jan said.

Harry was about to do a lot more than that when the gun came out. Low, hidden under the bag so no one could see, and aimed at Harry's gut. "Dumb move, Jan." Harry kept hold of the bag. "You don't want this kind of trouble."

Normally Harry would toss out his boss's name right now. Joey Morello was Vincent's son. People around the world knew the Morello name. You didn't mess with the Morello's. At least not more than once. Too bad for Harry he'd played Jan this whole time and never mentioned he worked for Joey Morello. Maybe then the guy wouldn't be so stupid.

Or maybe he would. "Do you think I care?" Jan said. "These horns stay with me. Get up and leave." He jammed the gun in Harry's side in case the message wasn't clear. "I will shoot you if I ever see you again."

Harry stayed put as people walked past ten feet away, oblivious to the threat. "I'm not leaving without these horns," Harry finally said. "We can come to an arrangement."

"This is the arrangement," Jan said. "You leave. I keep the horns and the money." Again, the gun in the ribs thing. "Now you go."

The dusters were around Harry's fingers now. The hand across his body where Jan couldn't see. "Bad choice, Jan." Harry shook his head. "I won't forget this."

Jan's mouth had barely opened when blue lights flashed off the opera house windows and sirens blared. The discordant noise drew his attention for an instant. Harry dropped his elbow by Jan to knock the gun down and held it there. Jan looked back at the same time Harry threw a left hook. The dusters cracked off Jan's jaw, knocking him off the bench. Harry grabbed the gun as Jan fell and then threw it over his shoulder into the waterway behind them. The backpack was still in Jan's grasp as he tumbled to the pavement. Harry dodged Jan's boot kicking out, gave him a punch to the gut and grabbed the bookbag as Jan gasped for air. The pack came free, Harry slung it over his shoulder and was off to the races.

He had the artifacts and his money. Now he had to keep his freedom. The cops were looking for a man in a bright blue coat, so Harry ripped his coat off and dropped it as he ran from the bench. He looked back to find Jan not yet off the ground, clutching his stomach as Harry darted between pedestrians and Jan was lost from view.

The pier he stood on jutted out from the mainland, offering spectacular views of the fjord but also creating a trap. If the police made it onto the wide pier before Harry got off, he was stuck, the water his only way out. Thankfully the narrow roads leading to him were clogged with all manner of traffic, slowing the police enough that Harry thought he could make it. He walked at a rapid pace, just enough below a run so people didn't take notice. A half dozen police cars with flashing lights approached the bottleneck he had to get through to escape. Harry dropped his gaze as tires screeched and the cars shuddered to a halt. Uniformed cops jumped out and ran directly at him. Harry stopped walking. So did everybody else, watching the cops race through the crowd. In Norwegian fashion, they parted to offer a clear path forward. Harry played along, staring wide-eyed as two officer brushed past his shoulders en route to the bench. They didn't give him a second glance.

Now he really picked up speed. It wouldn't be long before more police arrived. His call to an Oslo detective this morning had assured it. The anonymous warning of an artifacts deal occurring on the pier at a certain time in the morning grabbed the detective's attention. When Harry told him the deal involved two Viking drinking horns stolen from an active Nordic dig, the game was on. Norway took cultural repatriation efforts seriously. The chance to recoup two fantastic pieces like these horns couldn't be missed.

Getting the cops to show up was one thing. Escaping undetected was another. Harry never planned to steal the horns from Jan. No, he wanted Jan to keep the money. That way it looked like Harry had no part in this and his escape was mere luck. Considering Harry had leaned on a close friend to set up the meeting by assuring Jan the buyer was legitimate, it was the only way out that kept their cover story intact. Jan went to jail, Harry went free, horns in tow. That's where his escape plan came in.

Now on the mainland, Harry kept moving at pace across the plaza, headed for a series of pricey shops and office buildings until he came to a pedestrian bridge crossing on of the fjord's many tributaries. A commotion sounded to his rear. Police were headed back toward him. At least four of them, radios to their mouths as they ran. The crowds had thinned so Harry had a clear view as one pointed at him and started shouting in Norwegian.

"*Ryggsekk!*" The cop kept pointing, shouting the word again. "*Ryggsekk!*"

Harry didn't have to speak Norwegian to catch that is sounded an awful lot like rucksack. They were talking about his backpack. The only thing he couldn't drop. Harry took off.

A spring across the bridge sent other people bouncing off each shoulder. Across the water the foot traffic was even sparser. The cops were yelling at him and pointing as they sped up, forced to run in a narrow line through the crowds while Harry hit the gas and went at full speed into the urban heart of Oslo's waterfront business district. Glass and steel buildings leaned over him as he raced down the sidewalk. No more coats could come off to change his appearance. He had to outrun them and hope his plan worked.

Halfway down the opera house's rear—the place was massive—he barged through a couple standing beside a row of parked motorbikes. Vespas, the sort found across Europe. A particularly unimpressive model was step one of Harry's escape plan. He jumped on, fired the engine and shot out into traffic. The shouts of policemen faded as his engine whined, heading across another bridge and into the city. The cops chasing him on foot were nowhere to be seen when he looked back. Harry turned around and congratulated himself. He hadn't counted on Jan's entrepreneurial streak.

Two police cars barreled around the corner ahead and aimed straight for him. He veered left across an open plaza, people shouting as his motorbike hurtled through. He thumbed the horn to warn them. The tinny sound it made was scarcely audible.

"Out of the way!" Harry shouted, waving one arm. The people didn't need much encouragement. One older man was swept off his feet as another pulled him out of harm's way. "Sorry!" he called over a shoulder.

He made it across the plaza without killing anyone and bounced onto another street. An electric streetcar appeared on silent wheels in front of him, blocking any path across the road and forcing him to go right, further away from his pursuit and further from his planned path. Sirens grew louder behind him. The cops couldn't drive across the plaza, but he had only seconds until they would be back in sight, coming from either side if they were smart about it.

Time to improvise. Streetcar lanes occupied the center of this roadway, two tracks with fencing on either side and an open lane in the middle. He gunned the Vespa to a cross street and zipped over to the other lane, dodging into oncoming traffic and earning a blaring horn for his trouble. Two city busses idled in one lane ahead, back to back as they waited for the light to turn. A small group had queued at the stop to wait for their ride.

One cop car appeared several streets behind him. Another came around the corner blocks ahead. Harry darted between the two stopped busses and jumped the curb, bouncing to a halt beside wide-eyed riders holding coffee and shoulder bags. He hopped off his Vespa as the light turned green and handed the keys to the man standing closest to him. "Keep it," he said. The guy dropped his coffee.

Harry turned as the first bus motored off. The engine hardly made a noise, only a soft whine as it picked up speed. Faster than he imagined. Harry took off at a dead run as the other bus started coming for him, caught up to the first one and leapt at the back to grab hold of a bike rack, the bus accelerating as he did so he lost his grip with one hand and flailed around. The backpack stayed put until he recovered. Harry turned. The bus driver behind him had his mouth open. Harry waved. The lady waved back.

The police car coming at him zipped by in a flash. Harry held on as the bus bounced, one foot slipping off briefly before he recovered. The bus driver to his rear laid on her horn. Keep going. Just a few more blocks. That's all he needed to get things back on track.

His bus slowed. A stop, right when he couldn't afford it. He was halfway back to the opera house, to where his next safety net waited. Forget all the cops in the area. If he could get to that, he had a chance.

The bus stopped. Harry turned to find the driver behind him with a radio to her lips. She was selling him out. "Come on!" Harry shouted as he jumped off. He waved at her in frustration, and she dropped the radio. Apparently it wasn't every day a crazy man berated you from the rear of another vehicle.

Harry poked his head out from between the two busses, then ducked back. Two cops were on the other side of the street. They hadn't spotted him yet, not with all the foot and vehicle traffic, but he couldn't stay here. A streetcar approached from his left side, headed the direction he needed to go, and he had an idea.

He ran across the road to a stop as the trained pulled up and slid to a halt. The cops didn't see him. The doors opened, Harry slipped aboard, and as they slid shut behind him he let himself believe this could actually work. Jan in jail, Harry on his way back home, merchandise and money in his pack.

A uniformed police officer stood across the car. The officer barely looked up as Harry boarded. In fact, he barely moved, one hand on the safety rail, another in his pocket. Half the seats were full. The guy could easily see him. Yet all he did was pull out his cell phone and look at it for a moment. He pecked at the screen with two fingers. He didn't look directly at Harry. In fact, he was looking out the window. Staring intently, to be precise. A cloud covered the sun outside, turning the window into a mirror.

The cop's eyes were directly on Harry.

He didn't jump up as the train slowed. Didn't run for the doors. No, he waited until they were about to close before exploding from his seat and sneaking through them at the last second. The police officer wasn't fast enough, and the last Harry saw of him was the officer pounding his fists against the closed train doors as it pulled away.

The opera house stood to one side. He was nearly back where it started, a block from the bench where Jan had likely been arrested. Exactly as he'd planned. Minus the being chased by a dozen policemen, that is. Harry didn't try to hide as he ran onto the street, headed for waterfront café. He barely made it halfway when the streetcar screeched to a halt. He looked back to find the officer shoving the door open in the middle of the tracks, where he forced his way out and ran at Harry.

So much for the café. He had to lose this guy in the span of a block, and he had to do it now. The cop would have reinforcements on the way, most coming the waterfront ahead of Harry while this lone cop chased from behind. Harry looked left. Nothing doing. He looked right. A pedestrian bridge led around the café's far corner and out of sight.

The bridge. That was his ticket. He held the backpack straps tight as he ran full speed around the corner, putting the building between himself and the chasing cop as he ran onto the bridge. He'd noticed it while reconnoitering the area yesterday. All the bridges had drainpipes running down the side to keep water from pooling on the centuries-old stonework. Thick pipes, sturdy enough to hold a man. Or at least Harry hoped so.

He ran for the closest corner of the bridge. A look back found the cop nowhere in site. Harry slowed, leapt onto the thick stone barrier keeping pedestrians from falling into the water, and never stopped as he jumped for the drainpipe running down the bridge's side. For a long second he was weightless, floating through the air, then gravity took hold and he plunged toward the pipe, grabbing hold of it with both hands before his body crashed into the stone bridge with a jaw-rattling smack. He held on until his vision cleared, then shimmed down to where the pipe bent underneath the bridge. The sound of feet smacking on the sidewalk chased him as he moved hand-over-hand along the pipe until the bridge concealed him from view.

His breath came in ragged gasps. His palms shouted for relief from the rough metal pipe. Harry hung in place, feet swaying as he listened to the cop above him unleash all manner of Norwegian invective. Harry didn't have to speak the language to get the gist of it. The cop couldn't believe it. His target had disappeared. Vanished into thin air. The cop paced back and forth, yelling into his phone all the while. He fell silent. Harry held his breath. The water rustled beneath him until running footsteps again sounded from above, this time fading to nothing as the cop ran across the bridge toward the water.

Harry counted to five, then pulled himself out to the edge, where he grabbed a lip on the arched stone support and hauled himself up until one foot found purchase on the stone and he could slide across the pipe back to the road. Harry clambered over the fence and dropped in a heap to safety. He risked one look down the bridge while he army crawled for a patch of bushes and safety.

A small army of policemen milled about on the bridge's far side.

He stood and moved at a fast walk to the café door, going inside and juking between tables until he made it to a rear door. The sign on it declared *BARE ANSATTE. STAFF ONLY.* Harry twisted the knob and snuck through, passing a startled barista as he moved down the narrow hallway where he ducked out a side door and just as quickly snuck through a doorway adjacent to it, one propped open by a plastic crate. The cook sitting on said crate smoking a cigarette barely looked at Harry.

A bustling kitchen greeted him. Waiters shouted, cooks cursed, and steam filled the air. Harry kept his head down and hugged the wall until he emerged at the rear of a restaurant which overlooked the Oslofjord waters. Hectic, filled, it was the perfect place to get lost. He headed straight for a family restroom, getting inside and locking the door behind him.

Please be here. Harry's breath quickened as he lifted the tank lid.

Yes. The package he'd taped there earlier that morning remained in place. Harry ripped it free, unzipped the waterproof bag, and prayed to any gods who happened to be listening that it wasn't too late.

Police officers entered the restaurant overlooking Oslofjord's picturesque waters, startling diners and nearly upending a tray of drinks from a waiter's shoulder. They asked about a man who had come in, one wearing a backpack. Vaguely middle eastern in appearance, but not overly so. European, maybe. Average height, dark hair, solid build. No matter how many times they asked, none of the clientele recalled seeing anyone with dark clothes and pants on inside, certainly not with a backpack. The fuss soon died down as patrons got back to their meals and drinks, most wishing the cops would get on with it and leave.

No one remembered seeing a man who fit this general description walk out of the family restroom with a bag dangling from one hand. If they noticed anything, it was the wet suit he wore beneath his brand-new outdoors clothes, the sort a man wore when spending a day on the cold waters surrounding Oslo. If anyone recalled seeing him walk onto the entrance overlooking those waters, they didn't tell the cops. The man in question would have walked past any number of officers as he strolled down a walkway leading to the water's edge—and he definitely did—before retrieving a kayak from where it had been secured by the dock. No one, police or otherwise, noted this man slipping a backpack into his kayak before he pushed off and paddled slowly away.

If the cops had looked out onto the water, they might have seen the man making his way into the distance, though it would have been hard to pick him out among the other kayakers. This man paddled alone, headed for a motorcycle parked some distance away. A motorcycle which would take him to Oslo airport and a direct flight home to New York City, where the two souvenir Viking drinking horns in his luggage would turn out to be something far different than what he told the customs officials upon landing.

Chapter 2

Brooklyn

A fan spun slowly above them. Cirrus clouds of cigar smoke wafted and flowed on the ceiling, as they had for decades. Two men seated around a small table looked at each other. One's face was lined, his skin a roadmap of experience. The others was smooth as only a young man's could be. The dark circles under this young man's eyes betrayed him, though. He was a man with the weight of a family on his shoulders. The weight, in truth, of a city.

"I am sorry, Joey." Gio Sabella took a long pull on his cigar. "It is the best I can do."

"A month." Joey Morello looked at Gio over steepled fingers. "Not much time."

"You are lucky to have that," Gio said. "If it were not for your father, I suspect the decision would already be made."

"And who would it be?" Joey asked. "You?"

Gio shrugged. "It is not my place to say. You know I am not interested in replacing your father, god rest his soul." Gio crossed himself. "He guided us for decades."

"Until someone killed him."

"A killer who escaped." Gio laid his cigar in a crystal ashtray. He leaned forward in his chair. "Finding who murdered your father will not bring him back. It will also not put you in his seat. Not alone."

Joey lifted an eyebrow. "I'm listening."

"The families will follow strength and wisdom," Gio said. "Your father had both. In order for you to replace him, you must show this as well. Your own family is under threat. If you cannot stand up to one

326

man, and do it wisely, then I am not certain what to say."

That's all he said. It's all he needed to say. Gio's true message remained unspoken, and Joey Morello heard every word.

Gio stood, signaling the conversation had ended. "Be safe, young man." Gio accepted Joey's embrace, pulling him close so none of the bodyguards around the room could hear. "I believe in you," Gio whispered. "Show the families what you are made of."

The words rang on Joey's ear as he departed Gio Sabella's offices and got into the back of his waiting Mercedes. Fallen leaves stirred as Joey's driver took him back to his headquarters in Brooklyn, the sunlight falling through the cars bullet-proof windows doing little to warm his face. Joey hated to admit it, but right now his future hung in the balance, and the man who could push it any direction he chose? Gio Sabella. One of his father's closest friends, yet now Gio had given Joey an ultimatum. Even if Joey knew Gio was doing the right thing, it still stung.

Because Joey didn't know if he could do it. Gio made it clear. Find who killed your father. Joey had been trying to do that ever since the bomb exploded beside Vincent Morello's table in a restaurant. A table Joey should have been sitting at. He would have been, if it weren't for a phone call minutes before the explosion. The worst part was Joey knew who did it. He was more certain of this than anything in the world. The man who killed his father was also the same man now trying to push the Morello family off their turf. A man whose reckless actions threatened the peaceful existence between New York's crime families. An existence Vincent Morello had created.

Altin Cana, head of the Albanian crime family bearing his name. The Cana family had quietly declared war on the Morello family, causing trouble at their gaming houses, selling on their turf, sending the cops to their money laundering operations. All of it hit Joey Morello's bottom line, but even worse, it made him look weak. None of the other family heads wanted Altin to do anything but crawl back into the hole he'd come from, yet they didn't intrude. This battle was between the Morello and Cana families. Joey needed to prove he could lead his men the same way his father had. Vincent Morello had led not just his family, but the all the families in New York. Joey wanted to do the same. Gio had made it clear. If Joey wanted to lead them all, he needed to show he could handle his business.

Handle it intelligently. Starting a war was easy. And it was dumb. Gunfights and corpses were bad for business, and the leader of New York's families had one goal above all. Keep the peace so business could boom. Rich gangsters were happy gangsters. If Joey couldn't put an upstart Albanian into his place, how could he lead them all?

Joey's thoughts still churned when he arrived at his headquarters in Brooklyn, yet no answers were forthcoming. One question ran through his mind as he walked inside, greeting the armed guards before finding his office and falling into the oversized chair behind his desk. What would his father do?

He poured a drink from the bottle in his desk. A desk which used to belong to Vincent. The liquid warmed his throat when he drank, yet Joey didn't appreciate the smoky heat. How could he, when everything was crumbling beneath his feet? Vincent spent years preparing his son to take over the family business. Sure, his training was different than most people in his line of work. What other mobster went to business school? Yet the one constant was Vincent believed in Joey. Knew in his bones that when Joey's time came he would be ready. Now that time was here. What was Joey doing? Failing.

An empire given to him, and Joey botched the hand-off. All because of one reckless Albanian. A tree limb outside his window bounced as a bird landed on it. A goldfinch, its yellow feathers a spark of color against the urban backdrop. Yellow. The color of cowardice.

Joey set his drink down. Was he scared? No. He'd never admitted to being scared of anything in his life. That didn't mean he'd never been scared. Everyone felt afraid at one time or another. It's how you reacted that defined you. Vincent Morello came to America with nothing but his heritage, yet he rose to the top of New York's underworld, a force none could withstand. How did he do it? By working hard, sure, but there was more. He did whatever it took, and he didn't do it alone.

Vincent built alliances. Vincent fought dirty. Vincent won, no matter what. Perhaps Joey couldn't do it alone. That didn't mean he was destined to fail. It meant he needed help.

One problem. Mob bosses didn't always have the biggest circle of trustworthy friends. Associates? He had loads of those. Foot soldiers? Dozens of them. But people he could trust with his life? There were only a handful of those.

Joey's phone buzzed atop his desk. A name flashed on-screen. The name of a man he trusted above all others. A man currently in Norway, doing his part to keep the Morello's afloat. *Harry Fox.*

Harry filled a role few others in the world could. You could never have too many friends in Joey's line of work. Harry's work as the Morello antiquities hunter brought a set of friends he never imagined existed. Friends in the District Attorney's office, specifically the Manhattan Antiquities Trafficking unit, a team of law enforcement officers dedicated to stopping the flow of illegal artifacts which poured through New York. In order to do that, they used a time-honored police method. If you can't beat the bad guys, work with them. Harry Fox wasn't quite a bad guy, not really, so he worked well. Harry knew people they didn't. He went where they couldn't. In exchange for his help, the Trafficking unit looked the other way when Harry participated in questionable activities, which happened to pad Joey Morello's bottom line.

Harry Fox was one of a kind. He was Joey Morello's closest friend in the world.

Joey connected the call. "You back from Norway?" he asked.

Harry's response made him shift in his seat. His eyes narrowed as he listened. "You found *what?*"

To continue the story, visit Andrew Clawson's website at andrewclawson.com.

GET YOUR COPY OF THE HARRY FOX STORY
THE NAPOLEON CIPHER,
AVAILABLE EXCLUSIVELY FOR MY VIP READER LIST

Sharing the writing journey with my readers is a special privilege. I love connecting with anyone who reads my stories, and one way I accomplish that is through my mailing list. I only send notices of new releases or the occasional special offer related to my novels.

If you sign up for my VIP reader mailing list, I'll send you a copy of *The Napoleon Cipher*, the Harry Fox adventure that's not sold in any store. You can get your copy of this exclusive novel by signing up on my website.

Did you enjoy this story? Let people know

Reviews are the most effective way to get my books noticed. I'm one guy, a small fish in a massive pond. Over time, I hope to change that, and I would love your help. The best thing you could do to help spread the word is leave a review on your platform of choice.

Honest reviews are like gold. If you've enjoyed this book I would be so grateful if you could take a few minutes leaving a review, short or long.

Thank you very much.

Also by Andrew Clawson

The Parker Chase Series
A Patriot's Betrayal
The Crowns Vengeance
Dark Tides Rising
A Republic of Shadows
A Hollow Throne
A Tsar's Gold

The TURN Series
TURN: The Conflict Lands
TURN: A New Dawn
TURN: Endangered

Harry Fox Adventures
The Arthurian Relic
The Emerald Tablet
The Celtic Quest
The Achilles Legend
The Pagan Hammer
The Pharaoh's Amulet
The Thracian Idol
The Antikythera Code

About the Author

Andrew Clawson is the author of multiple series, including the Parker Chase and TURN thrillers, as well as the Harry Fox adventures.

You can find him at his website, AndrewClawson.com

or you can connect with him on Instagram at andrew.clawson

on Twitter at @clawsonbooks

on Facebook at facebook.com/AndrewClawsonnovels

and you can always send him an email at:
andrew@andrewclawson.com.